Alan Murray has published seven non-fiction books and has contributed to four award-winning television documentaries. His work has featured at international gatherings in the United States, Britain and France. He has also written short stories for print and radio. *Luigi's Freedom Ride* is his first full-length work of fiction.

LUIGI'S FREEDOM RIDE

A story of curiosity, love, hope and bicycles.

Alan Murray

FOURTH ESTATE

Fourth Estate

An imprint of HarperCollins*Publishers*

First published in Australia in 2014
by HarperCollins*Publishers* Australia Pty Limited
ABN 36 009 913 517
harpercollins.com.au

HarperCollins*Publishers*
Level 13, 201 Elizabeth Street, Sydney NSW 2000, Australia
Unit D1, 63 Apollo Drive, Rosedale, Auckland 0632, New Zealand
A 53, Sector 57, Noida, UP, India
77–85 Fulham Palace Road, London W6 8JB, United Kingdom
2 Bloor Street East, 20th floor, Toronto, Ontario M4W 1A8, Canada
195 Broadway, New York NY 10007, USA

National Library of Australia Cataloguing-in-Publication entry:

Murray, Alan, author.
  Luigi's freedom ride / Alan Murray.
  ISBN: 978 0 7322 9892 0 (paperback)
  ISBN: 978 1 4607 0255 0 (ebook)
A823.4

Cover design by Hazel Lam, HarperCollins Design Studio
Author photograph by Jacqui Murray
Typeset in 11.5/16pt Sabon by Kirby Jones

For Jacqui, Dugald and John

CHAPTER ONE

Freewheeling

Perhaps only flight in a glider can approximate the joy of cycling. There is, in cycling, a sense of serenity, of utter, spiritual integration of body and soul. Properly supervised, and with balanced medication, cycling can restore the insane to sanity.

— Verreker Boeg, *Cogs in the Wheel: The Therapy of Motion*, 1968

Even as his eighty-first birthday drew near, Luigi Ferraro was a handsome and stylish man. He'd use his long fingers to sweep his silver hair back from his high, tanned forehead; there was a raffish charm in this fleeting movement of fingers through hair. His knowing hazel eyes were framed in the gold of his slightly tinted spectacles, there was a calmness in those eyes. His brisk, firm handshake was always accompanied by a nod and the wisp of a disarming, engaging smile. His easy, unhurried manner said Luigi Ferraro was comfortable with himself and his world. Luigi, then, had the look of a man of uncommon resolve and resilience. A man with a story to tell.

His story began in the Tuscan village of Tescano in 1921, the year Benito Mussolini was elected to the Italian Chamber of Deputies. It would end half a world away in an Australian village, Diggers Cove, a cluster of houses strung like small knots along the ribbon of road that is the old Pacific Highway between Sydney and Brisbane. It was a story of endurance and sadness and great billowing gusts of joy. It was a story of the brutality of war, of travels by train and ship and bicycle, of stolen gold and, eventually, of the quietness of a soul content with what is and not concerned with what might have been or almost was.

Alone since the death of his wife in 1992, Luigi spent most mornings on the verandah of his weatherboard beach house at Diggers Cove. Inside and out, the walls were painted pale blue, and the door and window frames were blindingly white. The house was well maintained. It was also modest, save for the stainless-steel Italian kitchen appliances and cookware and the Italian marble benchtops his wife had insisted on. Australian women, she'd said, might settle for second best, even third best, when it came to husbands and kitchens, but she would not. The Ferraros had the money. She would have her kitchen.

Luigi's wife had been the keystone in the bridge that carried him across the sometimes trickling and sometimes torrential rivulets and rivers of life. Behind the brightness of her wide-set, dark eyes was a determination that could not be bested. 'Never argue with your mother,' Luigi once told son Enzo. 'She argues from the heart. You can argue against the head, but you can never prevail against the heart. Never.' More than the love of his life, Luigi's wife was his companion, his comrade for all seasons. She had the heart of a lion.

Luigi's house at Diggers Cove faced east across the endless ocean. Between May and November, whales on their northern migration swished through the waters off the lighthouse on the headland, Black Cape, a dozen or so kilometres from Luigi's verandah. Some mornings, Luigi gazed into the open space above the water, enchanted, unmoving, hypnotised by white horses and passing clouds. In the afternoons, he often read the cycling magazines he subscribed to, a dog-eared Raymond Chandler thriller, or one of the hundreds of copies of *National Geographic* rescued, over the years, from the Diggers Cove tip. The *National Geographic* stories took Luigi on journeys across the high, empty plains of Mongolia and the Russian Steppe, through the jungles of Borneo and the Amazon Basin, and along the Danube and the Volga, the Orinoco and the Yangtze.

There were other journeys, too. Journeys into swirls of sound that brought waves of memories of long-ago times and faraway places. The sounds came from Luigi's radio. It was permanently tuned to an FM station that broadcast classical music and brass-band concerts.

Sometimes, Luigi took the radio to his bicycle workshop — a garden shed where he built and rebuilt motorised bicycles — and found himself floating in a world somewhere between spanners and files and chain splitters and *Jerusalem* and *Pomp and Circumstance* and *The Messiah*. Transported by the music, Luigi would step back from his workbench and conduct an orchestra of tools and drills and rags. Beethoven's *Fifth* was a special favourite: *Da-da-da-daah*. Those opening notes had been the BBC call sign — representing V for Victory in the Morse alphabet — that heralded news broadcasts and their coded messages to occupied Europe in the war years when Luigi was a young man. Always, when the final notes of the *Fifth* had sounded, Luigi switched off the radio and stood, briefly, in the absolute silence of recollection. The notes of Beethoven's *Fifth* were those of another life. Then, sighing, Luigi would turn to his motorised bicycles. He was back in the present. There were brakes to adjust, spokes to be polished.

Each bicycle in Luigi's workshop was built around the frame of a Schwinn California Beach Cruiser. The lines were pure Art Deco. Perched on the crossbar of each frame was a copy of the compact fuel tank first seen in 1919 on the iconic Excelsior motorised bicycle. The Schwinn frame was big enough to provide the platform for the Honda two- and four-stroke engines that Luigi considered easily surpassed Michelangelo's *David* in grace and perfect proportion. The motorised bicycle was proof, Luigi believed, that God could inspire man to attain perfection.

Some afternoons he wheeled a bicycle from the workshop. He checked the tyres he'd checked the day before and then cycled towards the lighthouse on the cape. He powered his way up the long incline out to the grassy headland, stared at the ocean for twenty minutes, then freewheeled home. It was the magic moment of the day: wind in his silver hair, the almost soundless spin of the wheels beneath him.

Every downhill ride was a delight. The road from the headland ran dangerously close to cliffs that fell away, over narrow ledges, into the ocean. The ledges were alive with seabirds, mainly terns that Luigi had identified from Simpson and Day's *Field Guide to the Birds of Australia*. He liked the Latin names, and he'd sometimes say them aloud as he rode: *Sterna striata, Sterna sumatra, Sterna hirundo, Sterna albifrons, Sterna bengalensis*. The genus *sterna* sounded like the Latin declension of the verb 'to soar', and as Luigi recited the names, they evoked in him memories of the chanting of a black-robed priest of the old school.

The cliffs were a perfect take-off platform for the terns. They'd lean forward and fall into the nothingness. Their wings would splay effortlessly and the birds would soar, swept upwards on invisible swirls and spirals and thermals. Some days Luigi, his body a seamless and speeding extension of a fabulous, shimmering machine, would imagine himself as a soaring bird. Other days, in the blur of his own acceleration, he'd be transported back to his childhood in Tescano. He would become the boy who stripped and rebuilt his first bicycle in 1931, when he was ten years old.

That bicycle was a jet-black Hercules Popular twenty-one-inch Gent's Roadster. It was given to him by a young Englishman who was cycling to Rome. The journey had been abandoned in Tescano's cobbled piazza when the Hercules was deliberately clipped by a passing open truck loaded with a dozen Blackshirts, Mussolini's bully boys, who'd spotted the Union Jack stitched to the panniers on the bicycle.

Luigi had been playing handball against a wall of the long-abandoned carabinieri post in the Tescano piazza when he heard the truck accelerate. There were jeers and then the thump of metal on metal. Save for Luigi, none of the dozen or so villagers who saw the truck strike the bicycle moved. The Blackshirts might return, after all, and if they did, they'd certainly hand out a beating to any who helped a foreigner. Such matters, in Italy in 1931, were best left alone.

Luigi, his innocence a shield against fear, ran to the aid of the cyclist, lying dazed and bleeding by the fountain. He helped the man to his feet and took him home, where Luigi's mother, Franca, washed and tended the cuts and grazes and tightly strapped a rapidly swelling ankle. The fresh-faced man, speaking flawless Italian, said his name was Jeremy Forsythe.

For five days, Jeremy Forsythe, limping and sore, remained with the Ferraros — Luigi, his mother and his uncle Cesare. Luigi's father, an itinerant worker, had vanished from the village six weeks before his son's birth, in 1921. There were whispers that he had gone to Trieste to be with a woman he'd met during his military service in the Great War. It was widely held that he would be a dead man if he ever returned. A Tescano man would never desert his wife. Never. The scoundrel would pay with his life. Uncle Cesare, the village blacksmith and Franca's twin brother, said so. And all of Tescano knew that Cesare was a man of his word, of infinite patience and of uncommonly strong build. His hands, arms and shoulders had been shaped by the forge he sweated over. It was said that, as a sergeant in the war, he had killed four enemy soldiers with those bare hands.

During the time Jeremy stayed with them, the Ferraros learned that he had graduated from Durham University with honours in Romance languages a few months earlier. He'd planned to cycle to Rome before returning to England and entering the Royal Military Academy on the path to a commission in the British army. But the incident in the piazza had buckled both wheels of the Hercules, cracked the three-speed hub gears and snapped the bolt holding the front brake to the black frame. In his perfect Italian, Jeremy said he'd continue his journey by bus and train. Luigi could have the bicycle. With unbuckled wheels and mended brakes and gears, Jeremy said, breaking into four words of English, it would 'go like the clappers'.

Luigi whooped with joy at the gift. He was beaming. He had his very own bicycle. It had come all the way from England. He was sorry Jeremy Forsythe would have to abandon the Hercules in Tescano — but, with some work, the Hercules would soon be as good as new. Luigi would see to that. It would be the best bicycle anywhere. He would look after it forever; Jeremy could count on it.

CHAPTER TWO

Balance

*Like the bludgeon of Thor's hammer on white-hot
steel, the feet of our cyclists pushed our opponents
into the dust. Our young, Aryan warriors triumphed
and the medals were ours.*

— Dietrich Scheele, German Cycling Captain, Berlin Olympics, 1936

Rebuilding the Hercules occupied Luigi for most of the summer
of 1931. He toiled for weeks on end in Uncle Cesare's smithy,
in the lane that wound past the Ferraros' small, solid home.
The smithy had double doors. Pushed open, they allowed the
circulation of air around the forge. The whole place smelled of
oil and smoke and sweat and the vague scent of Cesare's lavender
hair tonic.

In the weeks before planting or harvesting, the smithy was
always crowded with implements to be mended. The focal point
was the forge and its wide chimney. The glow and flicker from

the fired-up forge reflected off the cutting edges of repaired or sharpened implements and cast shadows onto the walls of Uncle Cesare's modest empire.

Luigi would never know that the jerky, convulsive movements of these shadows sometimes reminded Cesare of the final, frantic writhing of the men he'd killed in those murderous close-quarter encounters on Italy's northern front in 1917. Cesare could remember, in every awful and secret detail, the staring, bulging eyes that pleaded for life. Another minute. Another hour. One more day. A last embrace with a wife, a mother, a child. Please, God. And always the pleas were ignored. This was war. There was no glory or honour in any of it. Most men died like frightened cattle facing the slaughterman's stained blade. When the memories came, Cesare shivered and turned his eyes away from the shadows on the wall. Yesterday was yesterday. It was best left alone. There was work to be done today. The shiver always puzzled Luigi. How was it that Uncle Cesare could feel cold in the heat of the smithy?

On the two anvils in the smithy, Cesare could fashion anything. A vague description, a rough sketch — in Cesare's hands, these were as good as detailed engineering drawings. These were hands that commanded and bent metal to his will and his skill. It was all, he believed, in the grip. A tightening or loosening of that grip would transform, say, a hammer from a battering, pounding bludgeon to a tapping, almost gentle instrument. A movement of the wrist, and tongs that had pulled molten metal from a bed of fire could caress and turn a bar of white-hot steel as softly as a mother turning a baby in a crib.

Beyond the circle of men whose business in life is machines and metal and moulding and millimetres, there is seldom mention of the grip. It is, among these ferrous freemasons, a close-held secret — like the secret of the cloistered few who know, beyond any shadow of doubt, that Christ, resurrected, lived out his days quietly in Roman Gaul after his many years in India.

Luigi often watched Uncle Cesare at work. He admired Cesare's skill and self-assurance. One day Luigi would be just like him. Indeed, by the time Luigi was ten, he could sharpen tools and mark cutting patterns on metal. He had his own corner in the smithy. Uncle Cesare said this special corner was just the place where a boy could rebuild a broken bicycle — a Hercules Popular twenty-one-inch Gent's Roadster, for example. He said Luigi could use any tool in the smithy. 'But it will be some time, if that time ever comes,' he said, 'before you master the grip.' Implicit in this observation was the master craftsman's view that the grip could never be known by a boy. Nor could it be merely learned. Patient years at the forge and the bench would not, of themselves, confer the grip. 'For the man of metal, the grip is like grace,' Uncle Cesare said. 'It is a gift from God.'

It was also Uncle Cesare's view that the skills of the truly accomplished cyclist were as much bestowed as they were learned. He had, some time earlier, recognised those skills in his nephew.

Before the arrival of Jeremy Forsythe and the Hercules, Luigi had learned to ride on a well-used ladies' 1923 Hirondelle Luxe Modèle No. 12 Pour Dame. The Hirondelle had been left in Tescano, like the Hercules, by an English person. She was Miss Queenie Bradbury, the quite beautiful, fair-skinned textile heiress of London and Staindrop, Yorkshire. Aged nineteen in 1927, she had arrived in Tescano with a chaperoned party of fourteen other girls from her Lugano summer school, the Else and Hilda Grichting Ladies' Institute of Fitness and Recreation. Like Jeremy Forsythe, Miss Queenie Bradbury had been cycling to Rome. However, Miss Bradbury's grand tour was halted not by a brush with a vehicle but by fatigue and badly chafed upper thighs. The distressed Queenie left her party in Tescano and proceeded to Rome by bus and train, standing for the entire journey. The Hirondelle Luxe Modèle No. 12 Pour Dame was left in the care of Cesare, on the understanding that it would be sent for or collected.

It was neither sent for nor collected. Cesare had eventually assumed ownership and begun instructing young Luigi in the skills of bicycle riding. Luigi was what Uncle Cesare described as 'a natural'. Under Cesare's guidance, he mastered balance, distribution of weight, the coordinated movement of ankles and knees to deliver maximum downward pressure, the correct positioning of the hands on the India-rubber grips of the handlebars, and the minuscule upper-body movements that steered a bicycle around wide corners. Importantly, the boy also learned that a bicycle must be kept in good order — clean, oiled, every part working with every other part.

Having learned to ride and to maintain the Hirondelle in perfect order, Luigi, aged ten, was ready to strip and rebuild his first, his very own, bicycle. The Hercules Popular Gent's Roadster twenty-one-inch model was a benchmark bicycle, setting the template for the legendary Hercules Safety Model series of later years. It was strong, functional and well finished. As a touring bicycle it more than matched any model in the Hirondelle range — gents' or ladies'. The name Hercules had been perfectly chosen by its English makers. It evoked an image of the mythical warrior of ancient times: a creature of immense physical power, a superhero who battled monstrous adversaries and survived terrible injuries.

The Hercules Popular Gent's Roadster could also survive terrible injuries. And as for monstrous adversaries, the Hercules, ridden with balance and steady, consistent application of downward pressure on the pedals, could defeat all but the steepest roads and tracks around Tescano.

The repair and rebuilding of the Hercules began with Luigi's survey of the damage the bicycle had sustained. He wrote on the back cover of his school jotter: *Luigi's Hercules Roadster 1931*. Then, on a blank inside page, he made an inventory of all that had been damaged. Even after Jeremy Forsythe's bruising brush with the vehicle loaded with Blackshirt Fascist bully boys, the frame of the Hercules was unbent, although scratched. True, there was some distortion of the front forks and some buckling of the wheels, but young Luigi discovered that the forks could be levered back into shape without causing any hairline damage to the metal. The buckled wheel rims could be straightened by gently hammering them between two flat pieces of wood. The bent spokes could be removed and straightened by hand in a vice. The brakes could be aligned, and brake pads could be cut from a worn, discarded wheelbarrow tyre Luigi had found in the smithy. The damaged paintwork could be renewed. Most of these tasks involved patient, detailed work.

The reward for Luigi's efforts that summer came during a balmy, seemingly endless autumn. The days were still warm and long enough for him to set off every Saturday on a bicycle journey of adventure.

The rebuilt Hercules devoured the hills. Luigi believed there was not a mount in all of Tuscany that could halt him. Once over the crest of each incline he sliced into the descent. Then, still standing on the pedals, he'd push and push and push. Faster and ever faster. Down and downwards, fingers well away from brake levers. He'd sit dead centre of the roads and tracks then crouch into every corner. He had, as Uncle Cesare claimed, a gift. He had what racing cyclists called a perfect line, a natural ability to sense the bend of a curve and fly into that bend with the easy bravado of a tightrope walker.

Now and then on his solo adventures he turned onto pathways that twisted upwards towards caves hidden from the naked eye. In some caves, the walls and roofs had flaked, revealing the perfect outline of fossilised trees. In time, Luigi knew every crevice and gully in the hills around Tescano.

And, in time, that knowledge would shape and change lives forever.

CHAPTER THREE

Entranced

There is no space for the freestyle cyclist in our Movement. Ours is the business of acting in concert as one. Each is a spoke in the bigger wheel, a tyre on the track of profound change.

— Randall Ochiltree, Convener, Glasgow Socialist Cycling Club,
    1938, letter to *The Glasgow Herald*

Half a world and most of a lifetime away from Tescano, when Luigi rested on the verandah at Diggers Cove after his glide from the headland, he sometimes wondered if bicycle riders passed into a trance where the only thing in their world was the mesmerising turning of tyres and the silver flashes from spokes. In the trance there was no past, there was only a sense that all life that had ebbed and flowed across the years was long ago and far away. In the trance there was no future. There was only the moment. The now.

Before resting on the verandah after the ride to and from Black Cape, Luigi always wheeled the steel steed into his workshop, drew out a rag from under the saddle, and wiped the frame and forks and wheel rims and pencil-slim exhaust. Then the bike was eased into the uprights of a bicycle rack alongside three quite magnificent, hand-built, two-wheeled machines: the Cape Cruiser, the Chingarry Champion and the Tindarah Tiger, names taken from local settlements and landmarks to the north and south of Diggers Cove.

Near the rack against the wall, under a thin cloth, was a shiny and ancient black Hercules, the talisman that had carried a much younger Luigi to and through some of the wonders and woes of life. Every day, he lifted the thin cloth, looked at the Hercules and stroked the saddle, just as a rider, saying nothing, strokes a horse after a well-run race.

Replacing the thin cloth, he surveyed, always with a sense of pride, his workshop. It was a model of order and neatness, a straight-edged jigsaw puzzle of perfectly jointed hardwood benches and brass-hinged boxes. The west-facing wall was made up of flyscreened sliding doors, which framed the vista that was Mount Disaster. Another wall was filled with a patchwork-quilt mural of the razorback ridges that held the village of Tescano in place. The mural bore the words *Ferraro Bicicletta*. It had been stitched together some years earlier by his wife as a birthday gift. Now and then he touched, ever so softly, the quilted mural and imagined he was touching the hands that had stitched it.

On the two remaining walls were wooden panels with hooks and the painted outlines of every tool in the workshop. In the middle of the workshop was a steel working table. Near the table were gas tanks and torches and a compressor. The gas torches were used for welding and brazing. The machines and tools were of European and North American origin — German power tools, American socket sets and wrenches, British screwdrivers and spanners, Italian precision measuring devices.

Like Uncle Cesare's smithy in Tescano, the Diggers Cove workshop was Luigi's modest empire. In this place he was master of his universe. He spent hours tidying what was already tidy or tightening a chain or polishing already shiny spokes. If he was stripping and servicing a bicycle he would first lay out the parts and tools he needed for the job. They were always laid out, from left to right, in the order in which they'd be used. They were laid out as a surgeon lays out the implements of his profession.

Some days, when he left the workshop, Luigi weeded around the rows of vegetables that grew in the garden first planted by his wife. He remembered how he'd watched her in that garden, stooping to tie a tomato plant back onto its stake, or standing upright, hands on hips, a quartermaster inspecting supplies. And he remembered how he'd listen, when she believed no one could hear, to her gentle, half-whispered monologues that encouraged sickly plants to recover.

Sometimes, in the late afternoon, Luigi wrote imaginary letters to her.

My dearest,

Your garden is, as ever, well tended, although some of the vegetables have wilted. I believe they miss the sound of your voice. Early today, before the warmth of the sun

shortened my shadow, I pulled some weeds from between
the straight rows you laid out so many years ago. When
that was done, I rode to the cape and sat watching the
birds. I saw you soaring in the sky we share. There are
nights when I see you in the space between the stars. And
when I see you there I feel the tears on my face. Then,
I taste the salt stinging a wound that weeps and never
heals. If only we could touch. One single touch to fill, for
one single second, the emptiness.

'Oh dear,' I hear you say, 'poor Luigi has become a
sentimental old man.' I talk to you every day. Sometimes
I say, 'Remember when ...' and I look sideways and
smile. But I can never escape my sadness and my sorrow
beyond dreams at the wound of your passing.

My eternal love,

Luigi

There were many letters like this. All were folded and kept in a shoebox by Luigi's bed.

At Diggers Cove the seasons dictated where Luigi spent his evenings and some early mornings. In the warmth of the daylight-saving months he sat, facing the ocean, on his front verandah. He sat there and wrote, in perfect copperplate, in his journal. The journal was a regular devotion. He wrote with the silver Montegrappa fountain pen he'd brought with him from Italy as a young man — a pen taken from the body of a German soldier beaten and shot dead near Tescano in 1944. Sometimes Luigi wrote of the birds he saw around the headland. Other times, perhaps on an anniversary, he wrote of a remembered birthday or a funeral. When he wrote of his mother, Franca, he remembered a woman of strong features and dark eyes, a woman who remained undiminished, though not unmarked, by the rod of life's caprice. He remembered a woman who showed kindness to strangers and, in her manner, gratitude for every breath she was granted by her God. Franca Ferraro had a good heart. She had, too, a determination to ensure that none who entered the Ferraro home would ever leave hungry.

In the cooler months of shorter days, Luigi moved inside to write his journal. He wrote sitting on a cane sofa, only rising in the course of the evening to prod the embers of logs in the pot-bellied heater that warmed the whole house. Then, with no words left to write, he surrendered to the night. Regardless of the season, he tugged the cord that swished the bedroom ceiling fan into life. He took a certain comfort from the sound of the slow-moving blades above his bed. The sound reminded him of the engines of a ship. He closed his eyes and, dreaming, smiled.

His dreams were, more often than not, of boyhood. He was ten or twelve or thirteen years old. He was with Leonardo Battaglia. He and Leonardo had been born in Tescano within days of each other. They had started school on the same day and shared a desk for all their years at school. At first, the friendship had been based on mutual self-interest. Leonardo was the son of Tescano's only baker, Santo Battaglia, and his wife, Madonna. As the son of the baker, Leonardo had easy access to olive bread, Luigi's favourite. He traded this with Luigi, who, as the nephew of Cesare the blacksmith, had easy access to small pellets of waste metal and discarded flawed nuts and washers from

Cesare's workshop. Leonardo used this blacksmithing detritus as ammunition for his slingshot. It also helped the friendship that Leonardo had a football.

Luigi quickly came to admire Leonardo. The baker's son had an eagle eye: he could load and fire his slingshot like a quick-on-the-draw Hollywood cowboy and boasted of an ability to 'hit the pink bit of a donkey's rear, dead centre, at twenty metres'. He was similarly accurate with the football: he would point to a mark on the wall of the long-closed Tescano fire station, say, 'Chipped brick halfway up' and, with his left or right foot, smack the ball bang on target every time.

When the football bounced back, Luigi sometimes said, 'Header, same brick', before clipping the worn leather ball with a sideways flick of the head that generally placed it close to, but seldom dead centre of, the target brick. Then they would play one-a-side football, dribbling, sidestepping, imagining themselves as star strikers for Firenze or Roma or Milano, imagining the roar of the big-city fans: *Ferraro weaves, left, right ... Battaglia blocks ... Ferraro regains the ball ... yes ... yes ... yes ... Ferraro scores! What a season this youngster is having ... Now it's Battaglia, confident, gliding down the wing ... superb play. They'll both star for Italy one day, mark my words.*

In the seven weeks of the summer holidays, the two were almost inseparable. Always on foot, until, aged ten, when they both had bicycles — the Hercules rebuilt by Luigi, and the Hirondelle that found itself on permanent unofficial loan to Leonardo — the boys would mount what they called 'expeditions'.

On these expeditions, the two were centurions, scouting well ahead of their columns on the lookout for signs of hostile tribesmen or for tracks that might shave some time off a day's march for the foot soldiers. They rode mainly in silence, hunched on their mounts. If they talked, they spoke in whispers lest any sound be carried on the wind. Often they communicated in sign language — a waist-high movement of the hand, a finger pointed towards a tree or an undulation in the ground, a signal to crouch or crawl.

Sometimes, however, physical contact with enemies was impossible to avoid. Barbarians sprang from nowhere and lunged at Luigi and Leonardo. The centurions triumphed, but always the fight would be a close-run thing. With the enemy laid low, the centurions turned and rode back towards their columns, clutching spear wounds to the upper arm or thigh. The pain was borne in stoical silence. Arriving at the vanguard of these columns, they brushed aside offers of treatment and rode directly to their commander. They reported their skirmish, bound their own wounds and rode back to the front ranks of the marching men. Broad-shouldered and with eyes fixed firmly on the road ahead, they were deaf to the admiring cheers of the soldiers, who, they knew, would follow them to the very ends of the earth.

Sometimes, tired of being centurions, the two friends became sinewy, hardy foot soldiers, cut off behind barbarian lines, desperate to avoid capture and torture. Always, after great hardship and courage, the two found themselves back among their own around the Tescano campfires. And always, the two would eschew the adulation of their comrades. No matter; their deeds would be celebrated in song and saga, and in the years to come raw recruits to Rome's legions would be urged, 'Never forget the Tescano Two.'

Tescano, for Luigi and Leonardo, was a place of legends.

CHAPTER FOUR

Cadence

*... and so we buried Titus Tescare on the slopes
below our winter encampment on the long march
from Gaul to Rome, our Mother, our Eternal City.
Chariot Master Titus was the most noble of the noble.
We called the place Tescano.*
— **Chronicles of the Remus Legion, 59 AD**

Tescano, during the boyhood days Luigi shared with Leonardo, had its own caterpillar-like cadence. If an imagined sound could characterise a village, the sound that characterised Tescano would be a near-imperceptible ticking, like the sound of cogs clicking into a bicycle chain. And like the wheels driven by the chain and the seemingly effortless motion that followed, the village passed smoothly through the days and weeks and months and years and centuries. The faces changed, but not the family names.

Some said the village had been there forever, that it had been the Garden of Eden, that from one of the now-fossilised trees in the caves in the hills Eve had plucked the apple that poisoned the world. It was said that after Adam's first bite, the trees turned to stone and never again bore fruit.

Bartolo Minoza, the local mayor and headmaster, who chain-smoked through every lesson he taught, would have none of this Garden of Eden story. A dottore from the University of Genoa, he was one of Tescano's two men of learning. 'Read the records,' he said to any who cared to listen during his wine-washed evenings in the small cafe in the piazza that marked the centre of Tescano. Few cared to listen. Minoza was not a Tescano man. He was a blowhard from Genoa. He was a Fascist who had been sent to the village by the Party. Everybody knew the mayoral election had been fixed.

Raising his voice and stabbing his finger into the air, he insisted: 'Read the records. Before the Romans came here, this was nothing more than a hill where a few farmers and their families lived. Peasants and pigs. It was the Romans who civilised them. The Romans first made it a winter camp. Then the winter camp became a village. Titus Tescare died of a fever here on the way back from Gaul. He was the greatest ever chariot master. Read the records! Garden of Eden — horse's arse, Garden of Eden. We are the sons and daughters of Roman warriors, not the spawn of the harlot poisoner Eve.'

Sometimes he would repeat this assertion to his pupils during history lessons. The idea that they might be the sons of Roman warriors appealed to Luigi and Leonardo. It sounded preferable to being 'the spawn of the harlot poisoner Eve' —

even though neither was then familiar with the words 'spawn' or 'harlot'.

Like many who embraced Mussolini's Fascism during the 1920s and 1930s, Minoza was economical with the truth, selective with the records that he claimed to have read and that he quoted. In truth, the place the Roman legions had called Tescano had been much more than a mere encampment of a few farmers and their families when Titus Tescare was laid to rest there in his finest robes.

In the days of Chariot Master Tescare, the settlement was a village of several hundred souls. With a turn of the head they could look down on their sloping fields and onto a track that snaked through the hills along a geological line of least resistance. The track linked the settlement to a spider's web of other villages of varying sizes, all no more than a day's walk away. Taken together, the villages and the people were part of a wider Tuscan culture that had its own currency and chieftains, its own ironworking and blacksmithing.

But this was a culture overwhelmed by an expanding Rome. It was trampled by countless Roman soldiers and cavalrymen and military engineers and quartermasters and slaves in chains, all of whom transformed a track between villages into a major military thoroughfare. However, as the power and influence of Rome shrank away in the fourth and fifth centuries the thoroughfare became a track once more. It was only widened again, as the world was widened, by the coming of the motor car.

None of these truths of an older, cultured pre-Roman Tuscany featured in Minoza's utterances. Taking his lead from Mussolini, he identified himself as a son of Rome, a son from the bloodline of Romulus and Remus who had been suckled on the milk of a mother wolf.

The other Tescano man of learning, the also recently arrived Father Gianni Genaro, was more circumspect. He said that only God knew where the Garden of Eden had been and that, in time, God might tell the Holy Father, who, in time, might tell his flock. Until then, all would remain a mystery.

Father Gianni's post-seminary studies had been completed at the Pontifical Gregorian University in Rome. Skilled in the translation of documents from Greek, Latin, Hebrew and Aramaic, his fluency also extended to Spanish, French, German and English. Once a rising star in the Vatican audit office, where his attention to detail had marked him as a man destined for bureaucratic glory, he fell from grace over a failed bet on the 1931 Italian Cycling Championships. Using millions of lira siphoned from a church-run fund to support Mussolini's Fascist Catholic Youth League, he backed a rank race outsider at fifty to one. The bet was based on a whispered tip from a fellow priest that the race was fixed and the rank outsider was a sure thing to cross the finishing line first. The sure thing proved disappointing on the day, as do many sure things.

Father Gianni was unapologetic. He told his audit office superiors he'd intended to use any winnings to support the wives and families of imprisoned and supposedly Communist trade unionists. He said Communists were merely confused Christians in a hurry to create God's paradise on earth. This was not a view shared by the audit office. Indeed, it was only the sympathy, support and influence of two of his former professors at the

Pontifical Gregorian University — both cardinals — that saved Father Gianni from excommunication.

That professorial influence flowed from the two academics' implied knowledge of a collection, held by Bishop Renzo Vigoro, a balding, strongly built man who was head of the audit office. It consisted of revealing photographic studies made the previous summer of teenage members of the all-boy Fascist Catholic Youth League at a gymnastics carnival near Naples. The professors suggested — to the principal private secretary of the Holy Father himself — that the head of the audit office, in his cups, had laughingly referred to himself as the Bishop of Buggeri, a fictional apostolic see, and had expressed a fondness for a weekly goats'-milk enema 'to flush the Via Faecessi free of sin'.

It was determined that all scandals should be avoided. A compromise was reached. Bishop Vigoro promised to avoid any more behaviour that might lead to gossip. Father Gianni was sent north to Tescano, by now a village of perhaps three hundred beating hearts, and admonished never to return to Rome. His two former professors, accompanying him to Rome's main railway station, Termini, and the train that would take him north, farewelled him with the words: 'From now on, be circumspect in all your words and deeds. This is God's gift to the wise. The Holy Father himself tells us that God's will is that we concern ourselves with souls.' Father Gianni said he would take the advice to heart. The professors doubted the sincerity of his response. Professors of the Gregorian, even to this day, doubt many things. Their doubts, because they are men of learning, are, more often than not, justified.

Father Gianni's charge in Tescano was the Church of the Blessed Seamstress. According to local lore, the Blessed Seamstress was a wretched, partially blind Judean, Martha of the Mount, who brought fleeting comfort, for a small consideration, to many soldiers of Rome's Jerusalem garrison in the brutal and troubled times of Pontius Pilate, Equestrian Procurator of Judea. It was said that after witnessing the sufferings of Christ she was so profoundly moved that she sat by the cross until the skies darkened; then, from her threadbare robe, she fashioned a shroud for the flayed and pierced body of the man who had been crucified between two thieves. It was said, too, that three days after the crosses and their victims were removed, Martha's sight was fully restored. Thenceforth, she led a life of chastity.

When Father Gianni arrived in Tescano, the Church of the Blessed Seamstress was without a resident priest. The church had been left vacant in 1931 by the loss of Father Paul Pedanti, a kind soul who had served his village for more than forty-five years but who, as he approached the seventy-eighth year of a life touched by grace, grew increasingly reclusive until he reached a point where he only communicated with his flock using a sheaf of handwritten notes, all of which said: *I have taken a vow of silence.* Concerned by this behaviour, Father Paul's housekeeper, Bella Colombo, herself aged in her seventies, finally used the presbytery telephone — an act of some personal courage, since she believed that only Father Paul was authorised, by the Holy Father himself, to use the phone — to speak to the hospice for aged priests in Pisa. Two days later, three men, all priests, arrived from Pisa. After sitting with Father Paul by the altar for several hours, the three priests, quite gently and quietly, helped him into their car. They carried with them a small wooden valise. It contained all that Father Paul owned in this world: a rosary that had belonged to his mother, some small religious ornaments brought back from pilgrimages to Rome and Lourdes, a Latin dictionary, and a slim, leather-bound volume of the writings of Saint Thomas, the disciple who had doubted. Then the priests and Father Paul drove off, down the hill and westwards, towards Pisa.

Some weeks later, mayor and headmaster Minoza was notified in writing, by the physician at the Pisa hospice, that Father Paul had gone to his Maker without uttering a word. He'd died in his sleep. The physician wrote: *He was, I suspect, simply worn out, too weary to speak, too thirsty for the taste of the waters of everlasting life to remain with us.* News of the passing of their priest brought great sadness to Tescano. There were so many stories to tell. The time Father Paul, smoking in bed, almost set fire to his presbytery. That terrible winter when he trudged through the snow to give the Last Rites to old Silvio at the Vendetti farm. Cesare recalled Father Paul, sleeves rolled up, in the smithy, sharpening tools for the harvest. Franca's eyes misted when she remembered Father Paul by her bedside as she drifted between life and death after the difficult birth of Luigi. That so many tears were shed was proof that Father Paul's earthly estate extended well beyond the contents of his small wooden valise.

Some of that sadness still remained when Father Gianni arrived in Tescano in the year of Luigi's tenth birthday. The sadness was evident in the new priest's first conversation with the elderly housekeeper. He asked Bella Colombo how the congregation remembered Father Paul and his good works in

Tescano. An astute man, Gianni wanted to know what he would be measured against and judged by.

'Father Paul was a saint,' Bella said. 'A saint. We were blessed to have him. Blessed. No one can replace him.' Then, realising she'd suggested the new priest was short of saintly, she clapped her hands to her mouth.

Father Gianni smiled. 'Oh, dear,' he said. 'Perhaps we should advise Rome of its error in sending me here. And while we await the reply, you can tell me of the light that Father Paul shone into your hearts.'

Bella nodded. She said Father Paul believed that most people in Tescano knew right from wrong and good from bad. Now and then, a few strayed — some might drink too much wine, others might speak unkindly of their neighbours. The divine mission of the priest, Father Paul had once told Bella, was to guide good souls to their heavenly reward and to warn those who strayed that they were walking to the gates of eternal chastisement.

'Well, there you are,' Father Gianni said to Bella. 'That's what I was told in Rome: concern yourself with souls. Those were the very words.'

Bella felt reassured and, in the days that followed, any who asked her about the new priest were told: 'He seems to be a good man. He has a way of speaking that touches the heart … and there is kindness in his face. God and the Holy Father must think well of Tescano to have sent us this priest.'

In the weeks before banishment and the train and bus journey north, Father Gianni had studied the place where he believed he would end his days, a displaced scholar of the Gregorian, a fading star — for every man, be assured, has his small, secret vanities — in the fading robes of a country priest. He accepted his fate. Tescano, he was certain, was God's will, just as his failed wager on a bicycle race had been God's will, too. Using the same logic, Father Gianni also came to the view that it was God's will he should remove a slim volume, *Essays on the Lore and Legend of Tescano*, from the restricted section of the central library of his alma mater.

There were thousands of books on the restricted list. The names of some were enticing: *Temptations and Myriad Devilries, Protocols for the Suppression of Lewd Tendencies, Exercises for the Containment of Bodily Tensions, Genitalia Diabolica, On the Altar of Sodom*. Other titles were more cerebral: *Secret Codes of the Heretic Painters, Icons and their Revelations of the Faith, Follies of Freemasonry, Estonian Madrigals and the Putrefaction Within, Findings on the Unclean Habits of the Laundress of Santa Monica*. The inside cover of *Essays on the Lore and Legend of Tescano* bore the official stamp of the Vatican Office of Linguistics and Theoretical Lexicography and the handwritten note: *Contents include references to heresy and the supernatural. Not to be removed from this place*. Father Gianni slipped the work into a sheaf of papers and, smiling in the direction of the domed glass ceiling, walked from the library.

From the heretical book, Father Gianni learned that the village was marked on the map as Monte Tescano. But to all — save for geographers and cartographers — who had stayed in or passed by the town from the times of the Remus Legion, it was simply Tescano. Maps in the book showed the narrow road that led to the village as a zigzagging affair that branched off the much wider Via Norde, which had been the main Roman route to Gaul. Marching north, the Romans had passed through the settlements of Baccanau, Vulsini, Clusium, Florentia and Pistoria before sighting the track that led away up the hill to the settlement they named Tescano.

The defensive walls built on the hill in Roman times had long ago become mounds of dross and rubble. Over many centuries, stones were removed from these defensive walls to be used in the construction of modest houses, and of what became Father Gianni's plain church and lodgings. They were also used to build the school and the ornate fountain placed on top of a well first sunk by the comrades of Titus Tescare. The well was reputed to be the deepest in Italy, and locals said it had flowed, without interruption, since the Romans had first tasted its waters and pronounced them to have healing and restorative powers.

The ornate fountain was in the centre of the Piazza Valsini, built and named in 1554 for the priest Vulvante Valsini. Father Valsini claimed to have restored the virginity of a maidservant by washing her uncovered body with water from the Tescano well. The father repeated the declaration of the Romans that the waters had holy and healing properties, a gift to the village from God. It was said that many fallen women were thereafter returned to purity by Father Valsini and the healing waters. Tragically, some years after the first reported restoration, Father Valsini died of a fever and a pox that could be neither cooled nor cauterised by the waters of the fountain. On the day of Valsini's death, according to *The Lore and Legend of Tescano*, an earth tremor had shaken the village, but the fountain remained unaffected. This was taken as a sign that Father Valsini had ascended to Heaven.

Earth tremors in the area were not uncommon. One tremor, in August 1914, on the very day the Great War began, damaged a wall in the school. The destruction was confined to a crack that ran the height of a wall in one of the two classrooms — the classroom for children aged six to ten. The crack had been plastered over many times but it remained visible. Only a small part of it was obscured, when Luigi was a pupil there, by a life-sized head-and-shoulders portrait of the dictator Mussolini, who had become Prime Minister of Italy in 1922. Three years later he styled himself Il Duce — Supreme Leader — of Fascism.

The older children were taught in the other classroom by headmaster and mayor Minoza. The younger children were taught by Salvatore Paglia, who was likewise not a son of Tescano. Behind his back, the children called Paglia 'Ferret Fartface', a reference to his thin, protruding nose and pursed, mean Borgia lips. But they were careful never to use the description within his earshot. Paglia was a young man easily enraged, and was feared, by many of his charges, for his backhanded slaps, which had loosened one boy's tooth and bloodied the eyebrow of another.

During their years at school, Luigi and Leonardo always shared a desk. Paglia, despite his rages, never raised a hand to either of them. Like most bullies, Paglia had an instinctive, self-preserving awareness of who could and who could not be bent to his will. He saw and understood that between these two boys was a bond that would see an injury to one as an attack on both. He sensed, in Luigi and Leonardo, two boys who had his measure. As a result, he would treat them always with caution, and sometimes with favour.

Unlike the chain-smoking Bartolo Minoza, Paglia was not a man of learning. He spoke in the rough, guttural tones that

31

marked him as a provincial from the southernmost toe of Italy. He had first arrived in Tescano in the late summer of 1926 as a member of a touring and tuneless Young Fascist League Trombone and Tambourine Troupe, in which he swaggered in his role of lead tambourinist. It was a role that saw him centre stage at every performance — like a cheerleader, his tuneless rattle held high and oscillating in one hand while the other jutted forwards and upwards in the absurdity of the Fascist salute.

After one sunset performance in the Piazza Valsini, Paglia had shared too many drinks with Bartolo Minoza. 'Young, well-proportioned men like you,' Minoza said, 'are the future of our Fatherland. Fit. Unafraid. Certain. Muscular.' Paglia had agreed with Minoza when the headmaster observed that he had much to offer. Indeed, Paglia indicated that he would welcome Minoza's guidance on how best to give of himself. That guidance was freely offered, and was accepted over still more drinks, long after sunset in the privacy of Minoza's home in a laneway off the Via Nera. As they entered, Minoza, because he was a man of learning, winked as he said to Paglia: *'Est vera amicitia inter homines'* — there is true friendship only among men. Paglia immediately understood the wink, if not the Latin.

The next day Paglia reluctantly departed with the tuneless ensemble for performances in Arretium and Arboretto to the north. Some months later, in early 1927, he returned to Tescano as a teacher. He had been selected and appointed to the role by a mysterious process, initiated by Minoza, to replace twenty-two-year-old Guido Gambaro, despised by Minoza as 'a weakling and a Red'. In late 1926, not long after the initial appearance of Paglia in Tescano, Gambaro was sacked, prosecuted, jailed and then drafted into the army after supposedly being found in possession of 'subversive, anti-State' Workers' Party leaflets. Gambaro died of cholera in Libya in 1931.

Paglia gloried in his status as both Tescano's new teacher and the foundation Sergeant-at-Arms of Tescano's local Cohort of Cobras, a State-funded Greco-Roman wrestling and body-building league for boys under twelve.

The Cohort of Cobras trained every Tuesday evening, on mats that were unrolled on the floor of the classroom with the crack that ran the height of one wall. It was the job of the younger children, every Tuesday afternoon, to push their desks against the cracked wall, making space for the evening wrestling. On Wednesday morning, first thing, they slid the desks back into place before singing, as Paglia beat time on his tambourine, the 'Giovinezza', the official hymn of the Italian Fascist Party. It was a rant that eulogised youth.

Some of Luigi's earliest memories of school and the desk he shared with Leonardo were of those Wednesday mornings when he sang:

Hail, people of heroes,
Hail, immortal Fatherland,
Your sons were born again with faith in the Ideal.
Your warriors' valour,
Your pioneers' virtue, today shines in every heart.
Youth, youth,
Spring of beauty,
In the hardship of life
Your song rings and goes.

And for Benito Mussolini,
Hip hip hooray,
And for our beautiful Fatherland,
Hip hip hooray.

Luigi enjoyed the singing. In general, too, he enjoyed school. The learning, if not the teachers. School was a place where there were books and maps and drawings of inventions and pictures of distant places.

By the time of his tenth birthday, Luigi was the best reader in his class. He was above average, too, in manual arts, a course for boys that centred mainly on carpentry and basic metalwork. The boys did manual arts while the girls learned sewing and baking in a course called domestic duties, supervised by a nun, Sister Maria Angela, who cycled to Tescano once every two weeks from the Convent of Santa Teresa, which lay at the mouth of a valley perhaps six kilometres away. The young Luigi believed that Sister Maria Angela was the most beautiful and good and pure of God's creations. Someday she would surely be a saint. If the word were given, Luigi knew he would die for her. God simply had to ask; Luigi would obey.

During the war that was to come, the Convent of Santa Teresa became a haven and a hideaway for Partisans and escaping Allied prisoners. And Sister Maria Angela became a heroine of the Partisans as the Cycling Sister of Santa Teresa, the only nun in all of Italy to be awarded the Partisan Service Medal and life membership of the Italian Collective of Touring Cyclists. These were high honours, indeed.

Luigi's above-average performance at school extended beyond reading and manual arts. He also excelled in writing and in geography. Teacher Paglia was particularly keen on writing, and he encouraged his charges to produce compositions describing their home life. 'Write everything,' he said each week. 'Write about your mother, your father, your sisters, your brothers. Write about the stories they tell, what makes them happy or even angry. Write about your dreams, your wishes. Remember, no secrets. Secrets are the black shadows of the soul.'

For Luigi, a boy with no father he knew and neither brothers nor sisters, writing opened the door to a fantasy world of rich uncles in America and cowboy cousins in Mexico who led seemingly fabulous lives: riding the ranges on palomino ponies, driving cattle across vast plains, sitting by campfires whistling or crooning or eating reheated beans, or sleeping under canopies of stars. He had read of such people and places in two books — *Tales of the Frontier* and *Real Men of the Old West* — that he'd discovered in the long-abandoned Tescano fire station.

Now and then, in his stories, he referred to his mother and Uncle Cesare. But these were passing mentions. *We live in a small house here in Tescano but my mother's sister lives in a big house in New York which is in America*, he wrote.

Paglia indulged Luigi's fantasies. They were harmless enough.

The stories, written every Friday afternoon, were collected by Paglia. They were returned to the pupils the following Monday, with a mark out of ten. Most Mondays Luigi learned that his efforts had been worth eight out of ten. Leonardo's mark was, consistently, six out of ten.

Luigi's eight-out-of-ten mark made him third from the top in writing. First and second places, week after week, went to the identical Fartini twins, Aldo and Waldo. They were seven months older than Luigi. Both were members of Tescano's Cohort of Cobras, and they were Paglia's favourites.

However, the Fartini boys would not outlive their youth. In 1937, their school days behind them, they volunteered for service alongside Franco's Falangists in Spain. They were members of a Fascist boy battalion, the Eagles of Empoli, that had been raised in the town, between Pisa and Florence, that gave the unit its name. The two never returned from Spain. Official reports reaching Tescano said the Fartini twins died as heroes in hand-to-hand combat with Spanish Republican irregulars. But there were rumours that Aldo's neck had actually been broken in an exhibition Greco-Roman wrestling tournament between the Eagles of Empoli and a Falangist unit, the Alicante Avengers of the Crimson Virgin. It was rumoured that Aldo, roundly disliked by the Eagles' wrestling coach as a cheat and a liar who bathed infrequently and was a poor excuse for Fascist boyhood, was deliberately mismatched with a much heavier and stronger boy, Manuel Strangozzo, from the Avengers of the Crimson Virgin. Strangozzo, it was later whispered in Tescano, had smirked as he snapped Aldo's neck 'like a dry twig'.

As for Waldo, the village stories said he fled from some Spanish Field of Mars seconds after his unit's first encounter with the enemy. Two days after his desertion, Waldo was captured and summarily executed on the orders of the wrestling coach.

But these were only village stories. Who knew if there was any truth to them?

Leonardo was not distressed by the stories of the Fartini twins. 'I never liked them,' he confided to Luigi. 'Teacher's pets. And you always wrote better stories at school. Even if they were all made up, you should have got ten out of ten. They were really good lies.'

Luigi's excellence in writing and geography during his school years was partly as a result of his having memorised the names of places on the map that hung on the wall of the classroom facing the portrait of Mussolini. The map showed Italy as the centre of the world — France and Spain and the Americas to the left, and Bulgaria and Greece and Asia and Japan to the right. During geography lessons, Luigi sometimes stood before the class and said then spelled out the names of places as Paglia pointed to them — Rome, Milan, Florence, Palermo, Tescano, Istanbul, Isfahan, Kabul, Bombay, Singapore, Sydney, San Francisco. As a reward, Paglia allowed Luigi to take home one of five dog-eared geography textbooks held in the school's 'library' — six single shelves that held perhaps seven dozen volumes.

On nights when he took home a geography book, Luigi read it by candlelight in the loft that was his bedroom. There was so much to read. So many places: Abyssinia, Algeria, America, Anatolia, Andalucia, Andorra, Armenia, just to start with the 'A's. The furthest-away place was called Australia. Luigi, alone, mouthed the word again and again: *Ow … straa … leeeaah*. It was bigger than all of Europe. He wondered what it might be like to cycle to that place at the very end of the world. One day, perhaps, he and Leonardo would go there. What an adventure that would be.

Certainly, Tescano was fine. It was home. It was his mother and Uncle Cesare and Leonardo and the kindly, clever Father

Gianni and the angelic Sister Maria Angela and the hills and their secret places. It was rust-coloured tiled roofs and the silver water of the fountain and the smells of the bakery and the forge. It was cats that visited every home and dogs that barked at every full moon. It was the village brass band that played at funerals and weddings and confirmations and on the holy days of saints and martyrs. But Luigi was learning that there were other places too. The places in the books and on the map on the classroom wall. There were grand cities and great rivers, and mountains that rose above the clouds.

Luigi often read until tiredness blurred his vision, and then he closed his eyes and drifted through a world of ships that crossed empty oceans and camel trains that crossed great deserts. For a boy who had never journeyed more than a day on foot or some hours by bicycle beyond his village, the very prospect that there were places such as these where the eye could see forever was truly wondrous. Then the dreams ended and Luigi woke for another day at school.

When there was no school and Luigi had no chores to do for his mother, he wheeled his Hercules into the sunlight beyond the two open doors of his uncle's smithy, where Leonardo waited with the Hirondelle. Depending on what had been studied in that week's geography lesson, Luigi might say: 'Looks like a good day for Bulgaria', or 'We might make Switzerland if there's no snow on the passes', or 'With a tail wind we could make Australia in a week. Easy.' Then they were off, into their own universe where no destination was too distant. Where a dream had only to be imagined to be realised. Saying and being were one and the same in the boys' private universe.

CHAPTER FIVE

Unity

We have a simple rule here. It is a rule above all other rules. We may leave our valiant dead on the field of combat but we never leave our bicycles. We are warrior cyclists.

— *Conscript Manual*, Army Cycling Training School, Livorno, 1939

Luigi's schooling finished when he was fourteen. He was needed in the smithy. Leonardo left school at the same time. He was needed in the bakery. Most days, Luigi was in the smithy, sleeves rolled up, by seven in the morning. Leonardo started his day in the bakery five hours earlier. On weekdays the boys seldom saw each other. But Friday and Saturday nights and Sundays were different.

Under Bartolo Minoza and Salvatore Paglia, one of Tescano's two school classrooms had become the local picture theatre, with two films screened on Friday nights and two on Saturday nights. Funding for the projector and the films came from the regional administrative office of the Partito Nazionale Fascista in Florence. The mayor and the hand-picked teacher, regarded in the regional administrative office as eager and sound Party members, had experienced no difficulty in securing the financial support. They presented the weekend showings as an opportunity to contribute to the Party's 'nation-building' programme. That programme, Minoza and Paglia said, was about 'going forward' in a 'new way' that 'turned its back on negativity'. During the fifteen-minute intermission between the feature films, Minoza and Paglia showed government newsreels. The feature films were the bait that reeled in an audience for the Party propaganda.

The feature films were, in the main, American westerns. That they were in English was of no consequence. The music and the action told the tale: ruthless cattle barons terrorising small ranchers, virginal sloe-eyed beauties in the clutches of saloon pimps, feathered warriors whooping around the embers of a burnt log cabin. Then, through the dust in the distance, a rider approaches, white Stetson firmly in place, a Colt Peacemaker in one hand, a sheathed lever-action Winchester strapped to a polished saddle. The ruthless cattle barons are scattered. The saloon pimps are felled by a single blow. The feathered warriors take to their heels. The virginal beauties swoon in the arms of the man in the white Stetson.

During 1935 and 1936, in the intermission between westerns, almost every newsreel featured Italian doctors and nurses distributing food to orphans of the Spanish Civil War or caring for the wounded. As the war in Spain progressed over the months, there was increasing coverage of events portrayed as 'Republican atrocities': burnt churches, brutalised nuns, priests shot down and left dying in the streets, crops and villages put to the torch by obviously godless Communists and Anarchists. There was, too, continuing coverage of the exploits of brave young Italian soldiers, who were bringing civilisation to the pagan multitudes of Libya and were prodding the black men of Abyssinia into the light of modernity. And, invariably, there were images of Il Duce, standing high on a balcony, hands on hips, looking down on a sea of adoring supporters; or, occasionally, sleeves rolled up, breaking bread and drinking wine with peasant farmers during a pause in harvesting. Here was a man of the people, for the people, with the people.

Entry to the film and propaganda night was free, and Luigi and Leonardo rode to the screenings astride 'Old Gunsmoke' and 'Mustang' — the Hercules and the Hirondelle. They watched both sessions on Friday night and both sessions on Saturday night. After the final Saturday session they'd walk out of the classroom-turned-picture-theatre bow-legged, hands hovering by hips, ready to draw their six-shooters and unleash volleys of lead into any miscreant who happened their way. Swinging into the saddle, they touched the front rim of imaginary Stetsons, nodded sharply and rode off into the night. No words were exchanged, for they were cowpokes, Kid Whiplash and Kid Lightning, whose nods and handshakes said all that needed to be said and whose steely, narrowed eyes scanned the shadows for Prairie Trash.

On Sunday afternoons they'd rendezvous at the bakery, check their mounts and ride down the zigzag hill from Tescano into the Badlands, alert for the telling smoke signals of Apaches in the hills or sightings of the gunslinging hired hands sent by cattle barons to harass and bully honest and hard-working smallholders.

But boyhood adventures, though long remembered, are short-lived. At fourteen or fifteen a boy can ride the range, vanquish the bad and rescue the weak. However, a bicycle can only exist as 'Old Gunsmoke' or 'Mustang' for so long. At sixteen and seventeen, a boy — a young man — has other pressing matters at hand. So, while the Sunday cycling continued, such conversation as there was now centred on the mysteries of women and on rumours relating to the enigmatic Widow Lola Volare.

She was not a woman of Tescano, she had arrived from places undisclosed in the year of Luigi's birth. If the rumours were to be believed, she was not a woman at all. She had been, so it was said, a serving soldier until she suffered an emasculating blow from a spiked German helmet in the Alpine campaigns of the Great War.

She lived alone in a small house in the Via Dolomare. Leonardo had heard that the Widow Volare was sometimes visited, in the hours of darkness, by Mayor Minoza, who was said by some to be Lola's 'fancy man'. When Luigi heard this, he was puzzled. He had never seen any 'fancy men' in Tescano. What, he wondered, might they wear — top hats, flowing robes, white gloves?

Finally, the Sunday cycling ceased altogether in late 1939 when Luigi and Leonardo, aged eighteen, received official notification by letter that they were to report as conscripts for military service. The letters were not unexpected. All Italian males, when they reached the age of eighteen, were required by law to undergo military training.

Luigi had never received a letter before. Sitting in the kitchen, he stared at the envelope then handed it to his mother. She would know what should be done with a letter. Opening the envelope, she read the contents slowly to herself then handed the single typewritten sheet to Luigi. 'They have sent for you,' she said. Then she turned away and quickly left the kitchen, raising her apron surreptitiously to wipe away tears.

Leonardo appeared in the doorway of the Ferraros' kitchen. He, too, was holding a single typewritten sheet. The contents of the two letters were identical, save for the names. Luigi and Leonardo were to go to the coastal city of Livorno on a set date. They would travel by bus. They were advised that there would be an initial training period of nine months. After that they would be assigned to regular units for eighteen months, or allocated to reserve units, where they would be liable to be called up for eighteen months' service. The notification described the circumstances under which a conscript might be afforded reservist status. Such status might be contingent on family circumstances, such as where a son was the family's sole breadwinner. Reservist classification might also be conferred where a conscript was required to work a farm or was essential to a family business.

Leonardo spoke first. He said the Fascists wanted a war and that he and Luigi might find themselves in the thick of it. 'Things are bad,' he said. 'If the war starts and I'm in the army and get sent to fight, I'm out. I won't be getting shot for the likes of Minoza and Paglia — loudmouths and bullies: *the Party this, the Party that*. If they want a war they can go off and fight it themselves. What about you, Luigi — what if you're in the army and there's a war and you get sent to fight?'

There was a chasm of silence between the two and Luigi shrugged. What could he say? How could he know what he would do if he was ordered to fight? He didn't know about such things. Uncle Cesare had been to war, but he never talked about it.

Leonardo pressed his question. 'I will ask Uncle Cesare tonight,' Luigi finally replied. 'If he wants to tell me what I should do he will tell me. And then I will tell you.' It was the closest Luigi had ever come to expressing annoyance towards Leonardo. Sometimes, Luigi thought, Leonardo was too full of questions.

That evening, at the kitchen table, he asked Uncle Cesare what he should do. 'Everybody must go for military training,' Cesare said sternly. 'If you do not go, they will come for you and they will take you away. In the last war, those who refused to go were shot.'

Dinner was eaten in silence after that.

On the morning of Saturday, 30 September 1939, Luigi and Leonardo boarded the twice-weekly bus that stopped briefly in Tescano on its journey from Florence to Livorno via Pisa. There were nine other young men on the bus when it reached Tescano. Along the rest of the route another eight were picked up. All were conscripts and all sat in silence, wondering what lay ahead. From Tescano to Livorno was a distance of a few score kilometres. It was the furthest Luigi and Leonardo had ever ventured.

The ancient port town of Livorno had been a melting pot for centuries. It attracted merchants, maritime traders and artisans from England, Holland, France, Spain and Greece. A place of lanes and canals and some grand houses, Livorno had two walled forts, the Fortezza Vecchia, near the harbourside, and the Fortezza Nuova. In the hills above Livorno was the Sanctuary of Montenero, a place where pilgrims sought solace and the intercession of the patron saint of Tuscany, Our Lady of the Graces.

Eventually the bus halted at the main gate of the conscript training facility at the Fortezza Nuova. The young men filed off the bus. A sign on what they'd learn was the guardroom said, in red, *Conscripts report here*. The conscripts entered and showed their conscription papers to a tall, strongly built, clean-shaven, immaculately turned-out sergeant. There were several long benches in the guardroom — more than enough seating for fifty souls. The sergeant nodded and, saying nothing, motioned to the conscripts to sit.

In the hours that followed, more conscripts arrived, until by late afternoon the benches were almost filled to capacity. The immaculate sergeant, a clipboard in his hand, finally spoke. 'When I call your name you will stand and identify yourself by your last name and by your given names. I will put a tick against your name and you will sit.' Then he began to read the names: Battaglia, Benzino, Capone, Convivante … Zevi …

The sergeant paused at Zevi. He looked up and fixed his eyes on the standing figure. 'Zevi, Jacob — are you a Jew?' he said.

'Yes,' the young man replied, a hint of trepidation in his voice.

The sergeant leaned forward. 'We've only ever had one Jew boy here before. Didn't last. Hanged himself after three weeks. Sit.'

Luigi, turning his head slightly, glanced at Zevi, who looked utterly alone, apprehensive, friendless. For the briefest moment, the eyes of the two met. With a wink and the hint of a nod from

Luigi, Jacob's apprehension eased. Perhaps he was not entirely alone.

Zevi's was the last name to be called before the recruits left the guardroom. They were marched, by the sergeant, to a bathhouse, where their hair was shorn. They were issued with overalls, shorts, singlets, black canvas gym shoes, underwear, two towels and a shaving kit, and were then ordered to shower.

Newly shorn and dressed in their overalls and gym shoes, they were assembled outside the bathhouse by the immaculate sergeant. There, hands clasped behind his back, another sergeant was waiting. This man was slightly built and less immaculately presented than the first, but the medal ribbons on his chest marked him as a man who had seen active service. The clipboard was signed and exchanged, and the immaculate sergeant — whose chest bore no medal ribbons, Luigi now noticed — marched off.

When he was just out of earshot, the slightly built sergeant said for all to hear: 'Big, useless bastard.' He addressed the conscripts. 'I am Sergeant Dante — Scalio Dante. I served with the Alpini in the Great War and I have fought in the deserts of Africa. I am here because I was sent here and because the army believes I am too old for the front lines — just as you were called here because the army believes you are young enough for the front lines. These front lines may well have already been drawn on maps we have yet to glimpse. For now, this is not my business or your business.

'You are now members of the Second Thirty-Ninth Training Division, my division. We are one of sixteen companies in the division. All will begin training on Monday. I will be with you and you with me for nine months. After that, nobody knows where anybody will be. Unlike the useless swine who marched you over here, I am a soldier, an old soldier. He is a coward pretending to be a policeman in an army uniform. He guards the gates with his louts and layabouts. Keep your distance. He and his kind are bad bastards. They should be put in sacks and used for bayonet practice. However, I do not believe this is likely to happen. The army seldom listens to my sensible suggestions. For now, remember this: if he lays a finger on you for no reason, I will deal with him. If he lays a finger on you for a reason — if you are drunk or disorderly or late back here after your first leave pass — you are on your own.'

Dante paused and eyed his conscripts, then continued. He spoke with passion. 'I am from Milan, and my passion is football. Each company in the training division has its own football teams, and at the end of five months we have a football competition, the Conscript Cup. Whether or not you gain passing glory on the field of battle is of no great consequence to me. Glory on the football field is another matter. This is the glory of real men. It is the glory of the spirit, the soul. It is the glory of fairness and respect and restraint. A fair man is not a soft man. Strong men and hard men are different breeds. Step forward any man here who disagrees.'

No one stepped forward. Sergeant Dante's tone, the ribbons on his chest and the dark intensity of his eyes suggested that disagreement was not being offered as a serious option.

The sergeant counted the men off into groups of eleven where they stood. 'We have four teams and four men to spare,' he announced. 'That means each team will have one reserve player.'

47

Pointing to each group in turn, he said: 'You will be the Wolves, the Foxes, the Lions and the Tigers.'

Luigi, Leonardo and Jacob Zevi were all in the Foxes. Luigi nudged Leonardo. 'The Tescano Foxes,' he said under his breath. Leonardo winked. Most of the conscripts who made up the Foxes were from Tuscany — from Florence, Empoli, Poggibonsi, Capannori, Porcari.

Sergeant Dante pursed his lips as he scanned the young men who stood before him. Some of them had the lean, strong build of footballers who could, after ninety muscle-wrenching minutes of play, endure thirty minutes of extra time and score the golden goal that clinched the Conscript Cup. Perhaps this would be his year.

Then the conscripts were marched, out of step, to a mess hall bigger than any single building Luigi or Leonardo had ever seen. It continued to fill steadily as the Second Thirty-Ninth, carrying metal trays with plates and mugs, filed along the line of laden food containers that fronted a huge kitchen. As a group, the conscripts then sat down on both sides of two long tables.

With food before them, the young men exchanged handshakes and names. Luigi had gestured to Jacob to sit between him and Leonardo. Jacob introduced himself first. He said his father was a master watchmaker and goldsmith in Florence and the family had been in the city for more than two centuries. Luigi and Leonardo said they were, respectively, a blacksmith's apprentice and a baker's apprentice. Their families had been in Tescano since before Christ.

When dinner was finished, Dante escorted the company to their dormitory barracks, the second in a long row of barracks built at right angles to the inside walls of the Fortezza Nuova. Each barracks had bunks for sixty conscripts. Linen, a pillow and two blankets were laid out on each bunk bed. Along the walls between the bunks were metal lockers, one for each conscript. Above some of these lockers were long, narrow windows that provided views of other dormitory blocks.

Sergeant Dante said each conscript should select a bunk. 'Lavatories and showers in there,' he said. 'Attend to your needs. After that, I suggest you rest. I have no objections to you playing with yourself if that is your inclination. However, the army and Il Duce are not favourably disposed towards you playing with each other.' Lights-out would be at 10 pm, and the conscripts would be wakened by a bugler at 6.30 am. 'I will be here at 7.30 am, by which time you should have washed, shaved and completed other necessities. In the morning I will show you, with my corporal, how the army makes beds. You will then be marched to the mess hall and from there you will be shown all the treasures of National Service Training Facility, Livorno.'

Dante explained that the conscripts would be medically examined on Monday and, if they were found fit for service, issued with uniforms and other items of kit. 'Our military doctors do not work on Sundays. If you have the misfortune to be sent to war and the double misfortune to be wounded, do not allow yourself to be wounded on a Saturday evening or a Sunday. Should you be wounded at such times, you will most likely bleed to death. For any who may entertain the hope of failing the medical examination on Monday, I suggest you drive that hope from your hearts,' he added dryly. 'Lazarus himself, unraised

from the dead, would be passed fit for service by our doctors.'
Then the sergeant turned and walked from the dormitory.

Leonardo led the selection of bunks for Luigi, Jacob and himself, hurrying to the far end of the dormitory. 'These ones,' he said. 'We're furthest from the door when Sergeant Dante or anybody else comes in, and we're furthest from the lavatories and showers, so the floor up here isn't dripping wet and people pissing won't keep us awake all night.' Jacob looked impressed and said Leonardo was obviously a thinker.

The dormitory lighting duly flickered and went out at 10 pm. A solitary light remained burning several metres outside the main dormitory entrance. Lying on his top bunk, Luigi thought of his mother and then of Uncle Cesare and the smithy and the bicycle adventures. The darkness of the dormitory concealed the trickle of his tears. There was no thought, there and then, of great travels to the furthest-away places on the map. Luigi felt so very far from home.

CHAPTER SIX

Pressure

A trumpet player who don't understand pressure just don't hit the sweet-as-pie notes. It's like a tyre. The right pressure and she runs cool and easy. Wrong pressure and she's flat and flabby as Grandma's chest.
— Xavier Nougatt, Panama Stars Swing Sextet, 1937

Luigi was awoken by the sound of the bugle. Looking along the length of the dormitory, he saw the friend from a boyhood that had ended walking towards him from the lavatories. Leonardo was already showered and shaved. Jacob was awake, yawning. Others were already awake or returning from their ablutions.

By 7.30 all had showered and shaved, and stood by their bunks as Sergeant Dante and Corporal Bernardo Bassanio entered. The corporal's tunic bore several medal ribbons. The bed-making lesson was brisk — bottom sheet tucked tightly under the mattress, pillow placed at the head of the bunk, sheet folded just below the pillow, blankets pulled tightly across the sheets. Corporal Bassanio was a master of the bed-maker's craft. Several conscripts were directed to follow the master's actions, watched closely by Sergeant Dante. All passed muster.

From time to time, Dante said, a junior officer might make a surprise inspection of the dormitory. 'Such visits are infrequent,' he added. 'Our junior officers spend more time with the tarts of Livorno than they do with their conscripts — it's either the tarts or the pox doctor.'

The dormitory floors and lavatory were to be washed and disinfected every evening before lights-out and every morning after the conscripts had showered and shaved. Every conscript would play his part in this housekeeping, Dante said firmly. There would be no shirkers, and bullies would not be tolerated.

Formed into ranks of three abreast, the Second Thirty-Ninth conscripts were marched to the mess hall. Half an hour later, the conscripts cleared their tables of plates and cutlery and cups, walked outside and were marched around the fort's facilities.

There was a large main square where marching and other drills would be learned, a gymnasium, and four sports fields where teams were already playing football. One building, its double doors guarded by four men in the uniform of the Military Police, was identified as an armoury. Another building was the medical centre. This sat next to a larger building, a warehouse for uniforms and equipment. Then there was the guardroom where the conscripts had first entered the day before, and accommodation for non-commissioned officers like Dante and Bassanio, and for junior commissioned officers.

Dante pointed to a substantial stone structure in a far corner beyond the main square and sports fields. 'That is the residence of our training commandant, Colonel Galileo Gonfalonieri,' he said. 'You will see him from time to time, walking alone with his dog, Nero. Both of them watch and know all that happens here. Where you see Nero you will see the Colonel.

'I served with the commandant in Africa. He is a brave and honourable man. Like me, he sees the hand of God in the feet of those who play football. He favours Calcio Venezia Football Club but I don't hold that against him. He is only an officer. I am not aware if Nero favours Calcio Venezia, but I would hope he knows better. He is a dog of some breeding and style.'

The following day was Monday, when the conscripts would have their medical examinations and would be issued uniforms. Before the 8.30 am medical examination, each conscript completed a form providing their details — name, age, place of birth, level of schooling, previous illnesses, any current illnesses, occupation, any particular skills, and details of immediate family members and their circumstances. Dante shrugged at the look of puzzlement on the conscripts' faces at this requirement. All of these details were already on record in the National Service Bureau in Rome. 'Everything is written down a second time in the army because nobody ever reads it the first time,' he explained.

In the section of the form asking for details of *any particular skills*, Luigi, Leonardo and Jacob wrote: *Bicycle repairs and metalwork*. This was Luigi's idea. 'If we all say we do the same things it gives us a better chance of staying together.' Jacob responded that Luigi, like Leonardo, was a thinker.

As Dante had predicted, none of the conscripts failed the medical examination. When the uniforms had been issued, Corporal Bassanio provided instruction on how and when they were to be worn. There was then a period of marching drill followed by a midday meal, a rest period of thirty minutes and a further drill, after which the conscripts returned to their dormitory, where they attended to the general cleanliness and tidiness of their quarters and then assembled for the evening meal. And so Luigi's first day in uniform was over.

After that, life at the Fortezza Nuova settled quickly into a routine of drills, marching, cleaning, washing, ironing and football training. The conscripts in Dormitory Two were a mixed lot. Unusually for a group of forty-eight thrown-together young men, there were no out-and-out dullards, slackers, loudmouths or bullies. Whether or not this had anything to do with Sergeant Dante's entreaties about teamwork and warnings about bullying and shirking can never be known. More likely, the members of the Second Thirty-Ninth simply accepted their shared and passing reality. They were conscripts. They belonged to the State. That was that. It was probable, too, that in Sergeant Dante and Corporal Bassanio they recognised two veterans who were neither overbearing nor over-enamoured of the military hierarchy. They had a job to do and it was to be done efficiently, without rancour and by the book. 'Sergeants and corporals look after men who look after their sergeants and corporals,' Dante said to the conscripts. 'Follow orders, take care of each other, don't disgrace us on the parade ground, and play like champions on the football field. We will do the rest.'

Much of the easy camaraderie that characterised the passage of the conscripts through their first month was forged on the football field. There were twice- and sometimes thrice-weekly training sessions that saw the Wolves, the Foxes, the Lions and the Tigers ready themselves for their own Sunday round-robin tournament.

From his very first touch of the ball in the tournament, Luigi showed himself to be a tidy and intuitive winger. He was fast, bold and determined. He could find space where none appeared to exist. He could trap a high ball with the thrust of his chest, kill the ball stone dead and then send it straight to centre forward Leonardo, who'd dribble, feint, dodge, duck and weave towards the goal. On the attack, with Luigi never far away, Leonardo was deadly.

However, while Leonardo was a killer kicker close in, it was Luigi who shone during the first thirty-minutes-a-half round-robin match, which saw the Foxes hammer the Tigers by three goals to nil. Watching Luigi from the sidelines, Sergeant Dante was transported. 'Magnificent. Magnificent beyond words,' he said to Corporal Bassanio. 'Watch how he moves. Like a hawk, circling, swooping, gliding. There is the hand of God in those feet.' Then, as Luigi swept a low, straight ball over to Leonardo, Dante shouted: 'Look at that! Perfection.'

While the goal-scoring credit from that first, revealing encounter with the Tigers owed much to the partnership between Luigi and Leonardo, the goal-saving credit belonged to Jacob. Between the posts he was like a coiled viper, ready and able to pounce in less than the blink of an eye. Twice he blocked driving, close-range attacks from the Tigers' centre forward, and on at least three occasions he sprinted forward, halting cannonball shots with his soft watchmaker's hands. This boldness in defence marked Jacob, in Sergeant Dante's sharp eyes, as a spirited goalkeeper of audacity and courage. Jacob Zevi, like Luigi Ferraro and Leonardo Battaglia, was a real find.

Of course, there was more to the first month at Livorno than football training and weekend matches. The conscripts, Dante and Bassanio may have wished it otherwise, but the army had different priorities, and these included drills on the parade ground, daily runs of five kilometres, and day and night marches, twice a week and in full kit, up and along and down the tracks and gullies around the hills beyond Livorno.

Luigi's physical strength during the marches was plain to see; uphill or down, on the flat or on winding tracks, he was constant and measured in his movements. Dante regularly used him as a pacemaker. Luigi's performance on the obstacle courses and the small-arms ranges was similarly consistent — although his ability with a rifle at three hundred metres was just overshadowed by Leonardo, who was easily the best shot in Dormitory Two.

Jacob, for his part, showed average small-weapons skills, but outstanding abilities in stripping down and reassembling single-shot, semi-automatic and automatic weapons. 'You get a feel for where things go,' he explained to Sergeant Dante. 'It's like watchmaking. You see with your fingers.'

At the end of the first month of training, a twenty-four-hour leave pass was issued. The forty-eight conscripts from Dormitory Two were assembled by Dante and Bassanio outside the Fortezza Nuova guardroom. All were paid half of their meagre conscript entitlements for one month. The other half was to be paid to their families.

Sergeant Dante addressed them. 'Two vehicles will transport you to the gates of the Fortezza Vecchia, close to the centre of Livorno. From there you can come and go as you please for twenty-four hours. After twenty-four hours, the same two vehicles will return you here. I warn you against unruly behaviour. The Military Police will attend to any disorder, and this will cause you some regret. However, should you engage in disorderly conduct, make sure you damage your hands and not your feet — your feet belong to your football teams.' As an afterthought, Sergeant Dante mentioned that the goalkeepers should also avoid damage to their hands. He cautioned his charges to eschew loose women and to show 'soldierly politeness' towards Livorno's mothers and children. The conscripts should stick together in small groups, he advised. Livorno, after all, was a waterfront town where ruffians lurked in unlit alleys.

The conscripts boarded the two waiting trucks for a journey that took less than fifteen minutes. Offloaded at the old Fortezza Vecchia, they divided into groups of three or four and ambled into the antiquity of Livorno. From a maze of lanes they emerged into the town's main piazza, where they drifted towards the cafes that punctuated the archways around the square.

Luigi, Leonardo and Jacob settled themselves into the metal chairs of the Trattoria Bersaglieri. Luigi and Leonardo had been drawn to the establishment by the sight of a bicycle bolted to a metal plate on the cobblestones near the table they chose. The trattoria had been named in honour of the renowned Bersaglieri, the elite corps of soldiers who fought as fast-moving units deployed on folding bicycles and, sometimes, on motorised bicycles and motorcycles.

Seated, the three young men glanced inside towards a marble-topped counter set in highly varnished wood. Behind the counter was a mirrored bar; fastened to the wall above the bar was a row of the feather-plumed hats that made the Bersaglieri instantly recognisable wherever they rode.

An aproned waiter, a stocky, one-eyed man of military bearing, delivered three glasses of water, and Jacob engaged him in conversation. The waiter revealed that the trattoria had been established in 1919 by Benny 'Mountain Man' Marconi, a revered veteran regimental sergeant-major of the famous wheeled fighting force. Marconi had returned from the Great War after losing his right leg in the ferocity of one of the countless mountain engagements in that murderous conflict. Discharged after months in a military hospital, and the eventual successful fitting of an artificial leg, Marconi had attempted to return to the regiment that was his life, only to find that there could be no role for a one-legged cyclist in the elite unit. However, all was not entirely lost, explained the waiter. Comrades past and many serving Bersaglieri had rallied around Marconi. Money was raised, a full pension was bestowed, and the Trattoria Bersaglieri was established.

From the outset, the trattoria had been a favourite gathering place of Bersaglieri stationed in the Livorno district. 'Since those first days,' the waiter said, 'the sergeant-major has given employment only to men who served the regiment with honour. All have remained here for the rest of their working lives, as will I. One of those men was Corporal Fabio Nardini. Blinded at the front, he was given work as a dishwasher. Sadly, washing kitchen knives, he accidentally slashed a wrist and bled to death alone and in silence.'

Puzzled, Luigi asked: 'Why did he not cry out for help?'

The waiter inhaled deeply and sadly. 'I have asked myself the same question many times. I can only conclude that Corporal Nardini did not wish to alarm our benefactor, or his customers. The code of the Bersaglieri is a code of sacrifice.' The waiter turned away.

Leonardo pulled some folded notes from the left breast pocket of his tunic. It was his conscript pay. From his right breast pocket he extracted a handful of coins and four or five notes, money he'd brought from Tescano. 'Right,' he said, 'money on the table. Let's see what we have between us.'

Luigi followed suit, producing his conscript pay and a few extra coins and notes. Jacob was next. First came the conscript pay. Then, fumbling, he drew a wad of notes the thickness of his thumb from an unpicked seam along the inside waistband of his tunic. 'I always carry a little extra,' he said. He slapped the notes on top of the contributions from Luigi and Leonardo. 'All for one and one for all … equal shares … just like Athos, Porthos and Aramis.' Luigi and Leonardo did not recognise the names. They did, however, recognise Jacob's largesse. Jacob smiled and raised a hand to attract the attention of the stocky, one-eyed waiter. 'We will have, for three,' Jacob said, 'whatever you choose for us.'

The waiter's choice was fish, lightly cooked in local white butter and served with pasta. The meal was delicious.

It was edging towards mid-afternoon when Jacob settled the bill. He tipped the stocky waiter generously before asking: 'And can you suggest where we three might spend the night? Before you answer, let me advise you that my two comrades here are, like your benefactor, bicycle men of the very first order. They have told me of their boyhood cycling adventures in the hills and valleys around their village, Tescano.'

It was settled in an instant. The Trattoria Bersaglieri had three modest rooms above the kitchen where the blind dishwasher had bled to death. Two of the rooms were being repainted. If Luigi, Leonardo and Jacob were prepared to share the third room, the establishment would be happy to oblige. Former regimental sergeant-major Marconi would be on the premises that very evening. He would perhaps share a glass with them. They were, after all, men in uniform. Much more than that, however, two of the three had just been identified as 'bicycle men of the very first order'. As such, they — and their comrade of as yet undisclosed talents — were always welcome. A price for the room was agreed. The three departed, promising to return after they'd explored Livorno.

From the Trattoria Bersaglieri, the three strode across a grand piazza and past its fountain. Here and there they saw others from Dormitory Two lounging in cafes, tunics open, or, like Luigi, Leonardo and Jacob, stepping out at a pace that suggested there was much to be seen.

The centre of Livorno was a place of grand mansions that had for centuries housed merchants grown fat on trade with France, North Africa, the Levant and places further east. There were parks with flowerbeds freshly turned over after the last blooms of autumn and a statue labelled *Monumento dei Quattro Mori*, but which gave no explanation for the fame of the four Moors alluded to. The three conscripts pushed on past the Museo Mascagni, which honoured composer and lyricist Pietro Mascagni, and through the closed stalls of the morning marketplace. They paused in lanes and alleys to whistle at the craftsmanship of handmade shoes or, at Jacob's insistence, to study the wares in the window of a jeweller or a watchmaker.

It was early evening when they returned as promised to the Trattoria Bersaglieri. As they sat down at the same table they'd left some hours earlier, a well-built, well-groomed man limped towards them from behind the bar. 'I have the honour to be Regimental Sergeant-Major Benny Marconi,' he said, 'Grand Companion of the Sons of the Alpine Foxes and Honourable Brother of the Legion of the Seriously Wounded.'

Marconi was an impressive figure. He had the confident bearing of a military man — upright, square-shouldered. The three conscripts rose automatically to their feet.

'Sit down, sit down,' Marconi said. 'I am informed that two of you are bicycle men of the very first order.' Luigi and Leonardo nodded, identifying themselves as the bicycle men. Marconi shook hands with them both, his grip vice-like. Turning to Jacob, he asked: 'And you, young man, what binds you to such admirable comrades?'

Jacob flushed, momentarily lost for words. Seeing his friend's embarrassment, Luigi spoke quickly, formally. 'Our comrade is a person of some modesty. He is uncommonly skilled in matters affecting small mechanisms — gears and chains, triggers, firing pins. His delicate touch would render him an excellent puncture man.'

Marconi looked admiringly at Jacob. 'A puncture man,' he said. 'Perhaps that is your calling. A most noble calling it is.

Many's the time when the Bersaglieri have rolled to victory on the backs of their puncture men. A good puncture man is beyond price. Few have the puncture man's steadiness under fire. Still fewer can sense the often hidden site of the puncture, the little prick that halts the leader of a Bersaglieri charge mid-pedal. I have seen many good men destroyed, rendered useless and broken by a little prick.'

Jacob and Marconi exchanged the warmest of handshakes. 'Soft hands,' Marconi said. 'The perfect hands for a puncture man. Hands that feel, hands that heal, hands that restore. The hands of a puncture man are the hands of a surgeon. As the surgeon touches a vein, an artery, a depression in the skin, so the puncture man touches the tyre and the rubber entrail that gives it pressure. And the injury speaks to him, like the surgeon, through his fingers. The puncture man has fingers that hear. God has blessed him with twelve ears.'

Marconi raised an arm and the stocky, one-eyed waiter of earlier in the day appeared. 'When you have eaten,' the sergeant-major said, 'I will return and you can perhaps tell me more about yourselves.'

Again Jacob entrusted the taste buds of the three to the care of the stocky waiter. The trust, as before, was not misplaced. The first course was Bouillabaisse Bersaglieri. The soup was rich with the scents of olive oil, saffron, bay leaf, garlic, parsley, thyme and cracked pepper. Then came the night's 'house special' — the Maestro Marconi Macaroni. The thickness of the pasta was mitigated by its softness to the tooth. The cheese sauce had the viscosity of slowly flowing lava. Served with the macaroni was Soldier's Salad, a mix of mild red onion, crushed garlic and quartered tomatoes.

Eventually, the comrades pushed themselves back in their chairs, replete, unlaced their boots and stretched out their legs beneath the plate-laden table. Marconi returned to help the stocky waiter clear the dishes. Once satisfied that the three conscripts had wanted for nothing, he suggested: 'Some drinks? We have local beer, spirits of several descriptions and origins, and our local San Francesco liqueur. We also have wine from the vineyards and presses near the Sanctuary of Montenero.'

Luigi and Leonardo admitted that they had only ever tasted the wine of Tescano. Neither had even heard of liqueurs. Jacob revealed a more sophisticated knowledge of alcohol, announcing that beer and spirits caused in him a flatulence that had the uncontrollable ferocity of a thunderstorm. 'That being the case,' he said, 'I am content with a wine of your choice.'

Marconi nodded approvingly. 'Not just a puncture man in the making, but a prudent and considerate puncture man of some uncommon sensitivity to the comfort and sensibilities of others ... As for your comrades, perhaps some new tastes are in order after the sharp wine of Tescano.' Wine was ordered for Jacob while, for Luigi and Leonardo, Marconi suggested beer and Vat 69 whisky drawn from a squat green bottle. 'Named for the Pope's telephone number,' Marconi declared. 'Vatican 69.' Luigi was astonished that the Holy Father's telephone number was so publicly displayed. But this, after all, was not Tescano. This was Livorno, with its forts and canals and fine buildings. This was another, grander world where things were done differently.

The drinks arrived, and continued to arrive. As the evening unfolded, some serving and former Bersaglieri entered the trattoria. Enlivened by alcohol, Luigi became effusive. He was holding court. There was, naturally, no mention of his tears of loneliness on that first night in Livorno. Instead, he told of Jeremy Forsythe and his gift of the Hercules. He spoke in great detail of the repair and restoration of the black bicycle, of his training under Uncle Cesare, and of the adventures of boyhood, the rides with Leonardo into the hills. He revealed that, having read much about the remoteness and exotic nature of a place called Australia, he was giving consideration to cycling there one day. For a bicycle man of the very first order, such a journey should present no serious difficulties.

There were cheers of agreement. *Bravo. Bravo.* Tables were slapped. Hands were clapped. Who there could possibly doubt the determination of this young, fit, self-assured bicycle man?

More drinks arrived and, with every swallow, Luigi sensed more strongly that he had arrived in the world of men, a world of shared confidences and bravado and invulnerability. An hour and another hour passed. Luigi's words slurred. His eyelids dropped. Marconi began to sing, and others joined in. It was their battle hymn of earlier days.

Bicycle men are we,
From snowy peak to sea
We smite the foe, we lay him low ...
Bicycle men are we,
Fearless warriors of the Alpine snow
Two wheels against the stubborn foe

Plumes in the wind, we forward fly
Our rifles flash, our foes must die.
Bicycle men are we,
From snowy peak to sea
We smite the foe, we lay him low ...
Bicycle men are we,
From snowy peak to sea.

There were several verses and they were all sung several times, each time more vigorously. There were other songs, too. But Luigi heard none of these. He had passed out quietly and without saying goodnight.

CHAPTER SEVEN

Tandem

*There's no such thing as a solo performance. We live
in tandem or we live miserably alone. I sing 'Land
of my Fathers' and I think of my late dad, Dafydd,
limping to the pit to make a crust for Mum and my
nine brothers and two sisters in our one-bedroom
house with the outside toilet and the coal fire. I
think of how close we were and how my dad was the
second pair of legs on the bike that got me here.*
— Rhys Evans, Welsh tenor, farewell concert, Swansea Metropole, 1967

It was the morning light seeping through the thin membrane of
his eyelids that eased Luigi towards consciousness. Then came
the awareness of dryness of mouth and throat. Luigi was looking
at a ceiling he couldn't recognise. He stretched out his arms
and felt the coldness of the stone floor where he lay flat under a
single white sheet. He wriggled his toes. His boots and socks had

been removed, as had his tunic, shirt and trousers. He had no recollection of when this had happened.

Luigi sat up. Leonardo and Jacob, on the double bed, also sat up. Leonardo rubbed his eyes; Jacob reached for the jug of water on the small cabinet next to the bed. The jug was passed from Jacob to Leonardo, from Leonardo to Luigi. Jacob, the only one of the three with a wristwatch, advised that it was 9.30 in the morning.

Then, out of the blue, there was a sound like tearing fabric. The room filled with the aroma of Maestro Marconi Macaroni. The rasping sound was repeated, and this time it was accompanied by the aroma of Bouillabaisse Bersaglieri and the dressing that had come with the Soldier's Salad. Flatulence had gripped Jacob. Without prompting, he made an admission: he had strayed from wine to beer during the evening.

He quickly got up and opened the room's two sets of deep double windows. The white curtains fluttered and there was one long, final rasp that ended with a whimpering sound, a rectal 'Last Post'.

'What happened?' Luigi asked. 'How did I get here?'

'Well,' Leonardo said, 'nothing happened. You talked about yourself and you fell asleep at the table. Then we carried you up here, took off your boots and socks and shirt and tunic and trousers, and you just snored.'

Luigi shook his head. Most of the evening was a blank.

Leonardo wasn't finished. People, he said, who passed out or loosed volleys of oxygen-devouring farts after they drank should simply avoid drinking. Luigi and Jacob shrugged self-consciously in the manner of chastised children. There was a short silence, interrupted by another flatulent squeak — this time from Leonardo. At that, all three roared with laughter.

They dressed and descended the narrow steps, then went out through the kitchen and bar of the Trattoria Bersaglieri. They seated themselves once more at the table they'd vacated some hours earlier.

Marconi approached, beaming. He couldn't recall a better evening, he said. 'And you, young Luigi from Tescano, such tales of the Hercules and Uncle Cesare! If I am ever in Tescano I shall make it my business to call on him. And your planned adventure to Australia — such a journey that will be. A fine young man and his bicycle against the elements. Such a journey. Such an adventure.' There was an obvious admiration in Marconi's tone. Thirty years earlier he would have savoured such a journey. But thirty years earlier he had two legs.

The one-eyed waiter arrived. He served cold water and, some minutes later, hot coffee. He asked how they'd slept, how they felt, what they might care to start the day with. The morning melted away. When Jacob offered cash to pay the bill, Marconi said there would be no charge for the room. It had, after all, only been used for a few hours.

At 11.30, there were more handshakes as the conscripts took their leave. Marconi solemnly advised that any failure of the three to return during their next and subsequent leave passes would be taken as a personal insult. The young men promised wholeheartedly that there would be no such affront.

Reaching the old Fortezza Vecchia, they found most of their comrades from Dormitory Two sitting along the sea and canal walls. Some stragglers appeared just as the two military trucks arrived to collect their conscript cargo. Little was said on the journey back to Fortezza Nuova. Some were tired. Others relived their brief encounters with waterfront women old enough to be their mothers.

The trucks halted by the main gates, where Sergeant Dante and Corporal Bassanio were waiting. Dante ordered the conscripts to form two lines. 'Good, good,' he said, when they were assembled. 'You have returned in good order. I have received no reports of unsoldierly behaviour.'

The two ranks were marched to Dormitory Two. They were now entering the second month of their training, Dante reminded them. The pace of that training would increase in the months ahead.

The sergeant and the corporal left. Some of the conscripts flopped onto their bunks. Others, including Leonardo and Jacob, sorted clothing for washing, drying and ironing.

Luigi wrote home:

Dear Mother and Uncle Cesare,

I am sorry for having taken so long to write. The army is a busy place. When I first came here I was lonely, even with the companionship of Leonardo. But now we have settled into our barracks at Dormitory Two here in Livorno and we have had a twenty-four-hour leave. Leonardo and I have a new friend. His name is Jacob and he is from Florence. Jacob is the goalkeeper in our football team, the Foxes. All of us in Dormitory Two seem to get along together and everybody does his share of keeping the place in what our Sergeant Dante and Corporal Bassanio call good order. We have regular football games, which remind me of the long-ago times when Leonardo and I pretended to be great football champions.

I will write to you again and keep you informed of any adventures.

Your affectionate son and nephew,

Luigi

As foretold by Dante, the military training became increasingly intense. The length of the night and day marches increased. There were bayonet drills twice a week. More time was spent on the parade ground.

There was also twice-weekly boxing in a ring formed by four benches in a corner of the parade ground. Gloved and wearing shorts and a vest, each conscript was matched with another for a two-minute bout. The corporal and the sergeant were vigilant, watching for the deliberate and unsporting scrape of glove lacing against lips or nose. Any low blows, kidney punches or wayward thumbs in eyes would see the offender ordered to complete another two minutes with a fresh opponent.

'Next to football,' Dante said, 'boxing is the most beautiful sport. Well-matched men with respect for each other, sticking by the rules, moving like acrobats. Duck, weave, dance, sway, feint, step back, forward, strike close in, from the shoulder, back again, cover up. Work on combinations — one, two; one, two, three. Bang. Bang. Bang. Move on the toes. Lean into the punch.

Tempt and confuse with the left, strike with the right. All the time the boxer is thinking — avoiding angry reactions, holding back, looking for a gap, making a gap. The boxer is in control of his actions. Boxing is the domain of the hunter.'

Of the three friends, Luigi was the tidiest boxer. He had a solid, square stance. His defence was tight and high and he was agile, hard to hit. Years in the smithy had given him broad, muscular shoulders and strong hands and wrists. A quickly raised forearm could deflect a high punch from an opponent, and blows from the side were brushed off by the sweep of a gloved fist. Yet even when he had clearly outmatched his opponent in a two-minute bout, Luigi was not overly aggressive. He would pick and choose his stinging blows, slowing and neutralising his opponent and letting the bout run its course to a standing finish rather than closing in for a knockdown punch. There was, in his boxing, a certain nobility, a decency of spirit. He did only what was required to win. An opponent should be defeated, not humiliated.

The second month of training passed in a whirl of running, shooting, drilling, overnight marches, map-reading, football training, weekend football matches, boxing, assault courses and kit inspections. Luigi wrote more letters to his mother and Uncle Cesare: the training had made him stronger and tougher, he was well, Leonardo and Jacob were well, the others in Dormitory Two were well. The Foxes had won two out of three football games, though one team, the Black Avengers from Dormitory Six, had once tripped and elbowed their way to a draw against the Foxes. Sergeant Dante had said that the Black Avengers were filthy swine and had no place in the Beautiful Game.

71

There was other news. There would be a twenty-four-hour leave pass at the end of the third month of training. The twenty-four-hour leave pass due at the end of the second month of training had been cancelled. There was some talk of Italy joining Germany in Hitler's war against Britain. There had been a visit to Fortezza Nuova by men in German uniforms. They had seemed to salute a great deal. They had worn polished black boots and clicked their heels. Luigi had said the Germans looked silly. Leonardo had said they looked more dangerous than silly.

The days steadily shortened. The evenings were cold and the two pot-bellied stoves in Dormitory Two were permanently lit. The mornings were sharp, astringent. Washed uniforms stiffened on clotheslines. Christmas passed with little fanfare. It was marked only by an open-air Nativity Mass on the parade ground. After the Mass, the routine of training resumed.

On the afternoon of Thursday, 4 January 1940, Sergeant Dante advised his charges that the following day they would be granted a twenty-four-hour leave pass. As before, they would be restricted to spending their time in Livorno.

Shortly after noon on the following day, Luigi, Leonardo, Jacob and their Dormitory Two comrades were driven to the Fortezza Vecchia. Once again they walked in small groups to Livorno's piazza with its fountain.

However, whereas before it had been nearly empty, this time the square was overflowing. Perhaps two thousand people stood shoulder to shoulder, craning their necks for a glimpse of a short, shaven-headed man in military uniform standing alone on a flag-draped timber platform at the eastern end of the piazza. The man declaimed in a powerful voice, hands on hips. He paused at the end of every sentence, an actor milking his audience for a response. The crowd's reply was uniform: 'Duce! ... Duce! ... Duce!' they chanted.

Luigi looked at Leonardo and Jacob. 'Is that him?' he asked. 'Is that him — Mussolini?' Both nodded.

Keen to get a closer look at the man whose face he had first seen on the portrait that hung in the Tescano school classroom, Luigi led the way through the crush. It was a slow journey, but people were willing to move aside for three young men in uniform. Finally they stood not four metres from the man himself. Only a row of black-uniformed bodyguards stood between them and the Supreme Leader.

It was Mussolini's manner that was impressive, rather than anything he actually said. He was strongly built and magnificently uniformed. His highly polished belt and long boots shone and reflected the winter light. His broad chest was, on one side, a flash of colour like a parrot in flight — red, blue, green, gold. He had more medals, Luigi observed, than even Sergeant Dante. Il Duce must have been in many battles, Luigi thought. Indeed, Mussolini had served with the Bersaglieri during the Great War.

With a patting, downwards motion of his hands, Mussolini urged quiet. Then he raised one hand and, with a finger pointed up towards infinity, he told the crowd: 'I have been with you every step of the paths we have trodden to glory for almost twenty years. I have been with you not by chance but by destiny. I have been sent here for you and for Italy. My destiny is my gift to you. My destiny has given you bread on tables that were once bare, wine in cups that were once empty, boots on feet that were once raw. My destiny has given you victories in battle. It has seen

Italians triumph over the Communist priest-killers in holy Spain. It has seen the idle and lazy put to work and it has seen the Socialist scribblers dealt with firmly. Their pens and pencils have been blunted. I will be with you forever ... it is your destiny to be with me forever. We are one. We are a single heroic heartbeat.'

The roar from the crowd was thunderous. 'Duce, we are with you! Duce, we are with you!'

Mussolini used the same patting motion to still the crowd. As he looked down, his eyes fastened squarely on Luigi, Leonardo and Jacob. He beckoned to the three to move forward and mount the platform. The young men looked at each other, dumbstruck. A bodyguard stepped forward and ushered the conscripts towards Mussolini.

Il Duce shook their hands and asked where they were from. Luigi only had time to say, 'Tescano and—' before the strongly built figure turned to the crowd and announced: 'From Tescano. They are from Tescano, the place named for the great Roman chariot master Titus Tescare of the Remus Legion, a place named for the most noble of the Sons of Rome. They stand before you, in uniform, as our finest, your finest, my finest. They are ready to drain their veins of the blood that flows through their bodies.'

The crowd roared: 'Duce! Duce! We are here!'

Standing behind and just to the left of the mesmerist, Luigi, Leonardo and Jacob felt the breaking waves of mass adulation. Looking into the crowd, Luigi saw Marconi and the stocky, one-eyed waiter five or six rows from the bodyguards. Luigi nodded and Marconi raised his clenched fist in salute. Following his lead, hundreds more raised their fists.

Il Duce was silent. Another word would have destroyed the

magic, the moment. He spread his arms, calming the crowd, briefly nodded to the throng, then turned, gesturing to Luigi, Leonardo and Jacob to follow. As they did so, there was the sound of a scuffle. Luigi turned to see a man near the front of the crowd grappling with four Blackshirt bodyguards. The man was shouting, protesting against the treatment of workers somewhere. He was punched and pushed to the ground by the Blackshirts. The beating continued after he was dragged out of sight into an alley near the rear of the platform.

Luigi hurried to follow Leonardo and Jacob. Behind the platform were several large black limousines and two military vehicles filled with heavily armed Blackshirts. Nearby were Military Police on their motorcycles, and seven or eight tough-looking men in felt hats, snappy suits and expensive overcoats. They looked like gangsters from a Hollywood film.

While Leonardo and Jacob stood to one side, Mussolini placed an arm around Luigi's shoulders. He said: 'The shoulders of a hard-working warrior of Rome. Shoulders that will carry, like Atlas, the weight of the world. Shoulders that can never be found on the riff-raff you have just seen removed. Scum. It will be some time before he sees his family again. Forget him. He is nothing. He is dung on the boot of a farmer. Now, tell me of your family in Tescano.'

Luigi hesitated. The closeness of Mussolini felt uncomfortable, almost threatening. Luigi could feel the strength in the arm around his shoulders. He sensed a great capacity for cruelty in this bald man.

Nervously Luigi told of his mother and Uncle Cesare and of the smithy and, of course, of the Hercules and its restoration and the cycling adventures with Leonardo. Luigi said that the people of Tescano were good people. They were the salt of the Italian earth. The conscripts at the Fortezza Nuova were also the salt of the Italian earth, he added.

Il Duce nodded as Luigi spoke. Then he said he wished to know more of the training at Fortezza Nuova, so Luigi spoke of Dormitory Two, of the football teams and of Sergeant Dante and Corporal Bassanio. The sergeant and the corporal were old soldiers who looked after their men. They were the salt of the earth too. Mussolini said that it seemed Italy was not short of salt. Then he laughed. On cue, the men in the felt hats, snappy suits and expensive coats laughed as well. Presumably they, too, were the salt of the earth.

Mussolini turned to Leonardo and Jacob, asking their names. 'Zevi,' he repeated after Jacob had spoken. 'That is not a common Italian name.' Jacob said his family had been in Italy for hundreds and hundreds of years. His watchmaker father had made timing devices for bombs in the Great War. Mussolini seemed satisfied. He ordered one of the men in felt hats to 'take the details of these Tescano boys'. Then he was off, into a black limousine that moved quickly away.

Their details taken, the three walked in silence into the rapidly emptying square and towards the Trattoria Bersaglieri. They were spotted, from a distance of fifty metres, by Marconi, and by the stocky, one-eyed waiter and a dozen or more patrons who had been part of the adoring throng. They stood up from their tables as one, applauding, cheering: 'Hurrah! Hurrah! Hurrah for the Tescano boys!'

The three were embraced, first by Marconi and then by the waiter and then by every patron. They had shaken hands with

Il Duce. They were the sons of the Remus Legion, Il Duce had said so. And they were there, in the Trattoria Bersaglieri. What an honour! To have stood alongside the Leader and then to have come straight to the trattoria of former regimental sergeant-major Benny Marconi! The Tescano boys would pay for nothing. Whatever they wanted — food, drink, a room for as many nights as they might need — was on the house.

Patrons crowded around the table where the three sat, warmed by the heat of a charcoal brazier and local fortified wine. The questions came in torrents. What was Mussolini like, really like? Was his handshake as firm and strong as it appeared to be? Did he talk of his Bersaglieri days at the front during the Great War?

Luigi, his confidence and inventiveness elevated — just as his lingering discomfort at the menace of Mussolini was dissipated — by the fortified wine, spoke for the other two. 'I have met no other like him. He has the handshake of a giant. It is an electric handshake that could power the whole of Livorno. He has eyes that could tunnel through mountains. He spoke fondly of his service with the Bersaglieri. He said there were no finer men in Italy. He had heard of this trattoria, the Trattoria Bersaglieri.'

There were nods and gasps and murmurs of approval. Luigi sensed he had touched on a great truth. Tell people what they want to hear, tell them they are brave and noble and important, tell them they have no equal, that they are special, tell them that they are what they wish they were. Tell them all those lies and they will love you.

Warming to his tale, Luigi went on: 'He spoke of Livorno. It has a special place in his heart. He came here as a young man and could never forget the goodness of the people. He said that only his duties in Rome prevent him from visiting all of Tuscany more often.' More nods and gratified murmurs. Drinks and even more drinks arrived. Luigi felt himself slowly rocking back and forth in his chair.

Marconi intervened. 'Clearly young Luigi is overcome by the events of this day,' he said. 'An afternoon sleep may be in order. This evening we can hear more.' Luigi stood and steadied himself. His two friends rose with him, Leonardo announcing that all three might benefit from a rest. Marconi said the three re-painted rooms in the establishment were at their disposal. They should each take one.

In the privacy of Luigi's room, Leonardo scolded his boyhood friend. 'The drink turns you into a braggart, Luigi. You make up stories, just like you made up stories at school. Il Duce is a bad man. He is the same as Minoza and Paglia. He said none of these fancy words to you.' But Luigi was not listening. He lay on the bed, snoring.

Some hours passed before the three, rested, returned to the company of Marconi and his patrons. Leonardo advised Marconi that none of the three would be taking strong drink. This was, he said, a time to refrain from excess, hard as that might be for spirited young men. There was more hard training ahead. There was the football tournament.

Marconi and his patrons said they understood perfectly. Luigi, Leonardo and Jacob were selfless examples of Tuscan manhood. It was no wonder at all that they had caught the eye of Il Duce. Mussolini knew good men when he saw them.

CHAPTER EIGHT

Traction

It's the point of engagement when the rubber meets the road. You feel the bite of the hard surface and the leg muscles strain. It's called traction. You push and push till it's over. You've won or you've lost. It doesn't matter. You gave everything because you got the chance and you took it. You grabbed it with both hands, right up to the elbows. No traction equals no life. It's that simple.

— Eddie Mortensen, Baltimore Monocycle Grand Champion, 1955

The following day, Dante's conscripts made an orderly return to the Fortezza Nuova, where they assembled for inspection and were marched to Dormitory Two. There, Sergeant Dante announced: 'Ferraro, Battaglia, Zevi — here in one hour, best kit, not a hair out of place. Training Commandant Galileo Gonfalonieri desires your company. Bring a biscuit for Nero the dog. The biscuit will

79

go down well with the dog and the commandant … and before you ask, I don't know why he wants to see you.'

The commandant's office was imposing, with bay windows opening onto the parade ground. Shelves along one wall were lined with sporting trophies — football, swimming, cross-country running, boxing. On another wall were framed photographs of scenes from the Great War. Three cruelly curved swords and several short, stabbing spears hung on a third wall. The office was equipped with two desks. On the smaller of the two desks a black Labrador sat upright, tail wagging, tongue lolling. Behind the second desk was the commandant. Luigi, Leonardo and Jacob saluted.

The commandant looked like a leader of men. His greying hair was cropped close to his skull. He was superbly uniformed. His perfectly pressed olive-green tunic bore two rows of medal ribbons. His brass buttons shone. His leather holster and belt had the lustre of varnished walnut. His hands were well manicured. Resolute, dark eyes, in a face that could have been hewn from rock, were cast over the conscripts and Dante. He motioned to the four to stand at ease and then, for two or three minutes, studied the contents of three fawn folders on his blotting pad. The folders contained the service documentation for Luigi, Leonardo and Jacob.

'So, you are the Tescano boys,' said the commandant at last. 'But only two are from Tescano. One is from Florence.'

Luigi began to speak but a sideways glance from Dante silenced him.

'No matter,' the commandant said. 'If those in the highest places say you are the Tescano boys, then you are the Tescano boys. You are whatever they say you are. If those in the highest places said, for example, you were the Marx Brothers or the Andrews Sisters, I would accept their word. If those in the highest places say they have been guided by destiny, who am I to think otherwise? Those in the highest places expect acceptance of their views. This has always been the way of things. It will never be otherwise.' There was a tone of resignation in his voice.

The commandant paused and then continued. 'I am informed — for I am informed of everything — that you spoke well of Sergeant Dante and Corporal Bassanio and of the training you are receiving here. I am told, too, by my old comrade Regimental Sergeant-Major Marconi — with whom I dine regularly and who has a telephone — that two of you are bicycle men of the very first order and that the third is a puncture man of great talent. For his part, Sergeant Dante speaks highly of your skills on the football field. And Nero seems to approve of you.'

The dog looked on, his tail moving from side to side like a windscreen wiper in a storm.

Luigi reached into a tunic pocket. 'We have some biscuits,' he said. 'The sergeant said Nero would be pleased to receive a biscuit.'

There was a smile on the commandant's face. 'Ah, the good Sergeant Dante. A mind reader of singular accuracy. A sergeant who knows the mind of his commandant's dog is a man of considerable influence. The officer class may have the authority and the best tarts, but the sergeants have the power. What do you say, Sergeant? Am I correct?'

Dante answered without pause. 'It is only the power to assist those in authority. As for the best tarts, I am obliged to accept your opinion. I have no experience of such entertainments.'

The commandant's smile broadened. Sergeant Dante, he said, was obviously a man of piety and virtue. He nodded, a sign for Luigi to offer Nero a biscuit, which was taken and swallowed in one swift gulp. Nero pawed Luigi's chest then licked his face. Luigi pulled more biscuits from his tunic. The commandant observed that Nero was a good judge of men, as, no doubt, were those 'in the highest places'.

In the minutes that followed, it became clear that the commandant was indeed well informed of the most recent events in Livorno. He knew everything — the Leader's invitation to the three to stand by his side on the platform, the back-slapping welcome at the Trattoria Bersaglieri, and Luigi's effusive recounting to the trattoria's patrons of the meeting with the Leader. The commandant said no harm had been done. Nothing had been said that was disagreeable, although he cautioned that conversations and meetings with those in the highest places should be treated with great circumspection. They should not be discussed with others in any detail.

The commandant said that those in the highest places had been impressed by the three. They had suggested, by telephone, that the Tescano boys might be well suited to training with the Army Cycling Training School near the Sanctuary of Montenero. How did they feel about that? A recommendation that the three should be admitted to the Army Cycling Training School was no small matter, the commandant said. 'It is not a school for any who might be lacking in resolve or manly character,' he said.

Leonardo spoke up. He said it was an honour to meet the commandant and to feed Nero, just as it had been an honour to meet the Leader during their brief leave. Leonardo, Luigi and Jacob were indebted to Sergeant Dante and to Corporal Bassanio for their guidance, fairness and leadership. They were proud members of Sergeant Dante's group of conscripts. Beyond question, the three would be proud — as two bicycle men and a puncture man — to train at the illustrious Army Cycling Training School near the Sanctuary of Montenero. The Bersaglieri trained at the school were the cream of the cream, without rival.

However, there was one reservation, Leonardo added. The three were members of the Foxes football team. There were other team members to consider, as well as the wishes of Sergeant Dante and Corporal Bassanio. They had the highest hopes for the success of the Foxes in the football tournament.

The commandant pushed himself back in his chair and drummed his fingers on his desk. The drumming of the fingers stopped abruptly. He said the loyalty of the three was commendable. Still, those in the highest places felt the Army Cycling Training School was the place for the Tescano boys, and the views of those in the highest places always prevailed. As for the football tournament and the participation of the Tescano boys in that tournament ... well, that would present no problems of substance. A number of the conscripts from the training companies, the commandant advised, were being deployed to other units in the immediate area. Normally such deployments were made after the first six months of compulsory military service, but times were changing. Regardless, the football tournament would be held as planned.

Leaning forward, taking the four into his confidence, the commandant said his old soldier's instinct — and a communication received that very morning and ordering the early deployment of conscripts — told him Italy was on the path to war. 'When this new war might happen,' Gonfalonieri said, 'I cannot possibly know. But it will be in no more than a year. It will be a war of machines, a war where there will be no distinction between civilians and those in uniform. Those who have never known war will see it in their cities and towns and villages and streets. And then they will never again imagine or speak of glory, legends, heroes or sacrifice. War is a filthy affair. Its cruelty can only be understood by those who have seen it. It is a cruelty that cannot be imagined. And war brings fear, fear of this cruelty that, even in brave men, brings the urge to flee. Bravery is not only to be found in facing the enemy ... bravery is the strength to hold fast against the fear, in every man, that causes him to run away from the enemy.'

Luigi, in all his days, never forgot the commandant's words. In time, he came to believe that courage in life, real courage, was not in the concealing of fear. It was in the refusal to be conquered by fear.

The commandant, ruffling Nero's ears, said that preparations for war were already underway. Italian forces in Libya had been quietly strengthened. On a recent visit to an elderly uncle in Genoa he had seen ships of the Italian Navy leave for exercises in the eastern Mediterranean. He had heard that Genoa's waterfront brothels — particularly one known by disapproving neighbours as 'Donna's Den for Dirty Men' — had done, literally, a roaring trade in the days prior to the departure of the warships. The commandant said it was common knowledge locally that the boot factory in Livorno and the uniform factories in the nearby town of Camaiore were working at full capacity to fill increased orders from the Italian Ministry of War.

The Army Cycling Training School near the Sanctuary of Montenero had, only a week earlier, taken delivery of five hundred new bicycles. The commandant had also been told that children in the workshops of the orphanage near the Sanctuary of Montenero were learning to make artificial legs and hands, as well as eye patches and crutches, and that the Murano glass-blowers in Venice had been called on to make glass eyes. It would perhaps be some consolation to the blinded, the commandant said, that they would have the most magnificent glass eyes in the world. Sightless glass eyes that sparkled like stars in the night sky.

Luigi, at that very moment, was lost in quiet puzzlement. He had never heard of a brothel and wondered if the 'Den for Dirty Men' it was a naval establishment where rugged salts of the high seas met and bathed in a convivial atmosphere of manly back-scrubbing before setting sail or raising steam. He pictured unkempt stokers, grimy from toil, arriving at the Den and being met by a black-clad, mothball-scented, motherly woman, before disrobing and immersing themselves in some great, bubbling Roman bath, and then emerging to find their uniforms clean and pressed, and a cup of wine and some sliced salami and local olives ready for their consumption before departure.

While Luigi was momentarily lost in his quiet puzzlement, the commandant continued. Half the conscripts would leave the Fortezza Nuova within the week for early deployment. The Tescano boys were among fifteen conscripts from various training companies who would attend the Army Cycling Training School. They would remain in their dormitory at Fortezza Nuova and would travel five days a week to and from their new assignment. The journey would take no more than twenty minutes each way. These arrangements meant they would be available for football training and matches at weekends.

The Tescano boys would begin their posting to the Army Cycling Training School the following day. When the need arose — and when those in the highest places had spoken — the Italian military machine could move with astonishing swiftness, the commandant observed.

At 7 am on Monday, 8 January, the military transport carrying fifteen conscripts from the Fortezza Nuova arrived at the Army Cycling Training School. The school occupied a large open concrete area about the size of ten football fields. Within this area, groups of fifty or sixty uniformed cyclists were riding in formation. Every few seconds there would be a series of shrill blasts from a whistle and the riders would change direction, turning sharply left or right or forming ranks six abreast. It was a balletic scene, a Bolshoi corps de bicyclettes. Beyond the flat, open area was a contoured obstacle course around which dismounted cyclists were carrying their bicycles over walls and across muddy ditches and up and down scramble nets. In the middle distance, paths snaked into the trees that fringed the school, and formations of ten or twelve bicycle-mounted men, in full battle dress, were speeding into the bareness of the winter foliage.

The Fortezza Nuova fifteen were met by an officer who introduced himself as Captain Guido Luchese. On the shoulders of his greatcoat were embroidered badges showing a bicycle in the colours of the Italian flag framed by gold lightning bolts. On the saddle of the embroidered bicycle was a representation of a cobra, rearing and ready to strike. Beneath the badge was the motto *Vae Victis* — Woe to the Vanquished.

Luchese, tapping the captain's insignia on the collar of his coat, said that badges of rank mattered little at the Army Cycling Training School. All that truly mattered was mastery of the bicycle, and the unbreakable, manly bonds that flowed from such mastery. Army cyclists were a special breed, he said. 'You have been selected for duty here because of information in your documents or recommendations from those in the highest places. I see some of you have been cyclists from an early age and that one or two have been members of junior cycling teams. I am advised that at least two of you are cycling men of the highest order and that we have the makings of an accomplished puncture man among us. All of this is good. It tells me you understand that the bicycle is every bit as much a living and breathing creature as a horse. As a horse has its habits and inclinations and disinclinations, so a bicycle has its very own ways. Here we talk to our bicycles as a cavalryman talks to his mount. And here we learn to listen to the language a bicycle uses to speak to us — the language of the tyre, the poetry of the turning wheel, the sonatas of the spokes.'

Captain Luchese outlined what lay ahead. An immediate tour of the facility and its workshops would be followed by an afternoon of introductory classes on bicycles and their parts. Within ten days, each of the fifteen would be allocated a bicycle, and riding ability would be assessed. There would be lessons in formation riding and bicycle assault tactics, particularly the V-Formation Thunderclap Advance that was guaranteed to scatter an enemy. Other, lesser-known tactics to be learned were the Scrambler Power Charge, the Arrowhead Pincer and the fearsome Sideswipe. These would be difficult and dangerous lessons. 'But no man among you will shrink from the challenge,' he said. 'I see this as I look into your eyes.'

There would also be instruction in night riding, rough-country riding and the negotiation of assault courses. Importantly, the newcomers would be required to learn 'Spokes in the Wheel', the official song of the Army Cycling Training School, which would be sung during formation riding. Captain Luchese crooned a bold, jaunty air:

We are the army's men of steel,
We are the spokes in a bigger wheel,
We ride by day, we ride by night,
We pounce with fearless, crushing might,
Honour we embrace with glee,
Our lightning strikes — the cowards flee.
They feel the wrath of the men of steel —
The power of spokes in a bigger wheel.

Luchese clicked his heels and executed a theatrical bow. There was spontaneous applause from the new arrivals, and the captain flashed a film-star smile. Luigi, Leonardo and Jacob sensed they were entering a fraternity rather than a military unit. The Brotherhood of the Bicycle.

In the hours that followed, the new arrivals were walked around the facility. Luigi was particularly interested in the workshops. There were tools of every description, including some he had never seen before. He paused several times, intrigued, to watch bicycles being assembled and stripped down by blindfolded young men. He was also puzzled to see similar operations being carried out by young men wearing thick gloves. A friendly sergeant in overalls, noting Luigi's obvious interest, explained that the bicycle man must always be able to tend to his steel steed, to make running repairs in the most adverse conditions, whether high in the freezing Alpine air or in the pre-dawn darkness before speeding downhill into the frenzy of battle. The bicycle man, the friendly sergeant said, was often only two wheels away from eternity. This, Luigi felt, was two wheels too close, but he said nothing.

One section of the workshops was set aside for the assembly of motorised bicycles. This fascinated Luigi — bicycles with engines! The friendly sergeant said the Bersaglieri were experimenting with Villiers 98cc two-stroke engines mounted on standard Italian Army bicycles. The Villiers was of British design, simple and most reliable. The Italian army had imported large numbers in the mid-1930s. Most had been warehoused, but now they were being pressed into service. A feature of the motorised bicycles, the sergeant explained, was the introduction of heavy-duty, solid rubber combat tyres. He said this with an air of melancholy, and added: 'Soon there will be a time when the skills of the puncture man are a thing of the past. So much is changing for the worse. What was valued is being cast aside.'

After the guided tour, the fifteen new arrivals assembled in a classroom whose walls were festooned with engineering drawings of bicycles and bicycle parts, and close-up photographs of torn pneumatic tyres, snapped brake shoes and bent spokes. There were also images of riders wounded in battle. A particularly gruesome picture from the Great War showed the hideous injury inflicted on a rider whose saddle, unbeknown to him, had been shot away in an ambush. Captain Luchese made a point of drawing the men's attention to that photograph. 'The Battle of Saint Teresa's Passage, 1917 — the rider, a Private Santo Santoro, was standing on the pedals going downhill when a sniper's bullet detached the saddle from the bicycle. Santoro was unaware of this and he sat down on the ragged saddle post. The rest you can see for yourselves — a man with two of what we have only one of. The lesson: one eye always on what is ahead and one eye always on your rear. Never forget Saint Teresa's Passage. It was to Private Santoro what Carthage was to Rome — a lasting pain in the arse.' Captain Luchese was obviously a man who knew his history and who excelled in its telling.

With the inspection and initial class over, the fifteen returned to Fortezza Nuova for the night. Before he bathed and slept, Luigi wrote home.

Dearest Mother and Uncle Cesare,

A few words to tell you my news. Leonardo and Jacob and myself have been selected for training at the Army Cycling Training School which is near here. We have been selected for this bicycle training because, in Livorno on leave, we met a person in the highest of places who decided we should be sent there for training. Our commandant said such meetings with those in high places should not be discussed with others, so I can say no more. Leonardo said people who reveal secrets can be shot by a firing squad and I have no wish to be shot. Leonardo has no wish to be shot either. As always, we agree on many things. I will write again.

Your loving son and nephew,

Luigi

In the morning, the Fortezza Nuova fifteen returned to the school. That day and several subsequent days were taken up with classes on bicycle parts and their functions and on the interaction between body and bicycle.

Most of the classes were given by the friendly sergeant whom Luigi had met during the tour of the workshops. The sergeant, whose name was Lorenzo di Canola, knew every millimetre of every part of a bicycle. He knew what purpose each part served and what horrors could follow the failure of any or several parts. He knew about tyres — solid tyres, pneumatic tyres, particular valves for particular tubes, tyres that were good in the snow and bad in the heat or good in the wet and bad on dry roads and tracks. He had an abiding interest in handlebars and a near-medical knowledge of the human muscular and skeletal systems where they interacted with the efficient operation of a bicycle.

'The relationship between the inside leg and the positioning of the pedal is no small matter,' he told his students. 'A single centimetre's difference can mean as much as a ten percent loss or a ten percent gain in pedal power. Then we have handlebars — a centimetre here or there, too high or too low, and the rider exerts less than perfect control. The correct saddle positioning is also important.'

His tone became sombre. 'Now, let us consider testicles, the wrinkled retainers of our Italian manhood. Our testicles are like our fingerprints: each is unique. As such, each man's testicles have their own relationship with each saddle. One man's testicles are another man's nightmare. Believe this, even if you believe nothing else. It is important, when you are allocated your bicycles, to ensure that the saddle is perfectly positioned for your unique testicles. A wrongly positioned testicle can be disastrous during formation cycling. A wrongly positioned testicle can cause a drift of two or three centimetres to the left or to the right, and at high speed such a drift will lead to collisions. Here we have found that those with what I shall call fuller testicles are the best bicycle men. Smaller testicles can kill and cripple. Fuller testicles can be a cyclist's salvation. Testicles are no small matter. Testicles are not to be sneezed at.'

Di Canola looked around the classroom. Nodding in the direction of Captain Luchese, who was present at every lesson, he added: 'However, I do not anticipate that these fine young men will fall short of the mark in the important matter of testicles.' There was a ripple of laughter from the conscripts.

With the first week at the cycling school under their collective belts, Luigi, Leonardo and Jacob resumed weekend football training and took to the field against a Dormitory Seven team. Like most teams playing that weekend, the strength of the Foxes had been depleted by the early deployment of some conscripts elsewhere, and it had become a composite team comprising Luigi, Leonardo and Jacob as well as eight members of the Tigers.

There had been some debate on what the composite team should be called — the Foxes or the Tigers. The matter was settled by the toss of a coin under the eyes of Sergeant Dante and Corporal Bassanio. The Foxes won the day. The team also won a handsome five-to-one victory against Dormitory Seven's Heroic Falcons. From the sidelines, Sergeant Dante and Corporal Bassanio shouted constantly, urging their players on. At every goal scored by the Foxes, the two punched their fists above their heads.

Dante was effusive with his praise. 'Look at that,' he bellowed. 'Look at that! My boys are naturals.' And with every shot deflected by Jacob, Dante cupped his hands around his mouth and roared: 'Look at him! A natural. The hands of a champion. The eyes of an eagle. The swiftness of a viper. The heart of a bull.'

When the Foxes left the field, shaking hands with the soundly beaten Heroic Falcons, Sergeant Dante called them into a circle. 'The championship is ours if you play every game as you played today,' he said, his eyes glowing with pride and excitement. 'You are naturals. Natural naturals.'

That natural ability shone through when the Tescano boys and the twelve others from Fortezza Nuova returned for their second, crucial week at the cycling school. This was the week when they were allocated bicycles and the assessment of their abilities as bicycle men began.

The bicycles used in training were black and rugged in appearance. The wheels were robust and slotted firmly into strong front and rear forks with nuts slightly larger than the nuts on standard bicycles. The extra few millimetres increased the ease and speed of tightening or loosening. The tyres were wider and had a deeper tread than most civilian bicycles. Above the rear wheel was a tubular steel rack where panniers could be strapped.

Sergeant di Canola ordered his new charges to mount and dismount, mount and dismount, mount and dismount at least a dozen times before he issued the order to mount and straddle the saddle, hands on handlebars. 'Testicle time,' he said. 'Toes touching the ground. Slide forward and back, forward and back. Close your eyes. Forward and back. Imagine your testicles. Every one of you should have a picture of a testicle in each eye. Left eye, left testicle. Right eye, right testicle. Now, left hand on left testicle. Adjust the testicle ... Right hand on right testicle. Adjust the testicle. Good. Very good. I see you are familiar with adjusting your testicles. I suspect you have been adjusting them for some time, perhaps since childhood.'

There were sniggers from the conscripts. Some were red-faced.

Turning to Captain Luchese, Sergeant di Canola announced, with the shadow of a smile: 'Well above average.'

After adjusting their saddles — fittingly by the loosening or tightening of two nuts — to the positioning of their private parts, the conscripts were ordered to mount and ride in single file, two metres apart and at walking pace, along a painted white line that ran the length of the flat, open area. Up and down, up and down they rode under the eyes of di Canola and Luchese. Then came individual sprints, followed by riding as a group, front wheels aligned.

The days following the allocation of bicycles flew by in a blur of drills and exercises. There were ever-increasing demands on the concentration and stamina of the trainees. Physically, they were being pushed to their limits. Muscles ached, joints stiffened. All wondered if they would survive the day, the hour.

At the end of each week, there was football training and the weekly football match on the sports fields at Fortezza Nuova. So it continued, cycling and football. Cycling and football. The Foxes advanced steadily towards the tournament final with more wins than losses and one draw against a team from Dormitory Four, the Tuscan Tormentors.

The cycling training advanced through formation riding to the negotiation of assault courses, and to track riding and night riding through the trees and hills around the cycling school. While the track and night riding in full kit were physically draining, it was the formation riding that made the most exhausting demands on concentration and raw skill. There were arrow formations, trident-shaped formations, triangular and phalanx formations, cluster formations, chisel formations. Each formation change, watched in silence by Luchese, was signalled by a series of blasts on di Canola's whistle: for instance, three long blasts and a short blast for the arrow formation; four short blasts for a chisel formation; two short blasts, three long blasts and a short blast for phalanx formations; four long blasts, a short blast and five long blasts for circular cluster formations.

There were several near disasters when riders either misheard or were completely confused by the whistle's commands. In one thrusting arrowhead movement the lead rider, a strongly built conscript from Milan, mistakenly veered left across the path of following cyclists; the almost instantaneous result was a tangle of swerving, skidding bicycles and colliding bodies.

When the men had picked themselves up and retrieved their bicycles, Captain Luchese called the riders together. 'These things happen,' he told them. 'You are better than most at this stage in your instruction. Remember some simple rules and you cannot go wrong. Surrender to your memory. Lessons forgotten are lessons that kill. Many cyclists die as a result of amnesia. Although perfection is elusive, daily progress is possible. Bruises and grazes and mishaps should not dent your confidence.'

The captain broke into song. '*We are the army's men of steel ... We are the spokes in a bigger wheel ...*' His charges sang with him. They sang with gusto. When the singing stopped, Captain Luchese was beaming. He recognised that, across the group, bonds were forming, brother was getting to know brother. There was mutual respect. Help was given when help was needed. There could be no doubt in Captain Luchese's mind: he was a leader of men. He suspected it was a gift. A gift like his good looks, his disarming smile, the sparkling dark eyes, that fine tenor voice. A gift like the grip. Luchese was, after all, a man of machines and metal and moulding and millimetres. Luchese and Di Canolo, in this respect, were cast from the same mould.

Away from the drills and the night exercises, one day a week was spent in the workshops that so impressed Luigi. The conscripts learned to strip and reassemble a bicycle, to improvise when parts were damaged or missing. Jacob's skill in stripping and reassembling light weapons was evident during the workshop sessions. Sergeant di Canola several times called other conscripts to watch Jacob at work. 'Look at the fingers. See how they move. Look at the hands, the touch,' he said. 'The hands of a young master in the making.' Privately he confided to Captain Luchese:

'One day soon young Zevi will have the grip. He is close, very close.' He added: 'The Ferraro boy may have it too.'

While it was true that Jacob had no conscript equal in the areas of stripping and reassembling, it was Luigi who excelled in repair work on the daily inflow of bicycles damaged during training exercises, and Sergeant di Canola encouraged others to watch him also. 'See how he works in silence,' di Canola said in a whisper. 'See the eyes. The eyes of an owl. And look at the slow, steady pressure on the fork. Not too little, not too much. The perfect touch.'

Luigi also attracted favourable attention on the rough and twisting tracks around the cycling school. After one energy-sapping night ride in full kit, Luigi was taken aside by Captain Luchese, who was glowing in his praise. 'You are a born bicycle man of the very highest order,' he said. 'When others tire, you find hidden strength. You are a man who drives the pedals and yet caresses the handlebars. Within you is a powerful and brutal master and, at the same time, a Casanova.'

Luigi was puzzled. He asked Leonardo that night: 'What is a casanova?' Leonardo explained and Luigi was relieved. He had thought it might have been a type of Livorno pasta.

The training continued. There were further twenty-four-hour leave passes. Luigi, Leonardo and Jacob revisited the Trattoria Bersaglieri where, on each visit, they were feted as honoured guests of former Bersaglieri regimental sergeant-major Benny 'Mountain Man' Marconi.

Three weeks before the end of the cycling training and the initial six months of conscription, Luigi wrote home:

Dearest Mother and Uncle Cesare,

In two weeks we shall be told our fate. Some of us will continue our service elsewhere and others will become members of reserve units. If I am to go elsewhere, I will serve for another year and a half. If become a reserve, I will return to Tescano and await any call to service. There is much talk of Italy joining the war. In one or two weeks I will be awarded my Army Cyclist badge and this gives me great pride.

The football games have been a joy. The Foxes are in the finals of the Conscript Cup. Sergeant Dante said we should win the game, which will be against the Black Avengers from Dormitory Six. We have played the Black Avengers before and they are as dirty as they are strong. Leonardo is well, as is our friend Jacob.

I miss you both and I miss Tescano every day.

Your ever-loving son and proud nephew,

Luigi

The final was played on Saturday, 16 March. There was a good crowd — perhaps six hundred — watching from the sidelines. A special bench was set aside for Commandant Galileo Gonfalonieri, Nero, several commissioned officers, and three other officers in the jackboots and field-grey uniforms of the German Army.

Sergeant Dante assembled his men on the sideline. 'You are the Foxes,' he said. 'Victory is within your grasp. The champion's trophy can be yours. You are the better of the two teams. The Black Avengers will play hard and dirty. Rise above them.' It was an order, not a request.

He shook each player's hand and the Foxes took to the field as the Black Avengers positioned themselves. A coin was tossed by the match referee. The Foxes kicked off.

With a swift, turning movement Leonardo flicked the ball to his right and to the feet of a Foxes forward. The forward moved ahead and crossed to Luigi, who was brought to the ground by a sliding Black Avenger's tackle. The referee signalled for play to continue despite the foul. With the Black Avengers in possession, play moved swiftly towards the Foxes' goal. One pass, two passes, three passes. Then a cannonball kick. Framed by the white posts, Jacob sprang forward like a lion, but he was body-checked to the ground by the Black Avengers' attacker and the ball flew between the posts and smacked into the net. There was a roar from the Black Avengers' supporters. Jacob picked himself up, winced and touched an eyebrow. There was a smear of blood on his fingers.

With the ball back in play, the Foxes regained possession. Three lightning-quick and deadly accurate passes saw Leonardo easily beat the Black Avengers' keeper.

At the end of the first half, the scores remained even. The pattern of play remained constant too. The stock-in-trade of the Black Avengers was the sliding tackle, the dropped shoulder and the ankle tap. Not one of the Foxes players was unscathed. Jacob's right eye was swollen almost closed. Luigi, heavily tackled several times, felt as though his left knee could fold under him at any minute. Leonardo's ears rang from a backhanded blow to the temple.

During the half-time respite, Sergeant Dante attempted to calm the rising ire of his players. Leonardo declared, to general agreement, that the referee was either blind or in the pocket of the Black Avengers. Luigi believed he'd be lucky to go the distance in the second half. There were mutterings about giving the Black Avengers a taste of their own medicine. The sergeant said they could outplay the Black Avengers without any need for dirty tactics. The Beautiful Game would triumph over the brutal game.

The whistle blew. The crowd roared. This was a Conscript Cup final that would be long remembered. An intercept by a Foxes winger saw the ball delivered to Luigi and on to Leonardo. Sidestepping a sliding tackle, Leonardo thumped the ball into the Black Avengers' net. By the final minutes of the second half the score was four to one to the Foxes.

A fifth goal was in the making when Leonardo was knocked to the ground unconscious by a swinging arm from an outplayed Black Avenger. In the blink of an eye, Luigi, moving to protect Leonardo, felled the arm-swinger with a hammering short and fast right cross and a scything left hook. Smack. Bang. An injury to one was an attack on both. It had always been that way.

Players from both sides ran into the fray as Sergeant Dante and Corporal Bassanio carried Leonardo from the field and laid him on the sidelines. The referee pushed himself between the brawling players. The linesmen were soon on the field too. It took their combined strength to stop Luigi's enraged attack on his bloodied opponent. Still kicking and shouting, he was dragged to the sidelines by three Foxes players, while two Black Avengers helped Luigi's foe to his feet. In all, four players from each side, including Luigi, were ordered off.

Play resumed for a few minutes until the final whistle blew. The Foxes were victorious.

Despite the ugly ending to the affair, Sergeant Dante insisted the winners line up to shake hands with the Black Avengers. 'We draw a line under the game here. What happened on the field is the business of the field. We are different teams but we wear the same uniform, we salute the same flag.' He added more sombrely, looking at each of the eleven young, tired faces: 'It may well be that those against whom you played, those who bloodied and bruised you, will be your comrades in other places at other times. Your disagreements are behind you.' On the other side of the field the Black Avengers coach was expressing similar sentiments.

The teams met on the centre line and shook hands. The player whose attack on Leonardo had sparked the melee apologised, and Leonardo, still shaky, nodded his acceptance. Luigi was reluctant to shake the offender's hand, until a stare from Sergeant Dante saw him accept the offered handshake.

Commandant Galileo Gonfalonieri and Nero, accompanied by the German Army visitors, then approached the two teams. Gonfalonieri congratulated Dante. It was a job well done, he said, and the Foxes had earned their victory. They had played with skill and courage. The Black Avengers had met their match. He handed Dante the prized trophy — a small, gold-coloured statue of a football balanced on the bayonet point of a rifle — and shook the hand of every player and the match officials. Then he saluted and left.

Back in Dormitory Two, a rapturous Sergeant Dante told his players they had been magnificent. Jacob said that the victory against the Black Avengers deserved to be remembered in song. A verse had come to mind. With Sergeant Dante's permission he began to sing.

We are the Flying Foxes,
We strike like sharpened steel.
Our boots are mighty weapons
That make Avengers reel.
Scalio Dante on the sidelines,
His urging spurs us on,
Before the Flying Foxes
Our foes are thrashed and gone.
Oh, watch the mighty Foxes,
Watch as they pause and sup,
Watch as they drink in glory
From this, the Conscript Cup.

Amid the cheering and back-slapping that followed, Jacob was hoisted onto the shoulders of his fellow Foxes.

A second rendition of his impromptu verse was cut short by Sergeant Dante. This was, he said, the finest of songs. But, there and then, there was other business to attend to. He had news for his men. Their conscript training had been shortened on the instructions of the Army High Command. Within a week to ten days they would receive their postings. In the meantime, they would continue their various deployments until dispersal.

As Dante spoke, the elation of victory on the football field suddenly gave way to a sense of impending loss — loss of comradeship, loss of shared lives.

The farewells began within a week.

At the cycling school, the group of fifteen from Fortezza Nuova graduated with the award of the Army Cycling badge. Captain Luchese congratulated each recipient. They should wear their badges with pride: they were now members of the Brotherhood of the Bersaglieri, and their code was bravery, decency and loyalty. The captain, with dampening eyes, said he might never again have such a fine body of young men under his command. 'You have become like sons to me, and I feel like a proud father,' he said.

Returning to Fortezza Nuova with their badges, Luigi, Leonardo and Jacob found a typewritten notice pinned to the door of Dormitory Two. The notice listed their postings and the postings of their comrades. They ran their eyes over the names. Luigi Ferraro, Leonardo Battaglia and Jacob Zevi were assigned to the Second Reserve Formation, Bersaglieri Intake, Army Training Cycling School, Livorno.

Sergeant Dante arrived at the door of Dormitory Two as the men scanned the list. Luigi turned to him and asked: 'What does this mean, Sergeant? Is this a good thing or a bad thing?'

Dante said that it was better than a good thing. 'Only the best of the very best are placed on the Bersaglieri Reserve. They are the men we turn to when all else has failed. This is a great honour. You will be the last to die.'

His voice dripped with sarcasm. He shook his head. Another war was in the making. Another generation of boys would be slaughtered.

The three would be returning to their homes on the morning of 30 March. As reservists, they would be subject to call-up at any time. They would also be obliged to attend, as required, training camps and exercises of one or two weeks in duration. They would be notified of such events by hand-delivered telegram.

That night, Luigi wrote home.

Dearest Mother and Uncle Cesare,

I will be home in Tescano on Saturday, 30 March. Along with Leonardo and Jacob, I have been made a reservist in the Bersaglieri and this means I can remain with you until I am called for. The district here has its hills and the sea and many grand buildings and the Trattoria Bersaglieri, but it will be a joy to see you and our own Tescano hills. I will arrive before noon.

Your loving son and nephew,

Luigi

On the appointed day, Luigi, Leonardo and Jacob took their leave of Dormitory Two and Fortezza Nuova. Before they left, Dante took the three aside. Tough and seasoned sergeant that he was, he seemed emotional as he said: 'The Foxes have been my best team ever, and you have been three of its best players.' Lowering his voice, he added: 'You have played the Beautiful Game in what will become ugly times. It is my hope that you will never see the things I have seen, but I fear otherwise. Be brave when bravery is needed and be cautious when caution is necessary. Above all, stand back from hatred. It is a fire that devours all that it touches. Hatred is the great destroyer of good hearts. Avoid anger even when anger seems justified. Show mercy when you can. Do your job when you must. Treat the fallen with dignity and respect.'

The conscripts, in the uniforms of their reserve units, boarded their bus. Luigi, Leonardo and Jacob sat together. The driver's door was slammed shut. Then the vehicle was off, through the gates by the guardroom and onto the road towards Florence. The stops along the way were brief — a minute, no more. The driver, winking, said he had business in Florence. A widow awaited his attentions. There would be no long farewells for his passengers.

Luigi, eyes fixed on the passing countryside, pondered Dante's parting words. He would, he was sure, treat the fallen with dignity and respect. He hoped, however, he would not encounter too many of them.

CHAPTER NINE

Braking

*Life is not a clear path, a single and unbroken
journey. It is a process of stops and starts, of braking
on the spiritual bends and holding fast on the
spiritual straights. Knowing when to brake is the gift
of Grace from God.*

— Father Bogdan Browne, SJ, *The Furnace Within*, 1987

As the bus from Livorno drew into the Piazza Valsini, the nine-
piece Tescano Men of Brass band, on standby for more than
an hour, launched into their signature piece, the romping tune
'Brave Sons of the Hills and Valleys'.

After embracing Jacob, solemnly pledging to maintain
contact by letter, and shaking hands with the other travellers,
Luigi and Leonardo left the bus and watched as it moved around
the fountain and rumbled back down towards the main road to
Florence.

Everybody was waiting there in the piazza. Schoolchildren. Local farmers. Father Gianni. Mayor and headmaster Bartolo Minoza and teacher Salvatore 'Ferret Fartface' Paglia. There was cheering from all around. A banner proclaimed: *Welcome home, our bicycle heroes.* The spring sun flashed on the Army Cyclist badges on the two young men's tunics. Both were kissed — Luigi by his mother and Uncle Cesare, and Leonardo by his parents.

Mayor Minoza brusquely pushed his way through the crowd. Two children squealed in pain as he stood on their toes. He ignored the squeals. This was to be his day, too. He was the mayor and he was a Party man.

Standing on a small step-ladder beside the fountain, Minoza adjusted his black tie and wing collar, then cleared his throat. 'Our Tescano boys,' he began, 'or rather *my* Tescano boys — for it was in my classrooms that they were taught the lessons of life — have returned to our bosoms. I have been told, for I have friends in the highest places, that these very heroes stood shoulder to shoulder with Il Duce in the piazza of Livorno. And I am told, by these same friends, that our boys, on the personal and direct command of Il Duce, were selected to attend the Army Cycling Training School at Livorno.'

There was more loud cheering. It was cheering for Luigi and Leonardo. It was not cheering for Minoza. Luigi secretly wondered if the mayor might be shot for his lack of circumspection in speaking of those in the highest places. He hoped this might be the case. Minoza was a boaster and a boozer. He wasn't even from Tescano. And there was something ... well ... suspicious in the way Paglia followed him around like a dog.

Now Paglia stepped forward. 'From our little school here in Tescano have emerged two of our finest,' he gushed. 'I am proud, as is our patriotic mayor, to have shaped the destiny of Luigi and Leonardo through our teaching and our example. As Party men and teachers, we have done our job well. Luigi and Leonardo are our gift to our Fatherland.'

There was a ripple of polite applause; deference to Party men was prudent in these times. However, neither Father Gianni nor any in the Ferraro or Battaglia families felt disposed towards contributing to that ripple, and Leonardo whispered to Luigi: 'What a pair of pigs.'

The speeches over, the Tescano Men of Brass blew their way through a short medley of martial tunes as Luigi and Leonardo were ushered towards food-laden tables and benches set out in rows before the doors of the Church of the Blessed Seamstress. By late afternoon most of the benches had emptied and the Tescano Men of Brass had ceased playing their instruments and had taken to drink.

In the weeks that followed, Tescano life folded over Luigi once more. There was much to be done in the smithy. Tools were repaired, sharpened and adjusted for the next season of ploughing and planting. Luigi saw little of Leonardo during this time, save for blue-sky Sunday afternoons of walking or cycling.

However, storm clouds were gathering elsewhere. Within three months of Luigi's return, Italy had entered the war alongside Germany.

The Friday and Saturday-night newsreels shown between feature films in the bigger of the Tescano school's two classrooms increasingly featured close-up images of Il Duce at rallies in Rome, Florence, Trieste, Naples and elsewhere. The camera would pan away from the great leader and sweep across a sea of entranced, chanting faces. *Duce ... Duce ... Duce ...* Luigi remembered Livorno and the hypnotised faces there, their adoring responses. The faces on the newsreels looked the same. They had the look of madness.

During their Sunday walks and bicycle rides, Luigi and Leonardo speculated on what they had come to believe was the inevitable arrival of the telegrams calling them to the colours. Leonardo thought that the call was not far away. 'Probably we'll get it in a month or two when they know how things are going. But it's not for me ... and not for you, if you have any sense. I said it before: I'm not getting killed for the likes of the mayor and Paglia and Il Duce.'

Luigi said they wouldn't be killed if they only went to Livorno. Leonardo, irritated, raised his voice. 'If it was only Livorno it would be fine. But it won't be that. It will be Livorno first and then somewhere else.'

Luigi pointed out that they might get shot for not answering the call. Leonardo said it might be a case of getting shot if they didn't go and shot if they did. He added: 'If they want to send me away somewhere, I'll go over the wall. Livorno, maybe. But nowhere else.'

Deeply troubled, worried that his closest friend might desert and would then be captured, shot and disgraced, Luigi sought out Father Gianni. The priest was, after all, a man of learning. The two sat before the altar.

'What if you knew somebody and you knew he would run away from the army?' Luigi said. 'What would you do to stop him?'

Father Gianni said that nobody could stop anybody from running away from anything or anywhere. Sometimes, he went on, it might be wise to run away. For example, if you were being chased by an elephant — although it was unlikely that elephants would have any inclination to attack Tescano. Still, in all of Heaven and Earth, stranger things had happened. People often ran away from things because they were afraid, and there was no shame in fear. However, Father Gianni said, it was important to understand the reasons for running away, and to remember that wherever you went you always took yourself with you.

Luigi pressed his questions. 'But what if you knew somebody who was not afraid and who was brave and good and still wanted to run away?' The priest said that in such a case it was necessary to know why, if a person was unafraid and brave and good, he or she might want to run away.

Luigi thought for a moment. 'What if the person just didn't want to fight in the army because he believed the war was stupid and that the only people who wanted war were people like Minoza and Paglia and Mussolini? And what if the person who wanted to run away believed any war would be lost by Italy?'

This, indeed, was a most serious question, Father Gianni said. It was a question that, in another form, Christ Himself had faced before His inquisitors. It was, the priest said, a case of rendering unto Caesar what was Caesar's and rendering unto God what was God's.

Luigi had no idea what Father Gianni meant. What had Uncle Cesare to do with this matter? He was a blacksmith. Father Gianni decided not to attempt to define the Augustinian boundaries of the Kingdom of God and the Kingdom of Man. It was a subject that, for centuries, had exercised minds far greater than his. He would pray for Luigi's troubled friend. Luigi should do the same.

Through the mild northern summer of 1940 Luigi prayed often for Leonardo. But with each month that passed without the anticipated call to service, the prayers became less anxious. Luigi felt it was quite possible that the war would be prosecuted without recourse to the services of him or Leonardo.

Autumn and winter came and went. Spring unfolded. In late May 1941, two telegrams arrived in Tescano. The war would not be prosecuted without recourse to the services of Luigi Ferraro and Leonardo Battaglia.

The telegrams were read in silence. Two Tescano mothers wept that day. Two Tescano sons were to present themselves at the Army Cycling Training School, Livorno. There they would join their Bersaglieri reserve unit. The telegrams advised that a military vehicle from Florence, carrying other reservists to Livorno, would collect the two from the Piazza Valsini, Tescano, at approximately 10 am on 3 June.

On that day and at that time Luigi and Leonardo boarded the bus. Leonardo, with some reservations, had decided to return to Livorno. The decision had been made easier for him by Uncle Cesare's observation that any who did not answer the call to arms could expect to be shot.

'Livorno is fine,' Leonardo told Luigi. 'I will go there. But beyond that … I will decide when I have to decide.'

On board the bus, Luigi and Leonardo embraced Jacob. He'd gained weight and now sported a pencil-thin black moustache.

They also encountered a few of their other comrades from the cycling school. There was some banal banter, the nervous bravado of young men unsure of what lay ahead.

They disembarked a few hours later at the Army Cycling Training School, where they were met by Captain Luchese and Sergeant di Canola. There were no salutes. Instead there were handshakes and smiles. 'Finally,' Luchese said to di Canola, 'we have some real bicycle men among us.'

The captain and the sergeant explained to the men that there would first be a four-week refresher course, focusing on physical fitness, proficiency in the use of small arms, and formation cycling. Then some weeks would be spent in the workshops. After that, the reservists would be assigned to duties either at the cycling school or in Bersaglieri units elsewhere. They could, of course, be posted beyond the Italian mainland, but that would be a matter for the Army High Command.

Captain Luchese said he was certain that none in the group would have any difficulty with the refresher course. He was correct. The lessons learned during the initial period of cycling training were remembered by all.

During the time in the workshops the reservists were given a special assignment: the assembly and maintenance of motorised bicycles using the Villiers 98cc engine. It was, Luchese said, an assignment that might last several weeks or several months.

Life in the workshops was something of a cocoon for Luigi, Leonardo and Jacob. The working day was seldom less than nine hours, but provided they abided by a 10 pm curfew, the Tescano boys could pass their off-duty time as they wished. Once or twice a week the three would cycle into Livorno and visit the Trattoria

Bersaglieri. The welcome from former regimental Sergeant-Major Marconi, his stocky, one-eyed waiter and the patrons was always warm.

After three months in the workshops, Luigi, Leonardo, Jacob and their comrades were issued with a seven-day leave pass and returned to their homes. Another seven-day leave pass was issued some months later, in early December 1941. During that second leave pass, Pearl Harbor was bombed by the Japanese, and America entered the war against Italy, Japan and Germany.

When the three returned to the workshops, the mood there was grim. Hitler had subdued most of mainland Europe and bloodied England's nose, but there was a sense that squaring off against America was another matter. 'The Americans have more of everything,' Leonardo told his two companions on their first night back at the cycling school. 'Once they get started there will be no stopping them.' Luigi nodded, recalling the men in white Stetsons in the cowboy films. Those men stopped at nothing.

Finally, three months after America's entry into the war, in early spring 1942, orders were received. Luigi, Leonardo and Jacob were to be stationed at the Bersaglieri and Infantry Supply Depot in Ancona, on the Adriatic coast.

Sergeant di Canola told them that they had landed on their feet. Ancona was about as far away from the front lines as it was possible to get. It was a tranquil place, not entirely unlike Livorno. The sergeant had, some years earlier, been stationed there for several months. 'The blue of the Adriatic will take your breath away,' he said nostalgically. 'For bicycle men there are few better places to pass the time on two wheels — the flatness of the streets and roads that wind by the water to the Portonovo coves, and the long slopes that take the rider up and up to the Church of Santa Maria ... such a place.'

The fact that Ancona was far removed from the front lines came as a profound relief to Luigi. It meant there was no immediate prospect of Leonardo honouring his vow to desert.

Jacob had his own reason to be pleased with the posting. He knew Ancona well, he told Luigi and Leonardo. 'My uncles, aunties and cousins live there in a big house not so very far from the main piazza.' He said his relatives were quite well-to-do: his uncle Adam traded in table silver as well as rubies, turquoise and sapphires bought from Jewish dealers in Tehran, while his uncle Arial, Adam's brother, worked in goldsmithing and traded in gold coins of mixed provenance. The Tescano boys, Jacob said, would borrow bicycles from the Bersaglieri and Infantry Supply Depot and visit them when on leave. 'We will be welcomed with open arms. It will be like a grand holiday. It will be perfect.'

Luigi raised his eyebrows. A grand holiday. He had never had a holiday, grand or otherwise. He knew of no person who had ever had a holiday. In Tescano there was always so much to do. Nothing, he imagined, could possibly go wrong on a holiday. Ancona, as Jacob had said, would be perfect.

CHAPTER TEN

Sprinting

*War is a bit like those silly cycling races where you
pedal at about zero miles an hour and then you go
like the clappers for half a minute. Either dead stop or
flat out.*

— Jeremy Forsythe, *Memoirs of a Partisan*, 1961

At first the posting to Ancona was, for Luigi, Leonardo and
Jacob, what old soldiers would have described as a 'cushy billet'.
The war was out of sight and, generally, out of mind. The three
spent their working days in the bicycle section of the supply
depot, which was part of a sprawling port facility of warehouses
for uniforms, medical supplies and vehicle parts, a magazine for
small munitions and an armoury for light weapons.

When the work was done or when the three had twenty-four-
hour leave passes, they were at liberty to explore the Adriatic
coastline on borrowed bicycles. They cycled the flatness of the

shoreline for hours. Sometimes they swam. Sometimes they slept on a beach, sheltered by rocks. Often, returning to the supply depot and the relentless movement of stores and men and machines, they wondered if the war would end before it reached Ancona.

Their own work at the supply depot was straightforward. It involved the receipt, warehousing and despatch of bicycles, spare parts and Villiers 98cc two-stroke bicycle engines. They were housed in one of several timber sheds within the confines of the port area. A few of those sheds were occupied by German Field Police. Leonardo suspected the Germans were watching for any pilfering by civilian dock workers or Italians in uniform.

The three were under the command of Quartermaster Sergeant Vince Vittoria of the Quartermaster Corps. Just because there was a war, he told them, was no reason to work themselves to death. 'Just keep the paperwork in good order,' he said, 'and check everything that comes in or goes out. Stow everything where it needs to be stowed. Get the requisitioned parts out on time and we'll all do very nicely.'

Some days, Luigi, Leonardo and Jacob never saw their sergeant. Other days he might appear for two or three hours before disappearing. They sometimes discussed whether he might be involved in shady business. Perhaps something to do with petrol, they speculated. Or spare parts. Though Leonardo added: 'Anyhow, it's none of our business, and it suits us for him to be our boss.'

Not unlike Livorno, Ancona itself was an amalgam of the truly grand, the ornate provincial, and the cobbled-together. At various times it had been a papal State, a fortress outpost of France, and — like Rome, Avignon and Florence — a centre of Jewish commerce and trade. The Citadel dominated the city but its real treasure was the Cathedral of San Ciriaco, which had been consecrated almost seven hundred years before Italians and the world had even heard of Mussolini. There were other treasures, such as a marble arch erected in homage to the Roman emperor and military genius Trajan, and the Churches of Santa Maria della Piazza, San Francesco and Sant' Agostino. From the harbour walls there were magnificent views of a serrated coastline that extended forever, held in place by the azure of a sea that had for centuries been a highway sailed by both traders and conquerors. To the west were equally beautiful views of the low, sometimes purple hills. Running along the hills were roads that wound towards hamlets and farms, imposing villas and mansions, all set in a crossword puzzle of fields and groves.

However, for Luigi and Leonardo, the jewels in the crown of Ancona were visits to the home of Jacob's relatives, whose gold and silver smithing and trading enterprises had first brought them to the city in the early 1800s.

On their first visit, it was obvious that Jacob's description of uncles Adam and Arial and their families as 'quite well-to-do' had been a significant understatement. The residence, on the impressive Via Renata, which ran from Ancona's Piazza San Giorgio towards the Citadel, was large and walled, and entry was through two wide Baroque wrought-iron gates. The main entrance opened onto a courtyard. Adam's family occupied the building on one side of the courtyard, Arial's family the other. The part of the courtyard that faced the main entrance was used as a common area — a place for shared meals or reading or lounging.

Luigi and Leonardo were welcomed warmly by the family. Jacob had recounted to his uncles his first hours at Livorno, the anti-semitism of the immaculately turned-out sergeant in the guardroom at the Fortezza Nuova, and the freely offered comradeship of Luigi and Leonardo. Adam said that they were living in times when Jews had few friends.

The two Tescano boys also met Adam's wife, Ariella, and daughter, Miriam, and the extraordinarily fetching Sarah and Zelda, the daughters of Arial and his wife, Batia. The household was one of harmony, courtesy and affection. As guests at the table, Luigi and Leonardo were always seated first.

Although conversation during meals was intelligent, lively and good-humoured, Luigi and Leonardo knew that the Zevis were concerned by the growing risk to themselves and their substantial material holdings. Arial said that wherever the Germans were in charge there were arrests and deportations of Jews to work camps. 'If the Germans take over here we'll all be finished. Sometimes I think we should get away now — take what we have and try to get to Switzerland.'

Adam disagreed: perhaps they should wait a little longer, he said, frowning.

Luigi said that there were hundreds of thousands of German soldiers on Italian soil. 'The Germans are already in charge. At the supply depot they are making everybody work longer hours. They watch us like hawks. They are bringing in more anti-aircraft guns. The war will soon be here, in your streets.'

The upgrading of the anti-aircraft defences was timely. The port area was bombed regularly in the first months of 1943. The men's visits to Jacob's family became less frequent, and there were signs on these visits that the Zevis were preparing to flee. Paintings and tapestries had been removed from walls. Furniture had disappeared. Packed crates were stacked in the courtyard.

Initially, the bombing raids on Ancona came every ten or twelve days. Then the raids became more frequent. Fifteen or twenty bombers would thunder over once a week, usually before noon, laying waste to any reconstruction undertaken since the previous raid.

It was such a pre-noon raid that saw Luigi, Leonardo, Jacob and Sergeant Vittoria thrown together in a venture that would take them away from Ancona. This raid was worse than any that had gone before.

They were counting crates in the bicycle section of the supply depot when the wail of the air-raid sirens began. The four dived under a long metal table. Other men working in the same area found shelter between rows of crated bicycles. The whistle of the falling bombs was terrifying. The ground trembled as the bombs found their mark, and debris peppered walls and vehicles. The blast from the explosions shattered windows into millions of shards of flying glass. Some men screamed. Others shook uncontrollably. Luigi curled into a tight ball, closing his eyes and covering his ears. He believed, in that moment, that he would never see Tescano again.

The rain of bombs fell for no more than fifteen minutes, but it felt like a lifetime. One end of the bicycle section took a direct hit. When the all-clear sounded, Luigi, Leonardo, Jacob and Sergeant Vittoria crawled from their makeshift shelter and looked around.

Dozens of men were obviously dead. Scores lay wounded or wandered in a state of shock. Luigi, Leonardo, Jacob and the sergeant worked together, looking for those still living and moving them clear of flames and rubble. Some gurgled their last breath as they were shifted. Others mouthed the name of a loved one. And there were those who simply stared in disbelief; they were about to die and it made no sense. Life was meant to be longer, surely.

It took hours to move the wounded and lay out the dead. Military ambulances arrived empty then roared away full. When the moving and the laying out were finally over, Luigi, Leonardo, Jacob and the sergeant sat in a tight circle on the ruins of a collapsed wall. The four looked at each other. They were stunned by the devastation. And they were stunned to have survived.

It was Sergeant Vince who spoke first. He took a deep breath, looked around nervously and said: 'What I tell you now places my life in your hands.'

Vittoria revealed himself as a Communist and a Partisan sympathiser. He had been a Communist since his service in Albania in 1941. There, he said, he had seen too many good Italians killed and too much German brutality against civilians. He had returned from the Balkans to a posting at the military supply centre in Milan, and it was there, during off-duty hours and nights in bars frequented by factory workers, that he'd drifted into contact with Communist Party organisers and sympathisers. These were the people who formed the backbone of the emerging Garibaldi Brigades of a ruthless Italian Partisan army. His subsequent posting to Ancona had seen him move from the fringes of Communist Party activity to a clandestine role as a procurer of arms and equipment for the Partisans. 'It is only a matter of time, a short time, before the Germans come for me,' he said. 'Somebody, somewhere, will be captured and tortured. My name will be revealed. It is as simple as that.'

The sergeant had a proposition for the three. He and three comrades had been preparing to leave Ancona that very day in a heavy vehicle loaded with supplies. The truck was parked outside the main gate of the port area, ready to depart. No bombs had fallen near that gate, but while laying out the dead he had seen the bodies of his three comrades. Luigi, Leonardo and Jacob, he said, could take the places of the dead and leave Ancona with him there and then, or they could stay and take their chances with the Germans and in the next air raid.

Luigi asked why the sergeant could not drive the truck away by himself. Vittoria explained that it was loaded with small arms, ammunition, some uniforms, medical supplies, canisters of fuel, and crates containing two-stroke Villiers engines for military bicycles. The regulations stated that such a load could only be moved under guard — two men in the back of the vehicle, and the driver and another man in the front cabin.

Luigi, Leonardo and Jacob exchanged glances. In the silence that fell between the three, the sergeant added that the paperwork for the movement of the vehicle was in order. 'I completed it myself, even used a copy of the head quartermaster's official stamp for the final approval.' He did not know their final destination, only that the vehicle was to be driven to Florence, where further instructions would be received. The journey would not be without its risks, he admitted, but as they had seen, Ancona had become a death trap.

Luigi said he knew nothing of the Communists. Minoza and Paglia had said that the Communists were evil anti-Christs. But, coming from Minoza and Paglia ... well ...

Leonardo shook his head. 'The Communists couldn't be as bad as those two loudmouths, who got us into the war in the first place,' he said. 'We should go with Sergeant Vince.'

Luigi looked to Jacob. 'Leonardo is right,' Jacob said firmly. 'We should go. We will die if we remain. But first I must see my family.'

The sergeant shook his head. 'There is no time for that. I know it is hard for you, but the danger is too great — for all of us.'

The Tescano boys reluctantly nodded their agreement, Jacob more slowly than Luigi and Leonardo. The sergeant returned their nods. 'Walk behind me to the gates,' he said. 'The guards will have better things to do right now than bother with us. And remember, when we leave here we don't exist anymore. We're missing in action. We're the bodies they never found. There's no coming back from this. We're on the run until we are among friends.'

Vittoria's prediction that the Germans at the main gate would be too distracted to check on comings and goings proved optimistic. The four were stopped by five guards in the uniform of the Military Field Police. While four of the Germans levelled their weapons, a fifth demanded identification documents. The papers were handed over, perused and passed back — all save those presented by Sergeant Vittoria.

'Vincent Vittoria ...' the German inquisitor said in heavily accented Italian. 'I have heard the name. Why might I have heard the name?'

Vittoria shrugged. All Italian names sounded the same, he said.

The questioning turned to what business the Italians might have beyond the main gates. Vittoria pointed to the truck parked just beyond those gates and handed the German a typewritten sheet of paper, listing supplies. The German read aloud: *'Twenty-four boxes of small arms, thirty boxes of small-arms ammunition, eight boxes of grenades, two boxes of morphine and syringes, four boxes of sterile field dressings, eight drums of motor spirit, field rations for four, bicycle engines and bicycle parts.'* Additionally, there were blankets, water bottles, camouflage nets, lengths of rope, all-weather clothing, boots, torches and batteries. The typewritten sheet indicated that the goods were to be delivered to a German reserve infantry unit near Florence. The German inquisitor was suspicious. 'Why all the way over there? There must be places closer where they can get this.'

Vittoria shrugged again. 'I just drive the vehicle,' he said. 'We were meant to be gone hours ago, before those bombers did their dirty work. Swine.'

Finally the German stepped back and waved Vittoria, Luigi, Leonardo and Jacob towards the truck. The paperwork was in order.

Vittoria motioned Luigi into the front passenger seat. Leonardo and Jacob were directed into the canvas-covered rear of the vehicle. 'If we get stopped,' the sergeant instructed, 'try to look like guards. Another thing: while there are just the four of us, I'm Comrade Vince and you're Comrades Luigi, Leonardo and Jacob.' He climbed into the driver's seat, started the engine and turned the vehicle towards the road, which seemed stitched, in places, to the coastline that ran north to Rimini.

At first, progress was slow. Some parts of the road were flooded with refugees fleeing towards the advancing Allied armies, which had by now pushed their enemies all the way from Sicily to well beyond Rome. Anything with wheels — carts, bicycles, prams, trolleys — was being pushed or pulled, loaded with hastily gathered possessions. Some had already been abandoned in the ditches alongside vehicles that, out of fuel, had themselves been cast aside. Lying around the forsaken vehicles and the broken carts were open suitcases, their contents strewn across the roadside dirt and gravel: family pictures in fractured frames and, now and then, a Christening gown or a wedding dress or a shawl of yellowing lace. Scattered among the vehicles and possessions were a few old people who had sat down to wait for death. Others, not old, had sat down to rest and had fallen, almost in the instant, into a coma of exhaustion.

No noise came from the columns of the fleeing. Even the children who walked or were carried by mothers or fathers were silent. On every face could be seen the hollowness of hunger, the blackness of terror, after their flight from the fires that now consumed bombed towns and villages.

Luigi felt numbed by what he was seeing. This was the war that Colonel Gonfalonieri had described. Here was the cruelty of it all. These fleeing people had done nothing to deserve such suffering. This was wrong.

At the port town of Senigallia, two hours after leaving Ancona, the vehicle's temperature gauge jerked into the red and steam shot from the front and sides of the squat bonnet. The truck came to a halt and Vittoria and Luigi checked the engine. The radiator hose had worked its way loose. It took the best part of two hours before the engine had cooled sufficiently for the hose to be reconnected, the radiator refilled and other hoses checked. Only then was the journey resumed.

Just half an hour later, however, as they reached Pesaro, a town that had once been a hub of Roman commerce, there was a flicker and then a flashing dashboard light to indicate that oil pressure was falling and engine temperature was rising once more. Again Comrade Vince stopped the truck, this time in a piazza not fifty metres from a police post. He raised the squat bonnet, and Vince cursed. 'No oil,' he said.

Two carabinieri left the police post and walked towards the truck. Vince threw up his arms theatrically and shouted at the three comrades: 'Useless! Useless bastards. I told you to check everything!' Then, to the carabinieri, he added: 'Conscripts. Useless! More trouble than they're worth.' He explained that the oil was low and they'd brought no spare tins.

The carabinieri were sympathetic. They told the conscripts to walk over to the police post. The taller of the two carabinieri said: 'Tell them we sent you and to give you three five-litre tins of engine oil. Better take plenty — you might have an oil leak.'

Vince was profuse in his thanks. They'd already had problems with the radiator. The oil problem was something they could have done without. That and the refugees on the road. 'We couldn't move for them,' he said.

'It's the war,' said the shorter carabinieri. 'These days my wife says everything that happens is because of the war. Her headaches, she says, are because of the war. We sleep in separate beds because of the war. Then she says she never sees me and that I'm out drinking, so I tell her it's because of the war. You'd think one war would be enough. But, no, they had to have a second one.'

Luigi, Leonardo and Jacob soon returned with the oil. The four comrades shook hands with the carabinieri. The truck hummed into life and Vince sighed with relief.

They continued north towards Rimini. From there they would push on to Forli and then turn west and into the mountains before winding down towards Florence.

With three, possibly four, hours of daylight left, Luigi and Vince, in the cabin of the vehicle, looked out on a world that seemed untouched by war and the horrors of bombing and the refugees they'd left behind. The dappled sky seeped into the sea on the line of the horizon. Here and there were small houses and fields that had been farmed for more than two thousand years.

In a passable tenor voice, Vince began a strong, manly rendition of 'Bandiera Rossa', the song that had been the optimistic anthem of organised labour in Italy even before the Great War:

> Forward, people, to the rescue.
> The red flag, the red flag.
> The red flag will triumph.

Hope, for Comrade Vince, continued to spring eternal. He assured Luigi that the comrades would eventually win through. All men and women would live a decent life. All would learn to read and write. All would have enough to eat, clean bedding, shelter, freedom to think and speak as they pleased. No head would be bowed. Vince hoped victory would come sooner rather than later, but either way, he knew it would happen. It had to happen. Communism was an exact science and science would always triumph.

Luigi said it seemed the Communists were nowhere near as bad as Minoza and Paglia had said they were. He wondered how he might become a Communist.

'It is simple,' Vince said. 'Within the heart of every man and woman is the heart of a Communist. You simply examine your heart and find the truth within.'

Luigi resolved to examine his heart.

The truck grumbled and rumbled on, skirting Rimini, and had begun to nose north and inland towards Forli when, dead ahead, they saw a German checkpoint — sandbagged machine-gun pits on either side of the road, a vehicle that blocked half of the road, heavily armed German soldiers. Two of them waved the truck to a halt. When the wheels stopped, four other Germans moved to the back of the vehicle.

Luigi and Vince were ordered from the cabin. Leonardo and Jacob climbed down from the rear. Identity papers and documents were inspected. The Germans were thorough. Every item in the rear of the vehicle was checked against the typewritten sheet handed over by Vittoria. Then came the questions: when had the truck left Ancona? Had the four seen anything unusual on the road? Why was such a load being sent all the way to Florence?

Vince feigned irritation. He had no idea why the material was consigned to Florence; he only delivered whatever it was he was told to deliver. God alone knew how many times their papers and documents had been checked since Ancona, and he'd be obliged if the truck could get on its way.

The Germans seemed satisfied. There were rumours of Partisan activity further ahead, they said, in the high country beyond Forli. It would be a good idea to pull over somewhere for the night and then tackle the high country in daylight. Vince thanked the Germans for the advice, and said they'd cover a few more kilometres before resting overnight.

Out of earshot, he spat: 'Fascist German bastards.'

CHAPTER ELEVEN

Endurance

We endure because life is only endurance. It is like the muscle-tearing bicycle ride with its hills and punctures and buckled wheels.

— Rev. Donald MacInnes, *Misery as the Maker of Men,*
Edinburgh, 1968

The late daylight of summer faded just as Comrade Vince swung the truck onto a narrow track that petered out, after a hundred metres, at a clearing. Luigi wondered how they had been lucky enough to find such a place. Vince confided he had made this journey many times.

Climbing down from the back and stretching, Leonardo observed that if Vince could find the clearing, so could the Germans.

'We are safe here,' Vince assured them. 'The Germans keep their distance at night. They jump at shadows and listen to rumours. The danger will come as we approach Florence. There are patrols everywhere around the city.'

The four spent the night on the soft earth of the clearing. At first light they were back on the road. A few hours would see them across and down the mountains and into Florence.

On the road that wound towards the high country it was slow going. The load was heavy and the vehicle had seen better days. The truck growled and rasped with every gear change. Luigi was silent, looking out on a landscape that reminded him of his boyhood and the adventures he'd shared with Leonardo, the Hercules and the Hirondelle.

His drift through warm memories ended abruptly with a scream of brakes and the skid of rubber on the mountain road. The truck had shuddered to a halt within less than a metre of four uniformed Germans, who had emerged from the nowhere of a perfectly camouflaged dugout. Luigi saw the SS insignia on their shoulders and black helmets. These were men not to be trifled with. More Germans, perhaps ten of them, now appeared behind the vehicle. Some were dressed in the leather coats of motorcycle riders.

'Leave this to me,' Vince whispered to Luigi. 'These pigs are the worst of the worst.'

Once again, identity papers and transit documents were demanded. A lantern-jawed sergeant read the names aloud: Luigi Ferraro, Leonardo Battaglia, Vincent Vittoria, Jacob Zevi. 'Which of you is Zevi, Jacob Zevi?' he demanded. Jacob raised an arm and the sergeant moved towards him. 'Jacob and Zevi. Jewish names,' he said. 'A Jew — are you a Jew?'

Jacob seemed paralysed with fear. Before he could respond, Vince cut in. 'A Jew?' he said, feigning amazement. 'He's not even a Catholic. He's one of your lot. He's a Lutheran. Can't drive, can't read a map. His people are from up on the Swiss border. They're all called Zevi and Mayer up there. Too poor to be Jews and too stupid to be good for anything. Bastards barely speak Italian. You can have him if you want. If we get stuck on a hill I might stick him under the wheels to stop us rolling backwards.'

The lantern-jawed SS sergeant cleared his throat and spat on the road. The identity papers and transit documents were returned to Vince. But just as the four were heading back to the truck, an SS officer appeared from the well-camouflaged dugout. He extended a hand towards Vince. 'The documents,' he said. 'Let me see the documents.'

The officer, a captain, examined and returned the papers without comment. While his men checked all the supplies in the vehicle, he asked about Ancona and the bombing raids and casualties there. Vince said that the port at Ancona was a mess, but that he had no doubt the tide of war would turn. Regular Italian soldiers like himself knew they could count on their German comrades to stiffen the line of resistance.

The SS captain rolled his eyes. A dismissive note in his voice, he said: 'We'll see when the time comes.' Then he added: 'There are Communists and other troublemakers in these hills. What you are carrying should not fall into the wrong hands. I will give you a motorcycle and sidecar escort of four men. They will ride ahead of you and behind you and will see you to the final checkpoint before Florence. Until then, you are under the command of my men. Do as they say. Do not stop unless they tell you to stop.'

The motorcycles, which had been invisible under camouflage netting, were wheeled onto the road and kicked into life. Then this smallest of convoys took off, the truck sandwiched between the front and rear escorts.

In the cabin, Vince told Luigi that when they got to Florence there would be a rendezvous and new documents would be provided, along with further instructions that, he suspected, would direct them beyond that city. Their final destination could be any one of four or five places.

Twice before the small convoy crossed the highest point of the hills and began the sweeping glide down to Florence, they were stopped at other German roadblocks. On both occasions the examination of documents was barely more than superficial.

'The SS flashes on the sidecars do the trick,' Vince told Luigi. 'They'll get us through anything.'

Some more hours passed before the vehicle and its escort swung left around a long, wide bend and there, abruptly, was the flatness of Florence. That flatness rolled away in every direction, well beyond the Arno River, well beyond the stunning dome of Santa Maria del Fiore and the clock tower of the Palazzo Vecchio.

At the point where the Tuscan countryside ended and began to fold into the city, the German escort waved the vehicle to a halt at another checkpoint. One of the SS escorts spoke to the regular German Army guards, then told Vince: 'We leave you here. Drive straight ahead. Go about your business.'

Ten minutes beyond the checkpoint, Vince stopped the vehicle on the hard shoulder of the tree-flanked road that scrolled towards the centre of the city. 'We should rest here for a few hours,' he said. 'Early afternoon is best for our arrival.'

The rendezvous in the city would occur at the Trattoria Signoria in Via Fortuna, a backstreet near the Palazzo Vecchio. Luigi, Leonardo and Jacob would remain in the truck while Vince entered the trattoria. What happened afterwards would depend on the instructions he was given. Vince had made several such journeys to and beyond Florence. It was unlikely, on past experience, that they would leave the city until dusk. 'That means we may be waiting in the city, out of sight, for some hours,' he said.

Jacob mentioned that Via Fortuna was fifteen minutes on foot from his family home. Would it be possible, he asked Vince, for him to visit his family? Vince was unsure. Everything would be dictated by the instructions they received. It might be that Jacob could spend a few hours with his family, but he would first have to wait for Vince to return with those instructions.

They set off again. Leaving the main road, Vince threaded the vehicle through a spaghetti knot of streets. The journey to the Via Fortuna took no more than twenty-five minutes. At the Trattoria Signoria, he swung the vehicle into a covered dead-end laneway. Parked well into the laneway, the truck was beyond the view of all but the most prying eyes.

Vince entered the back of the trattoria through a green door. When he reappeared, ten minutes later, he motioned for Luigi to bring Leonardo and Jacob inside, into a windowless storeroom. Upturned boxes served as seats for the four. Vince said they would wait for five hours before leaving, so Jacob could visit his family. He was in uniform and was unlikely to be stopped on the streets. Looking Jacob in the eye, Vince ordered: 'Return within five hours. Not one minute more. If you are late we will depart without you.'

Luigi and Leonardo dozed. They were exhausted, drained by the Ancona bombings and their dangerous journey. Four hours, almost five hours passed. There was no sign of Jacob. Then, finally, the green door opened and Luigi and Leonardo looked around, expecting Jacob, but then their jaws dropped. It was Father Gianni.

When the priest saw the two young men, his eyes sparkled and widened in astonishment. Turning to Vince, he said: 'My dear friend, God has led you to round up two of my sheep.' Vince shook his head, assuring Father Gianni that their presence had more to do with accident than divine design.

Leonardo began to mouth a question but Father Gianni shook his head and raised a finger to his lips. There might be time for talking later, but for the moment there was other business in hand. He handed Vince a sheet of paper. The document, he said, would allow the truck to pass through any German checkpoints on the western side of the city. They were to take the road that ran through Empoli. They would leave immediately.

Vince told Father Gianni of Jacob's visit to his family. Father Gianni said there could be no delays. It was time to go. There was no emotion in his voice. 'Reverse into the street,' he said. 'Wait for my car and follow me, but not too closely — maybe two or three hundred metres behind.'

Anxious, Luigi asked for a few more minutes. 'Jacob will be close. He will be on his way. I am certain. We cannot leave him.'

Father Gianni touched Luigi's shoulder. 'Every minute we stay we are in great danger. We must leave your friend to his own devices and to the will of God.'

Luigi looked at Leonardo, his eyes pleading for support. Leonardo inhaled deeply and shook his head. 'Father Gianni is right, Luigi,' he said.

Luigi followed Vince and Leonardo out to the truck. Vince reversed the vehicle into Via Fortuna. He waited until it was passed by a 1938 Fiat driven by Father Gianni. Then he followed.

Within half an hour they had cleared the German military checkpoint on the western side of Florence, and it was in the last minutes of daylight that both vehicles passed through Empoli.

Luigi's thoughts were of Jacob. Why had his friend failed to return? He'd given his word.

Darkness fell and eventually, mesmerised by the pinprick tail-lights of Father Gianni's car, Luigi slipped into a slumber, only to be nudged awake hours later by Vince. Blinking, he saw the pinprick tail-lights veer right. The truck followed, swinging onto a dirt track that wound upwards. Occasionally, the dimmed yellow headlights flashed across a landmark that seemed oddly familiar. Progress was slow, and thirty minutes elapsed before Father Gianni's car halted in the beam of a torch shone by a man standing in the centre of the track. The truck stopped less than a metre behind the car. Four or five other men appeared from the darkness and moved towards the vehicle. They were heavily armed and unshaven. They were Partisans.

Vince and Luigi climbed down from the cabin. The scent of the hills was pervasive. It was the scent of boyhood. They had arrived in the hills beyond Tescano, Luigi realised.

One of the heavily armed men shone a torch into the rear of the truck and Leonardo emerged. Then another walked towards

Luigi. 'Does it still go like the clappers?' he asked, in English, and broke into a grin.

It was Jeremy Forsythe. In his perfect Italian, he went on: 'I came back to check on the Hercules.' He laughed at Luigi's astonishment. Jeremy had learned of his return some hours earlier, he explained, when a coded wireless message from the Partisan proprietor of the Trattoria Signoria had advised of the truck's departure from Florence and listed its passengers. Speechless, Luigi stared at the Englishman.

Jeremy grinned again. Briefly turning away, he issued orders in the casual manner of a man who had never needed to raise his voice. The truck was to be moved to a cave three hundred metres away. Father Gianni was to return to Tescano. Then Jeremy motioned for the remaining men and Luigi, Leonardo and Vince to follow him along a winding track, into the darkness.

All the men were sure-footed on the path, and they moved quickly and quietly. All, it was obvious, knew the track — Luigi and Leonardo from their boyhood, Vince from previous journeys, and Jeremy Forsythe and his men from the hit-and-run life they had chosen in these Tuscan hills.

After ten minutes, the party had completed the steepest part of the climb, which led under a giant hanging rock into a cavern. The entry to the cave was well concealed by nets. A young woman held the netting aside for them to enter. The young woman was slim, Luigi noticed, and wore the Partisan garb of army trousers, loose-fitting tunic, boots and beret. Her dark hair was drawn back in a ponytail. In the half moonlight her face was quite beautiful — dark eyes, high cheekbones. Her holstered British Webley service revolver was slung from a webbing belt.

'You'd be no strangers to this place — almost your playground when you were boys, or so I'm informed,' Jeremy said to Luigi as the light from hurricane lamps projected the men's long shadows onto the rock walls.

'This was one of our secret places, mine and Leonardo's,' Luigi said. 'It was one of the best.' He glanced around the main cavern and then towards the maze of smaller passages cut by water and fault lines over hundreds of thousands of years. 'It's different,' he said. 'It used to be empty and dark. But now — look at it all … all the boxes … the lant—' Then the words stopped in his mouth.

Emerging from the darkness beyond the light of the lanterns was the figure of Uncle Cesare, his work shirt open, his work trousers, as ever, pockmarked by sparks from the big forge in the smithy. Cesare was beaming as he grasped Luigi and Leonardo in the embrace of a mountain bear. The three were locked together until Cesare released his grip and stepped back. He glanced towards Vince, smiling. 'My dear, brave comrade, we meet again.'

Incredulous, Luigi turned to Vince. 'Why in all these months did you never say a word of Uncle Cesare and the Tescano hills?'

Vince explained that to reveal the secret would have placed many lives in danger. Then Jeremy cut in. Questions and answers should wait until the new arrivals had eaten and rested.

In the meantime, Luigi should settle for news of his mother. Uncle Cesare said she was well but that she worried constantly. There were strands of grey in her dark hair. Every day she prayed at the Church of the Blessed Seamstress, for her son and Leonardo and their friend Jacob.

Leonardo asked for news of his parents at the Tescano bakery. Cesare assured him that they were in good health, but that they, too, worried every day. Leonardo and Luigi were in their prayers.

There was increasing movement of German SS troops across the region, Cesare went on. Danger was everywhere. Mayor Minoza and Salvatore Paglia were now in the pockets of the Germans, just as they had always been in the pockets of the Fascists. The pair were informers, but the day of reckoning for Minoza and Paglia was not far away. British, American, Polish and Indian troops were relentless in their drive north. The Partisans, working behind German lines, were making that advance easier.

'This is the ugliest of fights,' Cesare added. 'The Germans mistrust all Italians. And the Germans steal. They have been stealing everything — banks have been emptied, gold taken from churches. Whatever they steal, the Germans load up in trains and send north, up through Austria.'

The Germans had also been arresting Italian Jews. Cesare had no details, just the briefest of brief BBC radio reports, that very day, of arrests of Jews in Florence and Ancona. The Germans had a list of every Jewish family, and people who were arrested were as good as dead. They were sent away. There were camps in Germany where they were killed.

Luigi told of Jacob's disappearance in Florence. Jeremy said enquiries would be made; the Partisans had a spider's web of informants across the north. But it might be wise not to hope for too much.

There was silence. Jeremy's words had cast a pall over the small group.

The quiet was only broken when the young woman who had met them at the mouth of the cavern reappeared and said that the newcomers and Comrade Vince should eat and then rest. Jeremy introduced her to Luigi and Leonardo as Nunzia Costa. 'Nunzia is the only flower in this thorny place,' he said, half smiling. 'She came to us from Genoa and the comrades of the Garibaldi Brigades of which we have the honour to be but a small part.'

As Luigi looked at Nunzia he thought of the blooms that, every spring, brought great splashes of colour and life to the Tescano hills. To himself, he said, 'Fiore.' Flower. For a split second, Nunzia's eyes met his, and Luigi thought he detected a blush on her face. There may even have been the shadow of a shy smile. But the light was poor and it was impossible for Luigi to know.

As the visitors ate, Jeremy welcomed perhaps a dozen more men to the long, makeshift table. They were mostly young, unshaven and in their twenties, all in Partisan dress. None came from the Tescano area. They had taken to the hills for different reasons: some were Communists, others had deserted from the Italian Army. All offered firm handshakes and broad smiles. From them, Luigi and Leonardo learned that the cavern and its smaller caves and passages were home and headquarters to between twenty and thirty-five Partisans. How many were in the caves at any given time depended on the level of anti-German activity across the district. 'When the Germans are near here, we hunt and kill them here, and when the Germans are elsewhere, we hunt and kill them elsewhere,' said one of the Partisans. 'This is what we do. We think nothing of it. They kill good Italians and we kill bad Germans. It is simple.' Luigi felt the chill of that matter-of-fact declaration.

Fed and weary, Luigi, Leonardo and Vince slept on fold-down camp beds in one of the passages that ran off the main cavern. The night was cool and almost silent, save for the slow drip and trickle of water through the ancient rock formations.

As Luigi was falling into a dreamless sleep, he thought of the boyhood adventures in which he and Leonardo had tangled, in these very hills, with Barbarians and, later, Prairie Trash. But the wounds inflicted and the blood spilled in those long-ago days had only been imagined. This real war was miserable and cruel. Perhaps, when it was over, he and Leonardo would go away together. And if Jacob was alive he, too, would journey with them. They would go to the furthest-away place on earth. They would go to Australia. There they would be freed from the memories of such misery and cruelty.

CHAPTER TWELVE

Tactics

You take the right tack and you tick the boxes. That's why it's called tactics. Every race I ever won, and I won a few, I had a plan and I stuck to it. You don't just climb on the bike and pedal. You gotta see the race in your head.

— Stan 'The Man' Raymond, Golden Gears Champion, 1976

The next morning, Luigi was awakened by the sound of a low-flying aircraft. Seconds later, Leonardo and Vince were sitting upright in their camp beds, listening. Jeremy and Uncle Cesare appeared. There was nothing to worry about, Cesare said. German spotter planes flew over the hills every few days, but they could see nothing of the caves from the air. The only real danger for the Partisans was being spotted in the open — though even then, there was little an unarmed spotter plane could do unless there were German patrols on the ground nearby.

'They are looking for needles in haystacks,' Jeremy said. Luigi was puzzled. Why would the Germans be looking for needles in a place where there were no haystacks? It was an English expression, Jeremy explained. Luigi said that English was an odd language: bicycles went 'like the clappers' and needles were to be found in haystacks. He would like to learn more of these expressions. Perhaps Jeremy Forsythe could be his teacher.

And so began Luigi's initial education in the language he would come to speak for most of his life, a language he would learn, at first, through incomprehensible phrases — *freeze the balls off a brass monkey, bull in a china shop, red herrings, flat out, swings and roundabouts*. He proved an eager and adept pupil.

But on that first full day in the cavern there were other things to learn. 'There can be no return to Tescano until this is over,' Jeremy told Luigi. 'You and Leonardo have become Partisans by an accident of fate — just as the Hercules bicycle became yours by an accident of fate. Your only safety lies in remaining with us and fighting with us. We will teach you Partisan ways and we will all look after each other through thick and thin.' Where 'thick and thin' might be was a mystery to Luigi.

Within a few days of their arrival in the hills, Luigi, Leonardo and Sergeant Vince had discarded their Italian Army tunics and donned the garb of the Partisans. Luigi and Leonardo made a handsome picture: shirts open, sleeves rolled up, dark berets worn at a tilt. Each was given a British Army Webley revolver and twenty-four rounds of ammunition. They were also issued with the murderously sharp, slim-bladed, black-handled daggers carried by men of the Allied Airborne and Commando regiments.

Years later, sitting on his verandah facing the pounding ocean that shaped the scalloped coastline of Diggers Cove, Luigi was sometimes assailed by memories of what he saw and felt in the war that came to the hills around and beyond Tescano. The memories came and went for no particular reason. They had no obvious trigger. They simply arrived and crowded his mind. For hours at a time, sometimes for an entire day, he could think of nothing but the war.

He thought of the boundless ferocity of the Partisans, many of whom were trained by British undercover agents like Jeremy Forsythe. Jeremy, Luigi learned, had been commissioned into the Durham Light Infantry before the war. He'd been a regular, a captain, when the war broke out. Later he had volunteered for the Special Operations Executive. The new job fitted like a glove. 'All cowboys-and-Indians stuff, and you pretty much make it up as you go along once you're in the field,' he explained. 'None of this saluting and shiny boots and parades — just get in and get it done.' Masters of mayhem, the SOE agents ran Partisan networks consisting of small, tight-knit groups that were the eyes and ears of the Allies. They were also the purveyors of death and destruction behind the German lines. From camps hidden in the hills that were the unbending spine of northern Italy, the Partisans struck road convoys and trains and ammunition dumps. They struck railway yards and fuel stores. No quarter was ever shown. Germans were shot as they laid down their firearms. Wounded Germans were despatched — by blade and bullet and boot — where they lay.

The Partisan treatment of the SS units was beyond savagery. These were the Germans who killed hostages and burned whole villages without pity or remorse. The Partisans had no pity or remorse either. Some had lost fathers and mothers and brothers and sisters and comrades. They battered the Germans to a pulp. They cut off hands, noses, ears and genitals, and returned from raids soaked in German blood. It was on their hands and faces and boots. It was under their fingernails. It was matted in their hair.

The fallen were treated with neither dignity nor respect.

In the very worst times of crimson-hued memories, Luigi could smell the blood. He could taste it, like damp soil, in his mouth. When this happened, he tried to spit away the taste. Sometimes he succeeded and he could reflect, at peace, on fond, warmer memories — of the comradeship and the adventure, even the romance of Partisan life. He recalled how he and Leonardo, as accidental Partisans, would set off on scouting missions, sometimes with Jeremy and sometimes with Nunzia Costa, tramping along familiar tracks through those Tescano hills. When he remembered the missions with Nunzia he felt again, even as an old man, his first flush of attraction to her shadow of a smile.

He pictured, too, gruff Vince, whom Jeremy had designated the Partisan group's quartermaster, responsible for all the supplies stored in the cavern and its cool corridors. Vince gloried in the job, which saw him count, re-count and re-count again boxes of small arms, ammunition, explosives, detonators and timers. Sometimes he set off on foot for caves well away from the main cavern to check the stockpiles there — weapons, ammunition, medical supplies, boots, clothes, torches, batteries. Before every mission or raid, Vince was kept busy issuing weapons and ammunition, handing over explosives and field dressings. 'Shoot the Germans as many times as you wish,' he would say. 'We have more than enough bullets.'

Then Luigi's recollections turned to Jeremy Forsythe. To Luigi, the British agent had looked like a film star straight out of the westerns, the man in the white hat. Luigi was never afraid when he was with the brave, confident, commanding Englishman. There was a confidence in the way Jeremy spoke, the way he walked, shook hands and made eye contact, that inspired Luigi.

Jeremy had been parachuted into the mountain country between Florence and Empoli. His first task had been to coordinate a radio network in the north. With the network secured, he had shaped Partisan bands across Tuscany and at key points to the north into active service units of the Communist Garibaldi Brigades.

In the Tescano hills, Jeremy's contact was Uncle Cesare, who, having seen the horrors of the Great War, had resolved that this second war would only be ended by the death of Mussolini and Hitler. He had soon learned that he shared this view with Father Gianni. 'Our priest took me into his confidence,' Cesare told Luigi on his second night in the cavern. 'We went to the Convent of Santa Teresa, where he and Sister Maria Angela provided care and shelter for wounded Partisans and, now and then, escaped Allied prisoners. So I became involved, and this was how I came to meet Jeremy again. He remembered the Hercules and the small boy with his very own bicycle. Through Jeremy I came to know Sergeant Vince.'

He also met Jeremy's radio operator: a Scotsman, Sergeant Geordie Murray, who'd served as a forward signaller in the deserts of North Africa in 1942 before seeing action in the Operation Husky landings on Sicily and at Monte Cassino. After the fall of Rome he'd been pressed into service with the Special Operations Executive. It needed men like Sergeant Geordie — fast Morse men who never buckled under pressure, expert technicians who could fix almost anything that needed a battery and a current.

It was not a posting the Scot had welcomed, Geordie himself told Luigi during one late-night, lantern-lit conversation in the cavern. 'Not my bloody idea of a good time. That's the flaming English for you. Always use the Scots for the hard jobs.' Then he turned to Jeremy, nodded, and added in a thick accent: 'Mind you, there's the likes of the boss here … he's a toff, one of the old school, a gent.'

Luigi liked the sound of the words and repeated them aloud. 'Toff, old school, gent.'

In the daylight hours of their first week with the Partisans, Luigi and Leonardo barely ventured beyond the mouth of the cavern. But in the dusk, joined by Nunzia, they carried in small arms and ammunition from the military vehicle that had brought them from Ancona. The task was spread over several evenings.

It was on the third of those nights that Luigi sat with Nunzia beyond the overhanging rock that shadowed the entrance to their hiding place. Nunzia told Luigi that her home was in Genoa, where her father, Salvatore, was a teacher. He taught English and French. 'So I speak English and French,' she said.

After the war, Nunzia went on, she would travel to England and France. She would visit London and Paris. Luigi said he was also planning to travel. He would go away — not forever, but for a while — from all the ugliness he had seen. He would go away from the dead and the dying and the hopeless, the fires and the bombs. He intented to cycle to the furthest-away place in the world, Australia. It would take a few weeks if there were many hills.

Nunzia said it would take more than a few weeks to cycle there. She said that Luigi was a dreamer. Then, sensing she might have caused hurt, she added quickly that Christopher Columbus and Guglielmo Marconi and even Karl Marx had dreamed and changed the world. Being a dreamer was no bad thing. Her father had told her this. Perhaps Luigi Ferraro would change the world too, she said with a smile.

Luigi shrugged self-consciously. Nunzia's father, he said, must be a man of learning to know so much of dreamers who changed the world. He was, Nunzia said. He had attended university in Genoa and had survived the Fascist purges of schoolteachers in the early 1930s. 'He served in the last war,' Nunzia went on, 'and he won two medals for his bravery. He kept the medals in a frame on the wall of his classroom. He was very proud of them. One time when the Blackshirts came to the school and asked the teachers about loyalty, he pointed to the medals and said nothing. They left him alone after that. They knew my father had been a real soldier and that they were only ruffians and gangsters and bullies in black uniforms.'

Nunzia's mother had been a teacher until her marriage. Then she had raised Nunzia, her only child. Nunzia was now eighteen years old. Her mother had died a few months earlier. The doctor who was called to the family home said she had died from a heart attack. Nunzia's father sat on a chair and wept for a week. He neither slept nor ate. His awful sadness was beyond description.

Nunzia suppressed her own tears. The daughter became the parent and she held her father as a child holds a kitten. She was as tender as she was strong.

Luigi asked how Nunzia had come to be in the Tescano hills. She said that, like Luigi, she was an accidental Partisan. She had returned home from school one day and her father had told her she was to leave Genoa before night fell. 'He said Genoa had become too dangerous for us, but he didn't tell me why. I was to go to Milan and people there would take care of me. He said he was going away, too, and it was better if we were in different places. He said we would be together when the war was over. Whatever happened, wherever we were, we would find each other.'

One hour later a car had arrived at Nunzia's home. Father embraced daughter. 'There were three young men in the car,' Nunzia explained. 'I had never seen them before but they knew my father. They said he was a brave comrade. From Genoa we drove north to Voghera. From there we were to take the back roads to Milan. But outside Voghera we stopped at a farmhouse, where the man who was in charge said the plan had changed. They had learned, not two hours before, that the Germans had arrested some Partisans in Milan, the people I was being taken to. I could not go to Milan. As I waited to hear what would happen next, the men were taking boxes and crates from a barn and loading them onto a truck. Even though it almost dark I could see that the markings on the boxes were written in English. Then a voice asked if I could read English, like my father.'

It was the voice of Jeremy Forsythe. The British agent knew Nunzia's father, Salvatore. The two had met during Jeremy's secret visits to Genoa. Nunzia learned that her father had for more than a year worked as a Partisan wireless operator. He had taken many risks and been in constant danger. Nunzia's mother had also helped the cause, carrying messages and instructions to comrades in Genoa. She had been the bravest of women. That afternoon, Jeremy explained to Nunzia, before she returned from school, her father had been warned of a German operation to seize Partisans in Genoa. That was why he had tried to send Nunzia to Milan. 'But the information was wrong,' Jeremy told her. 'The raid happened in Milan, not Genoa. They arrested the people your father was sending you to. You were lucky but they were not. Your father is safe with some comrades.'

With the Milan plan abandoned, the car carrying Nunzia and the three young men journeyed towards Piacenza and then to Parma. From Parma the car turned towards Modena, and by the first rays of daylight Nunzia and her companions were in the hills above Vergato. The truck, driven by Jeremy and carrying weapons and men from Voghera, arrived one hour later. 'Soon we were at the camp of one of the Garibaldi Partisan companies,' Nunzia said, 'and I went from schoolgirl one day to Partisan the next.'

There had been maybe forty Partisans there, she said. Some of them had served with the International Brigade Republicans during the Spanish Civil War. Most of those who had served in Spain were Communists. A few were Anarchists.

As well as Jeremy and Sergeant Geordie there was another British man, who was called Sergeant Bob. Like Sergeant Geordie, Bob was from Scotland. He taught people about guns and bombs and how to kill Germans with a knife.

Nunzia, recounting her arrival and her first weeks with the Partisans, said that Jeremy, Geordie and Bob became like the big brothers she'd never had. 'When Jeremy and Sergeant Geordie came to the Tescano hills, I came with them,' she said. 'Sergeant Bob came a few days later. Sometimes when Sergeant Geordie and Sergeant Bob speak I have no understanding of what they are saying. Their English is harder to understand than their Italian. Jeremy says that people from Scotland speak in a secret code. But Bob and Geordie laugh and tell each other jokes, and that isn't bad in these terrible days.'

In the weeks that followed, Luigi and Leonardo — whom Jeremy had designated the unit's scouts — guided the Englishman along hidden tracks in the hills that had once, in more innocent times, been home to boyhood adventures. After one scouting mission, Jeremy returned to the cavern and told whoever cared to listen: 'Luigi and Leonardo are the world's first talking maps.' Hearing these words, Nunzia cast a fleeting glance in Luigi's direction. It might have been a look of admiration but Luigi was unsure.

Some evenings during those first weeks, Luigi and Leonardo sat with others in a circle in the cavern as Sergeant Bob stripped and reassembled weapons and explained the placement and detonation of explosives.

Uncle Cesare sat in the circle during some of Bob's sessions but his presence in the cave was infrequent. That presence, when Sergeant Bob was not sharing his deadly skills, was usually a sure indication that the Partisans were readying themselves for a hit-and-run raid on the Germans.

It was after one of Cesare's visits to the cavern that Luigi and Jeremy made their way, under cover of early-morning darkness, across the hills to the Convent of Santa Teresa. Partisan leaders from Florence and Empoli were there to coordinate an attack on a German train that would leave Florence, loaded with looted art treasures, within days, perhaps even within twenty-four hours.

Jeremy told Luigi: 'You will be my eyes in the blackness.'

Luigi was not admitted to the meeting at the convent. It was, Jeremy said, for his own good: the less he knew, the better. While the Partisans made their plans, Luigi passed some of the daylight hours with Father Gianni, who was also visiting the sisters.

As Luigi and Father Gianni sat together in the empty refectory, much of their conversation was about Tescano. There was some talk of the war and when it might end. Then Luigi spoke of what he'd learned at the cycling school, and how, when life returned to normal, he might open a bicycle shop — but only after he returned from Australia. 'It is the furthest-away place in the world,' he said. 'I will go there by bicycle. This place is filling up with bad memories. We will become prisoners of these memories. Far away, I think I will be free of all the things I do not want to remember.'

Father Gianni said it was never possible to be free of memories. 'But sometimes,' he said, 'it helps to be away from places that cause the memories to return.'

Luigi said he and Father Gianni should talk in English. If he was to learn English he should speak English. Father Gianni agreed. He had a flawless command of the language. Luigi's command was limited to what he'd learned through his earnest language sessions with Jeremy. Nevertheless, Father Gianni said he showed promise. He added with a smile that he was sure Nunzia would also welcome a chance to help Luigi with his English lessons. Luigi blushed. Father Gianni was a man who noticed things.

Leaving the refectory after lunch, the two walked through the grounds. The convent, which had been built during the early seventeenth century, was set on a gentle hill sandpapered smooth by the winds that blew down from the Tuscan high country. The enclosed fields running down to the road below the convent were mainly given over to a few rows of vines, medium-sized vegetable patches, a small pen for pigs and another enclosure for some dairy cattle. This produced enough to meet most of the food needs of the thirty-six sisters who lived in the convent.

Set apart from the main building were several small structures: a milking byre, a food storage barn, two or three equipment sheds and some outhouses. In one shed, Father Gianni revealed, were stored five of six bicycles that had been sent to the convent by a sister order, the Daughters of Coolamon Mor, in Oughterard, County Galway, Ireland. The sixth bicycle was ridden by Sister Maria Angela when she journeyed to the two-classroom school in Tescano.

'A truly wonderful tale,' he said. 'A few of the Daughters of Coolamon Mor, on a pilgrimage to Rome some years ago, lodged at our Convent of Santa Teresa. The Irish sisters commented that the roads and tracks around the convent and towards Tescano were as bad as the rough tracks in Galway, and said that bicycles were just the thing when it came to smoothing out such rough tracks. After the Irish sisters returned home they sent six bicycles to the Convent of Santa Teresa. You would only have been a boy in those times. But five of the bicycles have never been used. Every so often when he comes here, Cesare gives them a wipe, squirts a bit of oil here and there and pumps up the tyres.'

Entering the shed, Father Gianni drew back a linen sheet to reveal five Raleigh All-Steel Irish X Frame bicycles. The X in the name, he explained, represented the Cross of Saint Patrick, the patron saint of Ireland. Luigi was curious to know why they had never been ridden. Father Gianni shrugged. Maybe, he said, it was because none of the sisters, save Sister Maria Angela, had learned to ride.

Luigi said when the war was over he and Leonardo might teach the sisters to ride the bicycles. Father Gianni replied that Luigi had a good heart. He said good hearts were seldom to be found in the great and grand. The wonder of the world was that goodness was to be found not in the lives of the great and the grand but in the small lives of those who existed quietly, out of sight, their triumphs and tragedies hidden from the world. 'It is the small lives, tucked away, that reveal humanity in all its bigness,' Father Gianni said. Luigi thought Father Gianni had the most wonderful way with words. But, after all, he was a dottore of the great Pontifical Gregorian University in Rome.

Talk turned to Tescano. Father Gianni told Luigi that his mother and Leonardo's parents had been informed that their boys were alive and safe. Then he said that if some in Tescano had their way, Mayor Minoza and Salvatore Paglia might not be long for this earth. It was believed that their collaboration with the Germans had seen the arrest and disappearance of two brothers, Antonio and Guido Falcone, who farmed not ten kilometres from Tescano. Father Gianni added: 'Minoza and

Paglia, so it has been told to me, said the brothers were Partisans. But Antonio and Guido had nothing to do with the Partisans. I know this. They farmed and kept themselves to themselves.'

'What will happen to the mayor and the teacher?' Luigi asked.

'I suspect when the time comes they will not be spared, although my conscience will not allow me to wish them dead.' Luigi wondered how Father Gianni's conscience might view the work of the Partisans.

When the day passed and darkness fell, Jeremy and Luigi returned to the cavern. They arrived at their safe haven well before dawn and went straight to their camp beds. When they awoke it was close to noon. Jeremy called together ten of the comrades, including Luigi and Leonardo and Sergeants Geordie and Bob. There was work to be done. 'There are some Germans to be attended to and some stolen paintings to be collected from a passing train,' Jeremy told the ten.

Luigi's heartbeat quickened. Until that moment, the war had only ever come to him. Now, he was going to war. He thought of the words of Colonel Gonfalonieri and he feared he might run from the fray.

CHAPTER THIRTEEN

Execution

At the final moment Death will stare, unblinking, into our soul. Then Death will ask what we did in life — not what we planned, not what we thought about doing. Our actions are our epitaph. Our actions are the only words that speak for us when we are gone. Be sure they speak well of you.

— Janek Jaruzelski, *My War*, Warsaw, 1976

It was a simple plan. That night Jeremy would lead a group of ten to ambush a German train on a sweeping bend in the railway line that ran along the floor of the wide valley fifteen kilometres beyond the Convent of Santa Teresa. The ambush party would travel in the army truck brought from Ancona. Luigi and Leonardo were issued with rifles. Some others carried automatic weapons. All had revolvers. A unit of Partisans from Empoli would establish positions east of the ambush site. Some of the Empoli Partisans would block the road and railway line to prevent any German escape. Other Partisans from Florence would attack with Jeremy's men.

Intelligence from Florence advised that a German plan to send the looted paintings by rail north from Florence to Bologna and from there to Germany had been rendered impossible by Allied bombing along that length of line. Instead, the train would travel across country from Florence through Empoli to Pisa and from there to Milan then to Germany via Austria.

The train comprised a locomotive, two coal tenders, two cattle wagons and a guards' van. In one of the wagons were two or three large crates containing the paintings. The second wagon was carrying about fifty civilians. 'Probably politicals or Jews,' Jeremy guessed. The train was lightly guarded: there were two SS officers on board, two SS soldiers on the locomotive footplate and another two in the wagon carrying the looted art. There were, at most, eight other SS men in the guards' van. 'Remember, no Germans are to be left alive,' Jeremy added. 'They will kill us if we do not kill them. Everybody here must understand this. We have no place for prisoners.'

Luigi felt a shiver of apprehension and fear. Apprehension at the thought of taking a life, and fear that he might run away when the killing began. He remembered Colonel Gonfalonieri's words: *'bravery is the strength to hold fast against the fear, in every man, that causes him to run away from the enemy'*.

The day of the ambush passed slowly. Weapons were oiled. Bullets were counted. Bootlaces were tied and retied. Knives were sharpened again and again. There was little talk.

The yellow glow of the moon was dimmed by cloud when Jeremy's men and the Empoli Partisans moved into their attacking positions. Sergeant Bob and Jeremy placed explosives on the curve in the track, which ran through flat country flanked by small rocky outcrops and clumps of scrawny timber. Then they hid behind a small rise. Others concealed themselves behind the timber.

Luigi was one of a group of three hidden behind trees to the east of the track. His mouth was dry. His breathing was shallow and almost laboured. There were beads of cold sweat on his brow. He feared his comrades would hear his thumping heart. He peered into the darkness and saw the shape of Leonardo crouched in a group of three to the west of the track. Then ... the sound of the approaching train. The world became a swirling blur.

The action took ten or twelve minutes, no more. An explosion shook the ground. The locomotive and the two coal tenders lifted up in a flash and a cloud. The cattle wagons and the guards' van went in different directions. The guards' van reared up like a horse and then fell on its side. The wagon with the stolen pictures stayed upright but ran off the rails to the left. The other wagon rolled and rolled and rolled.

Partisans moved quickly from their concealed positions and ran towards the wreckage. Luigi ran too, but only because others were running. Some of the men made for the guards' van. The shooting, when it started, came from the Partisans. Germans trying to clamber to safety were shot. Their killing, to Luigi, seemed so easy, so effortless. A squeeze of the trigger and a life was gone. Luigi never fired a shot during that raid. He believed, in a swirling panic, that his rifle had jammed. His heartbeat hammered in his chest. Later, he discovered that the safety catch on the rifle was still on.

He stopped running when he reached the wagon that had rolled. Bodies, dozens of them, lay everywhere. Most were lifeless. Some were gasping their last breath. None would live to see another morning; their injuries were too terrible. They were the prisoners Jeremy had spoken of.

Then, a sight that came close to stopping his hammering heartbeat. Stepping over the bodies towards him, in the glow of the flames, was Jacob. He was gaunt, hollow-cheeked, unshaven, and his clothes were torn and soiled, but he had no obvious injuries.

Luigi stood statue-still and stared. This was a ghost, surely. A spectre. Something imagined in the heat of battle.

Then, from the corner of an eye Luigi saw a German — an SS officer — running towards one of the clumps of trees. He had a knapsack on his back. Luigi heard shouting: 'After him, after him … Kill the pig!'

The ghost, the apparition, began to run too. Jacob sprinted after the fleeing German. Luigi followed. The German stumbled and rolled, and Jacob was on him, kicking him in the face with a force that shattered his nose and split his lips. Luigi was surprised the kicking hadn't taken his head off. Somehow, through the blood, Luigi recognised the German. It was the SS captain from the roadblock on the way from Ancona, the one who had insisted on providing an escort. Jacob kicked him again. The German spoke in Italian, the words bubbling through blood. His knapsack, he said, contained gold coins and chains and bracelets and money. Please, he begged, take it. He slid the knapsack from his shoulders. A knapsack for a life, the German pleaded.

Jacob screamed at the man, his face contorted. Luigi had never seen such rage, such cauterising anger. It was the hatred Sergeant Dante had spoken of at Livorno: 'the great destroyer of good hearts'. Jacob turned, tugged at Luigi's holster and pulled the revolver free. He pushed the gun into the German's stomach and fired. When six bullets had been spent, Jacob dropped the revolver and picked up the knapsack. He said nothing, staring at the body, shaking.

Luigi was also silent. He was speechless at the horror of what he had just seen. The horror of death at close quarters and the horror of watching Jacob, his comrade, his friend, his companion in the Brotherhood of the Bicycle, despatch another human.

He felt, on his trousers, a warm dampness. Looking down, he saw in the light from the flames that he was spattered with German blood. He retched. He was still vomiting when two Partisans, Empoli men, breathless from running, stopped alongside him. They spat on the dead German. One of them reached into the German's tunic pockets and pulled out identity papers and a pen. The Empoli men kept the papers but handed the pen to Luigi. It was a silver Montegrappa. 'A souvenir,' one of them said.

Luigi and Jacob looked at each other. No words were exchanged. Their tears said everything. They embraced and, arms linked, walked back towards the carnage of the ambush.

Leonardo, standing over the bodies of dead Germans, turned and saw the two. The blood drained from his face and he ran to hug the trembling Jacob. Jeremy and the other Partisans gathered around the three.

'This is Jacob,' Luigi said. 'This is our comrade who became separated from us in Florence. This is a miracle!'

Jeremy replied that talk of miracles could be saved for later. 'We must leave here now. The Germans will come looking for their train. We must take what we came for and leave. Our new comrade will come with us.'

The stolen artworks, retrieved from the train intact in their crates, were taken in the truck to the Convent of Santa Teresa, where they spent the rest of the war until they were returned to their owners. The raiders remained at the convent for three days. Jeremy said they should stay out of sight. Germans would be swarming across the district, searching for the Partisans.

At the convent, Jacob spoke of how he had arrived at the Zevi home in Florence on that afternoon to find his family packing small suitcases and preparing to flee. They were hoping to reach Switzerland. They had received a telephone call from a rabbi in Ancona who said that Jews there had already been arrested and would be sent to Germany. Soon, he warned, the Germans would begin detaining Jews in Florence. The Zevi family in Florence should flee.

Jacob had been in the family home for less than two hours when German soldiers arrived and herded them into canvas-topped trucks. They were taken with hundreds of other Jews to a camp outside Florence. They remained there for four weeks, maybe five. He was unsure. Time had no meaning in that camp.

'Then we were taken to the railway freight yard and locked in sheds,' Jacob said. 'There were a dozen big sheds and hundreds of people were locked inside. Sometimes people were taken away. Families were separated. I was put in a shed with younger men. My mother and father were put elsewhere and I found out they were taken away after a few days. They may have been killed.

They may have been sent to Germany. I have no idea. Then I was put on the train with some of the others in our shed, and you know the rest of the story.'

He was silent, shaking his head. It was clear he would say no more.

On that first night after the raid, Luigi, Leonardo and Jacob slept fitfully in the convent shed where the bicycles, the gift from Ireland, were kept. In the morning, Luigi and Jacob told Leonardo the bloody details of the death of the fleeing German.

'He gave us this,' Luigi said, opening the knapsack to reveal a dozen small canvas bags. These were emptied onto the floor of the shed. They contained two hundred and sixty-five gold coins. Jacob recognised the coins as Russian, Austrian and British, and said they could be sold for their weight. In two pockets of the knapsack were twenty-five plain gold bangles and gold chains, thirty of them. Jacob said these were as good as cash anywhere in the world. There were also two thousand American dollars in small notes and one thousand pounds in British five-pound notes. This was a fortune. Luigi and Leonardo had never seen so much gold or money.

Luigi and Jacob said the contents should be shared three ways. Leonardo said that he had played no part in capturing the knapsack and he would not accept a one-third share. He would accept some dollars, no more. The three friends decided to hide the knapsack and its contents in the shed for now. They took a pledge of secrecy.

At the Partisan cavern after the return from the convent, it was agreed that the raid on the train and the recovery of the looted paintings had been a triumph. But it had not been without its cost. There was a resigned sadness that prisoners had died in the wreckage. War was cruel, Jeremy said. What had happened could not be changed. Thousands, tens of thousands, were dying every day. There was a job to be done, a war to be won.

Jacob, it was agreed by all, should remain with the Partisans. He was, after all, a trained soldier and Luigi and Leonardo's comrade-in-arms. He was also a man on the run with nowhere else to go. Like Luigi, Leonardo and Nunzia, he had become an accidental Partisan.

For these accidental Partisans, life in and around the cavern settled into a routine of sleeping, cooking, cleaning weapons and, in the evening, listening to BBC broadcasts from London and planning scouting sorties across the Tescano hills.

On some of these sorties, Luigi and Nunzia spent the daylight hours in the secret places of his disappeared boyhood, squeezing through narrow gullies, lying face-down on hilltops and outcrops, staring into the distance. Luigi insisted they speak in English as much as possible. Sometimes as they sat, Nunzia would point: *Hills … sky … clouds … trees … eyes … nose … ears*. Luigi would repeat the words.

Then, one day, Nunzia brushed Luigi's lips with a finger and said: 'Labbra … *lips*.' The fleeting touch of finger on flesh was exquisite. It was the touch of innocence in a time when innocence, for most, had been shredded by the baseness of war. Luigi soundlessly mouthed the words: Labbra … *lips* … *lips* … *lips*. And then, with a finger, he touched Nunzia's small, restrained smile. Her smile broadened, and she said, '*Kiss*.' Lips briefly, ever so briefly, touched lips. Then, silence.

On the return journey to the cavern there were no more new words. Hand found hand and that was enough.

On later scouting sorties, too, hand found hand. And there were evenings when the two scrambled to ridge-tops and watched the arrival of the soft Tuscan night and shy lips touched shy lips again. Then they talked of what might be when the war was over. Luigi's thoughts of Australia began to fade. He would open a bicycle shop in Tescano and he would repair bicycles in Uncle Cesare's smithy. Nunzia stopped talking of Paris and London. Perhaps her father could be a teacher in Tescano, she suggested. So, it was resolved. When the war was over they would never be apart.

By the winter of 1944 the conflict in northern Italy was entering its final stage. The Germans were retreating, destroying everything that might be of use to the advancing Allied armies — roads, railways, bridges, electricity lines, water pipelines. It was the job of the Tescano Partisans to harass that retreat.

Below the hills that hid the Partisans, the Convent of Santa Teresa sheltered more than a dozen British prisoners of war who had escaped from camps further north. Some, Jeremy Forsythe believed, had information that would be of use to the advancing Allies — the names of German units further north, the fighting strength of those units, their supplies of fuel and ammunition, the nature of their defences.

Assembling his comrades, Jeremy announced that Nunzia was being sent to the convent. She spoke English. She would collect information from the prisoners and then return. She would be gone for a few days. She would travel on foot.

Luigi walked with Nunzia for a few hundred metres before the two paused and held each other. She saw the anxiety in his eyes. She would take care, she said. She would return to him, safe and well. Then he watched her step into the distance.

Back at the camp he felt empty. How he loathed this war. He sat alone by the mouth of the cavern until Leonardo and Jacob sat by his side. Their words were well meant — words of reassurance that Nunzia could take care of herself, that there was no danger. Luigi knew otherwise. He simply knew.

Nunzia was taken by a German patrol almost within sight of the convent. The patrol then drove to Tescano, where she was thrown from one German military vehicle into another and driven away. Uncle Cesare reported that the people who witnessed this said she had been badly beaten. Some thought she might have been dead.

In the weeks that followed Nunzia's capture, the Tescano Partisans mounted half a dozen hit-and-run attacks on German convoys retreating north. They were quick and dirty affairs. The convoys were small, never more than a dozen vehicles, carrying one or two companies. The Partisans would initially strike at the first and last trucks and then hammer what was left in the middle. Sometimes the Germans tried to surrender, and they were shot with their hands in the air. Several times Luigi jerked the trigger on his rifle and watched Germans fall. He hated them for taking Nunzia. He had never felt such anger. He had no thought for his own life or death during these attacks. There was nothing heroic or brave about those final months of the war. Everything Colonel Gonfalonieri and Sergeant Dante had said was true. Their words haunted Luigi.

When the end of the war came to Tuscany, in the brisk spring of 1945, it happened quickly. Units of the British Eighth Army broke through the German defences of the Arno Line, which ran from just north of Livorno to a point below Florence. Some weeks later, the final German defences of the Gothic Line, running from the Mediterranean through Pisa to the Adriatic coast near Rimini, were breached, and all German forces in Italy surrendered.

The German surrender came two weeks after the arrival in Tescano of an advance unit of the British Eighth Army. The early-morning arrival was bloodless and swift. German motorised units in the area had fled days earlier. At first light, a squadron of lightly armoured Allied scout cars and two Bren Gun carriers roared up the hill. Tescano was liberated without a shot being fired.

The Partisans formed ranks of three and led the Eighth Army infantry units into the Piazza Valsini. There was cheering from the villagers. Spring flowers were showered on the liberators. Dogs barked. Cats retreated into kitchen corners. The bell in the Church of the Blessed Seamstress was rung. Jugs of wine were passed from hand to hand.

Luigi's war was over and he was home in Tescano. He was, some shouted, a hero. Leonardo and Uncle Cesare were heroes too. They had fought the Germans, had driven them away.

Father Gianni, standing on the rim of the fountain in the Piazzi Valsini, called for silence. There was, he said, another hero in their midst. He gestured for Jacob to stand by his side. 'This young man is Jacob,' he said. 'He has been with Luigi, Leonardo and Cesare through all that has brought us this day of liberation.

He is a new son of Tescano. He has lost much, so we must give him much in return.'

There were more cheers. Luigi's mother embraced Jacob. 'You will be another son to me,' she said.

Hours after the liberation, Mayor Bartolo Minoza and Salvatore Paglia were found by British soldiers, hiding in the bedroom of a long-abandoned house. For reasons that will never be known, the Fascist duo had failed to flee the approaching Eighth Army.

Minoza and Paglia, white with fear, were pushed into the Piazza Valsini at bayonet point. The crowd surged around them, screaming and shouting. There were cries for revenge. All in the village had come to detest the two for their open collaboration with the Germans. Father Gianni urged calm. The two should not be harmed. They should be bolted in the single cell at the abandoned carabinieri post and then handed over when the British Military Police arrived. Uncle Cesare agreed, adding that there was no need for a guard to be placed on the door. Minoza and Paglia could not escape, he was sure.

Afternoon slid into evening. The Piazza Valsini was alive with celebrations. Hoarded supplies of food were brought out and piled on makeshift tables. The Tescano Men of Brass played. There was no shortage of wine.

Finally, at midnight, Tescano fell silent. It had been the longest of days. When all were asleep, Luigi ambled, hands in pockets, to the empty piazza. He felt the softness of the night and he watched the stars move as the earth turned. He was numbed by sadness. Nunzia was gone. Jacob's family was gone. There seemed no sense in any of it. Life and death were like the toss of a coin.

He felt a ripple of remorse for his part in the bloody work of the Partisans. 'I should have been better than that,' he thought. 'We all should have been better than that.' A cat, on its nocturnal rounds, brushed against his leg. Then it, too, was gone.

Just after first light, a British soldier found that the bolt that had secured the single cell in the old carabinieri post had been undone. The mayor and the teacher were nowhere to be found. The floor of the cell was bloodstained. A single button, torn from a shirt, lay on the bloodied floor.

A search soon revealed the bodies of Minoza and Paglia in the abandoned house where they'd been discovered the day before. The two had been gagged and savagely beaten, and their necks were broken. Father Gianni was distressed when Jeremy took him to see the bodies. He said that rage and revenge were chasms in the human character. They were emotions that could be understood, but those who had taken the lives of Minoza and Paglia should ask for God's forgiveness.

Jeremy said nothing. The liberating soldiers said nothing. They'd lost too many comrades — good men — to be distressed by the death of two accused collaborators in a nondescript Tuscan village.

Some hours after the discovery of the battered bodies, the British soldiers departed. With them in the Bren Gun carriers were Jeremy and Sergeants Bob, Geordie and Vince Vittoria. Jeremy said they had work to do elsewhere. Some of the other Partisans would move on with the British too. The rest were free to return to their homes.

There were handshakes. Bob and Geordie said they were proud to have served with Luigi, Leonardo, Jacob, Nunzia and

Uncle Cesare. Jeremy said he would return, although it might be a few months before the day arrived. Sergeant Vince forced a smile. Then they were gone. The quickness of it all. The turn of a page. The blink of an eye. A single heartbeat. The world was different.

At dinner on that second night of freedom from war, Luigi sat with his mother, Uncle Cesare, Leonardo and his father and mother, Jacob, Father Gianni and Sister Maria Angela around the old wooden table in the Ferraro kitchen. Three chickens had been killed and roasted, and Leonardo's father had baked bread that, he said, was 'fit for a prince'. Luigi's mother had decorated the table with flowers and her finest embroidered napkins. Uncle Cesare dispensed wine and more wine. For Luigi, the evening ended in a haze. He slept that night at the table, his head resting on folded arms. Jacob slept on a broad bench in Uncle Cesare's workshop.

In the morning, Luigi woke and washed. He walked into the workshop, where Uncle Cesare was telling Jacob how Luigi had rebuilt Jeremy Forsythe's battered Hercules bicycle.

Luigi noticed that a button was missing from Uncle Cesare's shirt. He said nothing.

CHAPTER FOURTEEN

Planning

*Folks plan their lives 'coz it saves them from thinking
about death. I never planned a race in my life. I got in
the saddle and went like crazy till it was over. I did it.
I didn't plan it.*

— Nat Rozhko, Supreme Champion, Trans-Canada Coronation
  Cycle Marathon, 1953

Jacob remained in Tescano for almost a year. It was a stay made
necessary by two bouts of pneumonia and a lengthy episode of
nervous collapse. He was nursed from fevered near-death by
Luigi's mother. 'Everything has been too much for the poor boy,'
Franca said. 'Everything has gone from his life. There is little
fight left. He is skin and bone.'

Several times Luigi and Leonardo believed that their comrade
would die. Father Gianni, on his knees before the altar of his
small church, said earnest prayers. He reminded his Maker that

Jacob Zevi had suffered much and lost much. In prayer, Father Gianni always used full names. He believed it was always best to be specific in dealings with his Maker. He asked his Maker to recognise that Jacob Zevi was a young man of good heart. His was a life that should be spared. Father Gianni understood that his Maker was busy. There was much work to be done in rebuilding His world and the lives of His creations. But, please, might Jacob Zevi be spared? Surely Jacob Zevi deserved to grow old.

It seemed Father Gianni's Maker agreed, although Jacob's recovery was slow. By the time the second bout of pneumonia had passed, Jacob was only able to stand for a few minutes or take a dozen faltering steps without assistance. He was withdrawn and distant, and had to be coaxed to eat. Luigi's mother said if Jacob didn't eat he would turn into a scarecrow and people would talk: 'Franca Ferraro never feeds that boy Jacob,' they would say. She wasn't having that.

Often Jacob sat in the Piazza Valsini, alone, for hours. There was a shroud of despair around him. Father Gianni told Luigi that Jacob's was a spirit in terrible pain. He said that the pain of the body could be eased by potions and medicaments and the binding of wounds; for the pain of the spirit, the salves were companionship and compassion — even in the silence of watching and listening from the edges. And so these salves were applied, and it was the often-silent companionship and compassion of Luigi, Father Gianni, Leonardo, Uncle Cesare and Franca that, over time, rescued Jacob from the pit of his despair.

Bicycles, too, played their part in his return, although the ride was slow and uphill. The first turn of the wheel came on an afternoon in early 1946 when Father Gianni arrived at

Cesare's workshop to talk to Luigi. For some time, he said, he had pondered Luigi's kind-hearted offer, before the raid on the train, to teach the sisters of the Convent of Santa Teresa to ride the Raleigh All-Steel Irish X Frame bicycles that had been a gift from the sisters of Coolamon Mor in Ireland. Father Gianni had put the offer to the sisters. He explained that they held the view that while the offer was to be lauded for its kindness, it was not to be accepted lightly. With the exception of Sister Maria Angela, they said, none in their convent had ever ridden a bicycle.

One older sister, Sister Piety, had observed that Christ Himself had ridden on a donkey, not a bicycle, when He entered Jerusalem. Sister Maria Angela had responded that Christ was a man of His times. He had ridden a donkey because that was the transport then available. But the world had changed. It was quite likely that, with the passage of time, Christ would return to Jerusalem riding a bicycle. Sister Piety crossed herself several times. The very thought of Christ on a bicycle was beyond blasphemy, she said. That Sister Maria Angela could even imagine such things proved that riding a bicycle could place the soul of an otherwise kindly and devout sister in mortal danger. Sister Piety would pray for Sister Maria Angela.

The other sisters said that a period of prayer and meditation might aid them in this difficult decision. Riding a bicycle was no trivial matter if it caused dismay to even one of their number. The matter of the bicycles deserved their full and serious attention.

It was after two weeks of prayer, meditation and quiet discussion that a compromise, of sorts, was reached. All the sisters, with the exception of Sister Piety, agreed that three of their number who had shown 'modern inclinations' should learn to cycle, and that the two remaining bicycles should be given to Luigi as payment for his assistance. It was decided, however, that Sister Piety should carefully observe the novice cyclists and note any signs, however small, that their souls might be in mortal danger.

The sisters had also made mention to Father Gianni of the Villiers 98cc two-stroke engines, originally brought from Ancona, that had been stored in the convent since the end of hostilities. Perhaps Luigi, Leonardo and Jacob could make use of them, Father Gianni suggested. After all, the three were trained Bersaglieri, bicycle men of the very first order.

Then there was the matter of Sister Maria Angela's bicycle, which was in great need of care and maintenance. During the war, Father Gianni revealed, it had been ridden across countless kilometres of Tuscany by Sister Maria Angela in the service of God and the Partisans. The sister had risked life and limb as a courier between Partisan groups in the final months of the war. Her exploits had earned her great admiration.

One week after the sisters conveyed their decision, the bicycles and the engines were transported, in Father Gianni's car, from the convent to the smithy. All needed to be serviced. Also transported secretly by Luigi was the knapsack with its plunder. It had remained at the convent, concealed near the covered bicycles, since the days after the raid on the train.

For several days and nights, Luigi worked alone on the bicycles. Often during this silent, solo work, he thought of Nunzia. He imagined an unmarked and shallow grave in some field or by some roadside or in some prison yard. He thought of a face, a flower, covered by dirt. Sometimes he thought of ashes blowing through the branches of bare winter trees.

On two or three evenings, Leonardo came to the workshop and worked alongside Luigi. Sometimes Jacob came in and watched, saying nothing.

On the final day of his labours, after completely stripping and cleaning — every spoke, every chain link — the three bicycles to be used by the sisters, Luigi announced he intended to fit the Villiers two-stroke engines to the Hercules and to the two bicycles he'd received as payment from the convent. However, it was not a job for one pair of hands. Perhaps he, Jacob and Leonardo might work together.

The suggestion brought a trace of light to Jacob's sad eyes. He nodded. 'We should put the hands of a puncture man to good use,' Luigi said, winking, and was rewarded with a rare smile from his friend.

Most of the work over the weeks that followed was done by Luigi and Jacob. Leonardo helped when he could get time away from the bakery. Fitting the engines to the Raleigh bicycles was a painstaking task, with particular attention needed in the placing of the motor high on the inside of the frame. Similarly, there was much work involved in attaching the fuel tank and running fuel lines to the engine in a manner that gave the rider maximum freedom of movement. Jacob proved to be particularly adept at the most intricate aspects of the work.

However, the conversion of the convent bicycles to combined pedal and engine power was considerably less demanding than the work required to convert the Hercules. It soon became apparent that the engine was best placed low in the frame of the Hercules, which meant some steel mounts had to be attached, by welding. The precise placement of the steel mounts and the subsequent welding were tasks beyond even these bicycle men of the first order, and Uncle Cesare was conscripted to the job. For the engine to run properly the steel mounts would have to be specially made and expertly fitted, he said; a millimetre here or a millimetre there and 'disaster will strike like a thief in the night'. Then he advised Luigi and Jacob, his brow furrowing: 'It is the millimetre — not the centimetre or the metre or the kilometre — that brings men and their designs undone. It is the millimetre by which a spark plug fires or fails. All we have and all we are is that single millimetre away from disaster and nothingness. Take great care of the millimetre and the kilometre will look after itself.' Uncle Cesare, when it came to talk of metal and millimetres, had a capacity for eloquence, as might be expected from a man who had the grip.

At first, Luigi and Jacob had barely exchanged a word as they worked on the bicycles. But gradually Jacob began to speak. He had been thinking, he told Luigi, that he should return to Florence. If his family members were dead, he said, he would go far away. He would go to the Holy Land, Palestine. Many Jews had gone there before the war. Jacob said that he would pray at the Wailing Wall in Jerusalem. Then he would set up a business. It would be called 'Jacob Zevi, Watchmaker and Jeweller'. It would make and sell only the best of the best. A portion of the profits would be set aside for good works; perhaps he would buy bicycles for orphans.

Luigi talked too. If things had happened differently, he said, Nunzia would have come to live in Tescano. Nunzia's father would have taught there and Luigi would have opened a bicycle shop. Now, even though it was a fine place, Luigi felt he might leave Tescano. 'Australia is the furthest-away place from Tuscany,' he said. 'I might journey there. With a motor on the Hercules, it would be an easy ride.'

From the geography books at school he had learned that the main town in Australia was a place called Sydney. It had a harbour and a grand bridge, and there were animals called kangaroos that hopped everywhere because the ground was hot from the sun. There were also cowboys in Australia, and parrots, too. And there were many serpents. He told Jacob that one book had shown crocodiles, which probably lived in the waters below the bridge. Going to Australia, he said, 'would be a grand adventure and it would give me new memories ... to take away my sad memories of what we saw and did and what we lost here'.

With the completion of work on the motorised bicycles, the time for road-testing was approaching. But first there was the matter of the cycling lessons for the sisters of the Convent of Santa Teresa.

The stripped-down and reassembled Raleigh All-Steel Irish X Frame bicycles were returned to the convent in Father Gianni's car. Under the still-disapproving eye of Sister Piety, the cycling lessons were conducted by Luigi, Leonardo and Jacob on a flat pathway behind the convent. The three sisters who had shown 'modern inclinations' in their willingness to learn to ride were sisters Immaculata, Berenice and Maiella. All in their fifth decade, they were willing and able students. They crossed themselves several times before each lesson, and afterwards they said prayers of thanks for their safety. The prayers were directed towards Saint Christopher, patron saint of travellers.

The instruction of the three broadly followed the regime of the Army Cycling Training School at Livorno. Initially, some hours were spent in walking alongside the bicycles and in mounting and dismounting. Seat heights were adjusted several times, as were handlebars. Proper positioning of the feet on the pedals was emphasised, as was the safe use of brakes. With Luigi, Leonardo or Jacob gently supporting the handlebars, one by one the sisters found their balance and gingerly rode forward. Practice made elementary riding almost perfect. The next day saw the three riding single file, one metre apart, and turning with a measure of confidence.

On the fifth and final day of instruction, Luigi and Jacob decided there should be a formal ride from the flat area to the main doors of the convent, where Father Gianni and the non-cycling sisters were assembled. There were gasps as sisters Immaculata, Berenice and Maiella rode into view, their eyes bright, their black-stockinged ankles and calves clearly visible. The face of Sister Piety was a granite mask of reproach. Her fingers tightened and whitened around the rosary she had carried since her days as a novice. That she should have lived to see such things ... perhaps this was her punishment for some forgotten, and thus unconfessed, childhood misdemeanour, she thought.

Sister Maria Angela made a short speech. She said Luigi, Leonardo and Jacob had lived up to their reputation as bicycle men of the first order, and had also proven themselves instructors beyond compare. Jacob, while not of the Faith, had found healing and a family in Tescano. He would always be welcome there and with the sisters of the Convent of Santa Teresa. They should never forget that Christ Himself was a Jew.

The following day, a Saturday, Luigi, Leonardo and Jacob met at noon to commence road-testing the motorised bicycles. Luigi carried an emergency tool kit, Leonardo had brought some bread, and Jacob carried provisions provided by Luigi's mother. These provisions were not insubstantial: olives, pickles, cheeses, smoked chicken, boiled eggs, home-baked cakes and scones. Franca Ferraro, as Jacob had learned and as the other boys had known since childhood, was not one to risk any suggestion that those close to her would ever go hungry.

Franca and Cesare watched as the two Raleigh bicycles and the Hercules were wheeled into the sunlight, where they gleamed and flashed. Luigi assumed the role of commanding officer. 'Bicycle men, stand by your equipment,' he ordered. 'Bicycle men, mount on my instruction … Bicycle men, mount. Bicycle men, adjust yourselves to your saddles … Bicycle men, fuel switch on, disengage clutch, commence cycling, engage clutch.' In single file, Luigi, Leonardo and Jacob rolled into the piazza and round the fountain. They made one, two, three, four circuits of the piazza. The singing began:

> *Bicycle men are we,*
> *From snowy peak to sea*
> *We smite the foe, we lay him low …*
> *Bicycle men are we,*
> *Fearless warriors of the Alpine snow*
> *Two wheels against the stubborn foe*
> *Plumes in the wind, we forward fly*
> *Our rifles flash, our foes must die.*
> *Bicycle men are we,*

From snowy peak to sea
We smite the foe, we lay him low ...
Bicycle men are we,
From snowy peak to sea.

Then the Tescano boys swung down the hill onto the flat and cycled along the curving road past the Convent of Santa Teresa.

Beyond the convent they halted by a stream that ran along the edge of an overgrown field, and compared observations on the performance of the bicycles. There was agreement that the bicycles and the Villiers 98cc two-stroke engines were a perfect fit. All three bicycles positively purred when they were held, on the flat, at just below thirty-two kilometres an hour.

As he rode that day Luigi felt a sense of separation of spirit from body. Cycling freed him from everything around and within him. On a bicycle, Luigi flew through space and time. There were no memories to cloud or sadden the mind. The faster he went, the tighter the corners, the steeper the hill, the more there was only Luigi. The utter, absolute freedom of it all.

That first Saturday afternoon test ride was followed by another and then another. During a break in the third ride, Jacob, lying outstretched on the roadside, announced that he was now ready to return to Florence to discover the fate of his family there and in Ancona. 'It is a journey that has been delayed by my fear,' he said. 'I am still afraid. But I am ready to confront my fear.'

He said he would ride to Florence on his motorised bicycle. If Luigi and Leonardo agreed, he would take some of the gold bangles, chains and coins from the knapsack hidden under Luigi's bed and convert them to American dollars and British pounds on the black market. The remainder of the gold would remain in the knapsack in Tescano. Of the cash in the knapsack — two thousand American dollars and one thousand British pounds — Jacob suggested that half be given to Father Gianni. He could use the money to buy books for the Tescano school and to pay for work at the Convent of Santa Teresa. The remaining one thousand American dollars and five hundred British pounds should go in equal shares to Luigi, Leonardo and himself. As before, however, Leonardo declined to accept a one-third share. A few pounds and a few dollars would be acceptable, he said, but no more.

Jacob said that, depending on the unfolding of events in Florence, he would then return, at least for a while, to Tescano. He could be away for many months or as little as a few weeks. Whatever happened, he would write to Luigi and Leonardo.

Jacob's departure was set for a week later. The day before he left he handed Father Gianni the one thousand American dollars and five hundred British pounds, as decided. He assured Father Gianni that the money had not been stolen. It had been offered to him and Luigi by a German who, after making the offer, had suddenly died. Father Gianni was not entirely convinced that the whole truth was being told. But, as a man of learning, he understood that some matters were best left alone. Besides, Jacob meant well.

On the evening before Jacob's departure, he, Luigi, Franca, Cesare, Father Gianni and Leonardo and his parents all ate together once more around the big table in the Ferraro kitchen.

There was, initially, much laughter. Then, with the passage of the hours and pouring of the wine, came the grey mist of sadness. Jacob would soon be gone.

Slightly drunk, Jacob raised himself from his chair and spoke. He was unsure if he still had a family in other places. But he knew he had a family in Tescano. This family had taken him in after the war just as Luigi and Leonardo had taken him into their bosoms during the army training at Livorno. They had cared for a Jew in a time when the world cared nothing for the murder of countless Jews. The evening ended on those words.

The next day, his motorised bicycle fitted with panniers that carried enough fuel to give the Raleigh All-Steel Irish X Frame a powered range of two hundred and fifty kilometres, and with a small leather bag strapped to his back, Jacob said his farewells to Tescano. In the minute of his departure, Jacob pressed, unseen by Luigi, Cesare and Leonardo, a tight roll of banknotes into the hands of Luigi's mother. 'For your kindness,' he whispered. 'And for your goodness in bringing Luigi into this world. You gave him his heartbeat and his heartbeat helped give me life when I believed life had gone from me.'

Franca Ferraro kissed Jacob's brow. 'Remember to eat,' she said. 'We expect you back in Tescano, and when you return I do not want to see a scarecrow.' She handed him a bulging canvas shoulder bag. Jacob was surprised by its weight: perhaps close to four kilos. 'Some small things to keep up your strength along the way,' she said. 'Now, let me hold you before you go.'

Luigi, Leonardo and Cesare joined Franca's embrace. Father Gianni, watching, said that Jacob would be in his prayers, morning and night.

Jacob nodded, swung into the saddle, flicked the fuel switch and disengaged the clutch. One pedal, two pedals, three pedals. The engine spat into life. Twice Jacob circled the fountain in the piazza before he veered towards the road that sliced down to the flatness of the valley, and quickly disappeared from view. Soon the sound of the Villiers engine was gone too.

Later, with Cesare and Luigi back in the workshop and Leonardo back at the Battaglia bakery, Franca Ferraro counted the money: three hundred American dollars and one hundred British pounds. Two days later, after some thought, she mentioned the gift to Luigi and Cesare. Luigi's surprise was feigned to perfection. His mother said that how Jacob had come by such sums was a mystery — though he was, after all, the son of a well-to-do family in Florence. She revealed that she had given the money to Father Gianni. He was to use it for such good works as he thought fit. The Ferraro family already had much to be grateful for, Franca said, and what use could they possibly have for such riches?

Life in the Ferraro home and workshop slipped back into a Tuscan timelessness. There was work to be done in the smithy: farm equipment to be made or mended, doors needing hinges, axles and cartwheels needing straightening. The metal legs on the school desks were all replaced. Now and then repairs were needed to Father Gianni's car, and there was always work to be done at the Convent of Santa Teresa.

On weekends through the late summer of 1946, Luigi and Leonardo continued their motorised-bicycle rides. The two never ventured more than forty kilometres in either direction, an easy ride of no more than an hour and a half each way.

Some days they called in at the Convent of Santa Teresa, where they serviced the increasingly well-used Raleigh All-Steel Irish X Frame bicycles. Every day now, sisters Maria Angela, Immaculata, Berenice and Maiella rode to the Tescano school, with its replastered walls and considerably expanded collection of books, all paid for by Father Gianni, who had alluded to 'an anonymous German benefactor who wished to right some wrongs'. Since the demise of Bartolo Minoza and Salvatore Paglia, the sisters had stepped into the educational breach and now ran all the classes.

Imaginings of a journey to the furthest-away places continued to intrude on Luigi's thoughts. Some evenings, alone in his room with an atlas borrowed from Father Gianni, Luigi traced with his fingers the route that might be taken from Tescano to Australia. A journey to the furthest place on earth would require some planning. He could cycle to Florence and travel by train to Milan and then to Istanbul. He had never travelled on a train before, although he had helped in the destruction of one. He could then cycle from Istanbul to the Holy Land and Egypt. In Egypt, at a place called Port Said, it would be possible to board a ship to Ceylon and Australia. The atlas showed a shipping lane that sliced through the Suez Canal, down to the Gulf of Aden and onwards to Ceylon and Australia. Once there he would cycle around Australia. Then he would sail from Australia to Genoa or Naples and cycle home to Tescano. Such a trip, naturally, would require money. However, his share of the contents of the knapsack would take care of that.

Luigi shared his thoughts of great journeys with Leonardo during one of the Saturday rides. Perhaps, he ventured, Leonardo might consider accompanying him on this journey. It would be a grand adventure.

Leonardo said, quite sharply, that such a journey could be a grand adventure or a grand disaster. But it would be an adventure or a disaster that Luigi faced alone. Leonardo would remain in Tescano. There was the bakery to attend to. Anyway, what had happened to Luigi's plan to set up a bicycle shop, he asked, and what if Jacob returned to live in Tescano? Then there was Nunzia — what if she came back and Luigi was gone? Luigi was the best of comrades, but sometimes he never thought things through. Luigi was such a dreamer.

Luigi remained silent, concealing his disappointment. In his silence, however, Luigi remembered Nunzia's observation that night in the hills that being a dreamer was no bad thing.

Still, the prospect of travelling alone through strange lands was, even for a dreamer, no small undertaking. Perhaps, in time, Leonardo could be persuaded. Until then, Luigi's plans and dreams might best be set aside.

CHAPTER FIFTEEN

Pacing

*Life is about averages. Average price, average height,
average distance. Stick close to the average and you'll
be okay. You won't get a room with a view but you'll
get a room. An average sort of room.*

— Zane Barton, *Finance Fundamentals*, 1998

Luigi's dream of the grandest of cycling adventures was rekindled
by a letter from Florence. It arrived in early 1947. Jacob's business
in the city had been completed. Some mysteries had been partly
solved, and decisions of import made.

It had taken some months, but Jacob, through the Red Cross,
had finally learned that his immediate and extended family had
been sent to Germany. All had died in a place called Buchenwald.
The Zevi home and shop in Florence had been looted and burnt
in 1945 by the retreating Germans. With his family dead and
their home and business little more than charred shells, Jacob

had resolved to leave the city of his birth. The Holy Land was in his thoughts.

Jacob had other news, too. On the Via Lambertesca one day he had encountered Jeremy Forsythe. At the end of hostilities, Jeremy was assigned to the British Consulate in Florence. His task was to discover the fate of missing Tuscan Partisans who had served with British soldiers. Some weeks before the encounter with Jacob, Jeremy had received word that Nunzia's father had survived the war, serving with the Partisans, and had then returned to Genoa and to teaching. But there was no news of Nunzia. It was only known that she had been sent, by train, to Germany.

Jacob revealed that Jeremy would soon travel to Tescano. The visit would be in his capacity as an official of the British Consulate. Special Partisan medals — 'from the King of England himself' — would be presented to Luigi, Leonardo, Uncle Cesare, Father Gianni and Sister Maria Angela. Jacob had also been selected to receive this medal, and he would return to Tescano for the presentation.

So, sometime in the next few weeks, wrote Jacob, *I will return to Tescano. After that I will go to the Holy Land with my bicycle. I will start a new business there. Perhaps we should all cycle away together: Luigi, Leonardo and Jacob, the Tescano boys, on their biggest adventure.*

Four weeks later, while he was working in the smithy on a Friday afternoon, Luigi heard the distinctive sound of a Villiers 98cc two-stroke engine approaching and then stopping outside the wide doors of Uncle Cesare's workshop. He ran outside as Jacob cut the engine, dismounted and, arms outstretched, awaited Luigi's embrace and then that of Uncle Cesare.

Franca Ferraro, hearing the cries of welcome, ran out of her kitchen. She paused, hands on hips, and eyed Jacob before wrapping her arms around him. She said he looked like he hadn't had a proper meal since he left Tescano. She would change all that. 'People will talk,' she said. 'They'll say Franca Ferraro has a scarecrow come to live under her roof.'

That afternoon, Luigi and Jacob walked over to the Battaglia bakery, where Leonardo and his family embraced Jacob warmly, and then to the Church of the Blessed Seamstress. Father Gianni rose from his knees and beamed a smile that outshone all the candles around the altar. 'So, young Jacob Zevi,' he said, 'you have returned to your friends, whose prayers for your life were answered even by a busy God.'

That evening at dinner — with Father Gianni, Leonardo, his parents, Sister Maria Angela and Luigi, Franca and Cesare — around the big wooden table in the Ferraros' kitchen, Jacob spoke with great emotion of Florence and the loss of his family there and in Ancona. He would sell the fire-damaged Zevi family home and shop. He could never again live in the city.

Franca said Jacob should remain in Tescano for as long as he wished before he travelled on to the Holy Land. Glasses were raised in many toasts. They toasted Jacob's grand plan, and also Jeremy Forsythe, Franca and her wonderful cooking, the sisters of the Convent of Santa Teresa, Uncle Cesare, Father Gianni, Sergeants Bob and Geordie, and even the King of England himself. And there was a toast to Nunzia. 'Our absent friend and comrade,' Father Gianni said. 'Perhaps a brief moment of silence.'

The hours passed in reminiscences of boyhood and Livorno and the cycling school. Father Gianni observed that all of life was a journey of twists and turns: an unplanned twist here, an unexpected turn there. It was a mystery beyond words.

Emboldened by the wine, Luigi stood and cleared his throat. In recent weeks, he said, since Jacob's letter, his thoughts had turned to a journey he himself might make. If Jacob would have him as a companion, he would go with his friend to the Holy Land. Then he would strike out for Australia. Since his schooldays he had dreamed of making that journey across new countries and wide oceans. He would not be gone forever — a few months at most. Then he sat down, his face flushed with the wine and the realisation that his announcement had brought silence to the table.

When Luigi's mother began to speak there was a sharpness in her voice. 'And I suppose all this will be paid for by the bag of money and gold you have under your bed. I spoke of it to Father Gianni. He told me the bag was given to you and Jacob by a German who died suddenly and that some of what was in the bag has been used for good works. Then I understood how Jacob was able to give me money before he left for Florence.' While Luigi's decision to undertake a great journey was not a surprise to her, it was not an announcement she welcomed. 'But it would be a poor mother who did not know her son,' she went on, her voice breaking. 'I have seen the way you look at the book of maps. Of course I have the sadness of every mother whose son steps away and into the world. But I am not such a fool as to believe a mother owns her child.'

It was an awkward end to the evening.

Franca said little on the morning after Luigi's announcement. She realised that it would be folly to attempt to persuade him to remain in Tescano; Luigi, once settled on a course of action, was not easily diverted. She knew he would go and she resolved that it would be with her blessing. It would not do for Luigi to leave Tescano with a heavy heart.

In the days following, Jacob and Luigi talked of the journey. Uncle Cesare, asked for his thoughts, told them that a journey into the unknown would be no little thing. He had heard from the postman who came to Tescano every week that many Italians were leaving their homeland and sailing to Australia. Uncle Cesare could not imagine leaving Tescano. But it was Luigi's life and Luigi's choice.

Leonardo was less accepting. Sitting with Luigi and Jacob by the fountain in the Piazza Valsini, he wondered why Luigi would wish to leave all that was familiar. Tescano was their home. He and Leonardo had grown up here together. They had shared the same desk at school, the same boyhood adventures. They had served as brothers-in-arms with the Partisans. They were to receive a medal from the King of England himself. What more might there be to life? When Luigi said that there must be more, Leonardo stood and walked away.

For four days, he avoided Luigi — no mean achievement in a village as small as Tescano. Then came the weekend. Leonardo was watching from the doorway of the bakery when Luigi and Jacob wheeled their motorised bicycles from the smithy. He waved. Luigi and Jacob nodded, a signal that Leonardo should join them.

Together they rode their bicycles into the hills. Without exchanging any words, each had resolved that their comradeship should not be diminished by any more talk of grand journeys.

Three weeks after the night of Luigi's dinner-table announcement, a black Humber car bearing diplomatic numberplates arrived in

Tescano. As he stepped from the driver's seat, Jeremy Forsythe gave a theatrical flourish and announced grandly that he was there on the orders of 'those in the highest places'.

Two days later, a ceremony was held by the fountain. Medals from the King of England were presented to Luigi, Leonardo, Jacob, Uncle Cesare, Sister Maria Angela and Father Gianni. The sisters from the Convent of Santa Teresa applauded and the children from the school were given a day off.

In his speech, Jeremy said that without the courage of these brave Tescano souls, British agents sent to aid the Partisans and the people of Tuscany would have perished. There was much loud cheering and the Tescano Men of Brass launched into a rousing Tuscan march, 'The Cheesemaker's Daughter'. This was followed by the popular — even risqué — polka, 'Squeezing the Olives'. Children danced and ran and squealed. Food, much of it prepared by Franca, appeared on tables, much drink was taken and there was talk of instituting an annual Heroes' Day in Tescano, with perhaps even its own special song. Jacob suggested a title: 'The Fearless Foxes of Tescano'.

'Yes,' he said, 'some words are coming to mind.' He began to sing:

When dark days came, the bugle rallied,
And to the call the brave hearts sallied.
Not for them the bended knee,
They'd dare to fight, they would be free.
The Fearless Foxes of Tescano,
Their wings spread wide, swooped on the foe.
The Germans fled,

Dreams turned to sand,
And Tuscan hands freed Tuscan land.

Everyone agreed that Jacob was a poet of rare and locally unrivalled gifts. He was, it was noted by Father Gianni, a Florentine, and thus steeped in the wit and culture of that city.

Jeremy Forsythe stayed in Tescano for four days after the ceremony. They were days of recollections and walks into the hills. Sometimes Jeremy walked with Luigi and Jacob. Other times he walked with Luigi.

The first time the two set off together, Jeremy spoke of Nunzia. He said that many trains carrying prisoners from Italy to Germany had been attacked and destroyed by American and British aircraft. It was possible that Nunzia had died in such an attack. It was also possible that she had survived the journey and been taken to a camp in Germany. If she had survived the camp and it had been liberated by the British or the Americans, Nunzia would have been repatriated to Italy through the Red Cross. If the camp had been liberated by the Russians — well, that was another matter entirely.

'The Russians didn't mind taking our help in the war,' Jeremy told Luigi. 'They're not so friendly now the war is over. They've never let the Red Cross into the camps they liberated, and they've been reluctant to provide lists of survivors. Tens of thousands of those survivors were moved east into camps in Russia. Many are still there.' After a pause, he added: 'We can hope. It is better than nothing.'

On the day before the Englishman's departure, Luigi and Jacob spoke to Jeremy at length of their planned adventure to the

Holy Land and beyond. Even before it started, Jeremy advised, the journey wouldn't be without potential complications. There was the matter of passports. What once had been a simple task had become complicated by the destruction across Italy, in the final months of the war, of records of births and marriages and deaths. A telephone call from the British Consulate in Florence to Italian passport authorities in Rome might shorten a lengthy process — but Luigi and Jacob would have to be patient.

Once the passports had been issued, Jeremy said, the paperwork for entry to the Holy Land and for Luigi's entry to Australia would require attention too. 'I have a contact in the Australian Mission in Rome — that might help,' Jeremy said. 'Of course, they'll insist on a medical examination and chest x-rays; those could be done in Florence and sent down to Rome. They'll also want a character reference and I can sort that out. The Holy Land ... well, our Foreign Office looks after who gets into Palestine and who doesn't. A few words from me to our embassy chaps in Rome will pave your way along the paper trail.'

Then Jeremy cautioned the two: 'The Holy Land isn't the happiest of places right now. The British are caught right in the middle of a pretty bloody brawl between the Arabs and the Jews. Thousands of Jews who survived Hitler are trying to get in, and you can't blame them either. The trouble is, the Arabs were there first.

'The main thing right now is for you to understand that even a speeded-up passport process might take three or four months. My camera's in the car so I'll do your passport pictures now and start the ball rolling when I'm back in Florence. When the passports are ready you can come over and stay with me — there's plenty of room — and we'll do the rest of what needs doing.'

Jeremy left Tescano at dawn the following day. It was four months before he wrote with news that the passports had been issued. He had also made some progress in tracing what had happened to Nunzia after her transportation to Germany. Hopes should not be raised too high, he said, but neither should they be cast aside. He would tell Luigi and Jacob more when they arrived in Florence.

In the workshop, the motorised bicycles were readied for the adventure. They were stripped and cleaned and rebuilt. Spokes were tightened. Saddles were perfectly positioned. Panniers and rear racks were fitted. A small valise would be strapped to each rack. Engines were tuned and retuned. Handlebars and brakes were adjusted.

Then there was the matter of concealment of the gold coins from the knapsack. Some of the coins were sewn into the waistband of trousers and into the braces that held the trousers in place. Jacob said the two should buy hats in Florence; gold coins could be hidden in the hatbands. Cash would be carried in money belts worn next to the skin. Some plain gold bangles and chains from the knapsack would be carried in the lining of the valise on the rear rack of each bicycle. Jacob had learned of such places of concealment from his father.

Ten days after Jeremy's letter, Luigi and Jacob were ready to leave. On the evening before departure, Leonardo and his family and Father Gianni gathered with the Ferraros and Jacob in the Ferraro kitchen. Father Gianni offered prayers for those around the table and blessings for the two adventurers. Afterwards, tears in his eyes, Leonardo said he would miss his cherished comrades.

Jacob told them all that he would always hold Tescano dear. He had composed a parting song for this moment. He began:

When all seemed lost
When all seemed dark
A Tuscan voice from here said, 'Hark ...
This is your home,
Here are your friends,
Within Tescano your journey ends.
So here I came to life renewed,
Among these hills new hope was viewed.
All hail Tescano, mighty village,
Free from war and all its pillage.
And though I journey far and wide
My spirit still will here abide.

Father Gianni said it was beyond question that Jacob Zevi had an unusual way with words. 'I have read much over many years,' the priest went on. 'Much of what I have read was easily forgotten. Not so the words of Jacob Zevi.' Jacob flushed.

In the early morning, Luigi and Jacob wheeled out their bicycles and filled the panniers. Little was said at the point of departure. There were no lingering farewells. It was better that way. Emotions were best kept under control. Leonardo told the two that they shouldn't stay away for too long. Franca Ferraro said they should eat the food she had packed for them. Uncle Cesare said the motorised bicycles should be kept in good order with nightly inspections and maintenance. Father Gianni said the roads that led away from Tescano were the same roads that led back.

For a brief moment Luigi feared he might, at the last minute, withdraw from the enterprise. Perhaps this 'grand adventure' was nothing but a silly dream. Perhaps he should remain in the womb of Tescano.

Jacob saw the uncertainty in Luigi's eyes and, seizing the moment, swung into the saddle. Then the two were off. Without a backwards glance they cruised down the hill and turned west towards Florence. Luigi's fear was suddenly gone. There was freedom in every turn of the wheels. He wanted to cycle forever.

The two were in no hurry to reach Florence, stopping regularly to admire a view or eat some of Franca's more than ample provisions before riding off again. The motorised bicycles purred. The spokes reflected the rays of the sun. There seemed to be neither past nor future. There was only the joy of the moment, the purity of the present.

The two rode all day and took a room at a small inn at a village called Trabanto. Their faces burnt and tingling from the sun and the wind, they slept the dreamless sleep of angels. After another day in the saddle they were in Florence.

They easily found Jeremy Forsythe's house, a two-storey villa with a dizzying number of rooms — 'five bedrooms, three public rooms, a private library … take your pick,' Jeremy said. He gave them a tour of the house and introduced them to his cook and housekeeper, the Widow Maria Oscilante. She had started service with Jeremy some months earlier on the recommendation of a former Partisan.

That night, after dinner, and with Jeremy's gentle encouragement, Maria told her story. She and her husband, both Communists, had been with the Partisans in Florence. Both had been taken by the Germans. Her husband had died under torture. Maria herself had been savagely treated for more than ten days but had said nothing. Then she was loaded on to a train with Jews and other captured Partisans, and transported to a camp in Poland. On that crowded train she had met a young woman, Nunzia Costa from Genoa. In a German prison in Florence, Nunzia had been subjected to what Maria would only describe as 'unspeakable degradations'. Like Maria, Nunzia had revealed nothing to her German captors.

'The train journey to the camp lasted five or six days,' Maria said, without emotion. 'There was no food and hardly any water. We had maybe fifty Partisan prisoners in our wagon. At least twenty died before we reached the camp. We slept on the bodies of the dead. When we arrived, most in the camp were Russian prisoners of war. We saw them through the wire as we left the train. They were wretched souls, skeletons in rags.

'There were many sections in the camp: Russians in one area, Jews in another, gypsies and common criminals in another. We were in a section of the camp for what the Germans called politicals.

'There was no way of telling how long we were there. Time did not exist in that place. We measured our lives in heartbeats — hours and days and months and years belonged to another world. Towards the end, everybody knew the war was in its last stages. We could hear, day after day, heavy guns in the east. Russian planes would fly over our camp. Then, suddenly, the Germans just left. But we did nothing. We were too weak. We sat in the filth and stink and waited and watched people die around us until the Russian Army came.'

The first Russian units to reach the camp moved on quickly after setting up kitchens and providing some medical attention. Later, the process of clearing the camp began. 'It took months,' Maria said. 'Because we were in the section of the camp for politicals, we were sometimes questioned for days by the Russians, but we were fed and clothed and free to do what we wished within the electrified fence. Eventually I was sent west with some other Italians and we were turned over to the British. I think we were exchanged for some Russians who had gone over to the Germans. Others from our camp were sent east. Nunzia was one. I never found out why. The Russians never explained anything. Perhaps it was because it was obvious that she had an education, and the Russians were suspicious of anybody well educated. The last I saw of Nunzia was when I left to go west. She was frail. She rarely talked. I don't know what happened to her after that.'

For several nights afterwards, Luigi slept poorly. He was haunted by dreams of the horror of Nunzia's treatment by the Germans ... of her misery in some Russian camp ... of her death and burial in some unmarked grave.

It would be best, Jeremy said, noticing Luigi's drawn face and the dark rings around his eyes, to attend to the present. 'I have access to people here and there,' he said. 'The Red Cross, the War Graves Commission — the authorities who are trying to find missing people or resettle displaced people. There are millions who are not accounted for. I will do whatever I can to find Nunzia or news of her. For now, there is much to be done before you leave.'

Arrangements were made for Luigi to attend the medical examination necessary before an Australian entry permit could be issued. Meanwhile, Jacob arranged with a notary for the sale of the ruined Zevi property and the deposit of proceeds into a bank account. The men also needed to buy clothing for the journey. Hard-wearing clothes for cycling and lightweight clothes for train travel were the order of the day, Jeremy said. He knew just the place: a long-established tailor on the Via de' Bardi, a stone's throw from the Ponte Vecchio.

'A very good cutter,' he said, 'and a genius when it comes to the inside leg. Shouldn't take more than ten or twelve days between measuring and fitting. Appearances — and the right inside-leg measurement for comfort and ease of movement — are important when you're on the go. You need to look the part: dress poorly and you'll be treated poorly. Travel first class — always worth the money. Trains, hotels ... stick to first class. I'll make the arrangements. First class always gets better treatment, especially at borders. Eau de cologne, too. A whiff of cologne does the trick. It's the scent of money. It's the smell of belonging in first class.'

Four weeks after their arrival in Florence, the two adventurers departed. They would travel by train to Milan and there they would board another train for Istanbul.

At the railway station the three men exchanged firm handshakes. Jeremy's nostrils pinched at the spicy scent of cologne and he concluded that the two, unused to wearing fragrances, had substantially overindulged. He said nothing.

Instead, he nodded his approval as he eyed Luigi and Jacob. Indeed, they looked as they were meant to look, like young men of reasonable means and quiet self-assurance. Confident young men, off on an adventure.

CHAPTER SIXTEEN

Style

Style in cycling is like a fingerprint. The best riders have their own distinctive style. Style can take you just about anywhere, not just in cycling, but in life.

— Rory McLintock, Assistant Deputy Manager, Scottish
  Commonwealth Games Cycling Squad, 1982

Leaving the train from Florence, Luigi and Jacob wheeled their bicycles through the cathedral-like space of Milan railway station towards a sign that said *Istanbul Departures*. Each felt a shiver of excitement. Or maybe it was trepidation. There was no going back now.

At Platform Four they found their train, snorting steam like a war horse ready for the gallop into unknown territory. The sleeping compartments on the train were operated by the French Wagons-Lits company: 'It will be like a five-star hotel on wheels,' Jeremy had said when he presented them with their first-class tickets.

A white-uniformed steward led Luigi and Jacob to the open door of their sleeping compartment. 'Now,' he said, 'shall we say twenty minutes and I will return to escort you to your luncheon table?'

Twenty minutes later the two were ushered to the dining car and the table they would share with two well-dressed matrons. The women, Americans, introduced themselves as Miss Eugenie Dolan and Miss Katherine James. Miss Dolan volunteered the information that she had been a professor in Stevens Point, Wisconsin, with a speciality in the history of early Christian sites. Miss James, herself originally from Wisconsin too, had spent many years in the Middle East as the daughter of an oil man, and spoke some Arabic. Luigi said that he and Jacob were, respectively, from Tescano and Florence in Tuscany.

'Florence,' Miss Dolan sighed, almost swooning. 'Wonderful Florence, utterly magnificent Florence. All who visit Florence leave part of themselves there. Of all the places in the world to live, Florence would be my very close second choice after Wisconsin. Each has its own magic.'

There followed a gentle interrogation by the retired college professor. 'Really?' she said. 'You served with the Partisans? How truly dashing! How bold. How very Errol Flynn. How utterly George Sanders. The Partisans — my word.'

Luigi said he did not know of Errol Flynn or George Sanders, although it was quite possible the two had served with another unit of the Garibaldi Brigades. 'There were many English who came to our hills and mountains. I am sure our English friend, Jeremy Forsythe, would have known Mr Flynn and Mr Sanders.'

Smiling, Miss James asked what grand journey the two were planning. Luigi said that he and Jacob would be cycling to the Holy Land. Jacob would remain there. He would open a small business and would help orphans who did not have bicycles.

'Well,' Miss Dolan said, 'that seems to me to be a venture that is as admirable as it is unusual.'

Luigi, for his part, intended to travel to Australia. Miss Dolan said that her knowledge of the world did not extend to Australia. She did not feel this had held her back in life. Quite possibly, Australia was an interesting place despite its lack of any real history to speak of. The Holy Land was altogether another matter. It was a place of treasures.

Miss James agreed, and added: 'There's so much you'll simply have to see in the Holy Land. We might sit together for dinner tomorrow evening — seven o'clock, perhaps? You can tell us all about your derring-do with the Partisans and we can tell you of the Holy Land. What do you say?'

It was a kind invitation, Luigi said. He and Jacob would be pleased to join the ladies.

Later on that first night of their journey, the train crossed into Yugoslavian territory. Officials came aboard. Transit visas were stamped. Minutes later, the train was again in motion. It was a slow journey. Sections of the track were in poor repair. In the final year of the war, most of the rail lines in Yugoslavia had been either blown up by the retreating Germans or bombed by the advancing Allies. Progress was no faster when the train crossed into Bulgaria.

On the second evening, Luigi and Jacob joined Miss Dolan and Miss James for dinner at seven o'clock as agreed. There was some talk of Partisan life in the Tescano hills before Miss Dolan asked where the two young men might be planning to lodge in Istanbul. She immediately added that she and Miss James would take rooms at the Pera Palas Hotel. It was a first-class establishment, she said, where one was 'properly looked after'. Luigi, recalling Jeremy's advice to travel and lodge first class, said the Pera Palas seemed just the sort of establishment he and Jacob should consider.

Miss Dolan agreed. 'In plain American talk, the Pera Palas has class. It isn't low cost. But it's the best. And it caters to a good class of guest.'

Miss James nodded. 'One shouldn't look down on the less fortunate,' she said. 'But neither should one rush to share lodgings with them. Familiarity has, I do believe, always bred contempt.'

Another day and another night passed before the train pulled into the brightly lit Grand Sirkeci Station in Istanbul. On the platform, Miss Dolan took charge. A porter was despatched to secure three taxis — one for the Americans, one for Luigi and Jacob, and one for the motorised bicycles. Minutes later the taxis halted by the wide marble steps of the Pera Palas Hotel.

Miss Dolan and Miss James were escorted to their pre-booked single rooms on the first floor. Luigi and Jacob selected a double room on the second floor. 'An excellent choice,' the duty manager observed as he walked them to their accommodation. Then he advised that all accounts were to be settled in cash and that former hotel guests had included Britain's love-struck King Edward VIII, a tsar of all the Russias, the actresses Sarah Bernhardt and Greta Garbo, and the legendary spy Mata Hari.

Luigi wondered if the mention of cash payment and famous guests in one sentence suggested that the love-struck king or an actress had once departed in the night, leaving a bill unpaid. He wondered, too, if a tsar of all the Russias would have any information on the fate of Nunzia, who might still be alive and in the hands of the Russians. While he was not sure what a tsar might be, he sounded like a person of influence.

Luigi did not share his wonderings with the duty manager, who bowed slightly, cleared his throat and extended a hand, palm upwards. Luigi shook the upturned hand and the duty manager, failing to conceal his puzzlement, left.

From the wide balcony of their room, Luigi and Jacob gazed out on a dazzling panorama. To the left lay the glittering expanse of the Bosporus, and to the right the calm waters of the Golden Horn, past which the landmark basilica, the Hagia Sophia, dominated the skyline all the way to the Sea of Marmara. This was another world, another universe. This was a place to be explored, devoured. Breakfast could wait.

Jacob removed two concealed gold coins from his hatband. They would convert the coins to cash. They should also carry some US one-dollar notes. 'For small expenses,' Jacob said. Luigi said he might buy a gift for his mother. Jacob flicked him a coin and the two were on their way.

In the cavernous foyer, they strode to the marble-topped desk of the concierge, who addressed the two in English. He was, he told them, Abdi Abib, 'formerly of the Hotel George V in Paris'. The Pera Palas was at the disposal of its distinguished guests.

Luigi's request for a map was met with a knowing smile. 'A map. Of course,' Abib said. 'But allow me to advise that a map without a guide may leave you as blind men at the gates of Paradise. We cannot have that.' He produced a small map and tapped a finger dead centre. 'The Galata Bridge, the gateway to old Istanbul. I will make immediate arrangements for our most senior and knowledgable guide to meet you at the bridge in one hour. You should not hurry yourselves. Istanbul is best enjoyed slowly, at strolling pace.'

He raised a finger. A porter appeared and walked Luigi and Jacob to the main entrance. The ornate, heavy doors were pulled open by two men in hotel livery. Luigi and Jacob were, in the space of a footstep, in this other world they had seen from their balcony.

From the relative elevation of the Pera Palas they walked downhill towards sea level and the Galata Bridge, which spanned the waters of the Golden Horn, the freshwater estuary bisecting the old and the even older Istanbul.

At the bridge, the two were met by a well-dressed man. He introduced himself, in English, as Murad Suleiman, senior hotel guide. 'I am most pleased to meet you,' he said, 'and to share the delights of my Istanbul. It is a place where civilisations are interwoven. The threads of the East are joined with the threads of the West. It is a rich tapestry.'

Luigi courteously noted that Mr Murad had an impressive command of English.

'A product, in part, of my early schooling in Ankara and my time at the military academy,' the guide explained, 'but mainly from many months in hospital with some of the Australians who shot at me at Gallipoli. They were our prisoners but we made no distinction between our wounded and their wounded.'

Luigi said he intended to travel to Australia. Mr Murad said he knew nothing, really, of Australia, but if the Australians he had met were anything to go by, it was a place of fine soldiers. 'At the military hospital where I was sent to recover from my wounds,' he said, as they strolled into the Gordian knot of old Istanbul, 'there were many young Australians. I felt sorry for them. They were open-faced and some were quite innocent. They were honourable. They seemed brave. They bore pain with dignity and with a concern for the suffering of their fellows. This, to me, is always a sign of decency — concern for others. I would have been proud to have command of such men. I remember them as quite pure souls, these Australians. They had come halfway around the world to fight a war that had more to do with the English than it had to do with Australia. I also found they had a way with speech that was confounding in the extreme. It was like no English that I had been taught.'

The three continued walking until the great arched entrance to the Grand Bazaar appeared, like an open door to the fabled Aladdin's Cave. For four hours, Luigi, Jacob and Mr Murad wound their way past stalls and shops that purveyed shoes, slippers and soft sables; past pots, pans and painted plates, basins, bowls and bolts of cloth; past beaten copper, burnished bronze and buffed brass, carpets, cakes and confections. There was a brief interlude of half-hearted bargaining when Luigi selected and purchased two angora shawls. 'For my mother in Tescano,' he told Mr Murad.

The guide felt that Luigi had paid a price that was a shade on the high side of reasonable. Perhaps, Mr Murad suggested, he might be able to assist with any other purchases. There was much to see.

Luigi had no doubt there was much to see … so much that he wished out loud that they'd brought their bicycles with them.

Mr Murad beamed. 'Bicycles!' he said. 'Of course. I was advised by the hotel that you are cyclists and that your bicycles — with engines, I believe — came with you on the train journey. I was, myself, a bicycle man of some ability in earlier times. Today there is too much traffic to cycle in comfort around Istanbul, but I know a place you would enjoy. The Princes' Islands have no traffic. Büyükada would be perfect. Yes, indeed. Perfect. Can I recommend that we see the most famous sights of the old city tomorrow, and for the day after tomorrow I will arrange for you, your bicycles and, perhaps, a Pera Palas picnic lunch to be taken by boat to Büyükada?'

With the forward agenda set by Mr Murad, attention returned to the moment. Jacob's earlier excitement was giving way to fatigue. His shoes pinched and tiredness stung his eyes. He pointed to a tea shop. He would remain there while Luigi, if he wished, continued his explorations with Mr Murad.

In the El Dorado of the gold section of the Grand Bazaar, Luigi was bedazzled. At every turn were windows filled almost to overflowing with gold chains, bracelets, bangles, necklaces. He had never seen such things. They were more grand by far than the sacred gold goblets, incense burners and altar crosses in Father Gianni's Church of the Blessed Seamstress.

Luigi paused before one shimmering window. His eyes fixed on a bowl filled with intricately worked brooches, jewelled bracelets, elaborate rings, ornate Orthodox crosses. Necklaces and gold hair combs lay jumbled together. In the middle of this assortment was a miniature gold book delicately decorated with stones that still sparkled in defiance of obvious neglect. Luigi looked more closely. It was a locket.

'Russian gold,' said Mr Murad. 'Istanbul is awash with it. White Russians, the ones who resisted Communism, poured into Istanbul for many years. The lucky ones managed to bring their small treasures. They were sold cheaply. Local people see little value in Russian artistry and gold that is anything less than twenty-two carats. And much of the Russian gold is less than twenty-two carats.'

'So it is difficult to sell?' Luigi asked.

'It has been, since the war. Some Europeans used to buy it but the war stopped the visitors and few have returned. Perhaps you wish to examine this locket?'

Luigi nodded.

Inside the shop, the merchant was effusive in his welcome. His English was polished. In this glistening part of the Grand Bazaar, English was the second language of those who traded in precious goods. Certainly, his honoured guests could examine the locket, he said. A beautiful specimen. He speculated that the young gentleman had a young lady in mind.

'Yes,' replied Luigi.

And the lady was obviously beautiful?

Another 'yes' and the observation from Luigi that she had been taken away by Germans. 'Some days I believe she is alive,' he said. 'Other days ... other days I think otherwise. And some days I hope for hope.'

The merchant recognised the sadness in Luigi's eyes and in his voice. In his own life, he said, he had experienced the great sadness of loss. He would say no more of this loss but he believed hope was a good companion during times of sadness. The purchase of a small gift might, the merchant said, keep hope alive. In the Grand Bazaar, business was business.

The merchant handed the locket to Luigi and extolled the craftsmanship and elegance of the unusual design. He reached over and opened the locket to reveal delicate plates of glass, the size of a thumbnail, held in place by gold mounts. The merchant suggested a price. Luigi suggested another. There were several suggestions and several responses. Sensing the moment had been reached when there should be a move towards a firm transaction, Luigi reached into his pocket and drew out his single gold coin. He proposed an exchange.

The merchant examined the coin. Might it be weighed and tested? He soon returned. Yes, it was twenty-four-carat gold, and yes, the market price of gold might cover most of the price of the locket. Most of the price, but not the entire price. Luigi held his ground. His offer was sound, he said — one easily saleable coin with known value for one locket the merchant might take many more years to sell. The merchant pondered the proposition. 'We have an agreement, sir,' he said at last. Mr Murad nodded, satisfied that neither the merchant nor Luigi could have struck a better deal.

The coin, the locket and handshakes were exchanged. Luigi and Mr Murad returned to the tea shop and Jacob, then the three went to the Pera Palas by taxi. Taking his leave, Mr Murad promised: 'Sightseeing tomorrow, and cycling the day after.'

At reception, the duty manager handed a folded note to Luigi. The note advised that Miss Dolan and Miss James would be delighted if the 'young adventurers' would join them for a pre-dinner refreshment in the hotel's Orient Bar at 6.45. Fruit juice and tea would be taken. Turkish delight, too. There was a matter to discuss.

Returning to their room, Luigi removed the small locket from his pocket and showed it to Jacob. 'I will send it to Jeremy and he can send it to Nunzia's father,' he said. 'Should she return, he is to give it to her.'

Jacob examined the locket. He said it was an exquisite piece of work. 'How much?' he asked, then whistled in disbelief at the answer. 'One gold coin … never,' he said. 'This would have fetched four or five times that amount in Florence before the war. It would probably fetch close to that amount even today. And you say Russian pieces are bought cheaply in the Grand Bazaar?'

Luigi nodded.

With that nod, a seed was planted in Jacob's mind.

CHAPTER SEVENTEEN

Teamwork

Archie dropped dead in Turkey. Absolutely ruined the
honeymoon. Had to call off the trip. In those days
when all the trouble was going on with the Arabs
and the Jews and our chaps in uniform, a lady simply
couldn't travel unescorted in the Orient without the
risk of ... well, let's be plain about it ... there were
rough hands and uncut fingernails everywhere. One
shouldn't say more, at least not in mixed company.
— Lady Joanne Seaman-Franks, Personal Memoir, 1973

The tall, greying, well-groomed man seated with Miss Dolan and
Miss James at a corner table in the Orient Bar was introduced
as Timothy Winterman of the American Consulate in Istanbul,
formerly of the American Embassy in Rome. His handshake was
firm. Mr Winterman had the square jaw and straight back of a
man who might have seen military service.

'So you're the young adventurers I've been hearing about,' he said. 'Partisans reunited in a grand expedition. I met some of your boys when … well, enough said. It was the war — unhappy days for all concerned. Not the sorts of days we should burden these ladies with.'

Miss Dolan said that Mr Winterman was a fine son of the Wisconsin soil. 'A very dear friend from my carefree — and rather long ago — student days,' she said. 'We called at his consulate this morning.'

Winterman nodded. 'And a good job they did. Their destination isn't the safest of places right now.'

'That's why we asked you to join us tonight,' Miss Dolan explained to Luigi and Jacob. 'We find ourselves in what we Midwestern folks refer to as a pickle, a real pickle. It seems there's growing unpleasantness in the Holy Land between the British and some other parties there — something about local Arabs and those poor people who've been arriving from Europe. The Jews, I believe. Timothy tells us it would be folly for ladies to travel unescorted in such times. We might be mistaken for Englishwomen, and if that happened, there could be unpleasantness. We could find ourselves in quite a pickle.'

Luigi's head swirled. How could the Americans find themselves inside a pickle? English was such a strange language. Had he known the word, he would have described himself as bamboozled.

Miss Dolan went on: 'Timothy is rather concerned about the absence of menfolk and their protective ways on our travels—'

'The point is,' Miss James cut in, 'we would be obliged if you would consider joining us. As our chaperons, I suppose.'

Luigi's head continued to swirl. Perhaps the ladies would forgive him, he began, but he understood, from the Wild West films he'd seen as a boy, that chaperons were the leather trousers worn by cowboys. How might cowboy trousers assist the ladies?

Miss Dolan smiled an indulgent smile, the smile of a professor to a freshman. She said that 'chaps' was the name given to the rough garment worn by cowboys. The English also used the word 'chaps' to describe men of better than common breeding. Chaperons were an entirely different kettle of fish. Luigi remained perplexed but did not pursue the matter. He sensed that an explanation involving the nature of kettles of fish would confuse him even more.

'I'll get right down to tin tacks,' Miss Dolan said. 'We would simply ask that in the Holy Land you accompany us during our excursions. Of course, your expenses — first class, naturally — would be met and you would be rewarded for your time and effort.'

Mr Winterman, taking advantage of a pause in the exchange, said that the invitation to escort the ladies was not without its advantages to Luigi and Jacob. 'These are very troubled times,' he said. 'Any idea that you might cycle south through Turkey is unwise. The border area is a nest of bandits and cut-throats. Even for Partisans like yourselves, it is not the place to be.'

Luigi and Jacob exchanged some words in Italian. Jacob, joking, suggested Luigi might ask Miss Dolan to clarify the nature of any rewards that might be offered. Timothy Winterman, in perfect Italian, told Jacob he was certain that any rewards would be adequate.

'What Mr Winterman said of nests of bandits and cut-throats makes me think a change in plan might be considered,' Luigi said.

212

'And of course we would not wish for you ladies to be in danger. But it has been a long day for us. I think we will talk between ourselves and, I promise, we will answer in the morning.'

Luigi's promise of a prompt response was toasted in orange juice. 'Hard liquor,' Miss Dolan said, raising her glass, 'is the great remover. I'm sure you agree.'

Without knowing what hard liquor might remove or even what hard liquor might be, Luigi indicated his agreement. He was confused beyond words. Kettles of fish. The great remover. Pickles. Tin tacks. His modest confidence in his proficiency in English was being shaken to the core.

In their room after dinner, Luigi and Jacob explored the proposal. Luigi said that accepting the role of protectors had a certain goodness of purpose to it. Jacob, grinning, said the promise of material reward also had a certain goodness to it. There was, too, the matter of Mr Winterman's warning about safety in the Holy Land and Turkey's border country. Adventure was one thing, but falling foul of brigands was another. Jacob said he had not survived the war to end his days at the hands of such characters.

It was settled. Luigi and Jacob would become chaperons.

After a dreamless sleep, the two were awakened by a telephone call at 8 am. The concierge advised that Mr Murad would await the young gentlemen at the front desk at 9 am. A day of exploring the delights of old Istanbul, the concierge advised, lay ahead.

Luigi penned a note to Miss Dolan and Miss James and asked the concierge to deliver it to Miss Dolan. The note advised that Mr Ferraro and Mr Zevi would be pleased to travel to the Holy Land with Miss Dolan and Miss James. Arrangements should be discussed. A 7 pm meeting in the Orient Bar was proposed.

That evening, Miss Dolan and Miss James waved Luigi and Jacob to their table. 'We are delighted you will accompany us,' Miss Dolan said.

'Delighted,' agreed Miss James. 'No other word for it. You will be, I am certain, our mantle of safety.'

The arrangements, Miss Dolan advised, were being attended to. In a few days, all would be in place.

Next morning, a beaming Mr Murad, bicycle clips in hand, ushered Luigi and Jacob to the concourse beyond the hotel's front entrance. The two motorised bicycles gleamed. A third bicycle was nearby. Mr Murad pointed to the panniers and a picnic basket tied to the rear rack of his bicycle. 'Refreshments for our journey,' he announced. Then, with the air of a master of hounds before the hunt, he raised an arm and proclaimed: 'Let us begin!'

After swinging into the saddle, they freewheeled to the waterfront. There, a ferry took them to Büyükada, a jewel in the necklace of the Princes' Islands. The island was small but offered an infinite variety of cycling conditions. Hilly tracks veered off from narrow, flat roads. Scimitar-curved bends eased into slopes that offered a panorama of shore and ocean and sky. Here and there were villages with their goats and poultry and sheds.

Three hours into the island ride, Mr Murad brought the party to a halt on a grassy knoll shaded by a tall Turkish hazel. The panniers and the picnic basket were opened, revealing flasks of hot coffee and tea, and cold mineral water in stone bottles wrapped in damp muslin. There was bread and there were pickles, thinly sliced smoked meat, and confections, including, of course, Turkish delight.

When the three were refreshed, the cycling resumed. The afternoon passed in a swirl of curves and climbs and, from Luigi, whoops of utter joy as he breasted hills and, standing on his pedals, sped down towards the flat and eventually to the ferry that would return them to the mainland.

On the concourse of the Pera Palas, Mr Murad embraced his cycling companions. 'I wish you well on your journeys. As a younger man, I would have joined you, but ... too much coffee, too many cigars, the old wounds ...' He smiled. There was sadness in the smile.

Jacob pressed a gold coin into the hands of the guide. 'No, no,' Mr Murad objected. 'This is far beyond anything you should offer. Today I was, for a while, a young man again. Today I tasted and remembered the promise of youth.' But Jacob insisted, and finally the coin was accepted. Mr Murad again embraced his fellow cyclists and turned and left, heading back to his own, everyday life.

Three days later, Luigi, Jacob, Miss Dolan and Miss James assembled in the lobby of the Pera Palas. They were departing by train for Aleppo in Syria, a journey that would take thirty hours. After their accounts were settled, Luigi passed two parcels to the concierge. One, the smaller parcel, containing the locket purchased for Nunzia, was to be posted to Jeremy Forsythe at the British Consulate in Florence. The other, containing the angora shawls, was to be posted to Luigi's mother. A letter in the smaller package asked Jeremy, if he should visit Genoa again, to give the locket to Nunzia's father, who might then pass it to Nunzia if she returned.

Within the hour, the party had steamed out of Istanbul. A sense of freedom surged through Luigi again. With every click of the wheels, he felt as a soaring bird must feel between earth and the heavens. Seeing everything and touched by nothing.

In Aleppo, the four, awaiting their connection to Jerusalem, lodged for two nights at the welcoming and comfortable Baron Hotel. The Baron had hosted its share of luminaries, Miss Dolan said, among them President Theodore Roosevelt and aviator Charles Lindbergh, along with the emotionally tortured British adventurer T.E. Lawrence and novelist Agatha Christie. Luigi silently mouthed the word 'luminary', wondering if this might be something like a tsar of all the Russias. His admiration for Miss Dolan's command of her native language was growing.

On that first night in Aleppo, Luigi and Jacob rested well in their old-fashioned room. They woke to a morning that was clear and warm. At breakfast, Miss Dolan and Miss James said their preference was to remain inside the hotel until the cooler hours of the mid-afternoon, when they might venture outdoors in the company of Luigi and Jacob, their chaperons. The two young men nodded their agreement. They would spend the morning cycling.

The bicycles were brought from the baggage room and the two set off around a town dominated by Aleppo's Citadel, which, over the centuries, had seen conquering armies come and go. Luigi and Jacob stopped to rest on a low wall at the base of the Citadel, and watched another world pass by. A world of donkeys and old trucks that belched smoke, a world of passers-by whose names and lives the adventurers would never know, never touch. And despite all the comings and goings of strangers like them, the world around the Citadel would continue.

In the cooling mid-afternoon, Luigi and Jacob and the Misses Dolan and James walked to the Mosque of Abraham and to the top of the Citadel. Miss Dolan talked of kings and prophets and miracles but Luigi heard nothing. He was thinking of the passing parade of those who came and went without leaving a trace. He was thinking of Nunzia. Had she, he wondered, already joined the passing parade that Luigi Ferraro from Tescano would, surely, join one day?

In the silence of thought, Luigi understood, perfectly, that every heartbeat, every breath, every day of life was precious. Not one moment should be squandered. Moments existed to be seized.

The party left Aleppo the following day. Their train took them west to the Mediterranean, then southwards to Beirut and on to the Holy Land.

The railway line ended in the coastal city of Haifa. From there, the party journeyed south to Jerusalem in a private motor coach. It halted at the American Colony Hostel, built in the late Ottoman style with a series of enormous rooms around an open courtyard. Miss Dolan told Luigi that the American Colony Hostel was no ordinary lodging place. One past guest was none other than the great British hero Winston Churchill. The victorious conqueror of Jerusalem in the Great War, General Allenby, had also made the American Colony Hostel his base, as had an earlier prime minister of Britain, Lord Balfour. 'The ghosts of greatness are all around,' Miss Dolan said, rather grandly. 'Soak up the spirits. Bathe in the history.'

The party remained at the American Colony Hostel for ten days — several days longer than originally planned. There was,

Miss Dolan said, just so much to see. Miss Dolan wondered aloud if, perhaps, the forebears of Luigi and Jacob had once trodden the cobbles of the Holy City as 'standard-bearers for the legions of Rome'.

Although he said nothing, Luigi had his doubts. Surely he would have heard if any from Tescano had ever held aloft the standard of the Roman legions in Jerusalem. Mayor Minoza and Salvatore Paglia would certainly have made much of such standard-bearing.

In the days that followed, Luigi and Jacob were served a visual feast of historical and religious treasures selected by Miss Dolan. Yet for all the glories of Jerusalem and its past, Luigi could feel no real affection for the city. Behind the history and fabled miracles of the past was the obvious reality of the present. It was a city of dirt and poverty and overcrowding. Luigi was struck by the empty-eyed misery of its people and the palpable tension in the air. British Military Police were everywhere. Secretly, Luigi hoped Jacob would turn away from this place, perhaps even in the direction of Australia.

At dinner on the night before the women's departure from Jerusalem, Miss Dolan thanked Luigi and Jacob. They had, she said: 'Provided a mantle of safety in these exotic and troubled surroundings. That we have not been embroiled in any unpleasantness is testament to the wisdom of Mr Winterman's advice and, of course, your manly presence.'

Miss James said she trusted that Luigi and Jacob would continue onwards and upwards through life, and handed each one hundred dollars. Brushing aside their protests at this largesse, Miss James added that a further week's accommodation at the American Colony Hostel had also been paid for.

The women departed for Haifa the following day. There were farewell handshakes, in the American manner, as the women boarded their chartered motor coach. Miss Dolan insisted the two young men give serious consideration to visiting Wisconsin. 'It is, after all, the Land of the Free and the Home of the Brave at its very best ... and nothing short of bliss for bicyclists.'

Luigi and Jacob briefly raised their hats. The gesture delighted Miss Dolan and Miss James. Such courtliness, such civility, was rare, in their opinion, beyond Wisconsin.

As the motor coach drove away, Miss James confided to her friend: 'Oh, to be thirty-five years younger.'

Miss Dolan pursed her lips. 'Even ten years younger,' she said.

There was a sad, delicate longing in their words. The longing was for all those moments that had not been seized. So many of them. All gone. Forever.

CHAPTER EIGHTEEN

Preparation

The failures are those who don't prepare. Winners prepare and losers just wish. Give me an accountant over a dreamer any day. Accountants look at the angles. They're the guys who lay the road and the dreamers are the chumps who fall by the wayside. There's a hero in every accountant. Every journey needs preparation. Accountants do the hard, smart yards.

— Denver Manson Junior, inmate 873291, Leavenworth Federal Prison, Kansas, *Only Turkeys Pay Tax*, 2002

Luigi remained in Jerusalem with Jacob for six weeks. He felt a reluctance to leave his companion in this place where eyes seemed never to meet eyes. And within Luigi there was, too, a shiver of self-doubt, perhaps even a fear of the unfamiliarity of what lay ahead. But whenever the self-doubt arose, Luigi told himself he had come too far to abandon his journey. Besides, he would not be gone from Tescano forever.

The two took rooms in a clean, modest boarding house in the Jewish quarter of the city, and Luigi planned his onward route. He would travel first by rail to Port Said in Egypt. From Port Said he could secure passage on one of the numerous cargo ships that sailed, via the Suez Canal, from Europe to Colombo in Ceylon and, not infrequently, on to Sydney.

Several times during the weeks in Jerusalem Luigi suggested that Jacob might join him on the journey to Australia, but Jacob could not be moved. He would stay in the Holy Land. He would establish his business, Jacob Zevi, Jeweller and Watchmaker, and he would use a portion of his profits to help the needy.

The parting of the ways in Jerusalem was emotional. Jacob said he had never had such friends as Luigi and Leonardo. While Luigi was travelling, Jacob would write to Luigi's mother, who could then send any letters on to Luigi when he had an address. Each assured the other they would meet again. Luigi boarded the train for Port Said. Jacob turned away. Both felt desolate.

In Port Said, Luigi paid for a berth on the London-registered cargo vessel *Seringapatam*, which was bound from the Port of Leith in Scotland to Colombo and due in Port Said within the week.

Luigi was not unhappy to be leaving Port Said. It was a crowded, dirty, depressing place of beggars and rancid smells. A place where strangers offered Luigi the company of sisters and mothers and nephews — or at least postcard pictures of sisters and mothers and nephews.

The *Seringapatam* was commanded by Captain James 'Big Jock' Macauley, a red-faced, big-handed veteran of the North Atlantic convoys that had run the gauntlet of Hitler's submarines only a few years earlier.

Cargo aside, the *Seringapatam* had the capacity to carry twelve passengers. On this trip, however, Luigi was the only one. His modest cabin came with its own attendant, who serviced passenger accommodation after he had attended to the quarters and tables of Captain Macauley and his senior officers.

The attendant, Shug Hutchinson, was the first of the crewmen Luigi met when he boarded. After settling Luigi into his cabin and advising him that the Hercules had been safely stowed, Shug introduced himself as 'a Belfast man, an Orange Lodge man, a ladies' man, and your man for anything that's needed as we cross great waters and see God's wonders of the deep'. Then he winked and added: 'Anything that takes your fancy. I'm your man. You just say the word.'

Luigi said nothing. He sniffed the air.

'You'll get used to that,' Shug assured him. 'Paint and engine oil. First time on one of these?' Luigi nodded. 'We'll all be just grand ... at least for a bit,' Shug said with a wry grin. 'Flat as a tack for the next few days. Then we're on the open water, so you just keep a bucket handy and I'll have the mop just in case you have a wee slip, a heave-to, so to speak.'

Luigi had no idea what a 'wee slip' or a 'heave-to' might be.

An hour after the *Seringapatam* slipped her moorings, Luigi was invited to the bridge. Shug conveyed the invitation. Captain Macauley, Shug said, made a point of meeting every passenger. On the bridge, the captain unrolled a chart that showed his ship's route towards El Tina, El Qantera, El Ballah, El Firdan and into the Great Bitter Lake. From there, the *Seringapatam* would glide south towards the Gulf of Suez, the calmness of the Red Sea and the narrows of the Gulf of Aden.

Luigi recognised the captain's accent. He told the captain he'd served with two Scots in Italy during the war. The captain seemed pleased that an Italian had recognised a Scottish accent and had served with Scots in dangerous times. He said Luigi would be welcome on the bridge throughout the voyage. 'Just knock before you come in,' Captain Macauley said, 'don't touch anything, and don't get in the way … and don't believe a word that wee bastard Shug Hutchinson says.' With something approaching a smile, Captain Macauley added: 'He's a decent wee soul and a worker if ever there was one. I suppose he told you he was a big ladies' man?' Luigi nodded and the captain smiled again.

'I don't think he's that way inclined,' Macauley said. Luigi wondered what 'that way inclined' might mean. It sounded quite serious — a medical condition, possibly.

Back in his cabin, Luigi lay down on his bunk. The thump of the engines and the vibrations and oily scents of the ship sucked him into a sleep that ended some hours later when he was awakened by a tapping on his door. Shug Hutchinson advised that his dinner would be served with Captain Macauley and the ship's officers.

The captain and Luigi were joined at the table by chief engineer Billy MacBride, first mate Danny Blair and radio officer Tommy Ballantyne. Like Captain Macauley, all were Scots-born and all had served on the seas during the war. The handshakes were firm and the introductions brisk. These men of the sea reminded Luigi of Sergeants Bob and Geordie. They were no-nonsense, self-assured characters, men with a job to do.

Dinner was a matter-of-fact affair. Ballantyne said little that went beyond ritual politeness. As radio officer, he was used to his own company in the ship's wireless room just behind the bridge. Blair merely nodded. Ballantyne, Blair and the captain ate quickly then left. Ballantyne had messages to send to the shipping company's home offices in the Georgian grandeur of St Andrew's Square in Edinburgh — messages on the daily progress of the vessel, bunkering costs, provisioning needs at Colombo, engineering reports on scheduled maintenance. The captain and Blair had business on the bridge — housekeeping matters to log, charts and courses to recheck.

It was only when the three had taken their leave that the chief engineer spoke. He'd seen Luigi's bicycle being stowed. It was a grand machine, he said. He recognised it as an early-model Hercules. He'd had one himself, but never with an engine.

Encouraged by the interest, Luigi explained how the bicycle came to be his, how it had been restored to working order and how he was now taking it all the way to Australia. He said he'd been in the war with two Scots. He'd once helped them blow up a train.

But Billy MacBride was more interested in the transformation of the Hercules and the planned journey to Australia than the Partisan exploits. 'Aye,' the chief engineer said. 'Anybody can blow up trains. It's like fixing a fuse to a fart. Anybody can sail a ship, for that matter — no disrespect to Big Jock Macauley, as fine a man as ever pulled on a sock or buttoned up a fly. But engineering, that's another thing altogether. That takes brains. Now, I'll have a close look at your engine and you can have a close look at my engines. How about that ... does that sound like a bargain?'

In the plain-sailing days that followed, Luigi spent hours in the pounding cathedral that was the engine room of the *Seringapatam*, with its sixteen diesel engines. Everywhere were gauges and thin pipes painted bright red, and valves and switchboards and narrow companionways and tightly coiled rubberised canvas hoses. This was the kingdom of the marine engineer. A variation in pitch, a change in tone, and Billy MacBride would issue an order for oil to be squirted or wiped away. Then he would listen again. A bolt might be tapped with a hammer, a nut might be tightened. Perfect pitch would be restored. The chief engineer, like Uncle Cesare, was a man who had mastered the mysteries of the grip.

If Luigi was impressed by the chief engineer's world, MacBride was similarly impressed by the motorised Hercules. He pronounced it as grand a piece of cleverness and engineering as he'd ever seen.

During the glide south through untroubled waters, Luigi learned that MacBride had served his apprenticeship at John Brown's Clydebank shipyard. He'd also been a member of the local bicycle club, the Clydebank Chieftains Socialist Cycling Collective, before migrating to Canada in 1931. The highlight of the cycling adventures with the Chieftains had been the annual Tour de Trossachs, north of Glasgow. This was a tour for individual riders. The cyclists would ride for a day and rest for a day. From Glasgow it was a straight run up to Balloch at the southern end of Loch Lomond before the winding ride to Rowardennan and beyond, on forestry tracks that smelled of pine needles.

'It was a great time,' he said. 'We'd ride and camp out under the trees and the stars. All of us round a big fire, singing songs, telling stories. Planning how we'd change the world when the workers rose from their slumbers. Dreamers, we were. Dreamers. I did the Tour de Trossachs every year until I finished my apprenticeship and went to Canada. On the Great Lakes trade and the St Lawrence Seaway.'

Luigi knew that in Billy MacBride he had found a kindred spirit, a dreamer who had gone on great adventures.

'When the war started,' the chief engineer continued, 'I went back to the Clyde and joined the Wavy Navy — the Royal Navy Volunteer Reserve — as a third engineer on troopships. Went to North Africa and then India and the Far East. Far Cathay, we called it — Hong Kong, Macau, Shanghai.'

Luigi asked what his favourite place had been during his travels.

'Ceylon, that's the place,' said MacBride. 'White sand and oceans and reefs like you'll never see anywhere. That's the place for you and the Hercules. Have a bit of a break there. Plenty of time for a wee pedal around before you ship out. Give yourself a few weeks. Australia can wait. It's not going anywhere.'

If Luigi had a few bob, MacBride added, he could do worse than looking at putting himself up at the Galle Face Hotel in Colombo. The city had some fine hotels, but the Galle Face was the finest. MacBride and Captain Macauley had stayed there on previous spells ashore in Colombo and they had never been disappointed. On this trip, however, they would stay on board the *Seringapatam*. They had a busy turnaround of bunkering, unloading and reloading before heading home with a cargo of tea and teak. MacBride offered to ask Ballantyne to send a message ahead. 'The hotel people can pick you up when we get ashore,' he said. It was settled without further discussion. The Galle Face would be Luigi's Colombo bolt hole.

The pleasant, plain sailing that had been Luigi's introduction to shipboard life ended half a day after the *Seringapatam* rounded the Gulf of Aden and nosed into the first swells of the Indian Ocean. Luigi could feel the change in the movement of the ship. The *Seringapatam* slid into a slow, churning roll that became, in the days that followed, an increasingly sharp, shuddering pitch. Seasickness gripped Luigi. He retched until his ribs and stomach muscles ached. Cold sweat soaked his clothes. He was sure the ship would sink. By then, it was a prospect that was almost to be welcomed. Drowning would put an end to the sickness and the sweating.

Luigi, in his misery, imagined that in time the news of his death would reach Tescano. As there would be no body to bury, Father Gianni would hold a Requiem Mass for the soul of the lost son of Tescano. Luigi's mother and Uncle Cesare would weep. Leonardo would stand in silence, his mind caressing memories of his lost boyhood friend and comrade. The sisters from the convent would ride their bicycles to the Mass, and one bicycle, a black ribbon wound around the handlebars, would be leaned against the altar, riderless: a symbol of the cyclist, the adventurer, who would never return.

Jeremy Forsythe would travel from Florence to Tescano for the Mass. Asked to say a few words, he would clear his throat and speak. 'Fearless Luigi Ferraro was many things. He was a son, a nephew, a friend and a comrade. He was a bicycle man of the first order. Even as we are gathered in this place today I strain my ears and hear the tinkling of a bicycle bell. It is Luigi Ferraro arriving at the Gates of Heaven. The doors are opened wide and fearless Ferraro rides on to the broad meadows of Eternity. He has gone home to a place where there are no hills, no dangerous bends, no punctures or broken spokes ...' Jeremy's voice would trail off, choked with tears.

From that day until the end of all time, Tescano would be a village in mourning for Luigi. The mourners would file from Father Gianni's small church and there, by the fountain, would be standing an erect and lonely figure. It was Sergeant Geordie Murray. Resplendent in dark tartan kilt, campaign medals and dress tunic, Sergeant Geordie would snap a salute in the direction of the mourners, draw a pistol and fire six shots into the air. Then he would holster the weapon, turn sharply and march down the hill and into the distance.

Luigi's boyhood gift for fantasy was intact.

The ocean's onslaught ended a day before the *Seringapatam* made landfall in Ceylon. That night, for the first time in more than a week, Luigi sat at the captain's table. The radio officer, Ballantyne, advised that the Galle Face Hotel had been told of the estimated time of arrival of Luigi and his bicycle.

After the meal, standing on the deck in the warm half-light of the early evening, Luigi sniffed the air. He could smell the land somewhere beyond the horizon. It was a layered scent, dampness overlaid with a new fragrance, a sweetness like burnt sugar. With his back to the bow he looked westwards into the setting sun.

Then, suddenly, the light was gone, as if some celestial switch had been thrown.

Luigi slept deeply on that last night aboard the *Seringapatam*. When he awoke in the first light of morning, the scent of imminent landfall was pervasive. Shug Hutchinson knocked and entered. Captain Macauley, he said, would be pleased if Luigi would join him on the bridge for the arrival in Colombo. The *Seringapatam* would berth within the hour.

From the bridge Luigi saw, in the distance, the long line of cloud that floats above every large tropical island. The sea was almost flat. Even in the coolness of the bridge, Luigi could feel the rising heat of the day burning into the windows that gave Captain Macauley his one-hundred-and-eighty-degree view of the ocean. On the decks, crewmen were loosening the hatches. Derricks were being readied. The vessel closed on Colombo until the blur below the cloud became a great, green island. Its scent grew sweeter almost by the minute. Then Colombo was there to see — a city that started at the shoreline then swept back and back across the coastal plain, before spilling all the way up the hills of the hinterland.

The berthing was seamless. Luigi's voyage was over. The Hercules motorised bicycle appeared on the forward deck. Port officials boarded, checked the ship's documentation and crew papers, stamped Luigi's passport and left again. Then it was Luigi's turn to depart. He shook hands with the captain and Shug Hutchinson. Billy MacBride wished him safe travels. It was an abrupt farewell to the *Seringapatam*. She had delivered her passenger, safe and sound, and now the no-nonsense men had work to attend to.

Luigi walked down the gangplank. His motion was unsteady when his feet touched land. A small dark man, darker than any man Luigi had ever seen, dressed in white tunic and trousers, stepped forward. 'Captain Ferraro,' he said, 'welcome to Ceylon. The Galle Face Hotel looks forward to receiving you. Your bicycle has been attended to. Let me take your belongings. Please, this way.' Luigi was ushered into a car only marginally darker than its driver, the man in the white tunic and trousers.

The Galle Face was solid and imposing. A tall, dark-suited and raffishly handsome man in his mid-fifties smiled at Luigi from behind the broad reception desk. 'Captain Ferraro,' he said. 'Welcome to the Galle Face. Welcome, indeed. A telegraph message from your ship advised us of your requirements. It is our great pleasure to extend our hospitality to you, a man of the high seas, a man of rank — a leader of other men, and yet so young.'

Captain Ferraro's baggage would be attended to by a porter. His bicycle would be placed in safe storage. 'Naturally,' the handsome man added, 'the bicycle will be polished before it is stowed — below decks, as you maritime chaps say.'

Accommodation on the second floor was proposed. The rooms faced west and were cooled by the breezes of the Indian Ocean. Luigi nodded his acceptance. The man then asked how long Captain Ferraro might be honouring the Galle Face with his presence. There was much to see in Ceylon.

Luigi indicated that he had yet to learn when he would take ship from Colombo and commence his onwards voyage to Australia. Of course, of course, the handsome man smiled: while the captain commanded all at sea, on land he could only await orders. What Captain Ferraro's next ship might be was a matter for others 'in the highest places'.

There followed a brisk explanation of the services offered by the hotel. On the ground floor was a library and separate reading room. The reception desk would arrange the collection, washing and starching of laundry. Letters for posting could be left at the desk. Reception could also offer recommendations on tailoring services, although — and this was the handsome man's personal view — 'Ravith Fernando of Fernando International Styling is without equal, particularly in respect of the pinpoint accuracy of inner-leg measurements. He has a gift, a gift, for the sensitive matter of the inner leg. I understand this gift was recognised when, as a younger bespoke tailor, he spent a year in Florence with an Italian master craftsman, a cutter of great skill and an inside-leg man without peer in Europe.'

On the matter of general wellbeing, Luigi was advised that should, heaven forbid, Captain Ferraro need medical services, an outstanding physician, Dr Cornelius Finucane, could be called 'in less time than it takes to sneeze'.

A strongroom for the secure keeping of valuables was also available to guests. Financial and business services could be arranged through the Hindley Bank, a most reputable banking house; the Galle Face would be pleased to arrange transportation for Captain Ferraro to and from the Hindley premises. It was a short journey.

Luigi indicated that he would avail himself of the offer of transportation to the bank. He had some financial matters to attend to. The handsome concierge said that arrangements could be made within the hour. Hindley's would be told of his pending arrival.

In the meantime there was the small matter of payment. A necessary trifle. How might this best be arranged for the captain's convenience? Cash was generally the easiest way. English pounds were the preference of the hotel. A cash deposit against future charges would not be out of place.

The register was signed, a deposit was paid and Luigi was shown to his quarters: a bedroom, sitting room and bathroom that were jewels of comfort and restrained elegance. The floors were white marble. Ceiling fans whirred a welcoming coolness. The bedroom boasted a large four-poster bed. There was also a small desk with a leather-padded swivel chair, and a teak wardrobe. A door by the bed led to a bathroom with a deep claw-footed bath. A low table and a sofa and two armchairs occupied the centre of the sitting room. Each room had a large window and a door that opened onto a shaded private balcony.

Luigi sat on the bed and heard the crackle of the sheets. The starched linen was scented with sandalwood. This, surely, was the life. If only his mother, Uncle Cesare, Leonardo and Jacob could see him now: an honoured guest of the Galle Face. Luigi had yet to learn that, in grand hotels, the warmth of the welcome is in direct proportion to the perceived rank and wealth of the guest.

He counted his cash. He had two hundred British pounds — the proceeds of the sale of some of his gold coins in Istanbul and Jerusalem. He also had one hundred American dollars. From the band of his hat he unpicked four gold coins. He would exchange these at Hindley's for currency. Other coins remained hidden in the belt he wore every day.

Within the hour he returned to the reception desk and was driven to Hindley's. A florid, heavy man met him at the door of the grand premises and introduced himself as Arthur Holborn. 'Holborn of Hindley's,' he said. 'I am at your disposal, Captain Ferraro. Hindley's is here to help, and Arthur Holborn is the conduit through which that Hindley's help will flow.'

The exchange of the gold coins for British pounds was conducted in a small private room. The transaction was relatively brisk. Luigi had reason to be appreciative of this. Several times, Holborn of Hindley's apologised for his flatulence. 'Love the local food but it shoots through English tummy pipes a bit too fast,' he said, red-faced. 'And it doesn't rest too well with a nasty hernia from my time in the Army Pay Corps here during the business with the Nips.'

When Luigi returned to the comfort of his lodgings, a bottle of Gordon's Gin had been placed with an ice bucket by the bedside telephone along with several limes, two glasses, a small knife and a screw-top bottle marked: *Dudley's Ceylon Tonic: A tantalising taste for gentlemen of taste*. Luigi was tantalised. He poured and emptied three tumblers of gin and tonic. He lay on the bed under the swirl and whirl of the ceiling fan.

When he awoke, it was dark. For a moment, unsure where he was, he lay still. There was a rumble of thunder and then a snap of lightning that scratched the night. The rumble rushed closer and the monsoon storm, quite suddenly, enveloped the Galle Face. Great lances of water speared down outside.

Luigi sat bolt upright. He swung his feet over the bed and stood up. Sea legs made contact with terra firma, Luigi swayed, and, unable to steady himself, he tumbled onto the marble. His head made cracking contact with its hardness.

When he came to, his hair was glued to the marble by a smear of dried blood. Touching his head, just above the left ear, he felt where his flesh had split. The pain made him wince as he attempted to raise himself onto the bed. His left ankle was swollen like an inflated bladder. It took three attempts to move onto the bed. Then he again slumped into unconsciousness.

When he next woke, it was daylight. The pain in neither his head nor his left ankle had lessened. He reached for the telephone by the Gordon's Gin. 'Luigi Ferraro here,' he said shakily into the handset. 'I have fallen. Can a doctor be sent?'

'Certainly, Captain Ferraro,' replied a deep, calming voice. 'It will be attended to as we speak. You may count on this.'

Perhaps fifteen minutes later, there was a knock on the door. Luigi shouted that he was unable to move. There was the sound of a key in the door, and the raffishly handsome man from the reception desk entered with a portly man of fair complexion and medium height. The portly man, wearing a rumpled linen suit, white shirt and bow tie, was introduced as Dr Cornelius Finucane.

Luigi explained that he had fallen over. The handsome man was horrified that such misfortune had befallen Captain Ferraro. The doctor said he would examine his patient forthwith. The handsome man departed. A card was handed to Luigi. It confirmed that the medical man was Cornelius Finucane, MB, BCh (Dublin), FRCS (Dublin) and FRCP (Edinburgh).

'Better have a look at you,' he said. 'Start with that nasty crack on the head.'

Dr Finucane had the most delicate, soft touch. He said that the injury would, thankfully, not require stitches. An examination of the heavily bruised ankle indicated torn tendons but no broken bones. A strapping bandage would be applied. 'Then crutches or a wheelchair, I think,' the doctor went on. 'We'll get a chap to wheel you around. The locals are quite the thing at wheeling people around. They lap it up — gives them a sense of purpose. Wheel you anywhere you want. Born to wheel, that's what I say. Their little eyes fairly sparkle when they're pushing people along.'

Luigi said crutches would be sufficient.

The medical man's eyes settled on the bottle of gin by the bedside. It was a quarter empty. 'Oh dear me,' he said. 'It's always a worry when I see a chap alone with an opened bottle. Leads to terrible things, you know. Down the slippery slope. Tell you what, I'll join you for a snifter and then I won't be worried that you're drinking alone. For some chaps, one drink is one too many and ten thousand drinks are never enough. Poor buggers just can't stop. It's an illness, you know, solitary drinking.'

He casually observed that Luigi did not have the look of a maritime man. 'But,' Dr Finucane said, 'that's none of my business. It will be our little secret. Call yourself Admiral if you want. Most people here have a secret or two. The head chap down at Hindley's Bank was cashiered for fiddling the books when he was in the Pay Corps during the nonsense with the Nips. Spent the money on some widow bint. Blurted it all out when he came to see me about some rather rumbly, runny tummy troubles. He thought he was on the verge of passing away. Probably wanted to make a clean breast of it. Him being on the fiddle, you know.

Doctor–patient confidentiality prevents me from saying more. Hush, hush. Loose lips and all that.'

There would be no charge for today's medical consultation and treatment. Dr Finucane said that his retainer from the management of the Galle Face would cover initial costs. There would, however, be a small fee for subsequent visits — daily visits, he stressed, as the head wound would have to be cleaned and dressed. The firmness of the bandage would have to be checked.

Four large snifters of gin later, the doctor left, promising to see about the crutches. 'I'll organise a few powders for the pain,' he added. 'They might knock you about a bit. I'll pop in tomorrow.'

Within the hour, the powders arrived along with a pair of crutches. The bed linen was changed. The swollen ankle was raised on two pillows. By the time darkness and the nightly rains had arrived, Luigi had taken two powders. He was unable to move. There was no pain from either head or ankle. He lay on his back. He wondered if this was what dying might be like: a not unpleasant drift into nothingness.

In the morning, a light breakfast was delivered to the room along with a fresh bottle of Gordon's Gin and a fresh ice bucket.

Dr Finucane arrived not long afterwards. 'Grand. You haven't opened the gin,' he said. 'Well done. A little bit of willpower sometimes does the trick. Nasty business, drinking alone. Now that I'm here we can have one together. First I'll check that head of yours.' He removed and replaced the bandage. 'Good. Coming along fine. Now the ankle. Good. Brought some books for you. Books and a map. Tell you all about Ceylon past and present.

Something to pass the time before you get back on your feet. I'll just have a glass with you and then I'm off. I'll have some more powders sent up.'

It was early afternoon when Dr Finucane left Luigi, having consumed most of the gin. Alone, in the fog of the painkilling powders, Luigi thought of his mother, Uncle Cesare, Leonardo and Father Gianni. He thought of his own bed, Tescano's narrow streets, the hills, the colours, the smell of bread from the Battaglia bakery, the cycling adventures.

He reached for the notepaper and pen on the bedside table. In a shaky hand he wrote to his mother, Uncle Cesare and Leonardo. He asked forgiveness for not having written earlier. He wrote in rambling detail of all that had happened since leaving Tescano. He would probably remain in Ceylon for a few weeks, he said; he had been told there was much to see. Then he would complete his voyage to Australia and thereafter return to Tescano, never to leave. His mother, Uncle Cesare and Leonardo should write to him at the hotel. He wondered if there was any news of Nunzia, or if the time for hope had passed. As a hazy afterthought he mentioned his fall and the injury to his ankle. *Do not worry*, he wrote. *It is not a serious condition. My foot is in the hands of a good doctor.*

Visits by the good doctor settled into something of a pattern. Gin would arrive each morning, followed soon afterwards by Dr Finucane. Luigi suspected Dr Finucane ordered the gin to be delivered to his patient and then, after a wait of a few minutes, presented himself in Luigi's room.

Some days, during those visits, the two sat talking on the west-facing balcony. Luigi spoke of cycling in the Tuscan hills.

Dr Finucane recommended that when Luigi was fully recovered he should undertake some two-wheeled excursions along the Colombo coastline: 'Have a good squizz at those books and maps and get some idea of what there is to see. When you're a bit more nimble you can see the sights and exercise that ankle.'

Luigi followed Dr Finucane's advice. Most afternoons and evenings during his recovery from the fall were spent buried in, and transported by, stories and descriptions of Ceylon and coral strands and spice traders, of great overgrown temples, and elephants with their mahouts. Every night, Luigi slipped into sleep reciting the new words he'd learned that day: mahout ... native bearer ... tiffin ... elevenses ... chums ... char.

After two weeks, Luigi gingerly took his first steps unaided by crutches since the tumble. While the swelling of the ankle had diminished considerably, it had not disappeared. Gin and Dudley's tonic was recommended as a beverage during recovery. It helped thin the blood and would prevent clotting around the bruised ankle. But the beverage should only be taken in company. Dr Finucane would continue to 'pop in' to ensure Luigi would not be driven to solitary drinking.

Luigi remained at the Galle Face for eight weeks. It was a stay he would ever recall with the greatest affection. He would remember how the rains came and went until, after one storm, the monsoon was over. Then days and days were spent cycling along the great coastal roads south of Colombo. Thoughts of Tescano and Nunzia retreated to the edge of consciousness. The warm sun and the scented wind tanned Luigi's face. The Hercules purred. This was freedom. Luigi Ferraro could go anywhere. He could do as he pleased. Sometimes he would imagine he was cycling with his Bersaglieri brothers-in-arms. Alone on the road, he would purse his lips and whistle four times. Four short, shrill whistles. Then he would shout at the top of his voice: 'Bicycle men — arrowhead formation.' Sometimes he would sing: '*Bicycle men are we, From snowy peak to sea, We smite the foe, we lay him low ...*'

Surely, Luigi believed, there was never such bliss in all of time.

CHAPTER NINETEEN

Attitude

Attitude is everything for a chap. Chest out, head held high. To be the part you only have to feel the part, dress the part. Look the world in the eye and hold your ground.

— **Dr Cornelius Finucane, MB, BCh (Dublin), FRCS (Dublin), FRCP (Edinburgh)**

Two days before Luigi was due to leave for Australia, a letter arrived from Uncle Cesare. There was great concern that Luigi had not written more often. He should never again cause his mother such worry. The angora shawls were beautiful. Luigi's mother wore one every Sunday when she attended Mass. There were favourable comments, after every Sunday Mass, on the quality of the shawls.

All in Tescano were in good health. Leonardo was particularly well since the arrival of a new headmaster for the Tescano school.

Guido Cantare, a widower, had arrived from Empoli with his daughter, Carla. She was a pretty girl, aged eighteen. She and Leonardo had spoken many times. Several times they had sat, respectably apart, by the fountain in the Piazza Valsini.

Jeremy Forsythe had written to say that he had received the locket sent from Istanbul and that it had been passed to Nunzia's father. There was, Uncle Cesare wrote, no more news of Nunzia. All in Tescano sent their affection and all awaited further news. Luigi should never forget that he was a son of Tescano.

Attached to the letter was a note from Jacob, sent from an address in Jerusalem. Jacob had rented a small shop in the older part of the city to establish his business. Jerusalem was not entirely to Jacob's liking. There was increasing trouble between the British and the Jews. However, there was a brighter side. Jacob had made a special friend. Her name was Rachel Samuelovich. She had come to Jerusalem from Europe one year earlier. Her family had perished in Poland in the war. She was alone in the world. For all the sadness she had lived through, Rachel was like a flower in full bloom. Jacob nurtured the idea that he and Rachel might, in time, grow closer. They were both orphans. Maybe they would become orphans together. He hoped Luigi would write to the address in Jerusalem.

Luigi replied without delay — one letter to Tescano and one to Jerusalem. To his mother and Uncle Cesare, he wrote:

When you receive this letter I will be on my way to Sydney, the main city in Australia. I am interested to hear that Tescano has a new headmaster who has a pretty daughter. Perhaps Leonardo will take her cycling. Tell

Father Gianni and the sisters I think of them. I am sad
that there is no news of Nunzia. I will write to Jacob this
very day.

As always, your loving son and nephew,

Luigi

Then, to Jacob, Luigi wrote:

I am pleased you are starting your business. Maybe you
can tell me more of your friend Rachel. Leonardo has
become a friend of the daughter of the new headmaster
in Tescano.
*   The Hercules is as good as ever and I have cycled to*
many beautiful places. The people here are very black.
Many are poor, but they are kind. I will soon be sailing to
Sydney. A ticket has been arranged.

Your friend Luigi

Dr Finucane had insisted on assisting Luigi to secure that
ticket. He had, he said, friends in the shipping office. With the
payment of a gratuity and two cases of gin to a never-identified
third party, first-class passage was purchased on the British and
Oriental passenger ship *Colonsay*. Dr Finucane said that he had
moved heaven and earth to obtain, for Luigi, the only 'decent'
stateroom available on the vessel. It had taken 'quite some doing'.
    The less decent accommodation, he explained, had been taken
by migrants and their families looking for a new life in Australia.

'It would never do for a chap like yourself, a Galle Face man, to journey on the lower decks with these people — working class, rough types, cheap labour for a nation of convicts ... Can't imagine what you'll find there. Kangaroos and coarse people, I suspect. I've never met an Australian who wasn't up to no good. A bunch of twisters and confidence tricksters, that's Australians for you. The convict blood, you see. No breeding. No history. Solitary drinkers to a man, I'd wager.'

On the morning of his departure for Australia, Luigi exchanged five gold coins at Hindley's. Arthur Holborn wished Luigi bon voyage. A firm handshake was accompanied by a long, rasping sound. Holborn's 'tummy pipes' continued to be troubled.

The account at the Galle Face was settled. Arrangements were in hand to transport Luigi and the Hercules to the *Colonsay* — which the handsome man who had first welcomed Luigi to the hotel assumed to be Captain Ferraro's new command.

The handsome man seemed genuinely sad when the two bade each other farewell. 'You are of a better class than many who reside with us,' he said in a slightly hushed voice. 'Most turn out to be stinkers of the first order, especially the English. They have no equal as stinkers. They have been born to be stinkers.'

On board the *Colonsay*, a white-uniformed porter escorted Luigi to his upper-deck stateroom. Late in the afternoon, Luigi watched Ceylon melt into the distance. He felt a fleeting melancholy as the vibration of the engines pushed Colombo out of sight. The city had been a waking dream of warmth and breezes and fragrances. For some hours Luigi watched, from the top deck, the wash from the stern of the *Colonsay*. Later, in the dusk and then the darkness, the wash was luminous green.

Returning to his stateroom, Luigi unpacked. He spread his gold coins and currency on the turned-down bed. He had six hundred English pounds from the sale of gold coins, some American dollars, fifty-six gold coins and nine gold bangles. By no means were the financial straits dire. But they were narrower than they had been. The weeks at the Galle Face had not been inexpensive. Luigi resolved that there would be no fancy hotels in Australia and no first-class stateroom on the return voyage. He would seek modest lodgings in Sydney and on his further travels.

For all the comforts of the *Colonsay* and the stateroom, Luigi's voyage from Colombo to Sydney was miserable. Two days out from the scented isle, the ocean erupted in all its whitecapped fury. Not even the roughness of the latter stages of the journey on the *Seringapatam* could have prepared Luigi for this. There were days when there was no going back and no going forward, until finally, three days out from Sydney, the sea calmed once more and the misery was over.

The *Colonsay* docked in Sydney at eleven o'clock on a Tuesday morning. The sky was as blue as the skies over Livorno. Luigi scanned the shoreline and saw neither crocodiles nor cowboys. Nor were there any kangaroos to be seen. The berthing was slick, professional. Great hawsers knitted the ship to the quay. Gangways were lowered.

Luigi was directed towards customs and immigration desks in a huge waterfront shed. A sign on the shed proclaimed: *Australia welcomes New Australians.* Luigi's Hercules and luggage were inspected. A big red-haired man stamped Luigi's passport.

'You'll be right at home, mate,' he said. 'The place is filling up with Eyeties.' Then his eyes narrowed. 'Well, she's all yours. On your bike, Luigi.'

The new arrival felt welcome. The red-haired man had called him by his first name.

Luigi slipped his passport into his waistband and wheeled his bicycle through the massive sliding doors of the shed. Outside, he pushed the Hercules past a notice that said: *No standing at any time.* For several hours he walked. It would not do to break the law on his first day in Australia. If there was no standing at any time, there was no standing at any time. What a strange place this was.

Luigi spent his first nights in Sydney at a hotel in Annandale called The Plucky Digger. He arrived at the hotel after walking and wheeling the Hercules until it was late afternoon. A sign outside said there were rooms to let. He went inside to a public bar filled with men in undershirts. Australians, Luigi later learned, called these garments singlets. None wore the eau de cologne favoured by Jeremy Forsythe. The men looked like devils and they bellowed like pigs. When Luigi booked his lodgings, the Hercules was stored in a room with barrels of beer.

After three nights at The Plucky Digger, Luigi moved to a boarding house nearby. The woman who ran it, the portly and grey-haired Widow O'Connor, told Luigi she only took in Catholic boarders. And since Luigi was Italian, he was obviously a good Catholic. The Widow O'Connor would not have a Protestant under her roof for love or money. A fortnightly rent, payable in advance, was agreed. Luigi's small room was clean and the sheets were changed once a week. There was a crucifix nailed to the wall above the single bed. There was no shortage of food, on which fact Luigi remarked. He told the Widow O'Connor of the war-time food rationing in Italy, even when the fighting had ended. She said in Australia there was plenty of good, plain food — chops and steak and chicken and sausages and mince and mutton and pork and potatoes and carrots and pies. Australians liked pies. 'You'll get none of your fancy macaroni baloney under this roof,' she added.

Annandale, Luigi felt, had neither the excitement and swirling movement of the streets of Istanbul nor the scents and colours of Ceylon. It had one wide thoroughfare and a sprinkling of moderately grand houses. In the main, though, it was a place of tightly packed terrace houses. It was drab, but it would do, he decided. It was, after all, only the starting place, the point of departure for his exploration of Australia. The place of open space. The place in the books.

In those first weeks lodging with the Widow O'Connor, Luigi left the boarding house each morning on the Hercules. He rode everywhere — through the city and beyond to the west, towards the mountains. He rode around the north and south shores of the harbour. He rode to the cliffs at the Heads and faced an ocean that went on forever. Then, his back to the water, he looked at a land that went on forever. He resolved to see all of it.

Two months to the day after his arrival, Luigi left Sydney. He had told the Widow O'Connor he intended to cycle to the furthest-away point in Australia. The Widow O'Connor said that all Luigi had to do was to find a road that led north and to keep going until it stopped. Luigi would be welcome at the boarding house if he ever returned to Sydney.

The Widow O'Connor said Luigi should write to his mother, should attend Mass regularly and should avoid drinking, gambling and loose ways. God saw everything. All was written down and there was a day of reckoning for every sin. One day, Luigi would stand before his Maker. The fires of Hell never cooled, she said, and God wasn't easily taken in by the excuses of sinners.

On the day he left Sydney, Luigi rode and rode and rode for hours before he was in what Australians called 'the bush'. As he crossed the great Hawkesbury River, his spirits lifted. He had never seen such colours before. These were Australian colours. In some places the afternoon hills were purple and the sky was a shade of pale, almost transparent, blue. There were great red trees, grey trees, and trees that had been blackened by fire. Some trees gave off a scent that was sharp in Luigi's nostrils. There were birds everywhere. They shouted and screamed and screeched and soared and swirled — flashes of silver and yellow and mottled brown and red and green.

Most days, heading north, Luigi journeyed quite slowly, steadily. There was no hurry, no sense of urgency. He was free to travel as he wished. Within, there was a sensation — that boyhood sensation — of lightness, disconnectedness from all that had gone before. This was what he had craved for so long.

Here and there were roadside stalls and Luigi would stop to buy what fruit he could carry. The most he would journey in one day was a hundred kilometres. He did not use the engine all of the time. If the wind was behind him he would pedal.

There were, to Luigi, great distances between towns and villages on the road north. Unlike Tuscany where a few hours by foot or bicycle would get you to the next village, in Australia there could, even travelling by motorised bicycle, be a whole day between settlements. He might ride an entire day and see only a few dozen passing cars and a few dozen trucks. He would not, on the journey north, see another bicycle. Nor would he see a cowboy or a crocodile.

Reaching a town or a village in the late afternoon, he stopped for the night, sometimes two nights. Every town or village had at least one hotel. The names of these hotels intrigued Luigi: the Gay Digger, the Happy Soldier, the Bold Anzac, the Heroes' Rest, the Volunteer Arms, the Valiant Sappers, the Plucky Gunners, the Sacred Shore. He wondered if the army in Australia owned every hotel. Or perhaps wounded Australian soldiers were given money to buy hotels, just as Regimental Sergeant-Major Benny 'Mountain Man' Marconi had been given money to establish the Trattoria Bersaglieri.

Three times, unable to reach a settlement by nightfall, he slept by the roadside. These were uncomfortable, largely sleepless nights of strange noises and biting insects.

It was after the third of these uncomfortable nights that Luigi reached Black Bay. There was a soporific air to the place. Luigi felt this calm, this quietness as he cycled along Black Bay's single tar-sealed street. Rip Van Winkle might easily have lived there. The settlement had a shop, a garage that sold petrol, a few dozen houses, a one-teacher school, and a lighthouse on the steepness of Black Cape. It also had a small hotel, the Fallen Comrade.

Luigi took a room at the Fallen Comrade, paying in advance — first for two nights, then for another three. He was the only paying guest at the hotel and he slept, under a mosquito net, in a room that opened onto a verandah. From the single bed he could see the stars and the moon and wisps of cloud. He could hear the gurgle of the arriving and retreating waves. There was a sense of enchantment in this place, a feeling of comfort and safety.

Black Bay was what Luigi wanted Australia to be. It was better than the books he'd read in his boyhood.

CHAPTER TWENTY

Perspective

All of our time here is a journey. Point A leads to Point B, just like a race. Sometimes you slow down. You ease off and you get some sort of perspective and what was and what is and what lies ahead are clearer.

— Declan Flatley, *From the Podium to the Pit: A Cyclist's Ride from Hell* (privately published), Belfast, 1984

Black Bay became Luigi's comfortable cocoon. It was pretty. It was friendly. It was a place where time passed easily, seamlessly. Days tumbled into days and weeks folded into weeks.

During his first week in Black Bay, Luigi met Alfie 'Alamein' Arkwright, who'd served in the Western Desert campaigns in North Africa. Luigi had gone to Alfie's garage to ask if he could use some tools. After its long trip north, the Hercules was in need of stripping down.

There was an immediate camaraderie, an easy openness between the two men. When Luigi introduced himself, Alfie recognised the accent. Alfie liked the Italians he'd met in North Africa, he told Luigi. 'Bloody gents. Decent blokes, mostly. Didn't want a bar of the war. Happy as Larry when they surrendered to us. Wouldn't stop yabbering, poor buggers. The bloody Germans, though, they wanted a scrap. Kraut mongrels with their blond hair and blue eyes. Master race my bum — excuse the French. We were under Montgomery — Monty. Looked after his men, he did. That's his picture over there.' He pointed to a photograph pinned to a wall above a workbench. Then he snapped to attention and saluted. 'Bloody gent if ever there was one,' he said, a smile on his face.

Alfie had returned from active service deaf in one ear and minus his left leg — 'Rommel nearly did for me' — but with a job for life when his father, Les 'Lone Pine' Arkwright, died, leaving Alfie the family garage. 'Can't imagine living anywhere else,' he said. 'I saw the world during the war and you can have it. Foreigners and bloody deserts, that's what overseas is. No offence to you. Anyhow, I came back and I'll stay back. They'll take me out of here in a box. What about you? What brings you here?'

Luigi had been in the war, too. He recounted his brushes with the Hun, his time in the hills with the Partisans, the capture and disappearance of Nunzia. He recounted, briefly, how he'd built motorised bicycles and had worked in Uncle Cesare's smithy.

Alfie was impressed. Luigi had 'done his bit'. He said Luigi could borrow whatever tools he wanted — and, by the way, did he need a bit of work, a day here and there? Alfie could always use a hand. 'Come to think of it,' he said, 'I could always use another leg — a real one, not this wooden bugger. Ha. Ha. Ha. Another leg. Ha. Ha.'

Luigi said a bit of work would be just fine.

'You'll do,' Alfie said. 'We might even end up mates.' Luigi could live in the shed behind the workshop, Alfie suggested, and come and go as he pleased. It would be cheaper than staying at the Fallen Comrade, and the Hercules would be under cover and under lock and key. 'Not that lock and key matters. Who'd want to pinch it? Couldn't get away fast enough,' Alfie said. 'Ha. Ha.'

Luigi immediately warmed to Alfie, just as he'd warmed to Black Bay and its open spaces and fresh breezes, and — save for the ocean's roar and the squeal of seabirds — its quietness. Life in Black Bay was unhurried. Alfie said that this was because when God made time, He made plenty of it. Alfie said there was never a wrong time for a yarn. There was never a wrong time to stretch the legs. 'You never know who you'll bump into.'

Most mornings, Luigi used some of that abundance of time to walk the length of Black Bay's half-moon beach. On one slow stroll, he met Bruce 'Bullseye' Bertrand, and thereafter the two strolled together.

Bullseye was in his late seventies, the oldest man in the district. Yet for all his years, he was fighting fit and sharp as a tack. He'd been a sniper with the Colonial Infantry during the Boer War. 'Crack shot, I was,' he'd say. 'Crack shot. When I got a Dutchy in my sights he didn't go home for tea. It was like shooting crows on a telephone line. Never fired a bullet that didn't send a Dutchy to the Big Windmill in the Sky.' Back from the Boer War and too old for the Great War, Bullseye had for most of his days fished the waters up and down the coast from Black Bay. When the fish were elsewhere, he shot rabbits and sold them, skinned and dressed. 'These days,' he said, 'I take it nice and easy. A bit of a stroll then a couple of beers and then a snooze. Second verse same as the first.'

Luigi learned much from Bullseye on their walks along the beach. He learned that in Australia there were many creatures never named in the Tescano school's small collection of books. There was a rat that had a gold tooth. Another rat ran up drainpipes, and there was a dog that had two tails. Some people were two slices short of a loaf, while others wouldn't know their arse from their elbow.

On days when he wasn't working with Alfie or talking with Bullseye or cycling the coastal tracks, Luigi would sit, sipping homemade lemonade, on the verandah of the Black Bay general store. It was run by two spinster sisters, the twins Hettie and Betty Pretty, both in their sixties.

Miss Hettie and Miss Betty had taken what they called a 'shine' to Luigi when, passing by, he saw Miss Hettie holding a ladder while Miss Betty reached to scoop leaves from roof gutters. 'Please,' Luigi had said, 'let me help. This is not the work of ladies.' They were charmed in the instant. Such kindness, they said. And from that instant, they pampered Luigi with lemonade and home-baked biscuits. Without knowing it, they flirted with the newcomer. They asked, time and time again, for accounts of his travels. The sisters had never been further afield than Sydney. As children they'd been taken, four times, to the city's Royal Easter Show. In more than sixty years they'd spent fewer than thirty days out of Black Bay. Miss Hettie said that everything was so far away. Sydney was pleasant enough but it should have been built closer to Black Bay. The government never got anything right. Miss Betty agreed.

Luigi told the sisters tales of Tuscany and the Holy Land and Ceylon and Istanbul. The sisters wondered if the Turks in Istanbul had ever expressed any regret over how they'd shot Australians at Gallipoli. Luigi said he was sure the Turks felt deep sorrow at how they'd cast Australians from their shores. He said the Turks he'd met in Istanbul were very welcoming of strangers. Miss Betty and Miss Hettie were interested to hear that. They speculated that the Turks who'd fired on 'our boys' at Gallipoli had probably 'fallen in with a bad crowd'. It was very easily done, they believed.

Every few weeks, Luigi wrote letters to his mother and Uncle Cesare, and every few weeks he received replies. Luigi wrote of Black Bay and his work with Alfie. There was always something to be fixed — a car or a lawnmower engine or, now and then, a motorbike or a tractor from one of the farms beyond Black Bay. Two or three times a week, he and Alfie played dominoes and darts after work in the Fallen Comrade. Alfie was teaching Luigi to drive a car; according to Alfie, a mechanic who couldn't drive wasn't worth a cracker. What, exactly, a cracker might be mystified Luigi.

The letters from Tescano said that Father Gianni always mentioned Luigi in his Sunday prayers. Leonardo and Carla, the daughter of the new Tescano headmaster, had become close, and there was talk in Tescano that the two would become closer. The last few words were underlined. Leonardo often asked for news of Luigi and, just as often, said he would write to him. But

Leonardo had never been one for writing letters. The sisters were still riding their bicycles. Tescano was as Tescano had always been. There had been no more letters from Jacob. However, Jeremy Forsythe visited Tescano every few months. Sometimes he stayed in Luigi's old room, and other times he stayed in the presbytery with Father Gianni. On every visit, Jeremy talked about one day living in Tescano. It would be a fine place to end his days. Uncle Cesare and Luigi's mother felt Jeremy should avoid talking about ending his days anywhere. Such talk brought bad luck. But since the business of living in Tescano had been mentioned, perhaps Luigi should think about living in Tescano, too. He'd had his adventure now. There was much to be done in the smithy and Uncle Cesare was not getting any younger.

The pointed tone of the admonitions that his return was awaited and expected unsettled Luigi. His written response was a mixture of half-truth and prevarication. He was, he wrote, working most days with Alfie in his garage. Some days he worked at the Black Bay general store. Miss Hettie and Miss Betty were not in the best of health and they might not be in the best of health for some time. Luigi could not turn away from people who had shown him great kindness. However, he promised: *When all is settled here and I am not needed, I will return to Sydney and then I will buy a ticket to Italy. It is a journey of some weeks from Sydney to Naples or Genoa. Then I will take the train to Florence and I will cycle to Tescano.*

In truth, though, Luigi was torn. Of course he would return to Tescano ... eventually. But, in the way of many travellers, he was not yet ready to return to what he had left behind. And so he remained in Black Bay, and the seasons flowed like the waters of a stream: sometimes sparkling, sometimes quick, sometimes languid, sometimes lazy. Autumn was a sullen season of shortening days and crisp evenings. Winter gave way to the astringent breezes of spring. Then the long summer furnace lingered until the unsettled autumn days and evenings returned.

For Luigi, the coastal settlement delivered an easy and uncluttered life. There were his morning walks with Bullseye. There were afternoons watching, from the dunes, the seasonal migration of whales beyond the coastal breakers. There were bicycle rides along clifftop tracks. There was a variety of work to fill some hours and days — a few days' work with Alfie, a day behind the counter of the general store, a day here and there as a cleaner and yardman at the Fallen Comrade.

On one day each year, 25 April, the hotel became the focus of all attention in Black Bay. It was where the Anzac Day march began and ended. For at least a month beforehand, Alfie and Bullseye talked of little else.

There was also preparation. A military occasion deserved military planning. The route — the same one every year — was walked and rewalked and timed. The two flags, Australian and British, stored in Alfie's garage were ironed. Alfie's only suit was pressed too. Frayed shoelaces were blackened.

There was much speculation beforehand on the likelihood of rain on the sacred day, and on the prevailing winds. The possibility of high humidity concerned Alfie, too. High humidity caused chafing where artificial limb met scarred flesh below the knee. Chafing was no small matter for a marching man.

There was, too, the matter of Luigi's place in the march. He had served with the Partisans against the Germans. He deserved, Alfie said, to be in this special gathering of comrades.

Luigi said he was honoured to be counted as a comrade. But, sadly, he would not be in Black Bay for the big day. He would journey towards Sydney one week before the march.

His decision had been some months in the making. His heart had entertained the notion that he might stay in Black Bay for much longer, but his head had said otherwise. His mother and Uncle Cesare awaited his return to Tescano. There was much to be done in the smithy and Uncle Cesare was not getting any younger. With a resigned sigh and a shrug he told Alfie: 'The longer I delay, the harder it gets to leave. I will just have to imagine the march.'

Alfie wouldn't hear of it. 'It's the big day around these parts. An extra week is neither here nor there. Stay for the day and then get on your bike.'

Luigi was easily persuaded. His heart prevailed over his head.

The procession was led by a piper and a drummer, two farmers from the hills behind the coastal settlement. Like Alfie, they'd served in North Africa during the Second World War. Among the ranks of the marchers from the district were six veterans of the First World War. They had all fought in the trenches of northern France. 'Poor buggers,' said Alfie. 'They had it rough.'

The group assembled at the Fallen Comrade and marched the length of the main street three times. As a veteran of the Boer War, Bullseye led the procession. Luigi stepped out with Alfie. The piper, kilt swaying, played a march, 'The Black Bear', a spirited, jaunty air — perhaps a shade too brisk for the older marchers.

'This tune was the last thing I heard at Alamein,' Alfie said, 'before Rommel did for my leg. The regimental piper was out there in front, brave sod. And we just followed. Well, you would … a tune like that and you'd march to the end of the world.' He made a gargling sound, imitating the bagpipes, and said that the skirl of the pipes transformed mere men into warriors. Foes scattered in the face of these heroes.

Though he said nothing, Luigi suspected that it was the sound the enemies were fleeing, not the warriors.

The marchers, heads high, chests puffed out, strode past the garage and the general store, cheered by perhaps two dozen schoolchildren and a cluster of locals. Miss Hettie and Miss Betty applauded from the verandah of their store and waved a flag.

Luigi was unsettled by the cheering and the flag-waving. He thought of Ancona and the bombing and the Partisan raid on the train and the murderous attacks on fleeing Germans. He thought of the disappearance of Nunzia and the unimaginable cruelties she must have endured. He thought that, really, war was best forgotten. But this was not, of course, the time or the place to express such thoughts.

The marchers halted on the steps of the Fallen Comrade. The piper played a lament, 'The Dark Island', then led Alfie, Bullseye, Luigi and the dozen other marchers to the bar. Neat rum was the order of the day until the bar finally fell silent in the early evening.

In the garage, Alfie, memories unlocked by rum, sat with Luigi. 'You'd know,' Alfie said. 'It was bloody terrible. You'd know that. You'd have to. Not the mateship — I had the best of mates — but the noise and the screams and the fear … the bloody fear. You'd get in close and you'd hear the most frightening words in the world: *Fix bayonets*. Then it was on, really on. Jesus, it was horrible.

'Men wet themselves. Some ran away, poor sods. It wasn't their fault. There was blood and bits of bodies everywhere you looked. For days after a big show, blokes would curl up in a ball and cry. I still get the nightmares and I still think, sometimes, I would have been better off dead. Better off bloody dead and buried. At least it would be finished.'

Tears streamed down Alfie's face. Choking sobs shook his body. Then, gathering himself together, he said: 'I'm sorry, mate. It gets to me every so often. Now, not a word about this to anybody. Blokes shouldn't be carrying on like this.'

Luigi shook his head. 'Carry on all you want, Alfie,' he said. 'We're mates. You just said so.' In Black Bay, Luigi had learned that to be a mate, a real mate, was to be held in high regard.

In the morning, Luigi readied himself for his return to Sydney. He ate breakfast with Alfie, Bullseye and the Misses Hettie and Betty on the verandah of the general store. They would miss Luigi. Of course, he was welcome back any time. He was as good as a local.

Luigi told them that he would ride the Hercules south. There would be stops along the way, a few days here and a few days there. Then Sydney and a passage to Naples or Genoa, and then … and then Tescano. His Australian adventure was close to its end. He wished it could be otherwise.

Luigi exchanged mock-heroic salutes with Bullseye and Alfie, and embraced the Misses Hettie and Betty. They hoped Luigi would write. Bugger writing, said Alfie, Luigi should just turn up if ever he was in the district. Then Luigi was on the road, heading south, the wind pushing back his hair and reddening his face. The Hercules, stripped and reassembled and serviced for the journey, purred.

Within Luigi, as he rode, there was no sense of excitement at the prospect of a return to Tescano. He was not imagining the stories he would tell to his mother and Uncle Cesare and Leonardo and Father Gianni, or the sisters at the Convent of Santa Teresa. Nor was he imagining himself as an old man, Tescano's wise, living legend who had journeyed to the furthest-away places and then returned to the Tuscan hills to tell his tales. Instead, there was a sense of dullness, an empty, lost sensation.

He was in a no-man's-land between familiar places — between Black Bay and Tescano. There was sadness, perhaps grief, in the leaving of Black Bay. And there was a tremor of trepidation at the prospect of returning to Tescano, and the memories of Nunzia and their chaste first kiss in those surrounding hills. Tescano, Luigi suspected, would fold over him and it would be as if he had never been away.

Three days after Luigi left Black Bay, a letter arrived there. It was addressed to Luigi Ferraro, care of Alfie's Garage, Black Bay, New South Wales, Australia. Luigi's mother's name and address were on the reverse of the envelope. The letter contained news of Jacob.

Alfie returned the letter, unopened, to its sender. Luigi had left no forwarding address.

CHAPTER TWENTY-ONE

Chance

*I was ten seconds behind the Austrian rider, Zimmer.
There was no way I could win. Then, a magpie
swooped. Zimmer swerved and fell off his bike. The
race was mine. Chance, everything in life is chance.*
— **Patrick Gorman,** *The Luck of the Irish,* 1992

On the ride back to Sydney, the length of Luigi's days in the
saddle varied. When the distance between towns and settlements
was short, his day on the bike was short. When the distances
were longer, Luigi spent longer in the saddle. He did not spend
any nights in the open, by the roadside, as he had done on his
journey north. The bush by day was preferable to the bush by
night.

When the wind was behind him and the distance to be
covered was modest, Luigi cut the engine on the Hercules and
rode at an easy, steady pace. For longer distances, he engaged the

engine and powered through the hours of light, the astringent wind in his face.

He would miss this furthest-away place. He would miss the colours and the fragrances.

There were stops of one or two nights at Evans Head, Yamba, Grafton, Coffs Harbour, Nambucca Heads, South West Rocks, Hat Head, Winkle Point, Tuncurry and Woy Woy. The journey was unhurried. It was an experience to be savoured. Luigi was collecting memories. He told himself he would never pass this way again. He was going home to Tescano. He had made a start.

Sixteen days after leaving Black Bay, Luigi was in Sydney. There, he again took lodgings with the Widow O'Connor. Her eyes widened and her jaw dropped when she answered Luigi's knock on the door. 'Holy Mother,' she said, crossing herself. 'Here's me thinking you were long gone back to Italy or cold in the grave with that bicycle of yours. And here you are, large as life itself. But not so large that you couldn't do with a good feed. A haircut and a close shave wouldn't go astray, either. There's a bit of the bandit look about you, and that's no lie. A good bath and a scrub, that's what you need. Come in before people see you looking like God alone knows what.'

Luigi's old room was there for the taking. Of course, it would be a few shillings more than the last time. Nothing was cheap these days. 'And I've had the phone put on since you were last here,' the Widow O'Connor added. 'Tuppence for calls going out and a penny for calls coming in — not that you'd have many of those, you being a foreigner.'

The kettle was close to boiling. She was expecting a visitor. The new priest, Father John Macguire from the Church of Saint

Derla of the Dispossessed — 'not three streets from here' — would be along any minute for a cup of tea. 'The last one, Father Rohan Rafferty, passed away while yourself was on your travels ... not that you look the better for them, either,' she said. 'Father Rafferty was called to glory, as they say, this past while. He was never one for getting out and about, what with his bad hip and his trembles of a morning at Mass, poor soul. Father Macguire, now, he's out and about all the time. He's a bicycle man like yourself. Cycles everywhere. Well, not this last couple of weeks. Something wrong with the bike, so he tells me.'

In the Widow O'Connor's front room the questions came in torrents. Where had Luigi been? Had he been writing to his mother? What was he doing back in Sydney? Had he been a regular at Mass? And had he been working? The world was no place for idlers. By the way, the rent for the room would need to be paid two weeks in advance. There and then would be just fine. Oh, but it was grand to see him. And he was going back to Italy ... about time, so it was. His poor mother must have been beside herself while Luigi was on his gallivanting.

The spray of questions was interrupted by the arrival of Father Macguire, a Dubliner who could have been a tidy middleweight boxer in his day: broad shoulders, strong arms, big hands, some scar tissue above both eyes, and a nose that had been broken more than once. The luxuriance of the hair in his nostrils and ears suggested he was in his mid-sixties. His black suit was shiny from wear. He smelled of cigarette smoke and incense. A cup of nice strong tea, as ever, would be just grand, he said to the Widow O'Connor. And maybe a glass of dry sherry. Walking fairly dried up the throat. Of course he'd heard of Luigi. The

Widow O'Connor had mentioned 'the young Eyetie with the bicycle' more than once. Father John had a bicycle himself. But there was some trouble with the brakes … and the brake shoes … and the chain was loose … and there was a spoke or two missing.

'Wear and tear, for sure,' the Widow O'Connor said. 'There's you out there at all hours looking after the flock. Stopping the fallen from falling too far. You're a saint, Father John. A saint. There's not many around here that deserves the likes of you.'

Father John said that God's work, like other good work, was its own reward. Now, about that dry sherry …

He turned to Luigi. The parish bicycle could certainly do with some good work, he said, some expert attention. Luigi obviously knew about bikes and fixing them. He'd never been much of a man with his hands, he confided — apart from his amateur boxing days, back when he was a seminarian in Dublin. 'Boxing kept the mind and the hands off other matters.'

The Widow O'Connor flushed. The dry sherry would be right there. She was pouring it right now. That very second.

Father John, lighting a cigarette, wondered if Luigi might find the time to have a look at his bicycle. It was at the presbytery, 'just round the corner and a bit further on'. The Widow O'Connor said that nothing would be too much trouble for Luigi. He'd be delighted to pop round. And while he was there, the Widow O'Connor was certain, he'd be just as delighted to have Father John hear his Confession.

Father John said the day after tomorrow, in the morning, would do just the trick. Luigi said that seemed fine.

Between then and now he would visit shipping offices in the city to arrange his return to Italy. Ships carrying passengers from

Australia to Italy probably left every week, maybe even every few days.

Yet Luigi's visits the next day to half a dozen shipping offices proved frustrating. Berths on passenger-carrying cargo ships were booked several months in advance, while the passenger-only ships that left from Sydney once or twice a month were generally bound for Britain, not Italy. The next one sailing to Genoa — the *Stella Brindisi* — would be leaving in four weeks. Unfortunately, Luigi was told by the desk clerk at the offices of the Garibaldi Shipping Line, the last berth had been sold that very day. If only he'd been a few hours earlier. But berths were available aboard the *Stella Torino*, to Genoa, in nine weeks. A deposit, non-refundable, could be made there and then on a 'superior class' single cabin — 'not quite first class but certainly a bit above second class, and that's what you pay for, a better class of shipmates,' the desk clerk advised. No cheaper berths were available. The balance would be due two weeks before departure.

The deposit was paid. Luigi barely concealed his resentment as he pushed the notes across the counter. The cost was not an issue, and the balance would be more than covered by the sale of the gold coins that remained stitched into the band of his hat and concealed in his belt. It was the delay — nine whole weeks — that irked him. He had taken his time on the journey south from Black Bay, slowly becoming ready to leave, ready to return to another life. But now the grand adventure was behind him. There should be no lingering end. There should be no miserable wait, no counting the weeks.

The Widow O'Connor sensed Luigi's simmering frustration when he returned to the lodgings. 'You've the look of a man who's lost a pound and found a shilling,' she said. 'Out with it or it'll burn a hole in your soul.' He told her of the delay. Well, she said, if he had to wait all those weeks, he had to wait all those weeks. It was God's will. Some good always came out of God's will. Wasn't it possible that the boat he couldn't get on might sink, and where would Luigi be then? Lost at sea and his mother, poor soul, with no body to bury. Imagine how she would feel.

Now, about the room, the Widow O'Connor said: since Luigi would be there a bit longer he might want to pay a month in advance. That would be more convenient for all concerned. 'Saves you settling up every two weeks,' she added. 'Gives you a bit more time to yourself. You'll be busy getting yourself ready for that big trip ahead of you. A fair bit to do, no question of that.'

That night, Luigi wrote to his mother and Uncle Cesare, telling them of his ticket to Genoa. By the time his letter reached Tescano, he wrote, he would be close to leaving, and he would be gone before any reply from Tescano could reach Sydney. He would write to them again on the day of his departure. They would know, then, when he would arrive in Italy. To all in Tescano, Luigi sent his dearest wishes.

In the morning, Luigi went to Father John's presbytery. A bicycle leaned against the wall of the hallway that led to the kitchen. In the kitchen, Father John stubbed a Sweet Afton cigarette out in an overflowing ashtray. Then he immediately lit another. 'Three or four in a row always clear the phlegm first thing of a morning,' he told Luigi.

Nodding at the overflowing ashtray and then at the unwashed dishes in the sink, he said that his housekeeper had been 'poorly' these past few days. 'Near crippled by the sciatica,' he explained.

However, she'd be back by the weekend and she'd tidy things up. 'I'd do it myself but she likes to feel she's needed. She says that it wouldn't do to have a priest emptying ashtrays and washing the dishes when there's souls to be saved. And wouldn't I be the selfish one to stand in the way of her regard for the work of a man of the cloth?'

Father John asked Luigi to cast his expert eyes and lay his expert hands on the bicycle in the hallway. A cursory examination showed that new tyres were required, the chain should be tightened, and brake pads and brake shoes needed to be replaced, and some spokes, too. These parts would have to be bought, Luigi said. Father John frowned; there wasn't a bicycle shop for miles, at least not one that he knew of. But there was another bicycle in the presbytery shed. It hadn't been on the road for a long while. 'Not since one night when I was coming back from a burial and fell off. A bit too much of the unholy spirit,' Father John confessed, coughing. 'Anyhow, maybe there's parts you could use.'

The second bicycle was examined. The front forks and the back wheel were buckled beyond repair, but the tyres were sound, as were the brake pads. Spokes could be removed from the front wheel. It would take time, though, Luigi explained. Spokes were tricky. Brake shoes, too. The bicycle to be repaired should be stripped down, cleaned and reassembled. Then there would be a test ride and then, almost certainly, further adjustments. The positioning of the saddle was most important. Luigi did not elaborate on this latter point. Father John, after all, was a priest.

Luigi spent the remainder of the day, until late afternoon, stripping down and cleaning the bicycle to be repaired. When he returned the following morning to continue the work, there were three unfamiliar bicycles in the presbytery kitchen. Some of Father John's older parishioners had ridden to Mass the previous evening, the priest explained. 'Well, I'd barely mentioned, in passing, that this lovely young Italian bicycle man from the Widow O'Connor's was sorting out my bicycle when three of the flock, God bless them, wondered if you might be prevailed upon to have a look at *their* bicycles. So here you are; what do you say?'

That was how it began. In the weeks that followed, Luigi spent every day, until late afternoon, repairing bicycles at the presbytery of Saint Derla of the Dispossessed. No sooner had one bicycle been repaired than another would arrive. The word had spread across the congregation — 'faster than lightning from the heavens,' said Father John — that an Italian bicycle man of the very first order was repairing bicycles for a small donation to the church. Father John was astonished at how fast word could spread. If the Word of God could spread at even half that speed he would have no concerns for the immortal souls of the congregation of Saint Derla of the Dispossessed.

When Luigi arrived back from the presbytery in the afternoon, the Widow O'Connor was usually preparing to leave for Mass. Every evening, when she returned, she was beaming. That she'd offered the expertise of 'her Eyetie lodger' to cycling members of Father John's flock was a matter of favourable comment and praise. Her status at the Church of Saint Derla of the Dispossessed had risen substantially.

Often, Father John watched as Luigi worked. 'A handy young man like yourself,' he said more than once, 'could do worse than set up his own bicycle shop.'

Sometimes he encouraged Luigi to tell him about Tescano and his adventures on the land and sea journey to Australia. 'What a tale to tell,' Father John said when Luigi had finished his account. 'What a tale, indeed. It's a tale that yourself should write down one day ... all of these places you've seen! And here's me, never set foot outside Australia since I came out here from the seminary in Dublin. That wasn't yesterday, you know — it wasn't even the day before yesterday.'

Three weeks before Luigi's intended departure on the *Stella Torino*, and during what had become the regular morning tea break at the presbytery, Luigi asked if he might consult with Father John on a confidential matter. Father John said that nothing was too delicate for a priest who ministered to the congregation of the Church of Saint Derla of the Dispossessed. 'There's no sin I haven't heard about in Confession around here,' Father John said. 'Some of the stories would even curl the hair of a man of the world like yourself. Now, what particular sin did you have in mind — carnal, original, debauched or just run-of-the-mill?'

Luigi shook his head. The confidential matter related to money. He had some coins, gold coins, to sell. Their sale would pay for the balance owing on the berth to Genoa. Might Father John suggest a reliable buyer?

The priest pondered the question, looking momentarily wistful. 'I've never had to take care of such matters — more's the pity. The vows of poverty aren't all they're cracked up to be. And we'll stay away from talk of vows of chastity. Now, in the city, near the Town Hall, there's an arcade. The Queen Victoria Arcade. There would have to be some fancy jeweller or goldsmith there.' Directions were offered. Luigi said he would attend to the matter the following day.

It was late morning when Luigi arrived, on the Hercules, at the Queen Victoria Arcade. A sign proclaimed that the arcade was: *THE place in Sydney for fine goods, artworks, bespoke clothing and watches and jewellery.* Luigi touched his hat and his belt. He felt the outline of the gold coins he intended to sell. He wheeled the Hercules inside.

At the far end of the arcade, one particular shopfront shone and sparkled. Luigi quickened his pace. He parked the bicycle against the banister of a staircase that led to a mezzanine floor. Then he bent in close to the window of the shimmering shopfront. Behind the glass, reflections danced from rings to bracelets to necklaces to pendants to chains. He leaned closer, nose almost touching the glass, squinting at one particular piece that had caught his eye — a small gold locket, pearls on every corner. It was an old, unusual piece. It looked just like some of the pieces he'd seen in the Grand Bazaar in Istanbul.

Inside the shop, a man standing behind the counter looked up, then moved quickly towards the door. Luigi, his eyes fixed on the small gold locket, was oblivious to the man's swift, deliberate movement.

The door opened. A bell tinkled. Luigi turned. Eyes met eyes. The past and the present collided. There was silence and then a wordless, strong embrace. A passer-by veered to avoid the hugging men. 'Wogs,' she said, sotto voce.

The wordless hold continued below a sign suspended just above the glittering window display. The sign said: *Jacob Zevi, Jeweller and Watchmaker.*

Finally, each stepped back from the embrace and looked at the other. The two whooped like banshees, then Jacob whirled Luigi into the shop and through to a small workshop and office.

The two sat, then stood, then sat, then embraced again. Luigi's heart raced. This was impossible! Jacob was here, in Sydney. Here in front of him. Jacob Zevi!

Luigi poured out his story, higgledy-piggledy. The journey north. The cycling in Ceylon. The bicycle repairs for Father John. The coins to be sold for the passage to Genoa on the *Stella Torino*. The journey south. Black Bay. The lodgings with the Widow O'Connor. There was no order in anything Luigi said.

Jacob ruffled Luigi's hair. He put a finger to his lips and smiled. 'So,' he said, 'you are here because of my letter? I had almost given up hope.'

Luigi was puzzled, amazed. What letter? How could Jacob have expected …? What was he talking about?

'I wrote to your mother with the news that I had left Jerusalem and was in Australia,' Jacob explained. 'I told her about my life and my business here. It was months and months ago. But the mail goes by boat. Six weeks to Italy and six weeks from Italy. When your mother replied, she said she had sent my letter to you in this Black Bay place. She said you were returning to Tescano but she was certain you would first come to see me here in Sydney.'

Luigi shook his head in disbelief. 'I never saw any letter. It must have reached Black Bay after I left.'

Leaning forward, Jacob took Luigi's hands. 'And what of Nunzia?' he asked. His voice was soft.

Luigi shook his head. 'Nothing,' he said. 'She is dead. I feel sure of it. It is hard to think otherwise.'

Jacob looked at him closely. 'You have heard nothing ... or you feel nothing?'

Luigi said he could never, for as long as he lived, feel nothing for Nunzia. 'I think of that night Leonardo and I first met her in the Tescano hills,' he said. 'I think of our walks in those hills. I think of how our hands first touched. Her eyes, her words. How she told me I was a dreamer and that being a dreamer was no bad thing. I think of how we said that when the war was over we would be together forever. Then I think of the last time I saw her as she walked towards the convent. There has been nobody in my life since then. I think there will never be anybody in my life. That is how I feel ... and here I am, tears of sadness on my face where there should be tears of joy at seeing you.'

Jacob loosened his grip on Luigi's hands. 'There will be no work here today,' he said. 'One telephone call and we will go. A business matter.'

As Jacob picked up the handset of the wall-mounted telephone, Luigi left the small office and workshop, closing the door behind him. Two minutes later, Jacob appeared. 'All settled,' he said, locking the door of his shop. 'We will be off to my house.'

The two walked towards the ferry terminal at Circular Quay, Jacob wheeling the Hercules. They stepped off the ferry at Manly, on the north side of Sydney Harbour. Five minutes later they arrived at a solid, white, two-storey house with a red-tiled roof. The front garden was well tended. The house was in a street of similar houses, all suggesting material sufficiency.

As Luigi and Jacob walked up the path, the front door opened. A tall, dark-haired woman in her twenties stood there beaming, hands on hips. 'So you are Luigi and this is your famous bicycle!' she said, and explained: 'Jacob phoned.' Pointing to the garage, she added: 'Your precious bicycle will be safe there. And I have made a room in the house ready for you to stay with us.'

The woman was Rachel. She was Jacob's wife. Luigi, stunned, silent, self-conscious, offered his hand. Anything more than a handshake, he thought, might be too familiar. She was, after all, a married woman. She smiled at his reticence and clasped his hands in both of hers.

'Rachel Samuelovich,' Luigi said when he'd entered the house. 'I remember. Jacob wrote to me from Jerusalem. You were in the letter. Jacob sent the letter to my mother and she sent it to me. I was in Ceylon when I received it.'

In the living room, Luigi heard how Rachel and Jacob had met and how they came to be in Sydney. Rachel was from Warsaw. After the war, she was alone in the world. The Germans had seen to that. There was nothing for her in Poland, no marked graves where she could place flowers for those she had lost. So she had gone to the Holy Land.

She and Jacob had met in Jerusalem a week after Luigi left the city. Rachel had stumbled on a loose paving stone. Jacob had helped her to her feet. They had married two months later, and four months after the wedding they had come to Australia.

Rachel said the Holy Land was like the old Europe. There were great hatreds. It was not a place where she and Jacob could build a life together. Coming to Australia had been a good decision. In Australia, people lived their lives as they wished. Jacob had a good business. He was doing well for himself and Rachel and they would always have each other.

The talk turned to Luigi. It soon became clear that there was nothing of his story that Rachel did not already know — the Bersaglieri adventures, the bombing of Ancona, the Partisan raids, Jacob's escape from the wreckage of the train. She knew, too, of Nunzia and her disappearance. Jacob had told her everything.

When she mentioned Nunzia's name, there was a pause. She and Jacob exchanged the quickest of glances. They seemed nervous. Luigi saw the darting movement of their eyes. He saw Jacob give the smallest nod. Rachel cleared her throat. Luigi should sit down, perhaps, she suggested.

Then she spoke words that sent Luigi's head swirling.

'Nunzia is alive,' Rachel said, looking directly into Luigi's eyes. 'She has suffered much, but she is alive. I spoke to her after Jacob telephoned. I speak with her often. We have become close friends. She is here in Sydney with her father. And she and her father will be here this evening, in this room.'

The blood drained from Luigi's face. His heartbeat, in that instant, became a slow thump in his chest. There was a tingle of cold sweat on his brow. The room was swirling. He tried to stand up again and was steadied by Jacob.

Rachel told Luigi that if he was going to faint he should do it there and then. It would be preferable to fainting when Nunzia and her father arrived. Luigi needed to appear to his best advantage. Nunzia and her father expected to see a bicycle man of the very first order. It wouldn't do for such a man to fall on the floor. 'Now, upstairs,' she went on. 'Jacob will show you the way. First, a bath. Some of Jacob's best clothes have been laid on your bed. And give Jacob the telephone number of your lodgings. He will explain that from now on you are staying here, with us. Jacob will make arrangements to collect whatever you have elsewhere. No arguments from you.'

Amid all the swirling in his head, Luigi concluded that Jacob had married a most determined woman.

Soaking in the bath a few minutes later, Luigi imagined the arrival of Nunzia and her father. He imagined how he and Nunzia, his flower, might embrace — if they might embrace. And what they might say.

He remembered how Nunzia had looked when he had last seen her. And he wondered if, through all that she must have suffered, Nunzia had changed greatly — if her eyes had dulled, if her smile had vanished forever, if her head had been bowed by such terrible hardships. He wondered, too, if it was possible that her feelings for him had endured.

CHAPTER TWENTY-TWO

Revival

*I don't think we ever give up hope. Something way
inside whispers there's a chance. The noose was
around my neck when the reprieve came through.
And you know what ... I wasn't surprised.*

— Peter Anthony Montrose, *Back from the Gallows*, 1989

Clean-shaven, hair swept back, his borrowed clothes crisp, Luigi
waited in the living room. He sat, then stood, then paced, then
sat. Rachel that said all the pacing in the world wouldn't make
the clock tick any faster. Nunzia and her father would arrive
when they arrived, and not a second sooner.

Rachel was in the kitchen when the doorbell rang. Casting
aside her apron, she moved quickly to open the door. Nunzia
stepped inside, followed by a balding, wiry man.

Luigi's eyes widened. Nunzia was as beautiful as he
remembered her — as beautiful as she would remain until she

breathed her last. And she was wearing the locket, the Istanbul locket.

Luigi burst into tears. Nunzia burst into tears. Nunzia's father, even though he had never met Luigi, burst into tears. Jacob burst into tears. Rachel hid her tears in the kitchen. Somebody had to hold the line.

That evening there were so many tears that Luigi thought all of Sydney would be flooded. Eyes were dried and dried again. In the dusk, Luigi and Nunzia sat together on a bench in the garden, hand in hand. His touch was light, gentle. It was as if he were holding a flower.

Luigi remembered the first time they had held hands in the Tescano hills. Nothing had changed. He believed, he believed absolutely in that moment, that he and Nunzia would be together forever — for every day they breathed and for every day beyond whatever came after.

In the creeping cool of the evening, Nunzia told Luigi her story. Several times, as she spoke, she tightened her grip on Luigi's hand. Several times Luigi turned his face away, concealing his tears. The horror of it all. The cruelty. Nunzia had been brutally treated by the Germans after her capture. It would serve no purpose, she said, for her to tell Luigi the details of that brutality. Luigi was never to ask. He never did.

When her German interrogators had finished their work, Nunzia was sent north to a camp in Poland, near the border with Russia. Even after the Russians had liberated the camp, Nunzia and hundreds of others captured by the Germans had remained behind the fences. 'Most of the Partisans who served with Communist units in Italy, the Balkans, Greece and the

Ukraine were kept prisoner,' Nunzia said. 'The only people the Russians were more suspicious of than the English and the Americans were Communists who weren't from Russia. We were kept in the East for more than two years. We were not allowed to write any letters, but at least after the Russians arrived there was food. There were some doctors, too, but never enough. People died all the time — typhus, dysentery, or just despair. People died because they gave up trying to live. They sat down, closed their eyes and died. I thought I would die there, too. There were times when I was too weak to walk to the food lines; and when I did eat, it often stayed in my stomach for less than two minutes. There were fevers that lasted for days.

'I was skin and bone wrapped in rags when we were finally handed over in a prisoner exchange with the Americans — hundreds of us for five Germans the Russians wanted; that was what an American told me, months and months later in an American hospital.'

Nunzia remained in the American hospital for six months before she was transferred to a Red Cross camp for displaced persons. With no papers, it took the Red Cross four months to confirm her identity from the prisoner number the Germans had tattooed on her arm.

Released from the Red Cross camp with some money, some rations and a railway voucher, Nunzia returned to Italy and her father. By then he had all but abandoned hope that his daughter was alive.

The locket Luigi had sent to Jeremy Forsythe to be passed on to her father was there waiting for her. She would wear it until the day she died.

Reunited with her father, Nunzia had remained in Genoa for three months. What future they might have, the pair then decided, lay elsewhere — anywhere, as long as it was away from the past. 'I was ashamed of all that had been done to me,' she told Luigi. 'I wanted nobody to see me. I wanted to be invisible.' Luigi shook his head in silent disbelief at the absurdity of Nunzia's shame.

Nunzia and her father had sailed from Genoa to Sydney. They had set up home in a modest rented house near the Annandale post office. Like many migrants to Australia in those times, Nunzia's father could not follow his profession here. His qualifications — two degrees, one of them a doctorate, from the University of Genoa, and two language-teaching diplomas — counted for nothing. In Italy he had been a dottore, a man fluent in four languages. In Australia he was just another Eyetie. A reffo. A migrant looking for a job. He wondered, as he searched for work during his first days in Sydney, if migrants were encouraged to come to Australia only to make up the numbers; if migrants were no more than breeding stock. It crossed his mind that, maybe, migrants never really came to Australia. They simply left their homeland. Australia, for them, was a place rather than a country. Australia was not their past, and that was enough. It was better than what had gone before in their lives. The living was easier. That, really, was all that mattered.

Within two weeks of their arrival in Sydney, Nunzia's father had found employment in a small upholstery shop run by an Italian family from Cogoleto, west of Genoa. The job, stretching expensive leather over padded furniture frames, suited his temperament. Quality was the yardstick at Cogoleto Furnishings and Leather. The work was precise, unhurried. He could lose himself in it.

Nunzia found work in a city printery where the bread-and-butter business was invoice and receipt books, local bus timetables, betting tickets for on-course bookmakers, and business letterheads.

It was in the printery that she and Jacob had been reunited, some months earlier. Jacob was ordering stationery. Nunzia was behind the counter. Each was initially speechless at the sight of the other. Nunzia dropped the sheaf of papers she had been holding. Jacob, eyes wide, mouth open, stood absolutely still. He was seeing a ghost. Each felt the impossible was happening here, in Sydney, in Australia, the furthest-away place in the world.

A visit to the Zevi home had been quickly arranged. Nunzia and her father would come to Manly that very night. It was the first of many visits. Rachel and Nunzia had become close friends, while Jacob and Salvatore became what Australians called 'good mates'. This seemed to involve sitting on the Zevi patio, smoking cigarettes and discussing grand plans for a brick barbecue in the Zevi back garden.

'What else is there to tell?' Nunzia said.

She and Luigi returned to the living room, self-consciously unclasping their hands as they entered. They rejoined the talk around the table. Much was being said of how chance shaped lives.

Nunzia's father said he wondered what Luigi and Nunzia might do with the chance they had been given. He was a man given to wondering. He had, after all, been a teacher, a man of learning.

Nunzia blushed. It was the blush of the girl she had been in the Tuscan hills. It was the blush of innocence revived, innocence returning from the darkness of war. It was the resurrection of a wounded soul.

Luigi touched Nunzia's hand. He breathed in deeply, expanding his chest. He raised himself from his chair. He had a berth on the *Stella Torino*, he told them, sailing from Sydney to Genoa in three weeks. Chance had now cast doubts on that voyage. Nunzia — with her father's approval, of course — could settle those doubts. A nod would be enough, even the smallest nod, even the suggestion of a nod, and the *Stella Torino* would sail without Luigi Ferraro.

Nunzia had once said that Luigi was a dreamer. If Luigi had a dream, it was that this chance should not be wasted, that he and Nunzia should not again be separated. This chance had bestowed on Luigi something approaching eloquence.

Salvatore looked at his daughter. She nodded. It was by no means the smallest of nods. Jacob stood, whistling, cheering, clapping. Salvatore threw his arms around his daughter and Luigi.

Rachel, ever practical, brought the small gathering to order by tapping a spoon on the table. Luigi's mother and Uncle Cesare were expecting his return within weeks, she said. The events of the day, happy as they might be for Luigi and Nunzia and for all around the table, would cause great disappointment to Luigi's mother and Uncle Cesare. They must be informed.

A letter would take too long to reach Tescano. A telegram could be sent, but the arrival of telegrams sometimes caused distress. No, Rachel said, a telephone call would be best. Luigi should speak to his mother and Uncle Cesare.

Luigi said there was no telephone at the Ferraro house. People in Tescano had little use for telephones. They still spoke normally to each other. Luigi knew of only three telephones in Tescano — at the school, at the rebuilt carabinieri post, and at Father Gianni's presbytery. Rachel said Luigi should call the presbytery. Father Gianni could bring Luigi's mother and Uncle Cesare to the telephone. The call should be made in the morning, Rachel said. Luigi needed to think about what he might say. The call could be made from the shop before Luigi collected his belongings from the Widow O'Connor.

At midnight, with the last ferry from Manly to the city gone, Rachel called and paid for a taxi to take Nunzia and her father to their rented Annandale home. She and Nunzia would speak by telephone the following day. 'I will make arrangements,' she said, without disclosing what such arrangements might relate to. 'Leave it to me.' Luigi sensed that, in the Zevi home, much was left to Rachel. She was a woman who was comfortable with making arrangements.

On the doorstep of the Zevi home there were more embraces. Rachel said that this had been a day like no other. Lives had changed in the blink of an eye.

In the morning, Luigi and Jacob returned to the city and to the shop with the shimmering window display.

It took the telephone exchange twenty minutes to connect Luigi with Tescano 2, Father Gianni's presbytery. The telephone rang twelve times before it was answered.

'It is the middle of the night,' Father Gianni's voice said. 'What do you want at this hour? Who are you?'

The line crackled. Luigi suspected somebody, somewhere in the vastness between Sydney and Tescano, had brushed against a telephone post.

'This is Luigi Ferraro in Sydney.'

Father Gianni said he knew of no person named Sidney. It was the middle of the night. Didn't Sidney have a home to go to?

'No, this is Luigi Ferraro. I am telephoning from Sydney in Australia.'

There was a silence and then more crackling on the line. 'Luigi,' Father Gianni admonished, 'why didn't you say it was you? Why are you calling at this hour — is it bad news?'

Luigi shook his head, a gesture unseen in the darkness of Tescano. No. Hello. Hello? He wished to speak with his mother and Uncle Cesare. Hello?

'Wait, wait just one moment,' Father Gianni said. 'I must get my spectacles. I cannot see to speak on the telephone. Wait, here they are, right here in front of me. I could not see them without my spectacles. I can see to speak now. Luigi, all the way from Australia ... I will fetch your mother and Uncle Cesare. They will be sleeping. It is the middle of the night. Stay there. Do not move from where you are ...'

Lights flickered on around Tescano as Father Gianni thumped on the door of the home of Franca and Uncle Cesare. They should dress and come quickly, Father Gianni shouted. There was news, that very moment, of Luigi.

The door opened. Luigi's mother and Uncle Cesare followed Father Gianni across the Piazza Valsini to the presbytery of the Church of the Blessed Seamstress. A dozen others, roused from their sleep, hurried behind them.

With every step across the piazza, the rumours multiplied. Luigi Ferraro was home. He had returned, a prodigal in rags. He had arrived not ten minutes earlier. He would arrive in an hour. Luigi Ferraro had made his fortune. Luigi Ferraro was dead. Luigi Ferraro had met with a terrible accident on his way to Tescano.

The small living room of the presbytery was crowded, hushed, when Franca picked up the telephone handset and tapped the mouthpiece. 'Luigi?' she said, then dropped the handset when she heard her son's voice. Uncle Cesare stepped forward, picking up the handset. Uncle Cesare, all there knew, had been a sergeant in the Great War. He was a man well used to taking control.

As Luigi spoke, Uncle Cesare repeated his words. 'He is still in Australia,' Uncle Cesare said. 'He is well and he is safe. He misses his mother very much. He misses me, too. He misses Leonardo and the sisters at the convent and Father Gianni. He has been delayed ... His return has been delayed. He will explain. He hopes we are not angry. He did not know it was the middle of the night. It is still day in Australia ... He is with Jacob Zevi ... Nunzia Costa from the Partisans is also in Sydney, Australia, with her father, Salvatore. He is a teacher from Genoa. Luigi is overjoyed. He thought Nunzia was dead even though Father Gianni said he should never lose hope.'

At each revelation, there was a gasp around the room. Jacob Zevi, the young Partisan who had been rescued by Luigi and Leonardo, the young Partisan who had been near death and who had been nursed back to life by Franca Ferraro ... Nunzia Costa, the one who had been taken by the Germans, the one who had vanished ... they were all in Australia. Three people who had been in Tescano were in Australia. Who could ever have imagined such a thing?

The telephone handset was returned to Luigi's mother. 'Hello. Hello. Are you there? Hello ... The telephone line is very bad, but that is because Australia is a long way off,' Luigi's mother said, for the benefit of her audience. 'He can hardly hear me. He sends his love. Jacob and Nunzia send their love. He is with Jacob as he speaks to me this very minute. He says goodbye.'

There was a single click and then silence. In Tescano and Sydney, telephone handsets were replaced on their cradles.

In Tescano, few who were in the presbytery returned to their beds. The excitement of a call from Australia and news of Luigi had destroyed any prospect of sleep.

In Sydney, Luigi turned to Jacob. He could not hide his sense of guilt. 'My mother was pleased to hear I was safe but she was not pleased that my departure has been delayed,' he said. 'I could hear this in her voice, and I did not have the courage to tell her I might be long delayed. I said I would write. What can I write? That the sound of their voices makes me long to see them, but that I wish never to be parted from Nunzia?'

Jacob said writing would be the best thing to do. Difficult matters were often better addressed in writing. In the meantime, Luigi should return to his lodgings and collect his few possessions. 'I will be here when you return,' Jacob said.

Father John and the Widow O'Connor were drinking tea in the kitchen when Luigi arrived.

'I was worried sick out of my head,' the Widow O'Connor said, pointing Luigi towards the living room. 'Father John here has a kitchen near full of bicycles and here's us beside ourselves thinking it would be a fine thing for all concerned if, God forbid, there was nobody to repair those bicycles.'

It had crossed the Widow O'Connor's mind, she said, that Luigi — 'and yourself almost like a son to me' — might be lying drowned at the bottom of Sydney Harbour or might have been hit by a bus or, worse still, might be lying dead under a train. Why lying dead under a train might be worse than lying dead at the bottom of the harbour or under a bus made no sense to Luigi. Unless, perhaps, death by train was more bloody than death by those other means.

'The only thing that put me out of my misery,' the Widow O'Connor said, 'was that telephone call yesterday afternoon from your friend — Joseph? Jacob, was it? I'd just started making a nice mixed grill when he phoned, so that was two chops and two sausages and half a tomato wasted. And chops and sausages don't grow on trees, that's a fact. They might grow on trees in Italy, but not here they don't.'

The Widow O'Connor paused, briefly, to draw breath and then went on. 'This friend of yours who phoned tells me you're moving over the harbour to live with the well-to-do ... and there's a girl involved, he tells me, as well — a good Italian Catholic girl, I hope — Nancy, Nuncy, is that what he said her name was ...? Well, her being Italian at least she'd have none of that Australian inclination to funny business beforehand. You're a right dark horse, if ever there was one.'

Ignoring the implied question as to Nunzia's religious inclination and unsure of what, exactly, funny business or a dark horse might be, Luigi said that he, Jacob and Nunzia were friends from the war years in Italy and that Nunzia was a most special friend. She was so special, in fact, that Luigi had now delayed his return to Italy.

This was a revelation that brought the trace of a smile to the widow's face. 'Well, now, isn't it the truth that God works in mysterious ways!' she said. 'With you not sailing off to Italy you'll still be here to help Father John with the bicycles.'

There was another matter, she said, and that was the rent paid in advance. She couldn't find another respectable lodger at such short notice. She was sure Luigi wouldn't want a widow like herself to be out of pocket after she'd twice opened home and hearth to him when he was friendless and far from his family. Luigi and Father John exchanged glances and shrugged. Right, the Widow O'Connor said, it was settled. And, by the way, Luigi was more than welcome to drop in for a cup of tea when he was working on the bicycles at the presbytery. 'And when might you get back to that?' she asked.

Father John saw the rising flush on Luigi's face. He sensed Luigi's resentment at the Widow O'Connor's self-serving boldness. 'Myself and your man here will sort that out between us,' the priest cut in. 'He has the look of somebody in a hurry. We'll talk about it while I walk him to the bus stop. We'll get his things and be on our way.'

Outside, Father John said: 'She's a good woman. Her heart's in the right place but that's about all — she has an awful mouth on her and not that much of a brain.' He said he wouldn't be at all surprised if Luigi had better things to do than spend his days fixing bicycles and getting nothing for his efforts. Luigi would be better off opening a shop for himself. He'd said it before and he was saying it again. Father John winked. 'I could drum up business around the place, and you could see me right … a bottle of dry sherry every now and then would keep the throat moist after all the talking I'd have to be doing getting the customers in.'

Luigi, recalling the words of Dr Cornelius Finucane in Ceylon, said he had once been warned of the dangers of solitary drinking. The priest laughed. He was only having a lend of Luigi, he said. It was not an expression Luigi understood. In such circumstances, a smile — its falseness camouflaged with considerable difficulty — seemed the polite response. The two shook hands at the bus stop. No mention was made of when Luigi might return to the presbytery kitchen and the bicycles.

On the journey back to the arcade and Jacob's shop, Luigi imagined a sign that might hang above another shop. The sign would proclaim: *Luigi Ferraro, Bicycles and Repairs.*

CHAPTER TWENTY-THREE

Reward

Rewards in Heaven are just fine. But rewards down here, right now, are the Lord's way of saying you're on the right track for eternal life. The Godly get the Goodies. So get on your bicycles and pedal hard, brothers and sisters.

— Pastor Tammy-Mae Olsenberg, Prosperity Tabernacle, Creede, Colorado, 1984

Jacob and Luigi returned to Manly on the crowded ferry that cast off from Circular Quay at 6 pm. The early-evening return from the city was a routine that Jacob followed five days a week. On Saturdays, he returned at 1 pm.

Over dinner, Rachel drew from Luigi the details of the morning telephone call to Tescano and his promise to write to his mother and Uncle Cesare. Luigi should write to all his friends in Tescano that very night, Rachel said, and post the letters in the morning. The post office was nearby. Rachel's tone, that of a knowing, bossy older sister, indicated that this was an instruction rather than a suggestion.

Then her tone softened. Not two hours earlier she had spoken by telephone to Nunzia. It was Nunzia who had done most of the talking. Where was Luigi now? Wasn't he handsome? He seemed taller. And what a fine head of hair ... had Rachel noticed how Luigi swept it back with his fingers? Nunzia's father, never one to offer approval lightly, had said Luigi was a fine young man. Nunzia had hardly slept last night. How could she possibly sleep? Had Luigi said anything to Rachel? For the first time since that day of their parting in the Tescano hills Nunzia felt ... she wasn't sure how she felt. When might she and her father visit again — the weekend?

That evening, Luigi wrote three letters.

To his mother and Uncle Cesare, he wrote:

I could hear in your voice that my delay in returning was not the news you expected. But being with Nunzia in Sydney was not what I expected. Seeing Nunzia again has been a miracle. I am not sure what will happen next. I will stay with Jacob in Sydney for now. I will not be gone forever. Please do not be unhappy at my joy in finding Nunzia. Please write to me at Jacob's address.

To Leonardo, Luigi wrote telling of his reunion with Jacob and Nunzia. He said that he hoped he and Nunzia might never again be separated — although Leonardo should never forget that he was Luigi's oldest friend and one of Jacob's two best friends.

Nothing would change those truths. He said that Leonardo should write.

To Father Gianni, Luigi wrote of the reunion with Nunzia and Jacob, and of his work on the bicycles in the presbytery of the Church of Saint Derla of the Dispossessed. He wrote of Father John Macguire, observing that Father John was Irish and had not attended the great Pontifical Gregorian University of Rome. Perhaps this was why — with no disrespect intended to the Irish priest — Father John seemed less wise, less refined, than Father Gianni.

The next morning, Luigi walked with Rachel to the Manly post office. On the walk there and back and in the kitchen of the Zevi home that day there was talk, practical talk from the practical Rachel, of how Luigi might see the future unfold. It seemed, Rachel said, that, like herself and Jacob, Luigi and Nunzia were fated to be together. She thought that fate, when it was favourable, could make possible the belief that life was not without purpose or meaning.

Luigi could not imagine ever again being apart from Nunzia, he told Rachel, who said she could not imagine Nunzia ever wishing to be apart from Luigi. She doubted that Nunzia and her father would ever return to live in Italy.

'If that means me remaining in Australia,' Luigi said, 'then I will remain in Australia.'

Rachel asked how Luigi was planning to support Nunzia. How would they manage? Romance was fine, but there were practical considerations. Love was always more enduring and the pillow was always softer when there was food on the table. And then there was Nunzia's father. His daughter was all he had in the world. Had Luigi given any thought to Salvatore? He could not simply be left on his own.

Luigi, a serious note in his voice, said that making a living and looking after Nunzia and her father were no small matters. With great affection came great responsibility. He told Rachel of Father John's suggestion that Luigi open a bicycle shop, and his offer to help bring Luigi customers. In Annandale, where Luigi had lodged, there were many bicycles. He knew this because most of them seemed to end up in Father John's kitchen. But there was no bicycle shop.

Rachel nodded. 'Talk to Jacob,' she said. 'My Jacob is a man who understands business. Already he knows people here in Sydney. We were hardly here two weeks before Jacob knew people. It was the same with the shop in Jerusalem. When the Jews were killing the Arabs and the Arabs were killing the Jews and the British were being killed by anybody passing through the neighbourhood, my Jacob had Arab friends and Jewish friends and British friends. When he wishes, he becomes the lost puppy dog everybody wants to adopt. But you would know that, surely?'

Rachel was correct. Jacob Zevi, wherever he was, was seldom friendless for long. Yet Luigi had never, really, seen in Jacob anything that could be likened to a lost puppy. There was nothing of the lost puppy in the Jacob who had pumped bullets into the body of the kneeling, pleading German on the night of the raid on the train.

That evening, after dinner, Luigi and Jacob walked slowly along the north shore of Sydney Harbour. Jacob said that it seemed to him beyond doubt that Luigi and Nunzia would remain together in Sydney. He said Rachel shared this view.

She felt there might be no harm in her telling Nunzia of Luigi's idea to open a bicycle shop. At the same time, Rachel might also mention that Luigi had said Nunzia's father was deserving of the greatest consideration in any plans Luigi and Nunzia might make. Such consideration would show Luigi to be a man who would be as good and as caring a husband as Nunzia could find in ten lifetimes. 'When Rachel determines a course of action,' Jacob smiled wryly, 'she cannot be swayed. I would not be surprised if she told me to waste no time in making wedding rings for you and Nunzia.'

Luigi, feigning indignation, wondered aloud what his immediate role in the courtship of Nunzia Costa might be. Should he seek advice from Rachel? Jacob, smiling, advised him against it. Rachel should be left to enjoy her imagined role of matchmaker in a match that had in reality been made long ago, in the Tescano hills. In the meantime, Luigi should simply court Nunzia as Luigi thought Nunzia should be courted.

However, there was also the matter of the bicycle shop. On that matter, Jacob was pleased to offer advice. Setting up a business was no small step. The location and cost of premises were important considerations. Jacob understood that Luigi was looking at Annandale. There were no bicycle shops there. This was good. 'Competition is never good for business,' Jacob said. 'Only the customer benefits.'

Luigi would need to consider the question of buying or renting premises. There were other running costs, too — stock to be bought, tools and spare parts for repair work. Luigi would need money to pay himself wages while he built up the business. How might Luigi manage such things?

Luigi said he still retained a few of the gold coins from the German's knapsack. He also had some money saved from the work with Alfie and at the general store and the pub in Black Bay. And then there was the money he had intended to use to pay the remainder of his passage from Sydney to Genoa.

Jacob nodded. It was a start. He would make some enquiries. He knew some people, businesspeople. He had met them when he was looking for his own premises. These people might know of shops for rent in Annandale. Luigi should leave the matter of premises and expenses to Jacob. Nunzia, for now, should occupy all of Luigi's attentions.

In the twilight, Jacob and Luigi returned to the Zevi home, each satisfied that the past had started to give way to the future.

During the weeks that followed, there were other evening walks, sometimes with Jacob, but more often with Nunzia. This was a chaste, delicate courtship. A brushing, barely touching kiss, a sideways glance, a smile, a hand clasping a hand ... these were enough, these were more than enough. They were more than could ever have been hoped for.

On those evenings, Nunzia and Luigi ambled for hours. Sometimes they sat on rocks and watched the city across the water. Sydney twinkled like a diamond tiara, its lights reflected on the flatness of the harbour. That stillness, and the quietness of the evening, were regularly rent by the bows of departing ships and the baritone blasts of their sirens.

The sight and sound of these ships, slicing towards the open, endless water beyond the Sydney Heads, stirred in Luigi and Nunzia memories of their old world. For Luigi the memories were of boyhood and bicycles and comradeship. There were abiding memories, too, of the brutality of the Partisan war. For Nunzia the memories were of fear and hurt and darkness.

Neither shared their recollections with the other. Australia was their new world. No purpose would have been served by dwelling on the old. Instead, arms were linked and looks were exchanged and the silence of thought was broken by talk of what might be arranged for the weekend, or what progress Jacob might have reported to Luigi on the business of securing premises for a bicycle shop.

Some Sundays, Luigi passed the day with Nunzia and her father. They met at Circular Quay and walked through the Botanic Gardens. Sometimes they would picnic. Occasionally, Jacob drove the party up the coast to one of Sydney's northern beaches. He had become the owner of a Holden car. It was only used at weekends. At the beach, Luigi, Nunzia, Salvatore, Jacob and Rachel bought ice cream, or sat on the sand and watched the waves and the swimmers. This was a life that none who had lived through war in Europe could have imagined — a life of enough food, clean sheets, a roof, hot water, peace. Australia was a vast place of second chances, of clean slates, of fresh starts. A place of renewal.

Watching the waves and the swimmers, Luigi told Nunzia about the sign he'd seen when he first arrived in Sydney warning people not to stand at any time, and how he had walked and walked for an entire day. He told her how the city, beyond the harbour, had seemed dirty and untidy, and in the hotel where he'd spent his first nights the men were loud and coarse. Luigi had believed then that he might not remain too long in Australia.

But he was never one to quit. Now, he was glad he had remained. When others might have retreated, Luigi Ferraro had chosen to advance, had chosen to give Australia a chance.

'Yes,' Nunzia said, mischief in her eyes and a mocking reproach in her voice, 'I am sure Australia is most delighted that you have stayed. I expect you will receive a medal to go with the one you already have from the King of England himself.'

No more was said of how Luigi had given Australia the benefit of his initial doubts. And from that day onwards, Luigi endeavoured to avoid utterances that might have within them any hint of self-praise. When, very occasionally, these endeavours failed, Luigi could be sure of Nunzia's teasing admonition. 'Don't come to me fishing for compliments,' she would say. Nunzia would never, in all the years she and Luigi passed together, be one to allow even a hint of self-satisfaction to go unremarked.

In the weeks that followed the reunion, three letters arrived for Luigi. Luigi's mother and Uncle Cesare wrote that while the reason for the delay in Luigi's return to Tescano was understood, there remained an expectation that he would return *before too much longer.*

Father Gianni wrote that his heart had skipped several beats when he learned that Luigi and Nunzia had been reunited in Sydney. He had telephoned the British Consulate in Florence to tell Jeremy Forsythe, who was overjoyed. Jeremy continued to visit Tescano every few months. Father Gianni added that all in Tescano entertained the hope that Luigi would not be too long gone.

Leonardo wrote that he and Carla Cantare, the daughter of the new Tescano headmaster, were to be married by Father

Gianni. It was likely that by the time his letter reached Australia, Leonardo and Carla would be man and wife. Leonardo had at one time hoped that Luigi might have been by his side at the Nuptial Mass. However, he maintained the strong hope that not too much time would pass before Luigi returned to Tescano, and the even stronger hope that he would return with Nunzia.

For their part, Leonardo and Carla would live forever in Tescano. It was not as if he knew nothing of the wider world, Leonardo said. He had been to Livorno and Ancona, and had even passed some hours in Florence. But nothing he had seen on his travels could persuade Leonardo Battaglia that there existed a finer place than Tescano. If he and Carla were blessed with a son — a son who would learn to cycle as soon as he could walk, and who would be named Luigi Jacob Battaglia — that son would be raised as a Tescano man.

Perhaps Jacob might also return to Tescano. The village had no watchmaker or jeweller, Leonardo pointed out. Jacob might give this matter some thought. It could be to his advantage. Few in Tescano wore watches and none wore jewellery beyond wedding rings and religious medallions or crucifixes. A watchmaker and jeweller in Tescano would face no competition. It would prosper, just as the Battaglia bakery had prospered without competition.

Other news of great import for Luigi did not come from afar. Seated for Sunday dinner at the Zevi home, Luigi, Nunzia and her father were informed by Jacob and Rachel that the matter of the shop, and more, had been settled. Arrangements had been made.

Jacob placed a small metal box on the table but said nothing, immediately, of its contents. Instead, he said a lease had been secured on a shop and nearby house in Waterloo Street, Annandale. The owners — a Lebanese couple who had been in Australia for many years — had been among Jacob's first customers when he arrived in Australia. From time to time they sold gold. They also sold property. They intended to sell the Annandale shop and the nearby house in order to provide a dowry for a daughter who was to be wed. Part of that dowry, as their custom dictated, would be worn as jewellery, which they planned to buy from Jacob. Hearing this, Jacob had proposed to the couple that Luigi lease the shop and the house for one year. Jacob would guarantee payment of the rent, in advance, in return for an option for Luigi to buy both properties at the end of twelve months.

Jacob pushed the small metal box towards Luigi. It was not his intention, he said, lifting the lid of the small box, to offer Luigi and Nunzia a gift or a loan. The contents of the box sparkled, and Luigi was immediately transported to that day in the Grand Bazaar in Istanbul when he had first seen the Russian jewellery, the day when he had bought the locket that Nunzia now wore, the locket that Jacob said had been bought for a fraction of its worth.

Jacob explained that in Jerusalem, as in Istanbul, there had been no shortage of jewellery, some Russian and some Persian, that could be bought for its gold weight rather than the value of its craftsmanship. Jacob had brought several boxes of this jewellery to Australia, where he had sold numerous pieces for many times their weight in gold. Already, through people he knew, Jacob was considering the importation, from Jerusalem and Istanbul, of other such beautifully made objects. The people he knew had business dealings in both places. These dealings related to carpets and furniture, but it would not be difficult for them to also have dealings relating to jewellery. It was easy money, Jacob told Luigi, Nunzia and Salvatore. Pointing to Nunzia's locket, he added: 'And this money is being made only because of Luigi. Without that locket I would never have known of the Russian jewellery.'

The money from the sale of the contents of the small metal box would pay for the rent of the shop and the house for one year. It would also, after twelve months, and if the business flourished, pay for a deposit on the purchase of the shop and the house.

Rachel said there would be enough left to repaint the shop and the house, and to pay for repairs to doors and windows. The house needed a new bathroom, and the proceeds would cover that, too. And there was enough to pay living costs for one year and buy the stock and tools Luigi would need. This was a dream within a dream.

'For now,' Rachel went on, 'there are practical matters to settle. We will visit the premises, all five of us, tomorrow evening. There is little that could not be improved by a carpenter, two coats of paint, a plumber and a few weeks of work. Jacob, Luigi and Salvatore will attend to the shop and the stock and the tools. I will attend to the house with Nunzia. And now that a home and premises for the business have been attended to, there is the matter of the wedding.' None around the table, Rachel said, had any doubts that there would be a wedding.

No doubts were expressed. Luigi and Nunzia blushed. Salvatore, damp-eyed, said if only ... if only Nunzia's mother could be there, at the table ... If only she could see her daughter's smile, her blush, her happiness.

'Perhaps she can,' Luigi said, touching Salvatore's shoulder.

Rachel thought of the family she had lost in Poland. She inhaled deeply then collected herself. She and Nunzia would make the wedding arrangements, she said. Rachel had yet to discuss this with Nunzia, although she was sure Nunzia would welcome her assistance. They would speak with Father John Macguire. The bicycle business was in Annandale. The home was in Annandale. The wedding should be in Annandale. Then there was the matter of the wedding dress. The choice of style and material could not be made with the wave of a hand: several fittings would be needed. There should be no delay. Rachel had already spoken to a dressmaker, Martha of Manly. She had a good reputation.

Rachel said Luigi should write to invite his mother, Uncle Cesare and Leonardo to the wedding, even if it was beyond hope that the three would travel to Sydney. Luigi should also invite Alfie, Bullseye, and the Misses Hettie and Betty Pretty from Black Bay; he had talked of them often enough. Luigi might consider, too, an invitation to the Widow O'Connor. Rachel's personal view was that the widow — for all the shortcomings Luigi had mentioned to Jacob — had shown kindness to Luigi during his first days in Sydney and after his return from Black Bay. 'But that is a matter for you,' Rachel said. 'Far be it from me to interfere.'

Luigi and Nunzia exchanged glances. Far be it from them to interfere with Rachel's plans for their business, their home and their marriage. Of course, they said nothing. Rachel was, after all, a woman of considerable kindness, thoughtfulness and determination.

A wedding date twelve weeks hence was proposed by Rachel. Setting up a married home was not something that could be organised overnight. Nor was setting up a business an overnight matter. It would take two months, maybe three, Jacob said, to ready the shop for opening. The business would have to be registered. Luigi said it should be registered in the name 'L. and N. Ferraro, Bicycles and Repairs'. There was a six-week waiting period for new telephone connections. Receipt books would need to be printed. Stock would need to be ordered. Delivery would take weeks. Then there were the tools and the spare parts, and Luigi would need to set up his workshop. There was no time to waste.

As Rachel had instructed, the invitations to Tescano were despatched without delay, but none of the five was surprised — although all were disappointed — when Luigi's mother and Uncle Cesare wrote that they and Leonardo would be unable to attend the wedding.

While they were sad that they could not make the journey to witness it, Luigi's mother and Uncle Cesare believed the marriage to Nunzia would be the making of Luigi. It would, once and for all, put an end to any thoughts of adventures. Uncle Cesare had nothing but praise for Nunzia. He remembered her with great fondness and admiration. They understood that, wedding aside, the news that Luigi was to begin his own bicycle business meant a return to Tescano would, for some time, be unlikely. Nevertheless, Uncle Cesare believed it would not be long before Luigi Ferraro of L. and N. Ferraro, Bicycles and Repairs became a great success. When this happened, Luigi and Nunzia would visit Tescano.

Father Gianni's good heart had been warmed by the news of the intended wedding. The good hearts of the sisters at the Convent of Santa Teresa had been warmed too. And Leonardo had asked Luigi's mother and Uncle Cesare, when they wrote, to say that his and Carla's hearts had been warmed greatly. Rachel said Tescano appeared to be a place of uncommonly warm hearts. She wondered if it might be the Tuscan climate.

The response to the invitation sent to Alfie, Bullseye and the Misses Hettie and Betty was brief and to the point. Alfie advised that the four would be at the wedding *with bells on*. They would not, he said, *miss it for quids*. He said Luigi was *a real dark horse*.

Luigi understood, easily enough, that the invitation had been accepted. But he would have to ask Alfie when the two met why he might be wearing bells, and what resemblance Luigi had to a dark horse, or, for that matter, horses in general. The Widow O'Connor, Luigi remembered, had herself, quite recently, likened Luigi to a dark horse.

The Widow O'Connor was, in her own way, equally colourful in her acceptance. She would be delighted to attend the coming together of *a good Catholic couple*. She felt moved to recall Luigi's first appearance on her doorstep and his subsequent reappearance on his return from Black Bay. *Little did I know,* she wrote with a flourish, *that when I took you in, a stranger alone in a foreign land, I'd be setting you on the path to the altar of the Church of Saint Derla of the Dispossessed. Without me you would never have met the lovely Father John, and without the lovely Father John you might never have gone into the city and crossed paths with your Italian friend and the girl who will become your wife. It's not the first time I've felt that God Himself has used me as an instrument of His divine will. Please let me know if I should bring a plate.* This final sentence puzzled Luigi. There remained so much in the English language that he did not understand.

Initially, the matter of the wedding dress had unsettled Nunzia. Rachel said Nunzia should be wed in white. Nunzia was unsure. So many things had happened in the war. Rachel nodded her understanding. She said Nunzia might speak to Father John. A telephone call was made and a time set.

In the presbytery of the Church of Saint Derla of the Dispossessed, Nunzia talked openly for the first time of the war and her treatment by the Germans. As she spoke, it was as if a great dam of guilt and shame had been fractured. She told Father John of things that had never been told to another living soul. When there was no more to tell, she felt empty, drained.

Twice, while Nunzia spoke, Father John excused himself. 'I'll just get us another cup of tea,' he said. In the kitchen he blew his nose and wiped his eyes on a tea towel. He had never, even in the confessional of Saint Derla of the Dispossessed, heard of such wickedness.

When he returned from the last of these visits to the kitchen, Father John told Nunzia that what had happened during her darkest days counted for nothing. In the eyes of the church, Nunzia was as pure as the falling snow. Her wedding dress should proclaim that purity. All that had been taken from her had been restored.

*

The wedding, on a Saturday morning, was a simple affair. At the church, Alfie, Bullseye, the Misses Hettie and Betty, and the Widow O'Connor sat together. Jacob, Rachel and Salvatore stood behind the couple.

Nunzia was radiant. Her eyes sparkled. There was a joy, an innocence, in those eyes. Luigi had never seen such beauty — a beauty of the soul, the heart, the spirit. He mouthed the words, 'My little flower.'

Father John, his Irish lilt lending tenderness to his words, spoke elegantly. It was obvious he had not missed his calling. He said the job of a parish priest brought joy as well as sadness. The sadness came in times when he ministered to loss and waywardness. But the joy came when two people stood before God and sought His blessing on their union. Nunzia and Luigi, parted by war, had been reunited by a kindly God. Nunzia and Luigi, like others gathered in the church that day, had been blessed by the gift of continuing life. It was a gift that was given one day at a time, a gift to be embraced and shared. Every creature that lived on Earth came and went in the blink of an eye. The heartbeat was the only certainty of the moment, just as God's judgment was the only certainty of the inevitable, unknowable eternity to come. Father John was sure the kindly God who had reunited Nunzia and Luigi would, when the time came, set aside a place for the couple for all eternity. They would never be parted — now or in the time beyond time.

The rose-gold wedding rings, made by Jacob, were exchanged. There were embraces. Alfie applauded and was immediately silenced by a white-hot stare from the Widow O'Connor. The Misses Hettie and Betty, in starched floral dresses, nodded their approval to the window. Bullseye wondered aloud if, now that the ceremony was concluded, Father John might direct him to the dunny. At his age, he said, nature was a frequent caller.

Jacob, who had bought a camera for the occasion, took photographs on the steps of the church. Lunch was served in the Zevi home. There was much banter from Alfie about Luigi's time in Black Bay. 'I thought he was never going to leave,' he joked. The Misses Hettie and Betty said that, for their part, they had been sad to see Luigi go but were delighted that all had ended well. The bride, they agreed, looked as pretty as a picture. Bullseye excused himself several times during and after lunch as nature continued to call. Father John wondered if he might pour himself another sherry. The Nuptial Mass had left him quite parched. The Widow O'Connor inspected the Zevi house and garden and said Luigi obviously had 'well-to-do' friends.

At two in the afternoon, the bride and groom departed. Their one-week honeymoon would be spent far to the south, in Tathra. Rachel had made the arrangements. She and Jacob had visited Tathra twice. It was the perfect spot for peace and quiet, Rachel said, adding that it might be the last peace and quiet Luigi had for a while. The doors of L. and N. Ferraro, Bicycles and Repairs would open within the fortnight.

Taking their leave, Luigi and Nunzia embraced the Misses Hettie and Betty, and shook hands with Alfie and Bullseye. An invitation to visit Black Bay was issued. The Widow O'Connor extended to herself an invitation to visit the Ferraro home in Annandale. Father John winked and said that the Church of

Saint Derla of the Dispossessed was also open to visits by Luigi and Nunzia. He particularly recommended attendance for the sacrament of baptism, 'when the time arrives'.

Driving south in the car lent by Jacob, Luigi and Nunzia — Mr and Mrs Luigi Ferraro — passed first through Wollongong. South and further south they motored, beyond Kiama, Nowra, Jervis Bay, Ulladulla, Moruya and Bega. It was mid-evening when they arrived in the small coastal town of Tathra. In the full moonlight they stood on the timbered wharf and saw in the distance the white frothy wakes of fishing boats, and smelled the clean scent of salt.

They stayed in Tathra for six nights, in a small, cream-painted hotel that faced east into the rising sun, and they decided that one day they would live by the sea and they would have a vegetable garden and a house with a verandah. They resolved that in fair weather at their house with the verandah and the vegetable garden, they would watch the waves break and race and gurgle over the shallows. And when storms came they would, hand holding hand, marvel at the lightning forks and feel, under their feet, the pulse of the thunder. There would be no better place in the world, Nunzia said. Luigi agreed.

CHAPTER TWENTY-FOUR

Reputation

Getting the first customers through the door is easy.
Getting them back is the business end. It's not just
being good at what you do. It's how you do it that
seals the deal. That's what rings the bell on the cash
register. Reputation is money in the bank.
— Chad Barclay, *Business for Dummies*, 2001

In the days following the newlyweds' return from Tathra, Luigi, Nunzia and Salvatore moved into their newly painted Annandale home. Soon afterwards, the doors of the business were opened under a sign that said *L. and N. Ferraro, Bicycles and Repairs.* Salvatore had offered to assist, in the evenings, with book-keeping and ordering, an offer Luigi accepted gratefully. This was, after all, a family business.

But, family business or no family business, Nunzia insisted on keeping her job in the printery. Luigi attempted to persuade her otherwise. She was a married woman, he said. A husband should support his wife. Nunzia said she was happy to be a married woman, but not a kept woman. Besides, she was not one to stare at the wallpaper in the kitchen all day. So that was that ... and didn't Luigi have something useful to do? Didn't he have a tyre to pump or a saddle to adjust?

Rachel's prediction, made before the Tathra honeymoon, that Luigi would have little peace and quiet from the moment the shop doors opened was not entirely correct. As with every new enterprise, the earliest days were daunting. During the first three weeks of operation there were no customers, and Luigi's nerve was tested. Every day of those three weeks he stood behind the counter or just outside the door and waited, then waited some more. A dozen times he rearranged the workshop. He polished the tools. He moved two benches and then moved them back to where they had been a day earlier. Each night when he returned home, Nunzia and her father could read the disappointment on Luigi's face. Every night they smiled and said tomorrow would be better. But they never said which tomorrow that would be.

Twice, Luigi telephoned Jacob and said he feared this grand plan had turned out to be a grand mistake, that the Zevis' generosity and faith had been misplaced. During the second telephone call, Jacob said Luigi should speak to Rachel. She had answers for everything.

Rachel listened as Luigi told her he'd asked himself what sort of husband he was. 'A husband who can't support his wife, that's what sort of husband I am,' he said, answering his own question.

Rachel offered no sympathy. 'Stop this nonsense,' she said sharply. 'Instead of complaining that nobody has yet come into the shop, you should think of Nunzia and what she has come through. If you don't pull up your socks and get a grip you'll turn into a whinger — that's what Australians call people who do nothing but complain and feel sorry for themselves.'

When the telephone call ended, Luigi carefully pulled up both of his socks. He stared at them, perplexed. How would pulling up his socks change anything? But Rachel was not one to be ignored. He was also mystified by her instruction to get a grip. How, he asked himself, could Rachel possibly know of the grip? That, after all, was a matter for men whose business was machines and metal and mouldings and millimetres.

Three days later, however, L. and N. Ferraro, Bicycles and Repairs finally attended to its first customer. Somehow, the pulling-up of socks had changed business for the better.

'It's well and truly buggered,' Father John Macguire said as he wheeled his bicycle through the open doors. 'It needs fixing, and it's a paying job this time — pounds, shillings and pence on the nail, cash on delivery.' He gestured to the sorry-looking bicycle. 'Front wheel buckled. Back tyre punctured. Right pedal bent. Bus nearly ran me off the road last week. Didn't even stop. Wouldn't be surprised if the driver was a Protestant. Not a scratch on me, mind you. There's a special saint for Catholics on bicycles ... and there's more than a few of us.'

Luigi inspected the bicycle while Father John went on: 'Anyhow, I've been thinking, and here's what I've done. It'll give you a bit of a start.' Father John held up a sheet of paper. 'I wrote a few dozen copies and handed them out after Mass. There's some others I've sent round three or four parishes that wouldn't be all that much more than a few miles from here. I'd be gobsmacked if you didn't have customers breaking the doors down any minute now.'

This sounded ominous. Luigi had no wish for his doors to be broken down. Being gobsmacked, whatever that might be, sounded ominous too. He took the sheet of paper from Father John and read the handwritten words.

CATHOLIC BICYCLES AND REPAIRS
Father John Macguire of the Church of Saint Derla of the Dispossessed strongly recommends the services of L. and N. Ferraro, Catholic Bicycles and Repairs, Annandale, for all bicycle purchases and repairs.

Mr L. Ferraro, Master Craftsman, recently wed in the Church of Saint Derla of the Dispossessed, and a former well-mannered lodger with the Widow O'Connor of this Parish, personally attends to all customer needs.

A free Saint Christopher medallion, appropriately blessed, will be given to each customer — said medallion to be supplied by the aforementioned Father John Macguire.

All transactions strictly cash, as this is a young man just starting out on married life after a long engagement.

Luigi's thanks were profuse. He discerned the hand of Rachel in this affair, but he would never know for sure because he would never ask. There and then, though, he recalled a phrase he'd heard used by Jeremy Forsythe: 'Never look a gift horse in the mouth.'

By the week and then by the day, the customers began to arrive. Father John's sectarian recommendation had been heeded by pedalling parishioners young and old, both within and beyond the Church of Saint Derla of the Dispossessed. They were well pleased by the service they received. No repair was too big or too small for Luigi Ferraro. He was reliable. The work was always done on time. The prices were fair and, if Luigi liked the look of a customer, payment could be made at the rate of a few shillings a week. Luigi Ferraro was building a reputation, a good reputation.

Some evenings, with four or five bicycles to attend to, Luigi remained in the workshop for several hours. When this happened, Nunzia would bring him dinner and then watch as he repaired punctures, tightened chains, rebuilt caliper brakes, replaced spokes, straightened forks, and polished and repolished his stock. Nunzia watched a man confident and patient in his work. Without knowing it, she was watching a man who had mastered the grip — and, along the way, pulled his socks up.

Often, before he left the workshop in the evening, Luigi lifted the sheet that covered the motorised Hercules, which was stored beside some boxes. He touched the crossbar as a father would pat the head of his child. Then he replaced the sheet. Always as he replaced the sheet he would think, ever so briefly, of all the times and places shared by Luigi Ferraro and that bicycle. The wonder of it all. The wheels within wheels.

Eight months after the barren early weeks of the business, members of two local cycling clubs — the Annandale Non-Denominational Adventurers and the Agnostic True Wheelers — became regular customers, after being assured, in response to close questioning of Luigi, that the standard of service and attention afforded to non-Catholics matched that afforded to Catholics. Luigi told his questioners: 'In all my years as a bicycle man I have yet to learn the difference between a Catholic bicycle and a Protestant bicycle.' This, thought some Adventurers and True Wheelers, was an observation that showed Luigi to be a man who understood there was more to bicycles than their riders.

As regular customers, the members of the two cycling clubs looked to Luigi for inner tubes and valves and India-rubber brake pads and brake shoes and mudguards, and for advice on saddle and handlebar heights and the tensioning of spokes. They saw in Luigi a man who knew, truly knew, the joy and freedom of cycling, the delight of the open road.

Sometimes, as he was offering advice on the importance of the positioning of the saddle, Luigi would recount stories of the Army Cycling Training School at Livorno and the instructors there. Clearing his throat, he would begin a song from the Trattoria Bersaglieri:

Fearless warriors of the Alpine snow
We ride our rugged mounts, two wheels against the
     stubborn foe
Plumes in the wind, we forward fly
Our rifles flash, our foes must die.
Bicycle men are we,
From snowy peak to sea
We smite the foe, we lay him low ...
Bicycle men are we,
From snowy peak to sea.

The Annandale Non-Denominational Adventurers and the Agnostic True Wheelers expressed the view that Luigi Ferraro was 'a decent style of bastard'. Luigi understood that this was the highest of praise in a country where compliments between men avoided any suggestion of affection or fondness.

Regularly, Luigi rebuilt bicycles damaged on an Adventurers' or a True Wheelers' road run. There was a steady market for new bicycles, too. Some of these he imported from Italy and some from France. They sold well and for a tidy profit. Business was good. Within a year, he and Nunzia had enough set aside to make an offer on the modest Annandale house and the shop and workshop. Thus, Luigi and Nunzia Ferraro had a home that was truly their own.

They also had a livelihood that provided the security they would need to care for the child due in the second year of their marriage.

Eight weeks into her pregnancy, Nunzia left her job at the printery. The local doctor, Gordon Macrae, Inverness-born and Edinburgh-trained, explained to Luigi that events — unspecified — had not left Nunzia physically unscathed. It was certain there would be no second child. 'She's had a bad time of it,' Dr Macrae said. 'It's a miracle she's come this far. Between now and the confinement, herself needs all the rest she can get. Feet up. No lifting. Nourishment and rest. That's the prescription. Night or day, I'm up the road. You just get through this and count your blessings if you do.'

When Nunzia was delivered of a son, Dr Macrae said: 'A bonnie wee bairn with the right number of fingers, toes and other bits here and there. As fine as any bairn I ever delivered in Edinburgh.'

Luigi held the infant. He could smell the newness of life lying there in his arms. The fingers and toes and 'other bits' were tiny, but they were all there. Luigi touched his son's damp wisps of dark hair. Then he kissed Nunzia. 'Now I have two flowers,' he said. She heard nothing. She was sleeping, exhausted. It had been a difficult delivery.

The boy was named Enzo Cesare Leonardo Jacob Ferraro. Nunzia had baulked at a still-longer name that would have included Gianni, Jeremy and Gordon.

One week after the birth, the business was renamed 'L. and N. Ferraro and Son, Bicycles and Repairs'. Young Enzo took his first steps in the workshop. His first toys were some of Luigi's tools. Almost before he could walk, he could sit astride a tricycle. He was, Luigi thought, a tricycle boy of the very first order.

Luigi did as Dr Macrae suggested. He counted his blessings, of which there were several. He had Nunzia and he had Enzo. He had Jacob and he had Rachel. He had his home and he had his business. That a successful offer had been made on the home and the business premises owed much, Luigi believed, but never confirmed, to Nunzia's bookish father, whose approach to financial record-keeping was perfectly captured in his expressed view that there wasn't a tax department in the whole world that didn't already have enough money. 'I speak as one who was a teacher,' Nunzia's father said, 'when I assert that arithmetic creativity is a talent to be encouraged. You count your blessings and I will deal with the money that pays for those blessings.'

News of the blessings was regularly relayed to Tescano in lengthy letters, with photographs, to Luigi's mother, Uncle

Cesare, Father Gianni, and Leonardo and Carla. Enzo was a fine boy, Luigi wrote in every letter. He had the looks of Nunzia. He had the hands of Uncle Cesare. He had the good heart of his grandmother. He spoke English like an Australian. But, Luigi lamented, he also spoke Italian like an Australian.

In every letter, too, Luigi reported on the progress of L. and N. Ferraro and Son, Bicycles and Repairs. He longed, of course, to return to Tescano with Nunzia and Enzo, but that return would have to wait. He and Nunzia were, even as he wrote, completing the purchase of the narrow-fronted building that shared a wall with the shop and the workshop.

After much refurbishment, the narrow-fronted building became the Bersaglieri Cafe. Like the bicycle shop and workshop, the cafe prospered. The shop and workshop were Luigi's business but the Bersaglieri Cafe, Nunzia said, was hers. It was a welcoming, comfortable place that smelled of coffee and pastry and warm bread and hot milk. It was the second child Nunzia would never have.

The first regular customers at the Bersaglieri Cafe were drawn from the ranks of the Adventurers and the True Wheelers. Every weekend they arrived for a light breakfast before rides that would take them west towards the first slopes of the Blue Mountains or north towards the meandering Hawkesbury River.

In time, the Bersaglieri Cafe, with its Italian newspapers and sets of dominoes and playing cards, became the Friday evening and Saturday morning rendezvous of Italian husbands granted a few hours of leave by Italian wives. It became the place where Italian, in all its regional variations, was spoken, where the talk was of football and the Italian governments that usually came and went in the space of a football season. It was a corner of Italy in Annandale.

For Luigi and Nunzia, life assumed a warm, comfortable texture. The tick of passing time was unheard. There was the bicycle business and the cafe, and there was the delight of raising a son, and there was genuine affection and companionship in the Ferraro home. There was, too, some talk of the future and the house with a verandah and a vegetable garden, perhaps even a shed, a workshop, for Luigi. A house that faced an endless ocean.

One day. One day.

The news in letters from Tescano was mostly reassuring. Luigi's mother and Uncle Cesare were well, although Uncle Cesare seemed to tire quite easily and he was spending less time in the smithy. Leonardo and Carla were well. Carla was with child again after a miscarriage. Father Gianni had been unwell but he was well again, although a stroke had affected his left arm and hand. Sister Maria Angela rode her bicycle less often than she used to. She had never fully recovered from a bout of influenza. It seemed that her 'nerves' had been damaged and she seemed unusually prone to dark thoughts of the war. Sister Maria Angela, Uncle Cesare knew, had seen much more during her work for the Partisans than she had ever shared with others.

Tescano itself was unchanged. Uncle Cesare, Luigi's mother wrote, had once been told by Father Gianni that Tescano was a corner of earth where God, in His wisdom, had revealed, for all who cared to see, an earthly vision of the Heaven that awaited elsewhere. A world of light, a world where no shadows existed. Uncle Cesare, while he understood he should not disagree with a dottore of the great Pontifical Gregorian University in Rome, felt that Father Gianni's description of Tescano was rather too grand. Tescano was just Tescano.

Father Gianni himself, writing to Luigi, wondered when Tescano might expect to see Luigi, Nunzia and Enzo. The priest wrote, too, that he regularly corresponded with Jeremy Forsythe. The Englishman had left the British Consulate in Florence. He had returned to live and work in London. Nevertheless, he continued to visit Tescano at least twice a year. Father Gianni said Jeremy had promised to write to Luigi.

In time, Jeremy did write. He said he planned to spend a few more years in the British diplomatic service before retiring. He missed the scents and colours of Tuscany, and was giving increasing thought to spending his retirement there. Tescano or somewhere near Tescano, or maybe even Livorno. He might buy a house or rent a summer house. He had in mind something quite plain. A barn or a workshop that could be converted might do very nicely.

To Jeremy in London, Luigi wrote that he had been away from Tescano for too long. But, well, there had been businesses to build up, the bicycle shop and workshop, the Bersaglieri Cafe. Time had flown. No matter, Enzo needed to meet his grandmother and Uncle Cesare. No one in Tescano was getting any younger. There should be no more excuses, no more delays.

And so it was. Four weeks after his reply to Jeremy, Luigi wrote to his mother and Uncle Cesare:

We are to return to Tescano. We will stay for three weeks. We will take an aeroplane from Sydney to Rome then we will travel by train to Livorno, and from Livorno we will travel to Tescano by bus. The bicycle shop will close for the time we are away. Salvatore and Rachel will look after the Bersaglieri Cafe. I do not think Salvatore will ever return to Italy. He never says this, but I believe his memories of the war are too strong.

Every night when I close my eyes I see you all and I see the Tescano hills. I count the days until our return.

Your loving son and nephew and father of Enzo,

Luigi

The long journey by air from Sydney to Rome, broken by stops of several hours each in Biak, Bombay and Beirut, was not unpleasant in those days of wide seats and meals served on white china plates and coffee poured from white china pots into white china cups with white china saucers. From Rome, the train journey to Livorno took seven hours, and to Luigi the train seemed to stop at every telegraph pole along the line. It was early evening when they arrived in Livorno. They spent the night at a small hotel by the bus terminal.

Luigi rose early the next morning. While Nunzia and Enzo slept, he walked alone on familiar cobbles.

The Trattoria Bersaglieri had gone. It had been replaced by a pharmacy. A street sweeper, answering Luigi's question as to why the trattoria had closed, said that the proprietor had died a year earlier. Luigi said he had known the proprietor, who had been a hero of the Great War. The street sweeper said everybody in Italy had been a hero in the Great War and nobody had been a Fascist in the Second War.

Luigi ambled through the square where he and Leonardo and Jacob had stood alongside Il Duce. It seemed smaller. The harbour, though, was unchanged. In the soft morning light it was a timeless watercolour.

Luigi was silent on the morning bus journey from Livorno to Tescano. Enzo slept, his head heavy on Nunzia's shoulder. Behind closed eyes, Luigi played reel after reel of flickering pictures from another life. He was edging into sleep when he felt the bus slowly climb, then turn, then slow, then stop.

From outside, he could hear loud cheers. The Tescano Men of Brass began to play with great gusto. The Piazza Valsini was draped in flags and banners, one of which proclaimed: WELCOME LUIGI, SON OF TESCANO, HERO OF THE PARTISANS.

Stepping from the bus with Nunzia and Enzo, Luigi saw the beaming faces of his mother, Uncle Cesare, Father Gianni, Sister Maria Angela and Leonardo. There were embraces and cascades of tears. Luigi hadn't changed a bit, he was told. He was as handsome and kind-faced as ever he had been. And Nunzia ... such a beauty. A flower in bloom, that was what she was. Luigi should count his blessings in having such a fine woman by his side.

Enzo yelped with delight when he was hoisted onto the broad shoulders of Uncle Cesare. Two carabinieri officers offered snappy salutes as Luigi and Nunzia were walked, by Father Gianni, to the steps of the Church of the Blessed Seamstress. There, Father Gianni motioned for calm. The crowd hushed.

The priest pointed to one of the banners. A son of Tescano had indeed returned. He had left as a young man and now he returned as a husband and a father. Luigi had made his way in the world and had prospered in Australia. All in Tescano knew Luigi or knew of his exploits in the Partisans. Some of these exploits he had experienced with Nunzia, the girl who had become his wife, and with Leonardo, the boyhood companion who had become the finest baker in all of Tuscany, perhaps even all of Italy.

Father Gianni paused and nodded towards Carla, who stood, heavily pregnant, beside Leonardo. 'Of course,' he added, 'behind every great baker is the daughter of a great schoolteacher.' There was laughter and then sustained applause. The Tescano Men of Brass briefly broke into the jaunty strains of a polka. Father Gianni had such a way with words.

When the crowd was quiet again, Father Gianni continued. The people of Tescano had, he said, heard his story before. He had come to Tescano many years ago. He had come as a dottore from the great Pontifical Gregorian University and from a position in the Vatican audit office. The Gregorian had been a place of education. But Tescano had been a place of learning and of miracles great and small. These were miracles of kindness and friendship, of generosity of spirit, and of faith that hardships would pass, wounds would heal, and sons — prodigal or otherwise — would return.

Father Gianni recalled the boy who had asked questions and borrowed books and talked of journeys to places so very far away. He spoke of the young Partisan in the hills. He recalled Luigi's departure on his great adventure to the furthest-away place in the world. Then he stopped and stepped aside, motioning to Luigi to speak.

There were more cheers as Luigi came forward. He was, he said, overwhelmed and overjoyed. Truly, he had no words of worth to offer. The tears in his eyes said all that could be said. Then he was silent. Nunzia nodded. Her own tears were a wordless postscript.

The hour that followed passed in a crush of more embraces and more handshakes until, step by step, Luigi and Nunzia and Enzo finally made their way to the kitchen of the old Ferraro home, unchanged save for a new cooking range. Luigi's mother held her son and the daughter-in-law and grandson she was meeting for the first time with a tightness and strength that belied her years. Uncle Cesare looked on, arms folded, smiling.

That evening, in the kitchen, Enzo sat between his grandmother and Uncle Cesare, opposite Luigi and Nunzia. Around the table, too, were Leonardo, Carla, Leonardo's mother and father, and Father Gianni and Sister Maria Angela. There was one vacant place at the table but food was placed there nonetheless. The priest nodded, then tapped a spoon on his plate. In the instant, there was a knock on the kitchen door, which then swung open. There stood Jeremy Forsythe.

He had arrived earlier in the day, his visit planned since Luigi had first written of his return to Tescano, and it had been agreed he would enter the kitchen on the priest's signal. The Englishman threw his arms around Luigi and Nunzia then lifted Enzo high above his head. On a day of much squealing, there was more squealing.

The evening dissolved into a blur of chattering recollections of events that had, for years, been stored somewhere just beyond consciousness.

*

The visit to Tescano passed in what seemed like the blink of an eye. For Luigi and Leonardo there were weekend bicycle rides. The old Hirondelle and Sister Maria Angela's Raleigh X Frame were pressed into service. For a short time the two men were boys again, and their world was no bigger than the road that lay immediately ahead.

Some days Luigi spent quiet hours in conversation with Jeremy Forsythe. The Englishman again spoke of his hope of a retirement in Tescano. 'Long ago, my heart was stolen by this place,' he said. 'There is so much here to remember: the day I was thrown from my bicycle and you ran to help … your mother's kindness … Uncle Cesare's bravery and comradeship and the courage of Father Gianni and Sister Maria Angela and Nunzia … our time in the hills. But everything depends on what I might be able to buy or rent here.'

On other days, Enzo, Luigi, Nunzia and Father Gianni drank lemonade on the porch of the presbytery of the Church of the Blessed Seamstress. Father Gianni said that Enzo was a fine boy who was a credit to his father and mother. He wondered what the family's plans might be. Luigi's mother and Uncle Cesare, like all who breathed God's air, were not getting any younger. Uncle Cesare had told Father Gianni that he was getting too old for the workshop and that there must come a time when he would 'rest these hard old hands'. Had Luigi given any thought to returning to Tescano, not to live — for they understood that his life was in Australia — but to visit again? Luigi answered that the bicycle shop and the Bersaglieri Cafe provided a comfortable living. He and Nunzia and Enzo could afford to return for more visits. Father Gianni said he was pleased.

For young Enzo, during that first visit to Tescano, there were days alongside Uncle Cesare in the workshop, and for Nunzia there were walks with Luigi's mother — strolls to the bakery, visits to neighbours. Nunzia had been, Franca said, the salvation of her son. She had worried that she would never see him again. Only a saint could have saved Luigi from himself and his silly dreams of adventures. Young Enzo was an angel — full of smiles and funny faces and questions, but still an angel.

The day of departure, when it came, was, like the day of arrival, marked by damp eyes. But this time there was no brass band, no cheering. 'We will go quietly,' Luigi said. Before leaving, he promised his mother and Uncle Cesare that he and Nunzia and Enzo would return. The three left early in the morning, driven to Livorno by Father Gianni in his old car.

Three days later, Luigi, Nunzia and Enzo were back in Annandale wondering if they had ever been away. The exchange of letters between Sydney and Tescano resumed. Every few weeks a letter arrived and every few weeks a reply was sent. Days lengthened. Days shortened. Seasons came and went. Calendars were replaced.

From Tescano there was news of great consequence and there was news of little consequence. Leonardo and Carla had been delivered of a daughter. She was to be named Nunzia. Father Gianni had suffered a fall and there were fears that he might not recover from the pneumonia that had followed. There was a new carabinieri officer in Tescano. His name was Guido Rossi and he was a Livorno man, and had the most beautiful singing voice. He was Tuscany's answer to the great Italian-American tenor Mario Lanza. The school had been repainted and there were plumbing problems with the fountain in the Piazza Valsini.

From Sydney there was also news of great consequence and news of little consequence. Enzo was blossoming at school. He had learned to swim, too. He was 'a real little Australian'.

On the glowing recommendation of the Adventurers and the True Wheelers, Luigi became a member of the Specifications and Saddle Standards Sub-Committee (Standing) of the Sydney Amateur Cycling Fellowship. It was a position that afforded him considerable kudos within the Fellowship. He was, after all, a bicycle man of considerable overseas experience. In Sydney cycling circles, 'overseas experience' counted for much.

Nunzia — 'reluctantly and after much thought' — declined an invitation to serve on the Women's Auxiliary (Interim Refreshments Committee) of the Cycling Fellowship. She was committed, she advised the Auxiliary, to spending two evenings each week teaching English to Italian migrant women.

Nunzia's father embraced lawn bowls with the passion he had once poured into his dream of a world where the workers, united, would never be defeated. He had the determination and keen eye and fluidity of technique that some members of his club, the Annandale Royal Rollers Lawn Bowls Club, had told him were the marks of a late starter destined for local glory on the green. He had become an Australian. He had joined in. Joining in, he discovered, was all that Australia really asked of incomers.

Life slipped by. Time was a constantly flowing stream that washed away the minutes and the hours and the days and the weeks and the months and then the years. Life for Luigi and

Nunzia was busy, productive and rewarding. It was a life of contentment.

The Bersaglieri Cafe continued to prosper, as did L. and N. Ferraro and Son, Bicycles and Repairs. The returns were enough for the family to buy an imported Morris car and take a trip to Tescano every two years. The visits generally lasted four weeks. The welcomes, though always warm, were less grand as time passed. There was a perception, a product of the regularity of the visits, that Luigi merely worked in Australia, and that he and Nunzia and Enzo came 'home' to Tescano when work permitted.

Occasionally, between those visits to Tescano, Luigi, Nunzia and Enzo motored north to Black Bay. But with the passage of the years there were fewer and still fewer reasons for these journeys. Bullseye had died in his sleep. Age had finally wearied him. In his last weeks he barely stirred from bed. He had decided that, really, there wasn't much to get up for. He'd had a good run. He couldn't complain.

For their part, the Misses Hettie and Betty eventually sold the general store. They spent their remaining years in the Agatha Tresise Residential Home for Anglican Women in Coffs Harbour, well south of Black Bay. They were happy there.

Alfie took his own life. He hanged himself from a beam in his garage. At the inquest into the death, the coroner, himself a veteran of war service in North Africa, heard evidence from regulars at the Fallen Comrade that Alfie had become increasingly depressed over the last months of his life, haunted by memories of his war. In ruling that Alfie had taken his own life when 'the balance of his mind was disturbed', the coroner, a man of obvious compassion, said that Alfie was just as much a casualty of war as if he had died on the field of battle. He noted, too, that Alfie, a recipient of the Military Medal, had served with great courage and selflessness in the fight for King and Country.

The revelation that Alfie was a decorated man came as a surprise to the regulars at the Fallen Comrade. He had never mentioned the Military Medal.

He was buried in the Black Bay Cemetery, a windswept place that overlooked the ocean. A piper played the lament 'Going Home' and a bugler played the 'Last Post'.

Luigi learned of Alfie's death from a five-paragraph article on page nine of the *Sydney Morning Herald*. The small headline — *Black Bay Alamein Hero: Tragic Loss* — was spotted by Nunzia, who passed the paper to Luigi. He read and reread the story a dozen times. Then he closed the shop and the workshop for the day. He wheeled the Hercules into the street and rode to the great cliffs of Sydney Heads. For hours he watched, in absolute silence, the great ocean swell, and the gulls that soared and dived and soared and dived again.

It would take the passing of some years before Luigi could bring himself to lay flowers gently by the headstone that bore the words ALFIE 'ALAMEIN' ARKWRIGHT — MILITARY MEDAL — A FALLEN COMRADE.

'I will go when I am ready,' he told Nunzia. 'We do things when we are ready to do things.'

CHAPTER TWENTY-FIVE

Reflection

*There's birth and there's death and there's the bit in
the middle you can't ever really work out. So you
just get through the bit in the middle and leave other
people to try to work it out. It saves time. Anyhow,
you never know how long you have. One morning we
run out of afternoons. One afternoon we run out of
nights. If you want reflection, look in the mirror.*

— Ron Silvermann, *Velodromes and Victories*, 1975

Enzo was in the last few months of his mechanical engineering
studies at Sydney University when Uncle Cesare finally closed up
the workshop in Tescano. His tired old hands, he said, deserved
a rest. The workshop lay dark and shuttered for almost a year
before it was rented and refurbished by Jeremy Forsythe. He and
Uncle Cesare had talked of this possibility for some time. Thus
Jeremy made good on his decision to retire to Tuscany.

Leaving Enzo to his studies, and placing oversight of the business with Salvatore and Rachel, Luigi and Nunzia arrived in Tescano one month after Jeremy moved into the old smithy. The visit had been hurriedly planned in the week after Father Gianni telephoned Luigi and Nunzia to tell them Luigi's mother was unwell. She had been unwell for some months but had chosen, out of kindness, not to write of her illness in letters to Sydney. The doctor who every month travelled from Livorno to the Convent of Santa Teresa to attend to the health of the sisters also attended to the health of some in Tescano. Luigi's mother was numbered in his list of patients. The doctor had advised, earlier, that Franca's heart was failing — a consequence of rheumatic fever in her childhood. 'I am sad to tell you,' Father Gianni had said in his telephone call to Luigi, 'she is ready to leave us.'

For two days after arriving in Tescano, Luigi sat by his mother's bedside. Her eyes were closed and there was no movement behind her eyelids. She said nothing. Her face was as grey as her hair. Her breathing was shallow. But her grip on his hand was firm.

In the early twilight of the second day, her eyes opened, for a count of three or four. In those seconds, her grip loosened and Franca Ferraro was gone.

On the evening after the funeral, Uncle Cesare, head cupped in hard old hands, sitting silent and white-faced at the kitchen table with Luigi, Nunzia, Father Gianni, Jeremy Forsythe, Leonardo, Carla and Sister Maria Angela, sighed the longest sigh and, in the next instant, tumbled to the floor. When Luigi knelt beside him, there was no heartbeat in the broad chest.

Uncle Cesare was laid to rest beside the freshly covered grave of Franca Ferraro. It was as if two good souls in two tired bodies had held on to life until Luigi returned, and then, content that he had made his way in the world, had decided their time had come.

Luigi telephoned Enzo from the presbytery of the Church of the Blessed Seamstress to tell him of the death of his grandmother and great-uncle. That his grandmother had died was not unexpected. Enzo had been prepared for this. That Uncle Cesare had died too was a hammer blow. Uncle Cesare, the big man who had hoisted the young Enzo onto his shoulders, was supposed to go on forever. Uncle Cesare was immortal, eternal. There had always been and there would always be Uncle Cesare.

Nunzia then telephoned Jacob and Rachel with the news of both deaths. Jacob's grief was a grief beyond tears or words.

Luigi and Nunzia's return to Australia passed in near silence. It was the silence of loss. Luigi, on that longest of flights, looked out from his window seat into the whiteness of the clouds and then into the darkness of the night and then into the whiteness of the clouds as the aircraft sliced through day and night and day. He looked and looked, straining his eyes. There was nothing, nobody, there.

Luigi's only comfort on that return journey was the knowledge that Jeremy would now occupy the Ferraro house as well as the workshop and that he would send some of Uncle Cesare's older, smaller tools to Australia. 'An empty house dies of loneliness,' Luigi had told Jeremy when he invited the Englishman to move into the house. 'And unused tools are loyal servants without a master.'

Luigi and Nunzia would never again visit Tescano. There was a shared unspoken feeling that with the death of Luigi's mother and Uncle Cesare, the place was better remembered than revisited.

Of course, the letters continued to Leonardo and Father Gianni and Jeremy, and cards were sent at Christmas and Easter. Nunzia and Luigi proudly passed on news of Enzo. His mechanical engineering degree had led to a well-paid job at the Dysart Park open-cut coal mine in central Queensland.

Mention was made, too, of holiday journeys to places along the length of the coastline south of the Sydney sprawl. The journeys were made in the first automatic car Luigi and Nunzia had owned, a white, four-door Ford Escort. On those journeys, Luigi and Nunzia would stop and gaze at the white of the sands and the blue of the ocean and the purple of the coastal ranges, and at the weekend cottages and the fat birds that swooped into the froth of the waves. The south coast was fine, Luigi wrote in an Easter card to Father Gianni, but for all its grandness, it could never match the northern coastline.

He shared his observation with Nunzia. 'Well,' she said, 'perhaps we should look there for our house with a verandah and a vegetable garden and a view of the ocean. What is there to stop us?'

Luigi knew that Nunzia's question needed no answer — not since, some months earlier, the sudden death of her father, followed soon afterwards by Enzo's revelation that he was returning to Sydney. For too long, he said, he had been the absent Son on the sign above the bicycle shop and workshop.

Salvatore had died before a crowd watching the final of the Best Late Starter Tournament, played on the home greens of the Annandale Royal Rollers Lawn Bowls Club. The final bowl that would secure victory had barely left his hand when, sensing triumph, he gasped and fell dead at the feet of match referee Des Poulton, JP.

Nunzia's father was buried with full lawn-bowls honours. It was a moving affair that spoke volumes for Australian mateship. His white shoes, white trilby hat and a bottle of beer were placed on the Australian flag draped over his coffin. The bowlers sang their anthem, 'Roll Call in the Sky'. Nunzia wept until there were no more tears to shed. Luigi and Enzo wept too.

In the months that followed the funeral, resolve replaced grief. Enzo's return to Sydney to help with the business and Luigi's observation that the south coast could never match the northern coastline meant, Nunzia said, that plans should be made. Luigi understood. Nunzia was speaking with the heart. And her heart was set on a house with a verandah and a vegetable garden and a view of the endless ocean. If Luigi had a fondness for the north coast, Nunzia said, that was all well and good with her.

The two motored north to Black Bay, changed almost beyond recognition by waves of development, and to a meeting with real-estate agent Dougie Inkster. Two days after that meeting, Luigi and Nunzia made a cash offer on a small cottage and shed at Diggers Cove. 'Top spot,' Dougie said. 'Not too far out of town, but far enough for the quiet life.'

The offer on the cottage and shed was below the asking price, but it was a fair one, Nunzia said, hands on hips. Money, as far as she knew, didn't grow on trees. After all, the cottage would need a new kitchen and bathroom and an inside toilet. The shed needed straightening up before Luigi could use it as a workshop.

Luigi wondered aloud whether the offer would be enough to secure the cottage and the shed, but Dougie said not to worry — the deal would be a 'shoo-in'. He'd walk backwards to Bourke if it didn't go through. Luigi and Nunzia should leave the matter in his hands. 'You just get back down to Sydney and start thinking about living the dream,' he said. 'No worries. It's a cert. Dougie Inkster knows a sure thing when he sees one. Ask anybody around here. Dougie does the deal, that's what they'll say.'

Nunzia thought Dougie Inkster was what Australians called 'a bit of a shonk'. Luigi thought Dougie Inkster was what Australians called 'a fair enough sort of bloke'.

There was a brief detour on that return journey south. Without warning and without a word to Nunzia, Luigi drove through Black Bay and out to the windswept graveyard. He picked some wildflowers and laid them on the grave of Alfie 'Alamein' Arkwright. Luigi stared at the headstone. He remembered Alfie's generosity to a young Italian cyclist. He remembered Alfie's tears when he spoke of his war in the desert. It was a war that had never ended.

'We do things when we are ready to do things,' Luigi told Nunzia as they walked from Alfie's grave.

CHAPTER TWENTY-SIX

Horizons

*There comes a time when you look around and all the
people you journeyed with are gone. And you know
that one day, you'll be gone too. But it doesn't matter.
Others come along and ride the path and they all have
their own adventures. That's the best part, knowing
others are making the journey, having adventures,
turning the wheels.*

— Albert Foster, *The Bicycle Builder*, 2001

Work on the Diggers Cove cottage took longer than expected.
The new kitchen, bathroom and toilet had to be fitted. Doors
were rehung. Windows were replaced. A pot-belly wood-burning
heater was installed. The roof was repaired. Every centimetre
of wiring was replaced. New power points were installed.
Walls were painted. Floors were sanded. Verandah planks were
replaced.

Local tradesmen said not to worry about the time the work was taking. This was the north coast. It operated on north-coast time. Nunzia said if the tradesmen wanted to work on north-coast time, they shouldn't expect to be paid in Sydney dollars.

Eight months behind schedule, Luigi and Nunzia moved north. A cluster of perhaps two dozen people stood outside the shop and the Bersaglieri Cafe to farewell them — cyclists, customers, neighbours, Jacob and Rachel Zevi. Luigi and Nunzia would be missed, they said.

Enzo promised to be a regular visitor to Diggers Cove. He was also planning a visit to Tescano. Tuscany was, he said, the home of his heart. He was a Tescano man in all but birth. Luigi, his eyes suddenly blinded with tears, said Enzo was the finest son a man could wish for. He was a man with the grip. Enzo's eyes filled with tears too. As an engineer he had become familiar with the grip, and he knew there could be no higher praise for a man of metal. Enzo said that Luigi was the finest father a son could wish for. Nunzia said that Enzo had better make good on his promise to visit Diggers Cove. She nodded the same admonition to Jacob and Rachel. Doors closed and the white Ford Escort was gone.

Luigi and Nunzia, driving a safe distance behind a removal truck that carried all that was needed for life by the ocean, rolled away from Sydney. There were no backward glances. Something had ended and something else was starting. The business had been signed over to Enzo, but of course the name would remain — L. and N. Ferraro and Son, Bicycles and Repairs — as would the name of the Bersaglieri Cafe.

Beside the cottage with the verandah, a vegetable garden was planted. One day folded into the next. Weeks folded into weeks. Months into months, then years into years. So it went.

With the passage of those years came the passing of more lives in Tescano. The living, breathing past was disappearing. The march of time was trampling a rare vintage. Sister Maria Angela succumbed to pneumonia. Jeremy Forsythe and Father Gianni both passed away in their sleep. The sad news came in letters from Leonardo.

There was other news, too. Tescano had a new priest, a Tuscan man, Father Renzo Rinaldi. He reminded many of Father Gianni. And a visiting English painter, Eustace Oldham, FRSA, had asked Leonardo about renting the Ferraro house and Uncle Cesare's smithy. Leonardo wrote: *Mr Oldham is quite famous, I have been told. I do not believe he will be any trouble when it comes to paying the rent. I will wait until I hear from you and I can look after any arrangements.*

Luigi and Nunzia agreed that the house and the workshop should be rented to Mr Oldham. The rent should be modest, enough to cover the cost of maintaining the buildings in good order. No more was necessary. After all, Nunzia said, the Ferraros were comfortable enough, and better off than most. They had a small home and a vegetable garden by the ocean and enough to eat and a good son in Enzo. They had each other. They had companionship. Their wedding vows had been honoured for richer and poorer, in sickness and in health. They had loved and cherished and they had forsaken all others.

In the shed behind the cottage, Luigi motorised Schwinn bicycles with two-stroke Honda engines imported from Japan.

Each bicycle was a work in perpetual progress. Buyers were never sought. Every so often, he stripped and rebuilt the old Hercules. These activities were encouraged by Nunzia. They brought Luigi genuine and obvious contentment. There was a profound peace and certainty within him. Luigi knew, beyond any doubt, that with Nunzia and the Diggers Cove cottage and the workshop and the bicycles, his Freedom Ride had reached its final destination.

Nunzia shared Luigi's contentment. She had her vegetable garden. She had her sewing, a craft she had taken up some months after the move north, and which saw her produce quite marvellous quilts, mosaics of beautifully stitched and cleverly cut and contrasting fabrics. In her sixties, Nunzia had learned to drive, and every Thursday she drove to Black Bay to pass the day in the backroom of the Odds and Ends fabric shop with a group of her stitching sisters, who styled themselves the Northern Mature Lady Quilters' Co-operative.

There was a trickle of regular and welcome visitors to the north. Enzo visited every five or six weeks, and he and Luigi would ride up to Black Cape or fish from the beach or walk by the ocean. Jacob and Rachel visited twice a year.

Letters from Leonardo arrived when there was news to tell. His daughter had married a baker's son from Livorno. *One day*, Leonardo wrote, *the Tescano bakery will be theirs.* He wrote, too, that the Tescano priest, Father Renzo, had revealed himself, in late middle age, to be a cyclist of some prowess and achievement. As a younger man he had been Seminarian Cyclist of the Year in Padua. After a lapse of many years he had, Leonardo wrote, returned to his only other passion beyond the priesthood. It was now a fact of Tescano life that Wednesday was Father Renzo's cycling day. No weddings or funerals could be held in Tescano on that day. Nor would Father Renzo be available to hear confessions on Wednesday. Instead, rain or shine, the priest would take to the hills on his bright yellow British-built Raleigh Racer Roadster. As for the last rites, Father Renzo said, if Tescano people were to pass away he hoped they might try to avoid meeting their maker on Wednesdays. His words were always spoken with a smile.

Luigi seldom ventured far from the shed or the house by the sea. Of course, there were the regular rides to Black Cape and walks by the water. Sometimes he'd fish from the beach or from the rocks. Each week he'd dump his rubbish at the Diggers Cove Landfill. Every few days he'd pass an hour or two with neighbour Nev Grainger, a retired bus driver. Mostly, though, Luigi was content with his own company and the company of Nunzia. Few words passed between them. Fond glances and smiles sufficed. What, really, was there left to say?

Standing on the verandah, eyes sweeping the horizon, Luigi would look towards the sky and he would see faces in the scudding clouds: his mother, Uncle Cesare, Jeremy Forsythe, Father Gianni, Sergeant Dante, the players of the victorious Foxes football team, Sergeants Bob and Geordie and Vince Vittoria, and Nero, the Livorno commandant's dog. Dear, hungry, drooling Nero.

In 1992, Nunzia died. She had been weeding her vegetable garden when she fell to the ground. There was no last gasp. No final cry. Luigi, working in his shed, heard the sound of Nunzia's fall. Kneeling, he cradled her head in his arms. The ambulance men, called from Black Bay, said death had been instantaneous, probably a heart attack or a massive stroke. Luigi removed the locket from Nunzia's neck and held it tightly, perhaps trying to feel in it the pulse of a life that had ended.

Nunzia was cremated and her ashes placed in a blue and white porcelain urn that sat on the windowsill of the showpiece kitchen during the day and by Luigi's bed during the hours of darkness. Each night when he closed his eyes, Luigi would say: 'Goodnight, Nunzia, goodnight.' Each morning, as he moved the urn to the windowsill in the kitchen, he would say: 'There, look at the goodness that grows in your garden.'

The months after Nunzia's death were months of awful sadness. Countless times Luigi believed that he would be overwhelmed, that it must be possible to die from grief. He thought he might die in his sleep and he thought that would be no bad thing. Hearts could, indeed, break and shatter into a million pieces. He could feel the sharpness of those broken pieces in his chest. Often he felt as a sailor might feel on the blackest of boiling oceans under the blackest of black skies. He was lost and full of despair.

Neighbour Nev, himself a widower, sat with Luigi through many days of sadness, often saying little or nothing. His presence was a profound comfort. When Nev did speak he showed himself to be a man of uncommon insight. 'It never goes away, the sadness,' he told Luigi. 'We just get better at living with it. But we're always just one blink away from tears. That's the truth, mate, and it never changes.' With such wisdom, Nev Grainger could quite easily have become a dottore of the great Pontifical Gregorian University.

It was Nev who pulled Luigi from the grinding slide into despair. He said that grief offered choices: Luigi could forever lament a future without Nunzia or he could treasure the memories of what he had been given, memories of the life he'd had with her. 'What we have is the past and the present,' Nev said. 'The future is something we imagine, something we hope for. Nothing wrong with hope, but there's no guarantee. Life doesn't come with a guarantee. Treasure what you have and what you had with the missus; there's no good and no peace in "what if" and "if only".'

And that was what Luigi began to do. He treasured the memories. He counted his blessings. He reminded himself that there was much worth remembering. From time to time there were tears that could not be blinked away. Mostly, though, there was gratitude. Really, he had been blessed.

In late 2002, Luigi, writing in his occasional journal as he sat on the verandah, closed his eyes for the last time. Some hours later, Enzo, arriving from Sydney, found the body of his father. Luigi seemed to be sleeping. A silver Montegrappa pen lay on the floor. It had slipped from Luigi's right hand. Dangling from his left were Nunzia's locket and chain. An ambulance was called. Luigi's body was removed to the Black Bay mortuary. The death certificate said that Luigi Ferraro, born in Tescano, Italy, in 1921, had died of cardiac arrest.

Enzo, Jacob, Rachel and Nev attended the cremation in Black Bay. There was no service. Instead, Enzo, his voice wavering, read aloud the last words written in Luigi's journal.

I have become very tired these recent weeks. Everything to be done in this small life has been done. Everything that should be felt has been felt. I close my eyes today, as I close them every day, and see Nunzia, beautiful and kind beyond words. I think of how much she gave to me. Her lips move and I see the shape of her words. They are asking me to be with her and all the other companions of the journey. I am content to go. I am ready.

Eight months after the cremation, Enzo returned to Tescano. He borrowed Father Renzo's Raleigh Racer Roadster and cycled into the hills. On an outcrop above the mouth of a cave, he cast the ashes of Nunzia and Luigi Ferraro to the winds. He watched them blow away. First grey and then gone. For some minutes he stood, alone and in silence. Slowly, and without a backward glance, he returned to his father's village and then to Australia.

In 2005, Enzo Ferraro sold the Sydney shop and workshop, the Bersaglieri Cafe, the family home in Sydney and the Diggers Cove cottage. Now middle-aged and still unmarried, he returned to Tescano a man of some means. He brought with him a box of tools, the same tools that had been sent to Luigi after Cesare's death.

What had until then been Enzo's second home now became his only home. He had thought of the return to Tescano every day since he scattered his parents' ashes in the hills.

In Tescano, Enzo met thirty-three-year-old Rosa Rinaldi, the youngest sister of Father Renzo. Rosa, who had been widowed, childless, one year earlier, had come to Tescano to spend the early summer of 2006 with her brother.

Married by Father Renzo in the Church of the Blessed Seamstress, with a frail and ailing Leonardo and Carla watching on, the two set up home in the old Ferraro house, vacated some time earlier by its tenant, the famous English watercolour artist Eustace Oldham, FRSA. It was said that one of the painter's works — *Sunlight and Shadows: The Tescano Forge* — had sold for many thousands of American dollars in New York.

Uncle Cesare's workshop was reopened and a sign erected over the big double doors. It said: *L. and N. Ferraro and Son, Bicycles and Repairs.* Within a year the sign had been repainted to read: *L. and N. Ferraro and Son and Grandson, Bicycles and Repairs.*

In 2008, the great Italian cycling classic the Giro d'Italia passed through Tescano for the first time in the history of the race. Since then, the Livorno to Tescano stage has become a feature of the blue-ribbon event. The sign outside Uncle Cesare's workshop is seen, every year, by an estimated forty million television viewers. Some of those viewers, keen cyclists, visit Tescano in the cooler autumn months after the Giro. Under the sign outside Uncle Cesare's workshop is a shining motorised Hercules bicycle. It is the subject of much discussion among those visitors.

The success of the business owes much to that fleeting, almost accidental, television image of the curious sign above the workshop. It is Enzo and Rosa's hope that one day the business will be run by their son Luigi.

The generosity of Enzo and Rosa has rebuilt the presbytery of the Church of the Blessed Seamstress and has built in the Tescano hills a small marble memorial bearing the names of the Partisans and those who risked everything to help them. The memorial sits on the outcrop above the cave where Enzo scattered the ashes of his mother and his father.

From time to time, Enzo and Rosa lay flowers in front of the memorial. Always on such visits, Rosa wears a small, sparkling locket. She knows only that it once belonged to young Luigi's grandmother and that it is precious beyond words.

Enzo and Rosa are contented and they have the hope, through their son, of a far horizon. Contentment and hope are no small things.

ACKNOWLEDGMENTS

Historian, author and journalist Dr Jacqui Murray, who lived in the Middle East for many years, provided invaluable information on Istanbul, Syria and Palestine. Her contribution was central to the development of several chapters of this story.

The late John Foss provided advice on historical and technical aspects of bicycle-building. Along the way he became an avid reader of early drafts of this work of fiction. John was a fine friend and a man of humour and vivid imagination.

Margaret Kennedy, a consummate professional and principal of MKA, was as patient as she was generous with her time. Her lucid observations and always constructive suggestions contributed greatly to the telling of Luigi's story.

At HarperCollins, Catherine Milne was supportive beyond words. Editors Amanda O'Connell and Clara Finlay were simply the best.